The Enormous Arrival

New Discoveries in Southern Fiction Series, No. 1

The Enormous Arrival

Sally Poole

Authors Choice Press
San Jose New York Lincoln Shanghai

The Enormous Arrival

All Rights Reserved © 2001 by Sally Poole

No part of this book may be reproduced or transmitted in any form or by any means, graphic, electronic, or mechanical, including photocopying, recording, taping, or by any information storage or retrieval system, without the permission in writing from the publisher.

Authors Choice Press
an imprint of iUniverse.com, Inc.

For information address:
iUniverse.com, Inc.
5220 S 16th, Ste. 200
Lincoln, NE 68512
www.iuniverse.com

The following work is fiction and the characters cannot be construed to resemble any person living or dead.

ISBN: 0-595-19070-7

Printed in the United States of America

FOR
MARION MONTGOMERY
INSPIRING TEACHER, FEARLESS WRITER, FAITHFUL
FRIEND

Nightgirl put on soft shoes
Tiptoe cross a moonlit floor.
Colored girl sing the blues
Don't want to love no more.
White girl whistle down the wind,
Come a knocking at my door.
Don't know where she been
Don't know what she come here for.

Night girl, light girl, bad girl, sad girl
Don't want to love no more.

Morning break when evening gone,
Birds start singing, squirrels go feeding,
Man go working, she's alone.
Washing dishes, thinking, needing,
Missing, wishing, hoping, dreaming
Till the tears come down.
Day beginning, heat's a'steaming,
Then the screen door slam.

Who that come and where he been?
It don't matter, just come in.

I

The first time I saw Jim play ball I had to sneak in because the colored (that's what we were called to our face) weren't allowed onto the bleachers. Jim was anything but somebody's golden-haired, blue-eyed boy. His hair was dark brown and tightly curled, almost kinky. His skin was naturally tan. Instead of electric blue, his eyes were focused brown; I heard somebody who didn't like him describe them as "beady."

I was squatting beneath the bleachers so nobody could see me. It was the day I saw him on the field. You had to think of King David because of the way Jim was. He moved about the field like it was no big deal. There was also a Goliath, much bigger boy who squinted and singled Jim out. I tensed because you could see he was a bully and had Jim in his sights.

Somebody passed the ball. It was in the air. Jim suddenly appeared and snatched the pigskin as it seemed to hover like a brown blimp above the scrimmaging teams. The bully dived. I sucked in my breath as his vast body stretched towards Jim's legs. But it was in that instant that Jim leapt.

You see, Jim had a way of doing something surprising like that. It was as if the Lord God had choreographed the moment. The big guy slid forward as other players scurried out of his way. Brown slush splattered up in front of him as he bulldozed forward. When he came to a stop, his face was covered in mud and Jim was gone down the field, nimble as a rabbit, springing in long leaps rather than running.

Jim was amazing. He was also a white boy, and his name was Hall. Everybody knew he was a Hall because his grandmother and granddaddy hadn't ever married. Jim's father, Henry Hall, had taken his mother's name because Jacob Freikas hadn't bothered to adopt him or marry his mother, Dora.

Well, it wasn't easy growing up a bastard in Lawson County. I can vouch for that. Still, when you're inside the experience, it never is as bad as it sounds from the outside. First of all, nobody had expected Jacob Freikas to marry Dora Hall.

Dora was just white trash. She had walked into town one dusty day all by herself. Jacob had taken her in, but everybody knew there was a limit that a respectable merchant could go. There was also the fact that Jacob Freikas was a Jew. Not that anybody really knew what that meant, but they figured that his religion didn't allow him to marry somebody like Dora.

All I know is what people told me about all that because Jacob and Dora were dead before I came along. People in town still talked about Jacob, though, as if he were alive. He had made quite an impression being the only Jew who ever settled in Lawsonville, Georgia.

When I was young you could still hear people reciting jokes Jacob had told. People liked to remember him and his peculiar manners. They told the story of Jacob and Dora, too.

Jacob's store had been down on Emancipation Street, which is where us coloreds shopped in those days. Jacob's customers weren't mostly of the colored persuasion, though, because the white women valued his honesty.

Catfish Wallace claimed to know that Jacob Freikas had emigrated from Russia. Nobody knew exactly where a drunk like Catfish had gotten such information, or why he was so confident it was correct. When he told the story, Catfish usually managed to imply that he and Jacob had been secret drinking brothers.

There were few people with German names in Georgia back in those days. Black and white, everybody was a Taylor, Smith, Cantrel, McCormick, Jones, Steeples or Lawson.

Coloreds remembered Mr. Jacob, which is what they called him, with nostalgia. "It was a sad day when Mr. Jacob died," Aunt Ida Mae would sigh when I came back from shopping with a piece of spoiled fruit or some meat with too much fat hidden on the underside. "He treat us good. You didn't get no spoiled meat nor nothing like that when he was alive." That was Aunt Ida Mae's opinion.

So there was Jacob Freikas getting up early in the morning when he would recite a Psalm, then working until late at night and no suitable marriage partner in sight. It was into this picture that Dora Hall came barefoot, unwashed, and silent. One day she was just there, sweeping the sidewalk in front of the store.

People didn't know where she'd come from, who she was, or what she had in mind, and she wasn't about to say. She was long-legged, thin, and silent by nature. She was like dozens of sharecropper folk who passed through town destitute, dirty, sometimes begging. They rarely spoke.

Dora was soon a fixture around Freikas Mercantile. She was always busy, always fussing around with something, not at all lazy and good-for-nothing like people had come to expect of her kind. Coloreds liked it when Jacob would call, "Dora get this woman some good tomatoes!" Dora always did her best to find the best. She didn't seem to know the difference between black and white.

Dora worshipped Mr. Jacob. She had no other religion. God only knows where and how she grew up. She knew no more of Baptists than she did of Jews. People were just people to her, neither high nor low, Christian nor pagan, rich nor poor. Except for Mr. Jacob whom she adored.

When a woman loves a man like that it's just a matter of time until a child comes along. That's how little Henry showed up. Nobody even knew Dora was pregnant until she was seen nursing little Henry in the back of the store, but it was no surprise. People had seen the way she looked at Mr. Jacob.

Of course, there was virtually no resemblance between little Henry and his father. Where Mr. Jacob was handsome and broad-shouldered, darker skinned and brunet, little Henry was pale, long and angular with pale blue eyes. He had a nose that was longer than it should have been by the strength of his chin, more like his mother, awkward, silent, and sullen.

When Jacob Freikas died in 1939 just before Germany invaded Poland, Mr. Golucke, who was still serving as Clerk of Court though he was about eighty-five, acted as executor of his will. In his official capacity Mr. Golucke declared that Dora Hall was as good as Jacob Freikas' common-law wife, which meant that Henry Hall was none other than his son, and Dora was entitled to his full estate.

After the Freikas' store was sold, Dora used the money to buy and equip a farm outside town. It was a place of some hundred and fifty acres. Upon it sat a rambling, unpainted clapboard farmhouse with a rusty tin roof and porch running across the front. There were also two barns, three milk cows, and sundry other livestock, including a fine hog. She bought a freight wagon and two mules to round it out.

It was obvious that coupling with Jacob Freikas had been the smartest thing Dora would ever do because it raised her out of the sharecropper and tenant class and put her square in the farmer class. Henry joined the ranks of those small farmers still trying somehow to make a living raising cotton, while all the world had long known that cotton could be grown more cheaply in places like Egypt or India.

The Hall place really was sort of in a far corner of the county, bordering the Coosa National Forest which the Roosevelt Administration had just created out of some of the swampiest, sandiest, most worthless land in Georgia. That is where I was born, in a little ramshackle community known as "The Ridge." It's also how I first came to meet Jim, long before I saw him play ball.

People thought Henry Hall married beneath him when he took Corley Whitlock's sister for his bride. She was a whining sort of woman and lazy, too, everybody said, just like all the Whitlocks. There was no doubt about it. The Whitlocks were a miserable, mean lot that ran a broken down old mill on Sugar Creek. They were known mostly for feuding, drinking, and not paying their bills on time.

Now Jesse Lee Whitlock hated colored folk though Henry Hall didn't. Henry was not an unfamiliar figure at The Ridge and my Mama was his favorite concubine. Mama asked me more than once to go play down by the creek when Henry Hall came to call, both before and after he married Jessie Lee.

Jessie Lee was a scourge to colored children who strayed onto her farm. If she was out in the yard and near enough to them, she'd take her hoe and sling it at them. Otherwise, she'd just throw rocks or scream and holler for them to get off her land.

Knowing all of this is important because, if you didn't, you wouldn't ever believe that Jim Hall came from two such people as Henry and Jessie Lee Hall. It would be like believing that a beagle and a hound dog had produced a gorgeous collie.

From the very start, when he was still hardly more than a little child, Jim was totally different than his parents. Where they wore suspicious, pale blue eyes in their faces, their heads covered by matted, dirty light brown hair with blond streaks, Jim had trusting, warm dark brown eyes and thickly curled black hair that glistened in the sun. Where their chins were weak, noses long, his nose was straight and well-proportioned, and his chin was chiseled out of granite.

Jim was friendly and outgoing while Henry and Jessie Lee were churlish and taciturn. Jim was as graceful as they were maladroit. He was intelligent and inquisitive though his parents acted stupid and ignorant. Finally, he was kind and interested in people, generous to a fault and fearless when protecting children from bullies.

The old people in town saw Jacob Freikas in Jim and said so. Miss Barleycorn, who never married and served as the town telephone operator, would purse her lips, adjust her glasses and allow that Jim was the "spittin" image of his grandfather.

The retired Methodist pastor asserted with confidence that Mr. Jacob Freikas was manifest once again in his grandson and that the whole town could be grateful to the Lord for managing such a feat in his infinite wisdom.

From the very start Jim Hall knew how to get himself talked about, loved and admired. People went on about him from the time he could walk. Not only was there always an unmistakably endearing manner expressed in his voice and bearing, Jim enjoyed the town's approval, sought it, responded with respect, warmth and heartfelt kindness wherever he could.

In one way, this story is about Jim because I loved him from the start and everything about him, and I never stopped. Not even yet.

II

Henry Hall had gone in to Mama, and the cabin was making all those noises, the wood groaning and the whole thing kind of rocking on the stones that undergirded the floor. Mama sounded like she was having fun. She'd sing out in her fine contralto, and Henry Hall would come in behind her in his baritone, and they created an ecstatic duet.

Mama had beautiful teeth, and maybe that's one reason she liked to smile like she did. Mama could have been a movie star she was so beautiful. When a man would come up and see her sitting on the porch and smiling, it'd take his breath away. He'd stand there sometimes for minutes like he was struck dumb. Men were crazy about Mama, and not just Henry Hall but lots of white men.

Our cabin was one of a dozen or so that were thrown and patched together out of sundry materials. It was a motley assembly of shacks, outhouses, and chicken coops. Animals had free run of the community, the chickens and other foul pecking and eating the insects, the hogs rooting, the dogs lounging, running with us children, or simply howling. It was a great place to be a child.

Later I found out how the Ridge was founded by runaway slaves at the end of the Civil War. It was a place of refuge for coloreds. Everybody who had a reason to get away from town went there. Everybody who had crossed some white person made at least a stop there. There were no men in permanent residence, though. Even the older male children just sort of disappeared when they got close to puberty.

It was among these shifting constellations of children that I spent my first five or six years, while Mama made a living for both of us by keeping her pallet ready for white hunters thirsty for an ample dose of her gorgeous body and luscious love-making.

Much of what we did to pass the time was play chase, and it was in those games that I discovered my speed. Even as a little child I was fast. I could dodge anybody, and I often found myself far out alone and ahead of the pack. Then I would stop and listen. When I didn't hear them shouting, I usually went down to the creek and played by myself.

One day while I was playing in the water of the creek Jim came up. He was a couple of years older and rather big for his age. When he said, "Hey," I was startled. I leapt up and was ready to take off running. "Don't leave," he said.

There was something in his voice that kept me there. We got along fine and met again several times before Mama decided to leave me and go off up north.

After Mama was gone, Uncle Cajus and Aunt Ida Mae came and got me and took me to live with them in the little servant cottage behind Lawson Hall. That was when I first went into Lawsonville, Georgia.

We approached town from the west. When you come over a knoll on the road, you can see Lawsonville tucked into a kind of hollow. Lawson Hall is sitting up on a softly rounded hill to the north looking down over the town. From below on Main Street you can't see it because of the thick, large oaks. The railroad lies along an axis from east to west and skirts the southern edge of town.

The courthouse dominates downtown with its late Victorian, red brick towers and the two clocks that never agree, one in each tower looking in different directions, always at least an hour and twenty-five minutes apart.

The white school – Robert E. Lee Institute—and playing fields are just south of the rail line. The colored school – George Washington Carver Consolidated—is back out of sight behind a bend of forest. Confederate Park is nestled to the south of the First Baptist Church and the cemetery. The Confederate Museum is next door to the home of Alex Stephens, the Vice President of the Confederacy.

The stores of Main Street are lined up in contiguous order marching along the raised sidewalk. The stores to the right as you look down form a perfect square, the backside facing Emancipation Street and the colored district.

The stores to the left flank of Main are a single rank with the hotel at one end and the picture show at the other. Behind it are residential houses detached and seated in their own fenced yards.

People don't think you can remember much when you are six, but I remember coming over that knoll and looking at the town. It's very dense in my mind. I also remember driving up to Lawson Hall that first time.

I was sitting on the front seat of Judge Lawson's Buick with Uncle Cajus driving. Actually, I think I was standing and looking over the dashboard because there were no seat belts in those days. We drove through the gates and passed the weeping willows dragging their hair in the pond. There was the long sweep of gravel drive and the house in front of me.

Lawson Hall was nothing like the Southern mansions everybody knows from "Gone with the Wind" or other romantic films about the South. The central core was really a sort of partially raised Piedmont cottage built of bricks the slaves had formed with their hands and baked themselves. The brick were generously mixed with stone to save work, and that made the walls irregular and rough with different stone and brick textures, the earth tints varying widely from one part to the next.

Even as a child I knew that Lawson Hall was a lovely home. The best thing about the place was that it really wasn't pretentious the way so many of the Doric mansions built during the heyday of cotton production in the 1840s and 50s were.

There was no columned-portico dominating the central entry of the house. Rather a metal roof sloped down over the porch to provide the shade necessary to cool streams of air sucked out of the yard and into the house by the working of gravity and heat.

It was plain once I was inside it that Lawson Hall had been built with a shrewd eye to keeping the interior of the house as cool as possible during the long summer days in Georgia. The large rooms were dark and soared twenty feet to a ceiling clothed in eternal obscurity. The wings were built later by different Lawsons.

The current scion, Judge Lawson, loved nothing better than to retire to the library wing where he lived a rather hermit life, except for when he had to go out on his court docket in a four county district. Later you will see how I discovered in the secret attic above his library the genealogical documents that explained the mysteries of my origins.

When Randolph Lawson arrived to build the house, Lawson County was still Cherokee Indian territory. Long-staple cotton had brought him from Charleston and drawn him away from indigo and rice agriculture. He was depicted in the huge portrait hanging in the hall at the front of the house, standing with his hand propped on a broken column while some invisible wind blew his closely cropped, Regency hair.

Randolph had been not only a high born gentleman of Charleston society, he served as plenipotentiary to German courts and was briefly senator from Georgia. Later I found the portrait reproduced in my Georgia history text when I found myself back in Georgia in high school.

I cried my heart out the day Uncle Cajus came and got me at the Ridge. With Mama gone, I didn't mind leaving the Coosa National Forest, but I was afraid I would never see Jim again. Losing both Mama and Jim was more than I could bear.

"Hush, now, honey," Uncle Cajus crooned as we drove into town. "It's gone be all right. We gone take care of you now."

When Uncle Cajus stopped the Buick in back of Lawson Hall, I scrambled onto the gravel drive and looked round. I will never forget the moment because to me I was standing in a place more wonderful than I could ever have dreamt.

My highest standard had been the unpainted Hall farmhouse that I had seen from a safe distance one morning. I had never even imagined that people could build places of mortar, brick, and stone, but even the stables at Lawson Hall were masonry.

Uncle Cajus soon disappeared into his chores, and I was left to play about and shift for myself. I found a gym set with swings and a slide not too far from the screened porch on a flank of the Hall. It seemed to have been waiting for me, and I ran down and began to climb.

"Niggers aren't allowed on my gym-set!" The voice was sharp and nasal. I was too high up to jump down, but, as I turned, I saw Laura Lawson for the first time. She was standing on the screen porch. "Get off!" she commanded, and then she headed for the door and steps. I tried to hurry down and get away before she got outside, but I'd got myself more tangled in the confusion of bars and crossbars than I had intended.

The first thing I knew, she had me around the waist and was pulling. I felt this awful fear that I'd come tumbling down. Without really thinking about it, my foot went up automatically and shoved at her. She grunted and screamed, and, when I looked around, she was sitting spread-legged in a flowerbed.

Before Laura could get back up, I was running across the gravel parking area to the kitchen where I sought the protection of Aunt Ida Mae. Laura was close behind, and, as I hid behind my aunt's broad expanse, she wailed, "She kicked me down in the mud! See how she messed up my new blouse!"

"Why, Folly Steeples, ain't you ashamed of yourself," Aunt Ida Mae said, pulling me out into the open.

All my attempts at explaining were to no avail. It was clear that Laura was the mistress at Lawson Hall. My word didn't count. Aunt Ida Mae ordered me to my room in the cottage behind the main house. She stood on the back porch and watched me as I went hangdog to my punishment.

Later I realized that she was also making certain Laura Lawson didn't bully me on the way. Being colored was a tricky business. Often you had to seem to be on the white person's side while you were actually protecting your brothers and sisters.

It wasn't any time after my arrival that Aunt Ida Mae pushed me in front of her into the dining room while the Lawsons were eating at the long, formal table. "This here is Folly," she said, patting my head. I saw Laura Lawson stick out her tongue and then go cross-eyed at me.

"Hello, Folly," Miss Ellen said. "How old are you?"

"I'm not right sure," I told her. "Mama never told me exactly, but I usually say I'm six."

"Well, Ida Mae, she'll be able to help some with the chores soon, I'll bet. She's a big girl."

"Yes'm," Aunt Ida Mae said. "She shore can. She's smart as a whip."

It was the first time I'd gotten a good look at Judge Lawson. He had a really disconcerting way of turning his face to you but without looking. His abstracted blue eyes were actually rolled up to the top of his eye-sockets, a lot of the white showing at the bottom, so that he looked like a cross between a zombie and some dyspeptic saint searching the sky for God.

Miss Ellen had a kind of leathery skin and a generally disinterested manner. It gave you the feeling that the rest of us were not real to her, like we weren't actual human beings but props or scenery on a stage where she was the only real actor. Miss Ellen was the last person I thought who'd ever take an interest in me.

Of course, the truth is that what happened later didn't really mean she took an interest in *me* personally. It had more to do with her obsession with tennis. That's what brought us together. Miss Ellen was outdoors most of the time. She was always trying to get somebody to come up, so that she would spend the day playing them on one of the two courts out by the stables.

Tennis occupied for Miss Ellen the place most people reserve in their hearts for some *body*. She wore her short little tennis dress around the house and everywhere else. It was pretty near being her uniform. It didn't matter to her that she was a little old to be showing so much leg. Also when she sat down you could see her panties shining.

Still, I couldn't help myself. I had watched her play, and I loved the game before I ever held a racket in my hand. Finally, I just couldn't help myself. I went out to the pavilion where she kept the equipment and found myself a racket. I took a few balls and started practicing on the backboard. Soon I was slipping down at one point or another to practice every day.

At Lawson Hall everybody had her own sphere of influence. Miss Ellen's was on the courts. Ida Mae commanded the realm of the kitchen. She cooked and supervised cleaning, too, and there were three or four other coloreds who came once or twice a week to do her bidding.

Uncle Cajus drove the Buick for the Judge when he had to go out on his docket and kept it waxed and in good repair. He also supervised the yard work crew when they came up and played at being butler when there were guests or dignitaries.

The Judge would come out of a morning. Uncle Cajus would hold the door of the Buick open. Judge Lawson would say, "Good morning, Cajus," and Uncle Cajus would answer, "Good morning, suh." Then Judge Lawson would put up one spindly leg, grab hold of a strap inside the back seat and pull himself in. As he settled himself in the seat, he'd ask, "Cajus, you got a dime this morning for a coke while I'm in court?" "Yassuh," Uncle Cajus would reply. "I got the change I needs."

If they ever varied their exchange, I didn't hear it. That's the way everything ran at Lawson Hall. It was regular, predictable, and according to long-standing tradition.

I was given the dusting to do, which is one of the things Ida Mae thought I was up to at my age. When she saw how well I did that, she gave me other chores. Pretty soon that was a tradition, too, because traditions were made very fast at Lawson Hall.

Next to tennis, I liked to work. I loved dusting the furniture and oiling it until the deep mahogany shone. I also took out the trash for Aunt Ida Mae. We burned it out behind the stables, away from the tennis courts.

As long as I was busy and within shouting distance of my guardians, I was fairly secure from Laura Lawson's abusive intrusions. It was when I strayed too far from them that she appeared, my inexorable nemesis, to torment me.

Laura seemed always to know when I was alone. It was really hard to find times to slip down to the tennis courts without being discovered. I think it was my unquenchable need to feel the racket in my hand that made me risk it.

Laura was about three years older than I, so you can guess that she was also around the same age as Jim Hall. She was not just knock-kneed. She had freckles, and her eyes were set close together. That made her look cross-eyed at times, though she could also cross her eyes when she wanted to mock me behind Aunt Ida Mae's back.

Laura had a very short waist and looked at times a little out of balance because of her long legs. You wondered where God found room to put in all her guts and organs in such an abbreviated trunk.

I'm not sure I really hated Laura Lawson at first, but she definitely was a terrible nuisance. I dreaded any encounter with her. My main effort was actually directed at avoiding rather than despising her. If she came by while I was dusting in the house, she'd stick me with a pin from behind or pinch me. If I screamed, she'd simply lie and claim I was spoiled and trying to get attention.

Once she had a woven, Chinese device she asked me to put my finger in. "It won't hurt. We'll see who can pull hardest," she said. I could have kicked myself when I did it because my finger got stuck. The weave drew tight and imprisoned my finger. While I was trying to pull the poor member out, Laura dug her fingernail into it until it bled.

By the time Miss Ellen came down one day and found me hitting the tennis ball against the backboard, I'd gotten pretty good. The wood felt comfortable in my hand, like it belonged there. I knew the solid "pock" when the ball struck the center of the catgut mesh.

She must have watched me a good while. Finally, she said, "Your backhand needs some work."

"I didn't mean to," I said in knee-jerk fashion. I whirled about and almost threw the racket away just to have the evidence of my crime out of my hand.

"It's okay," she said. "Wait. I'll come around and show you a better grip."

She came onto the court. I was so embarrassed I couldn't look her in the eye. But Miss Ellen didn't notice my discomfort. She was only thinking about how she could improve my grip. She took my arm in her hand and adjusted my grip for the backhand with the fingers on her other hand: "This way," she said. But the racket was really far too big for me. That's why I'd been using both hands.

A couple of weeks later she came out with a smaller racket she'd had made and presented it to me. "That ought to fit better," she said as she handed it to me.

Laura was watching. When I caught sight of her, the back of my head, inside my brain, burned. It was because I knew Laura would be sure to think up something to do to me. Somewhere, around some dark corner, something would happen. It would hurt, too.

Laura was terrible at tennis. Her long legs were uncoordinated. She could neither dodge nor run. When she moved into a faster gait, she looked like a diseased antelope. Her limbs just didn't seem to be put together with any grease.

Miss Ellen occasionally had her try her hand at tennis, but the racket looked out of place. The worst thing was that Laura could never keep her eye on the ball. She was probably thinking about how she looked.

I knew from the start that Miss Ellen wasn't interested in me but in my ability to play the game. That didn't matter to me, though, because I shared her love. Let's just say that I was a kind of natural. Not only was I fast on the court, but I could use the racket with accuracy in a way the children I played against rarely could.

During the next year or so Miss Ellen trained me. When she thought I was ready, she mustered every tennis-playing child in a fifty-mile radius. Their mothers would drive up in their Lincolns, Cadillacs, or Packards. The girl or boy my age would approach me curiously, some sullen, others smiling.

The boy I liked most beat me the first five games. He had a shock of orange hair and a grin like a leprechaun. "Ready to get whipped," was what he usually said as we were about to start. When I finally beat him, he came up to the net smiling his crooked smile, "Play pretty good for a girl," he said, holding out his hand.

Most of the children, especially the girls, weren't so personable. Our contact was limited to the court. When we stopped for lemonade, they usually pouted. That was because I was usually beating them. Sometimes I liked to drive the ball almost down their throats for good measure.

"Don't be so aggressive," Miss Ellen cautioned once after such a finale. "You're making it hard enough for me to find people to play."

"They don't like to come back?"

"You're getting a reputation."

"Don't you want me to win," I asked.

"Yes, I do," she said simply.

She never said anything about me being colored, so I didn't know for sure if that was why the children were so cool. I suspected they might have guessed or that that was the gossip going around. My status was, under any circumstance, obviously ambiguous because Miss Ellen never explained, so far as I knew, or made up a lie or sought to invent a story.

Once I started beating the boys, I gained confidence. There was just something about white people. They weren't up to par on the court, no matter how hard they tried. Some girls almost bit their lips. I could see in their faces how they were bound and determined to defeat me. They tried so hard, too. I enjoyed beating them.

Once a father came with his son, probably because he'd heard from his wife how I'd beaten the boy. He jumped up in the middle of a set and started hollering, "Her backhand. Force her over in the left corner! Don't let her beat you!"

In those days it was really a total violation of the game to get excited on the sidelines. People just didn't do it. Miss Ellen scowled at the man.

The end of summer came, and I was scheduled to begin back in the third grade at George Washington Carver Colored Consolidated. Miss Ellen was playing me, interjecting corrections and coaching as we played. During the break, she said, "We've run out of people to play. Nobody around here can challenge you."

At the time I didn't know how that would change my life.

III

It was just before school began, too, when Jim Hall appeared again. It happened when I was coming back from getting sugar for Aunt Ida Mae. I'd ridden my bike down and was pedaling through the neighborhood before reaching the gates to Lawson Hall. Suddenly I came around a corner, and there was a bunch of white children blocking my way. They all lived on that street.

A large, fat white boy stepped out of the crowd and grabbed the handlebars of my bike. I had dismounted when I saw the group was blocking the street. Laura Lawson was there, too, holding back a little, but it was plain she was the one behind it and in charge.

What I was doing is looking around trying to figure out how to make a quick exit when the fat boy yelled, "No nigras can go through here today!" He was grinning as he approached.

I had the sugar in the basket of my bike. "I gotta bring the sugar back to my aunt," I said.

"Sorry," he said. "No nigras allowed through here." Before I could grow weary with him repeating himself and long before I could figure out what to do, he reached out and jerked my bike right out of my hands. He pulled it with him, backing off, and then he pushed it over in the ditch. When he'd done that, he turned back to me and dusted his hands off.

All I could do is stand there with my mouth open. Then I saw the bag of sugar rolling out of the basket and coming to rest flat and brown, half on the street, half on the grassy margin. I took a deep breath. As he grabbed for me, I dodged.

I still remember the meanness in his eyes. It was a sort of spark of joy. He was having fun, but I got away, snatched up the bag of sugar, clutching it to me like a football. Then I was headed out at full run right toward them all.

They moved in unison toward me shouting, "Get the nigger!"

If I hadn't been carrying that bag of sugar, they'd have never stopped me. I dodged them like they were standing still. For a few moments I was having fun, too, especially when a couple of the boys dived to clip me, missed, and ended up looking stupid on the ground. The dead weight of the sugar slowed me just enough for somebody finally to hit me from behind.

The pain was sharp in my legs as I went down. The sugar left my hands, carried into the air by its own dead weight. My brain told me that they were piling on top of me. My lungs told me I couldn't breathe. I thought I was going to die, and I only regretted that Aunt Ida Mae would miss the sugar I'd promised to bring her.

Just about the moment I thought I couldn't stand the pain any longer, things got lighter. Then I was sitting up, blinking my eyes (there were little circles dancing in front of me). I didn't stay there long, though. As soon as I realized I was free, I jumped up.

That's when I saw Jim Hall. He was tossing the children around like they were dolls. The fat boy rushed him, and he sidestepped and tripped him at the same time. Next he gave him a solid kick in the rump, shoving him sprawling and rolling over somebody's front yard. The fat boy let out a loud yelp.

Laura Lawson was standing at a good distance away. She was bending forward, indignant and cawing like a crow: "What are you doing, Jim Hall? Get out of here! This isn't your place! Go back to your dirty little farm!"

When Jim had tossed the last boy into a somersault and rolled him out of the way, he turned in Laura's direction. He was laughing, "What does it look like I'm doing? Don't nobody fool with this little girl. You hear! None of you. She's my friend. Anybody who bothers her, gets it from me."

"I'm gonna see that you get fired from your job," Laura threatened. "I'll get my daddy to get Mr. Hendricks to fire you."

Jim laughed at her, then came over to me, put his hand on my shoulder. "How are you. Didn't know I'd see you again. Heard they brought you into town. What happened?"

"My mama left," I said. "I got brought into town by my uncle and aunt."

"You live up at the Hall then?"

"Yep."

He looked over at Laura Lawson. "Hey, that's too bad. Got to put up with her?" I nodded. "Well, you better get that sugar on up there before Ida Mae is fit to be tied." Jim laughed. I thought I'd never heard anybody laugh that nicely.

"Thanks," I said.

"Hey, nothing to it. Tell me if they bother you again."

"Will you be around here?"

"I work at Mr. Hendricks' store now. He give me a job after school and on Saturdays."

I think I must have grinned at that. "So you'll be here in town all the time?"

"Yep. Delivering groceries like right now." He nodded, indicating the delivery bike parked back in a driveway. The front wheel was smaller than the back to accommodate the huge delivery basket that was full of brown bags of groceries.

"Good," I said. I picked up my bike, put the sugar in the basket and headed up the hill. I looked back a couple of times. Laura Lawson was still standing there staring after me. Jim was gone.

It all happened that fall. I think Miss Ellen was partly frustrated because I didn't have a lot of time to put into training and because she couldn't get anybody to come play me. Maybe word got out that I was going to the colored school.

Miss Ellen kept saying that I was at the top of my game. She itched to get me into some real competition. So she invited the pro from Augusta over to watch me play.

His name was Eric, and he was Swiss. A dark reef of hair encircled his head just above his ears, but the dome was like polished bronze, utterly bald, not even a waft of fuzz to disturb the smooth reflections of light mirrored there. He spoke a British English with a fairly heavy, sing-song German accent.

After Miss Ellen demonstrated my prowess, Eric played me himself for awhile. I could feel him holding back, watchful, testing me in the corners, trying my backhand, gauging my strength and accuracy in the serve.

"She's a natural, isn't she," Miss Ellen called. Eric nodded, but he was careful about passing out judgments too lightly. Tennis was a serious business to him. If he agreed, the expectations of his client might soar out of reach.

"Yes, not bad," he said as we gathered to drink the lemonade waiting on us.

"Not too bad," Miss Ellen cried. "Are you kidding! This kid is the best I've seen."

"She shows promise," Eric admitted.

"More than that. She's a natural."

"You've been working with her two years. You said so."

"Sure I have."

"Her ability is not natural. She is trained. You're a good coach, Ellen."

Miss Ellen wasn't interested in the compliment. "I've got a lot of talent to work with," she insisted. "Real talent." Eric sipped his drink. Then Miss Ellen came to the point, "Do you think I could get her into the tournament next spring?"

Eric tensed. He had trouble swallowing the lemonade he had just sipped. Once he managed, he had to cough and clear his throat. "Ellen, I don't beat about the bush. You know that."

"Sure, that's what I like about you."

"Good. I will tell you then. No, she can't play in the tournament."

Miss Ellen's face fell. She was not used to being contradicted or refused when she expressed a desire. She began to tremble, not too noticeably, but I saw it. "Why not," she said after a struggle to regain her composure.

Eric shook his head slowly and said very quietly, "You force me to say this in the child's presence, and I don't like it. She's colored, Ellen."

Then something happened I'd never seen before. A rouge color began to spill into Miss Ellen's face, starting at the hairline and coming down like a tide moving over a tan beach. I would have guessed that you couldn't see her blush because of her leathery tan, but I was dead wrong. "Who told you that, Eric," she asked, her voice cracking.

Eric looked at her without expression. "Everybody knows, Ellen. Surely you are aware of that?"

"Everybody?"

"Everybody."

"I don't believe it."

"Have you no idea what other people are thinking, what they know, what is obvious to them? How do you think you can hide this sort of thing? It means nothing to me. I find it…" he sought the appropriate term, "absurd," he said with some finality.

"Well, then—? If it's absurd, Eric, why—"

"No 'well then.' It is not up to me. I did not make the rules, Ellen, but they are there, and they won't change because we don't approve. I merely work at the club."

"These are rules that keep a player like her from the courts, Eric," Miss Ellen said with more passion than I'd known she possessed in her entire being. "They are wrong!"

Eric shook his head slowly, "I agree. But that does not matter. You know she cannot be entered. There is a color bar. Why must you even ask? Did you think I would lie for you and risk my job?"

"To hell with the color bar," Miss Ellen cried out. She stood up. She was thoroughly excited and angry. She had completely missed Eric's point. She was only thinking of her own plans.

"Not to hell with the color bar," Eric contradicted.

"Why?"

"Because we don't make the rules."

"Then why obey them?"

"You are rich, Ellen. I must work for a living. I cannot afford to do exactly as I please. It is a luxury to do that."

"But rules like that should be broken!"

"By somebody else. I refuse to lose my job for nothing. Nothing would change. The color bar would not be broken. It would merely be a humiliation for this child, and I would have to leave Augusta and look for something else."

"You're a coward," Miss Ellen blurted. I flinched as if she'd hit me and then looked at Eric in fear and embarrassment. Miss Ellen had gone too far. I remember it like a frame in some home movie that stopped: Eric underwent a metamorphosis. His expression hardened. He stood up.

"Until now I have indulged you because you love the game. Now I have had enough," he said. The way he said it, I knew it was final.

"I thought we were friends," Miss Ellen said. There was something uncertain in her voice. She was beginning to realize that she had overstepped the boundaries.

Eric reached down and picked up his racket, set down the empty glass with his free hand and started walking. "You thought we were friends," he said over his shoulder. "Very funny."

"Eric, it isn't funny," she said as she leapt to her feet and vaguely began to follow behind him. "Friendship isn't funny."

He stopped at the gate and turned around. Miss Ellen was moving so fast that she had to stop quickly to avoid running into him. It was almost comic – for a second.

After starting back to escape the collision, Eric gathered his dignity. "Friendship," he spoke the word carefully, a world of contempt shaped in his clipped manner. "You rich women know nothing of friendship. We are not your friends. We are there to spoil you. When we refuse to do your bidding, you despise us."

"I—" Miss Ellen began, but her shoulders slumped. She was out of fuel. She had never heard anything like Eric was saying before.

"Try to remember that there are other people in the world beside yourself. Goodbye, Ellen," Eric said, mustering a dignity meant to admonish her. He stepped through the gate, threw open the door to his little yellow MG, plopped himself down into it. The motor ground to a start, he threw it into gear and left in a hail of gravel that made Miss Ellen turn and bend over as if shielding herself against a heavy wind.

That must have been when Miss Ellen made her decision to take me up north to live. Aunt Ida Mae was against it. I heard her whispering loudly to Uncle Cajus after they thought I was asleep:

"That woman gone take this chile away up north, Cajus. We gots to stop it."

"Why we want to stop it, woman?"

"Cause it ain't right."

"Why ain't it right?"

"Cause she do it just cause it please her. She ain't doing it for the chile."

"How you know what Miss Ellen doing anything for, woman? Hush and go to sleep.""

"You gone just let her do it, ain't you. I see that now. You just gone let her do it."

"What's so bad about it. She'll take that chile up there and get her an education. That can't be bad."

"She be taking her up there so she can play that rich folks game. When she's tired of it, she'll bring the chile back. What do you think about that?"

"What's wrong with the chile going with her. She'll probably get to go to a white school and get a good education."

"What good that gone do her when she's back here? She'll be like a fish out of water. This won't be home no more. She'll talk different and won't fit in with the life she got here."

"Aw, hush up now. It late. I gotta sleep."

Aunt Ida Mae continued to grumble inarticulately until they both went off to sleep.

Uncle Cajus was right, of course. No matter what Aunt Ida Mae thought, there wasn't much anybody could have done. If Miss Ellen wanted to take me off up north, who would stop her? My own mother had gone up north herself and left me behind. What had she cared?

The thing is that I wasn't sure I minded leaving Georgia and segregation. I kept thinking about them saying I'd go to a white school, and the thought of being white was appealing. If I were white, I could play all those snotty, spoiled children and whip their britches off them. One thing I knew for sure. That would be fun.

Laura Lawson wasn't finished with me, though she pretended to be really friendly during the last couple of weeks. She fooled me good, too. I thought she had had a change of heart because she smiled and didn't stick me with a needle when she passed nor play some other trick.

Shortly before our departure, I was walking to the court to practice with Miss Ellen. I had on my pretty little white tennis outfit, complete with canvas Keds. The rubber sole wasn't very thick in those days.

"Bet I can beat you," Laura said, showing up on the gravel. "Let's race to the courts."

"Wanna race," I asked.

"Sure," Laura said.

I got a spurt of speed and headed across the gravel. The October cool had taken the sweat out of running. As I dashed, I thought how good it would feel to leave Laura far behind. She was not a fast runner. I could easily beat her. And that's when I felt the pain shoot up my leg.

I will never forget looking down at my foot and seeing the big nail sticking right up through the canvas of the shoe. Horror spilled over me, coursed through my arteries. I began to scream long before the awful pain got to my brain.

"Pipe down," Laura said.

I screamed louder and hopped around on my good foot. I held the wounded foot up in my arms, cradling it. I was crying out of anger as much as pain because I knew Laura had played another joke on me.

Miss Ellen came running from the tennis court. Later the tetanus shot hurt as bad as the nail. Dr. Veazey brought out one of those huge, horse needles and stuck it in my arm. People said I could be heard clear to the courthouse.

It was pretty plain to everybody that Laura had planted the nail and challenged me to race knowing the chances were good I'd step right on it. I suppose I could have missed it, but I've always believed she had several nails in the gravel and had removed and hidden them.

The next afternoon when I got home from school, Aunt Ida Mae's eyes were really big with lots of white showing, so I knew something was happening. It turned out that Miss Ellen was shouting at Judge Lawson in the library wing.

As I nursed my foot, she shouted a long time, but she wasn't able to bully him into spanking Laura. He did decide to send Laura off to a school in Virginia, but that wasn't anything special. Lawsons went off to school in Virginia usually, anyway, so I doubt if it had anything to do with getting the nail stuck in my foot. There'd be no revenge for me.

In Connecticut Miss Ellen took a stone house on a quiet street not too far from the tennis club. I don't remember the name of the place. I don't really remember anything well or just in patches, probably because of the accident. It is all kind of a haze with clear spots, like moving through a fog but finding places where the fog is suddenly gone.

I remember that I was embarrassed about not having a father. My friends would ask me where my father was, and the devil would really tempt me to lie. But I fought it because I knew I'd just get myself into a bind later. "I don't have a father," I'd say.

"You don't have a father," they'd croon. Their eyes would bulge, and they would look at each other like I'd just said a bad word or something. Everybody must have had a father in Connecticut. They just couldn't imagine not having one.

I figured saying I had no father was better than saying I had no mother or even worse telling them I was really colored. Their eyes would have bulged then, for sure.

What I can remember about those first months in Connecticut is how careful I had to be not to let a vowel slide or to start swaying with my hips or dancing or making other colored movements. I remember being pretty worried that I might make a slip, and I did, too. Sometimes other children seemed to notice but mostly they didn't. I was careful never to repeat anything I did wrong.

I don't know how long it took me to learn everything, especially how to talk like a Yankee without having to think about it, but it finally became second nature to me. I also learned to walk like the other white children.

The way you do it is this: You just don't sway and then you tuck your fanny in a little and walk straight ahead. My voice got where it didn't go whirling up into soprano registers in that explosive way colored people had back in Lawsonville, Georgia. In Connecticut you just kept this kind of dry nasal tone like all the Yankees around me, kind of like you're just singing one note.

It's true that I often had mixed feelings about being white. I missed playing chase. I missed Aunt Ida Mae hugging me into her vast corpulence. I missed Uncle Cajus's wonderfully warm bass thundering across the lawns.

First it was hard being white in Connecticut because, I'm telling you, those Yankee whites didn't fool around. They were very serious about academics and getting everything right. You couldn't wiggle around in your desk, either, and they didn't laugh nearly as much as my people back home. Once you got adjusted, though, it wasn't so bad.

I missed most the AME Methodist-Episcopal service on Sunday. In Connecticut Miss Ellen took me to an Episcopal church because that's who owned the school I was attending. It was part of the bargain, I think, that we go there. The church was a stone Neo-Gothic building about half a block from my classroom.

I liked the banners all hung out and hanging down in a long row on either side of the sanctuary. The cookies they served after the service in the parish hall were good, too. There were also the colorful vestments the priest wore for each season.

I thought that our own Reverend Smothers would have been very envious of those vestments because he liked to put on as much color as was decent. The service in Connecticut was, on the other hand, very different from the AME Zion church, or any other colored church I knew about.

Instead of somebody standing up and saying, "Amen, brother," people got up and down in unison. Their faces remained, on the whole, impassive like they were bored and just going through the motions, or like they were involved in some very private business. They knelt, and they jumped up. Then they knelt again.

Everything was done according to the instructions in the red book. It was like they couldn't have thought how to do anything themselves, so they needed to get it all out of a book. Nobody uttered a word unless it was printed in that book, not one single, stray "amen."

So that's the basic difference between white people and colored people, I thought. Colored people are playing it all by ear, whereas white people like to follow the book word for word, verse by verse. If you miss a word, it throws them all off. They get really bothered, while colored people invent the story as they go. If they can't think of anything that makes sense they just shout, 'hallelujah.' White people have memorized how it ought to be, and they want to be careful to get every word just right.

I guess that if everybody hadn't been getting up and kneeling down and getting up again, a lot of people might just have dozed off in the pews. The pews were so angular and hard, on the other hand, that might not have been possible. The wood wasn't hewn to human contours.

The longest period you had to sit was when the Rector (which is what they called the preacher) gave his sermon. He kept it pretty short compared to the sermons I'd heard back home, but even that would leave a pain in the butt.

The Rector was a tall, handsome, white-headed man who had very white skin and looked like he spent a lot of time getting himself groomed and dressed in the morning. After the service he would stand in the doorway of the church, so that you couldn't get out without shaking his hand; yet, no sooner than you'd taken his hand in yours than his eyes had wandered to the next person.

The thing I learned is that life as a white person isn't as much fun as being colored. It seemed hard for white people to laugh much as a rule. I knew the Judge didn't laugh and Miss Ellen had hardly ever been able to muster a single smile, but somehow I hadn't realized it applied to the whole white race, as well. The drunks in Lawsonville, Georgia had, for instance, laughed raucously out at the bench where they sat across from the courthouse.

In Connecticut a majority of white people need to resort to heavy drink before they can get into laughter at all. There was a hard edge to being white that was new to me, something unforgiving and metallic. It would be hard to put it in words, but I got the feel for it. I'd say the difference in being white and colored is the difference between stainless steel and a nicely oiled wood.

There were times, especially during the first months (which I remember better than the last couple of years), when I just thought I couldn't handle it. This white thing got to me. The last thing I ever would have done is make Miss Ellen ashamed of me, so I kept working at it and finally became a good student and almost a real white person.

Organization is what I learned in Connecticut. Organization became second nature to me. The most important thing about being organized is to do what needs to be done *now*. Not later. Not tomorrow. *Now*. And get it all right, just like in the book. Once I learned these two things, my problems were over. At some point, I reached the stage where not being organized made me uncomfortable. When I finally reached the stage where not getting something precise bothered the dickens out of me, I knew I was as good as white.

I am sure my progress on the tennis circuits was steady and satisfactory because, if I remember anything at all, it is that look on Miss Ellen's face. She was about as satisfied as I had ever seen her before, and I was glad that my playing made that possible.

I mixed my playing. When I really wanted to beat my opponent good, I played colored. I improvised. I played by instinct. If it felt right, I just did it. When I wanted to win but not too much, I played white, calculating, keeping the whole court both in my mind and in my eyes.

Miss Ellen told me to call her "Aunt" Ellen in public, but in private I kept on calling her Miss Ellen, and she never told me to stop it. We had this fiction that we maintained for the world, and it molded us into a solid phalanx against everybody else.

Miss Ellen was always a good coach. She never lost patience. She sometimes showed a very thin smile when I did something really right. When I won a challenging tournament, I even saw her almost laugh.

As a child loves whoever is there for her, I loved Miss Ellen. She had no idea how to return my affection. There was no way she could have known. Everybody said that her father had been the meanest man in Georgia. Even so I knew that she loved me – after her fashion.

When you have an accident like we had, it isn't any surprise that there might be long stretches of time when you don't remember anything at all. That's the way it was with me. It was a partial amnesia.

I didn't forget the geography, mathematics, and English I learned, but I forgot the process of learning it. I forgot most of the part of my life I spent in the stone house and at school. I forgot the names of the friends I had made. What I didn't forget is how to speak standard, Yankee American.

I got a prize at some point in school. I still have it. It is a certificate that designates me an honor roll student. I can't tell you exactly how I received the certificate, nothing about the circumstances. Was my name called in an assembly or did the teacher just hand it to me, or did they send it through the mail? I don't know.

If I can't remember the events, I sometimes remember the feelings attached to them. I remember what it felt like to hold my racket. I remember the exhilaration of moving across the court, how it felt as I balanced on my feet. I remember how it felt to win. I liked that feeling a lot.

When I won big that last time, we had come to the place at the head of the table. Miss Ellen's plans for me had culminated, in one respect, but were beginning in another. Nobody made big money on the tennis circuit in those days. Money didn't matter to Miss Ellen. It was the sport that counted, and I was headed for the big time.

"We need to celebrate," Miss Ellen said. Her voice had something girlish, a slight dash of hysterical jubilance I'd never heard there before. She had drunk a couple of glasses of champagne in the lobby as people stopped to congratulate us. When we left the club, she whistled. She even seemed to notice the valets who brought the Jaguar up from the parking lot.

Speeding is what Miss Ellen did when she was particularly elated. In no time at all we were speeding along a winding cliff road. Far below us in the semi-darkness, the surf crashed through the jagged rocks. "When you've beaten everybody and are at the top, Folly," she cried above the wind, "you need to eat lobster."

Eating lobster meant driving the coastal road to a restaurant built on an outcropping of the sheer cliff. She had taken me there before, and we had sat at a table by candlelight eating seafood. It was her favorite getaway, and that is exactly where we were headed that night. It was the closest Miss Ellen ever got to romance.

She was whistling, and there was no way I could let her know that we were driving too fast. How could I spoil her mood? So I just started shutting my eyes around the hairpin turns and prayed that we would reach the restaurant safely.

I remember exactly what she was singing when the truck and the motorcycle rounded the curve ahead of us. It was "Dancing in the Dark." The motorcycle and the truck occupied both lanes. I remember thinking how odd it was because there were only two lanes of pavement. The rest was void, dark and empty space with just enough daylight to see them coming at us.

The motorcycle was passing the truck, I suppose. Before we could do more than see what was happening, that same reckless young man was driving up over our hood. I saw the red bandanna he was wearing. The rest is a confusion of disconnected images and sound of crashing steel and collapsing glass.

IV

One morning I woke up in a blinding white light that struck me like a careening train. I squeezed my eyes shut. Medicinal odors penetrated the darkness. I opened the left eye very slightly. Pungent doctor smells made me wrinkle my nose. When I opened my eyes again I saw a big, round black face in front of me, and I heard Uncle Cajus's voice say: "I think she's a stirring! Nurse, she's waking up!"

Judge Lawson had sent Uncle Cajus up to get me. He was staying in a colored boarding house not too far from the hospital. Through him I learned that even in Connecticut there was a colored world separate from the white world in which I had been living.

There were supposedly no laws that required the separation between one kind of American and another. The colored world was a refuge offered from the ubiquitous indignities to which colored people were subjected in the course of a normal day even in Connecticut. It was clear to me in Connecticut that coloreds actually preferred the separation.

The two weeks I remained in the hospital, Uncle Cajus played out an elaborate fiction and insisted on my joining him. He was the family retainer sent up to get me, the young Missus.

Once I woke up and heard two nurses talking about my situation. Their voices were indignant. "Can you believe they just sent up that old colored man to get her?" And, "They say the woman killed was really her mother." Then, "These Southern aristocrats are pretty sick." And, finally, in a whisper, "Sometimes I wonder if she's really white. There's something about that child…"

When I was discharged from hospital, we stayed a night there before taking the Silver Comet via New York and Washington to Atlanta. Judge Lawson summoned me into the library on my arrival. He sat behind his desk. "Sir," I said interrogatively, as I opened the door.

He looked up – and up until his faded blue eyes turned to the ceiling. He hadn't changed. It was still the same disconcerting feeling of being interviewed by a zombie. "Sit down, Folly," he said. I dutifully walked over to the chair.

There was a long pause after I settled down upon the seat. Judge Lawson fumbled in his desk, took out his pipe, filled it from the tobacco tin. He tapped the tobacco down. The aroma drifted my way. It was the delicious Walter Raleigh honey smell so familiar from my childhood.

Judge Lawson took out a match from the box, his long, white fingers accentuated in the act; then he scratched it on the abrasive strip running alongside the box. The flame burst into life, and he thrust it up to the pipe and began to puff.

As smoke rose out of the bowl, Judge Lawson leaned back in his chair, squirming around until he was slumped in his favorite position on the base of his spine. He propped his knees against the desk. "Was the trip down comfortable," he asked, still looking at the ceiling.

"Sir," I started, rousing myself from the semi-stupor into which I had fallen during the long process of his filling and lighting his pipe, "it was good. Uncle Cajus and I did fine. Thank you for sending him to get me."

The Judge wrapped his gigantic hand around the bowl of the pipe and took it out of his mouth. He sat regarding it in affectionate silence a moment. It was certainly a tool of pleasure for him. The next thing he said in his high-pitched tenor was "How did it happen?"

"The wreck?"

"Yes. Miss Ellen..." he stumbled a moment, looked down now at the desk, "how—did she?"

I told him about the accident without saying anything about Miss Ellen's speeding. He seemed satisfied. Thrusting the pipe between his thin lips and clamping down upon it with his teeth, Judge Lawson puffed several times until he looked like a coal-burning freight train.

After that he began to speak at intervals through his teeth and from the side of his mouth unencumbered by the pipe: "You've broken your right arm in several places, I hear?" And, once I nodded satisfactorily, "Went to a very good school, too?" I nodded. He puffed; then, "Take any languages?"

"French," I said.

"French!" he exclaimed. "That's not what I'd have taken."

"My advisor told me to take it," I explained.

"Advisor." Judge Lawson took his pipe out of his mouth and grimaced. "Never good to listen to advisors. They never know what's good for a person. Now I'd take German, if I were you. That's what I'd take."

"Well, I'm not going to go to that school anymore," I said. "So I guess there won't be any problem."

"That's true," he said, looking slightly confused. "All the better. Er, I mean, good for what I wanted to ask you."

"Yes," I said.

"See here, Folly, girl, you know I read German. Did a lot of it at Harvard. Still do. I read a lot. It's an interest of mine."

"Yes, sir."

"So here's the thing: I thought you might want to join me. In reading German, that is. You see?"

"I doubt I'll have time," I answered honestly. "I have school now at George Washington Carver—"

"That shouldn't take so much of your time," Judge Lawson said emphatically.

"Well, it does, actually. I go early in the morning and get back about three fifteen or so. I take a short cut. But then I have to help Aunt Ida Mae—"

"Help," he said, his tenor taking a shrill, indignant rise.

"Yes," I said, thinking that he should know. He'd seen me often enough doing the dusting, sweeping, and other chores.

"Well, you ought to be able to take some time from that, then."

"That'll just leave Aunt Ida Mae more to do, and I don't think I'd like that," I said.

"I'll speak to her."

"How often did you want to do this," I wondered.

"It'll take at least a couple of hours a week, don't you think? I mean, you've had French, haven't you? You know language isn't easy to get the fundamentals of – and I'd want you to make pretty rapid progress, so that we could discuss things, don't you know."

I was astonished. I had never seen Judge Lawson talk so much in my life, not to anybody. "I'll ask her," I said.

"No, that's fine. I'll talk to her myself."

"I wouldn't want her ending up with more work."

"No, don't you worry about that. And I'll give you twenty-five cents an hour. Per meeting, I mean."

That is how I began to learn German with Judge Lawson. It was at the beginning of the eleventh grade, my reentry into George

Washington Carver, my return to Lawsonville, Georgia, and five months after my sixteenth birthday.

As it turned out, and I don't want to sound conceited, the work my classmates were doing at George Washington Carver was stuff I'd done long before at my Episcopal Day School. Mainly what I found myself doing at school was wasting time. Biding time, you could call it. But I wasn't learning anything. Except maybe how to talk colored again.

Now the people in Lawsonville, Georgia were no better and no worse than anywhere else. Take Harry Dale, the Principal of George Washington Carver. He was one of a kind, a dandy dresser and a tall man with narrow hips who bore some resemblance (at least in the figure) to Fred Astaire. He was the best-paid colored man in the county and had a master's degree from Columbia University.

When Harry Dale had come to town with his wife, Rhonda Dale, they had been the most elegant couple anybody had seen, black or white, in at least a generation. Rhonda Dale was descended from Thomas Jefferson, and her father was way up on the GS scale in some Washington governmental office. In fact, Rhonda Dale was practically white except for her hair, plus she had a dazzling smile and perfect teeth.

What I heard was how Rhonda Dale had breezed into town in her two-toned Pontiac not recognizing from anything how the whites might feel about her being so beautiful, driving such a nice car, wearing such uptown clothes, and speaking better and clearer American English than any of them could. It was like she was deaf and dumb, in a way, and it made you wonder how a person could be so indifferent to things around her that could really affect her (and finally did).

Her sojourn in Georgia was just bound to be fairly brief, under the circumstances, or just about as long as it would take for the worst of the whites to think up some way to humiliate and embarrass her. Yet, Rhonda never gave any sign that she suspected anything. Not right up until it actually happened.

The first thing that offended was Rhonda's descent from Thomas Jefferson. I don't know how the word got out. Rhonda didn't brag. It did, nevertheless, and it got to the wrong white ears, too. Outrage is a mild way to put how the UDC women and the Women's Club ladies in Lawsonville felt about such a claim. It was as bad as some colored woman coming in and saying that she was the great-granddaughter of Jesus Christ; white people were bound to take offense.

The second and, perhaps, most unforgivable thing about Rhonda Dale was her beauty. Not that it offended the men. They didn't mind colored women being beautiful. But their wives did. They felt that a colored woman ought to look as African as possible. It was only decent. If they could have, the white ladies of Lawson County would have prescribed by law that every colored woman in Lawsonville should wear a bone through her nose, walk with a bouncy strut, talk in a lazy, sassy fashion and carry baskets of laundry on her head.

Short of somebody throwing acid in her face or running over her with a bulldozer, it looked like Rhonda Dale's beauty was there to stay. Her elegance appeared to be just as integral a part of her person as her good looks. Her accent sealed the bargain and made her totally offensive. But what really galled was that the white women sensed they weren't really real to Rhonda Dale, the way the local native is never real to a visiting person from the center of civilization. They knew that Rhonda Dale found Lawsonville and all its inhabitants, black and white, a little quaint, perhaps, if anything.

Rhonda Dale would come into a store looking like a film star, dressed like Old Atlanta, and speaking like somebody with a distinguished education. At first the white clerks and customers almost swallowed their tongues and popped their eyeballs. Later, Rhonda's absent-minded disinterest seemed more like arrogance. It made them really mad. They wanted to make her notice that they really were superior.

The thing is, if a colored woman could be so beautiful, elegant, and well spoken what good was a system that was supposed to reserve the privileges for whites? Rhonda Dale threatened the very foundations of Southern segregation because she looked more like Scarlet O'Hara than any white woman in the county.

Rhonda Dale's blithe manner added insult to injury. If she could have only seemed a little self-conscious and guilty about her qualities, it would have made a lot better impression on the white community. So what Rhonda Dale did do not too many months after her arrival (and I was still in Connecticut and just pieced all this together from hearsay) was walk innocently into a fatal trap.

It was a trap set by the ladies of Lawsonville led by one of the self-appointed grande dames of the town, Miz Dubbie Happity. One thing you could say about Dubbie Happity: She was a woman of substantial parts. Her bosom was an ambitious affair extending far out in front of her. It looked more like an advancing single front than two separate and distinct breasts.

Miz Happity cultivated a commanding air that had been developed and strengthened by her experience running the local laundry. Her vocation had given her ample opportunity to lord it over the colored women who did the hard work for her. She had no mercy, and they had no choice but to accept her abuse at the very meager wages she paid them. The alternative was always, for the colored women of Lawsonville, not to work at all. Which left Miz Happity with a gigantic Miss Napoleon complex.

Miz Happity knew immediately what she wanted to do with Rhonda Dale. She had only to look at her. After that, it was a matter of a couple of months for the ladies, under her leadership, to set the trap. Not that it was completely unanimous, however, for there were some women who resisted. Emily Conyers refused, for instance, to allow her store to be the site of the "incident."

Such resistance notwithstanding, there were others more than happy to offer their stores as venues for that drama of revenge and humiliation. Purly Goodfellow owned Goodfellows, a store she had very shrewdly managed since her husband's death, and she was in an excellent position to be obliging. Rhonda Dale knitted at home and was, therefore, a regular customer at Goodfellows.

The Goodfellow store sat squarely across from the courthouse just on the corner of Main and Justice Streets. It had a venerable presence in town, though it had undergone some mutation since Purly's husband had died ten years earlier. The old man would never have stooped to specializing in women's knitting supplies.

Rhonda Dale came in at regular intervals to replenish her supply of knitting goods, so the conspiracy had only to bide its time. They set up an alarm system and remained on the alert.

When it happened, Purly phoned Miz Dubbie at her house two blocks away, and she came running. The great bulk of a woman entered the store huffing and puffing from the strain of hurrying. Everybody in the store shrank from the scene, but Rhonda Dale took no notice. She was as usual dreamily fingering the merchandise and not noticing anything around her. Somebody said she was even humming softly to herself.

She had gathered a few items and then started for the cash register. That's where she ran into Miz Happity. "Excuse me," Rhonda Dale said, becoming dimly aware of the ominous presence of the enormous white woman blocking her path.

"No, excuse me," Miz Happity enunciated in a loud, threatening voice. "Are you going to put yourself ahead of me, gal?"

"No, not at all," Rhonda said, ignoring the ominously denigrating form of address Miz Happity used. Rhonda then stepped back a step or two to give Miz Happity space to continue with her business (without seeming to care what it might be).

Nothing she could have done would have sufficed for Miz Happity. She could have given her fifty feet of free space. The die were cast, thumbs were down, and Rhonda's fate was sealed. "You can't get out of this, gal," Miz Happity declared at the top of her lungs, thrusting herself, bosom first, at Rhonda. "What you need is a lesson. Here in this town we don't tolerate uppity nigras!"

"Please, go ahead," Rhonda urged. Her gorgeous eyes had widened, and she realized an audience had gathered in surrounding aisles, faces leering, eyes hungry to watch the kill.

"I will go ahead," Miz Happity cried, "but not because a colored person lets me!"

People were murmuring and nodding around her as if a moral point had been forcefully made in a sermon. Rhonda Dale waited a moment or two and suddenly turned, hurrying back to replace the items she had held in her hands. Then she left the store.

"That ought to do it," Miz Happity announced to the small crowd. But she was wrong. Rhonda Dale did not leave Lawsonville the next day or even the next month. She was seen again and again stepping out of her two-tone Pontiac.

The men on the Board of Education got wind of the scene at Goodfellows and became worried. Harry Dale had, you see, been part of a scheme to avert disaster by proving to the whole country that the rule of "separate but equal" was not a lie.

"Look here," they would explain, "coloreds in this county have a fine new school and a principal with a degree from Columbia University in New York." The point they were trying to make was that Lawson County coloreds had equal rights.

When the board members came out of session smoking the stumps of their cigars and looking grim, they each went to their separate domicile. Once inside the walls of their homes, they told their wives that such harassment of the Negro principal and his wife would have to cease.

That was all well and good except that Miz Happity escaped admonishment altogether since it was she who ruled at home. She was as much autocrat in her home as she was at the laundry. Nobody crossed her. Least of all a husband. Her opinion of the town menfolk was no higher than her assessment of the colored community. She had been heard often to articulate that view in the most straightforward manner, saying: "Men in general are no better than Nigras. They are lazy, sorry, and usually up to no good!"

When it became apparent that the incident at Goodfellows had not vanquished Rhonda Dale, Dubbie Happity decided to step up the campaign and masterminded the final *coup de grace* that sent Rhonda packing.

It happened at three p.m. on a Friday afternoon. It was on that day that Rhonda, responding to a very nice invitation she had received through the mail, came up the steps of the Liberty Café. Inside several of the more militant ladies were waiting to ambush her. Standing in the vanguard of this little clique of warriors was the hysterical and nearly senile Cecilia Bonum, who was the eighty-four year old owner of the venerable eatery.

Cecilia Bonum was the product of a generation and mindset that would have considered George Wallace soft on Civil Rights and segregation an imprudent step away from slavery. She had been known to swear that she would slit her own throat before she would serve a Negro at her counter or one of her tables.

Age had dimmed more than her vision and left her with an obsessive determination to oppose what she generally called "any Communist plot." In the last stages of her delusions, Miz Bonum would be observed ejecting out-of-town patrons who spoke with a Northern accent, declaring to all and sundry that her tables were occupied even when the place was half empty.

As the unwary wander haplessly into the mouth of roaring lions, so Rhonda Dale smiled wistfully to herself as she mounted the steps to the café. She was proving herself to be one of those abstracted persons too busy with her own thoughts to give the world its due. Her wistful smile reflected her quiet pleasure at the odd invitation she had received the day before to attend a coffee that morning at the Cafe. Her husband, Harry, had expressed his doubts about the anonymous invitation, but all had fallen on deaf ears.

If Rhonda Dale had thought about it at all, she had seen it as a clumsy attempt by the local yokels to apologize for her treatment at Goodfellows. They want to show they're sorry, she whispered to herself. It was only right that she condescend to sip the hot liquid of good fellowship with them.

It was, of course, a dastardly plot, nastily conceived and consistent with the most noxious traditions of the rural South. No sooner had poor Rhonda opened the door and entered the Café than Cecilia Bonum launched at her like a rocket off a catapult, crying at the top of her creaky voice: "No niggers is allowed in my café!"

Rhonda Dale was thrown back against the door in a collision with the juggernaut. Cecilia's flailing hands got tangled in her victim's necklace, and this set off somewhere in the clouded corridors of her geriatric brain the notion that Rhonda was her assailant. "Help! Help," Cecilia screamed, "she done caught my hands and is trying to tie me down!"

Rhonda and Cecilia might very well have rolled and kicked about the floor of the Liberty Café for some time had not Vince

O'Doole very reluctantly set his coffee cup down and gone to separate them.

Vince was a mechanic at Mark White's garage, a man of gentle persuasion who hated violence and had become a Quaker just before World War II. He wrestled the two women apart and finally stood the shaky Cecilia upon her feet. "Thou better go while Thou canst," he told Rhonda gently.

Standing up the fight came back into Cecilia. Too blind to see Vince clearly, she tried to beat him away, crying, "Now she's a smearing nigger grease on me!"

Rhonda Dale took Vince's advice and beat a hasty retreat out the front door. Catfish was sitting on the bench outside and described later to anybody who would listen how Rhonda Dale flung herself into her Pontiac and left the town square with the straight eight engine whining out its familiar lament in each gear until she was out of sight.

In the months that followed, whenever somebody asked Harry Dale about his wife, he would explain that Rhonda's mother had taken ill up in Washington, D. C. She had had to hurry home to nurse her. To the question when she was to be expected back, Harry might look just a little pained and say, "Oh, it won't be long. It won't be long..." His answer became less convincing, however, as the months became years.

Members of the Board of Education and other politically savvy men in town held their breath for a couple of months, fully expecting Harry Dale to resign his position, pack his bags and leave in angry protest at the violence done his wife. Gradually, however, they relaxed. Harry Dale did not resign. Inexplicably, he stayed on sans wife and continued to occupy his comfortable brick residence alone.

It is said that the leading members of the colored community were as relieved as those of the white community were that Harry stayed. Harry was part of a strategy proposed by federal senators and representatives to stay off integration. As I mentioned before, men in high office had advised the county elite that it was time to do more than give lip service to the well-worn legal principle, "separate but equal." Otherwise, integration was certainly coming, they predicted.

The local response to the warning had been to build the new buildings that housed George Washington Carver Colored Consolidated. Harry Dale was another of their concessions to necessity. Nobody could doubt his credentials since he had an M.A. from a major Yankee university.

The colored business community, the deacons of the AME church, and all the older colored people were as much afraid of change as the whites. They especially did not want strangers coming into town to lead sit-down protests and other disturbing demonstrations, get the whites all in an uproar and then leave the mess as they went off to another place. Who was to say that anything that changed would not change for the worse. At least folks knew where they stood the way things were.

Change, Deacon Cassius Brown had told the AME Zion Church the Sunday after Rhonda Dale disappeared, had never been for the good. People who called for change always made promises, but those promises had always been broken. He cited some Bible verses that seemed to support his contention about the Hebrews grumbling and wanting change and how it always displeased God.

The oldest members of the colored community told stories of how white people from up north had come down after the Civil War to emancipate the colored and ended up just getting them in more trouble than before with the KKK and so forth. "Yankees burnt our houses and stole our chickens just like they done with the whites," the oldest woman in Lawson County insisted in a peepy, trembling voice while her great great grandchildren held her on her feet. In short, the consensus was against rocking the boat.

V

It was this Harry Dale, who had been a de facto bachelor for four years, who was now standing in front of me about to speak. He had stopped me in mid stride, and now he was saying, "Folly?"

"Yes, sir," I answered as evenly as I could as I wondered how he knew me by name.

We were standing in a mid-September heat wave, in the open, treeless lawns between the main school and the gym. It is difficult to exaggerate Harry Dale's glamour. He towered over me, but he didn't take up much volume. His voice was powerful but soft and kind, at the same time. His presence shimmered in a gloriously courteous aura, and I felt that I was being addressed by a demigod emerged from the ether of the cosmos.

As I looked up into the distinguished Mandarin features of his aristocratic face, I almost gasped. Seldom did one see so many admirable features combined in a single human being. He almost didn't seem real.

"I'd like to speak to you in the office. Right after P.E. Is that okay?"

"What," I asked breathlessly, realizing I had not listened.

"Come to my office," he said smiling.

"I have P.E.," I said.

"After P.E."

"Should I change out of my gym shorts first?"

"No. No, just come right to the office."

"Yes, sir."

He smiled reassuringly, turned and hurried away. I stood looking after him. Behind me Chandra startled me by growling, "I know what he want." Chandra was a large, big-boned, vulgar girl who had made it plain that she didn't like me. I also heartily despised her. "He want some of that good, young, high-yellow poontang, baby-cakes."

I sniffed my contempt as I swung away to hurry to the gym. But Chandra was not about to let me off so easily. She jogged alongside me grinning and mocking me with, "That what he want, you little Yankee shit. He smell your good, tight pussy. That's what a black man like."

"He isn't black," I sneered. Stopping at the door to the gym, I whirled about to confront her with a defiant, "You are beneath contempt!"

"What you say," Chandra sneered back, unimpressed. The words were lost on her, but she knew it was an insult. "Listen, you watch your tongue. I gone wipe up the road with you fancy little ass!" As I turned to go into the building, she caught my arm and gave it a quick twist to show me just how willing she was to cause pain.

In the locker room our P.E. teacher Miss Blair asked me what Mr. Dale had wanted, and I told her I'd have to go see him. Within the hour I was standing in the front office of the school taking the full brunt of Miz Battle's withering scorn: "Why you standing like a statue, gal, and you still in your gym shorts. Get your dress back on!"

"Mr. Dale told me to come right away and not to change," I answered with less confidence than I'd have liked.

Miz Battle squinched her nose up until it was almost tucked under her eyes. She seemed to be considering the unlikely prospect that a student might actually be telling the truth. Then she instructed me in the tone of one speaking to an idiot or a murderer, "So he tell you to come in your shorts?"

"Yes, m'aam," I answered, my tone sagging.

"Then what you waiting for? Go on and knock on his door if he waiting! Don't be wasting my time lolling around here in the front office!"

"Yes, m'aam," I said as I hurried by her.

Beyond a short, dark hall, I came to a door with a brass plate tacked on it. Upon the plate were emblazoned the words, "Harry Dale, M.A., Principal."

I knocked.

"Come in," a voice beckoned from within. When I tried to open the door, however, it caught upon an Oriental rug laid on top of the wall-to-wall carpeting.

"Just straighten it out and shove," Mr. Dale instructed. When I was unable to make it work, he stood and came around the desk to help.

"I'm sorry, sir."

"It happens all the time," he shrugged. "Sit down, Folly."

He stood leaning slightly against the desk and looking down at me as he arranged objects on his desk. I felt a flutter in my stomach and became conscious of my shorts and tight athletic t-shirt. The material stretched much too tightly over my newly sprouted breasts. I crossed my arms in a futile effort to cover them better.

Harry Dale smiled very leisurely, as if he were enjoying taking his time. I was torn between resenting my breasts and being pleased my person somehow gave him pleasure.

What Harry Dale did next is extract a cigarette, put it in his mouth, take out a silver lighter and light it. His movements were elegant enough to have been choreographed. His fingers were long and slender, his wrist almost delicate. I had to think to shut my mouth.

"Well," Harry Dale said as he let the smoke drift out through his nostrils. "You've been in Connecticut. Gone to school there?"

"Yes, sir," I replied.

"Country Day School. Episcopal."

I nodded but refrained from another yes, sir.

"Yes," Harry Dale nodded. His eyes wandered over me again. "I went to a school in Chicago. Did you know that? No, I don't expect you did. It's in my biography, though. The one in the school yearbook." He walked back behind his desk and sat down. Even in sitting his shirt retained its crisp creases.

"I haven't seen the school yearbook," I said.

Harry Dale leaned back comfortably in the large leather chair. His eyes came level to my face and fixed there. "My parents were ambitious. They sent me to Chicago to live with an uncle who had done very well," he said. "That's how I got out of the South and got a good education."

"Oh," I said, feeling the inadequacy of my response. I longed to rise to the occasion, to respond somehow in kind, with generosity, courtesy, elegance. I wanted to be debonair like Harry Dale, to be his match; yet, I knew it was impossible.

His eyes searched mine, and I had the feeling he was looking for a sympathy, an equal knowledge, a shared experience. "So you probably find the work here at George Washington Carver much too easy. Your teachers tell me you are bored."

"Oh, no—"

"But too smart to admit it. I understand," he said, raising his hand in a languid gesture, "I understand. I didn't come back to finish school here, but I can imagine how it must be. I went on from my school to Columbia. That's in New York."

"I know," I said.

"Dear Folly," he mused, smiling quietly, "what a vast change this must be. Now we are both back here, aren't we?"

It was impossible to see that we shared, in any fashion, experience. He had stayed up north, gone to college there, only chosen as an adult to return. His experience seemed so vastly different, he was so beyond anything I could be that I was simply puzzled that he imagined he found common ground. "Yes," I said rather weakly, "here we are."

"Both in Georgia."

"Yes."

"I have a plan for you, Folly. I think it might help your boredom," he said.

"I'm not really—"

"You don't have to be diplomatic with me, young lady," he interrupted. "I don't expect you to say things around me you don't feel."

The words ground to a halt upon my tongue, and I cocked my head sideways a little as I wondered what it was all about. What did Harry Dale have in mind? What did he mean?

"I want to offer you a student assistant job."

"Student assistant," I asked.

"Working in the office. Miz Bargain can use your help. I can see from your grades that you were a good English student. You can spell?"

"Oh, yes, sir!"

"Write well?"

"I think so."

"Good. We can use you here. You'll learn some office skills along the way, so there'll be some challenge. Office skills never hurt in the job market." He looked at me and said, "Well, what about it?"

"It sounds good, Mr. Dale. But I don't have the time. I really don't."

"Don't have the time? Your teachers have told me you have nothing to do. You already know everything they're teaching."

"Yes, sir, but I have to help at home with the chores, and Judge Lawson is teaching me German."

"Judge Lawson," Harry Dale pronounced the name with due reverence, and I saw he was deeply impressed.

"He's teaching me German."

"Did you have German in Connecticut, Folly?"

"No, sir. French. But it is a hobby of Judge Lawson's. He likes to do it, and I think I'm getting something out of it."

"Ummmm," he said. "What if I said that you can earn something with the work here?"

"How much?"

"Fifty cents an hour," Harry Dale announced.

"Oh, I am sorry, sir. That's not enough."

"Not enough?"

"No, sir. Student office assistants got a dollar an hour at my other school."

"A dollar an hour!" Harry Dale was visibly shaken, but he quickly recouped. "Folly, this is Georgia not Connecticut. A dollar an hour? Are you sure?"

"Oh yes," I said, feeling a chill seep down from my hairline as I thought it entirely possible he might pick up the phone and call Connecticut. It was a bold, spontaneous lie. I had no idea why I had said it, but I couldn't back down at that point without looking like a complete fool. Besides, a dollar an hour might make it worth my while.

"Okay then. But we must keep this between ourselves," Harry Dale said. He sprang to his feet, mashed his cigarette stub into the large, bronze ashtray on his desk. I took the cue and got up. "Miz Bargain will work the schedule out with you, Folly. I'm sure you'll be lots of help to us with the office work."

"I hope so, sir."

He opened the door and stood waiting. I passed very close to him as I left. The pores under my hairline were dilated and sending little crinkling, piercing sensations to my brain. It was obvious that Harry Dale wanted me to work for him very much.

Chandra was waiting for me that day just out of sight of the school building, but she wasn't alone. She brought along an entourage of girls, each one eager to get at me. I hadn't realized I was so unpopular until I saw their sullen stares. When I put up a spirited resistance, one of them tripped me. When I got up, I got pushed back down.

"Hey, that's not fair," I cried. "You're ganging up on me."

"You're ganging up on me," Chandra mocked. "Talk like a white girl, don't you. Think you're so smart."

The girls were circling me with keen, smiling eyes. Chandra and I were in the middle of the circle facing off. They were all eager to get in a good kick. I saw how ridiculous the word "fair" must have sounded away from the teacher-imposed rules of the playing field. It was pretty plain that I'd have to fight the whole bunch and not just Chandra alone.

I knew I should rush at the weakest link and try to break out and run, but I hesitated because of my arm. I wasn't sure about my condition after convalescing so long, and I was scared to get my arm hurt. I also knew that hesitating a minute was the wrong thing to do. They sensed it in one accord and rushed me.

I don't think from the pain in my side that more than one of them got in a good kick. I used my legs and feet but only the first few minutes. After that there were too many to aim or do anything by design. I was flailing, trying not to be brought down. If you're down with that many against you, it's over.

It was about that moment that Jim Hall appeared again in my life. He came into the midst of the circle like some dynamic force of nature. Girls were tossed about screaming. When he got to Chandra, there was a contest. She had more strength than most girls. She grabbed him by one arm. He picked her off the ground and flung her about, but she hung on.

One of the girls came up behind me and got me by the hair. I reached back and was able to grab hold of something and pull her around. It turned out that I had her by the ear and hair, and she screamed. When I let her go, she actually ran. I stood there delighted.

Jim finally shoved Chandra into the field that flanked the road. She tumbled and rolled from the force of his thrust, coming to rest bottom up, her head squeezed under her torso. When she righted herself, she began to curse. Jim laughed. "Get on," he hollered shooing her off like you would a stubborn cow.

"You white son-of-a-bitch," Chandra cried. Jim feigned at her, and she turned and ran. She stopped a hundred yards or so into the field and shouted something, but Jim ignored her. I saw her stoop to pick up something. When she threw it, I said, "Watch out," and we ducked. But whatever it was, it didn't come close. Chandra wasn't much of a thrower.

"Thanks," I said. I must have been beaming at him, though I could feel some pain in my side and back jabbing at me and must have winced, too.

"Hey, you hurt," he wondered, bending over near me.

"Naw, I'm okay."

"Hey, sport," he laughed, "welcome back to Lawson County. Pretty rough here, huh? Bet it's worse than up there in Connecticut."

"Yeah, you can say that again," I agreed.

"What was this all about?"

"She just doesn't like me. I don't know why."

"Yeah, you could see that. She's strong. Probably a bully? You better keep away from her, sport, for your own safety."

"She's a bully, all right. Believe me, I've tried to stay away from her."

"I still bet you put it to the test somehow, am I right?"

"Not really. Well, maybe I did say something that set her off. I guess that's right."

"Here in Lawson County somebody's always fighting. It's the way a lot of young people pass the time. The meaner you are, the better people like it. There's nothing they like better than a good fight."

"You saved me once before, remember?"

"Sure, think I do. You were a little tyke then."

"You weren't so big yourself."

Jim laughed again, then he walked across the road and lifted up the delivery bike he had been riding. The front tire was smaller than the back to allow room for a giant basket. The words "Hendricks' General Store" were painted on the metal plate running from the handlebars back to the seat.

"You're still working for Mr. Hendricks?"

"I don't just work for him. I live in the store. There's a room above the feed room."

"You live in the store?"

Jim seemed proud of the fact, "Yeah. My old man got after me, and I had to leave home and come into town."

"Oh," I said. I was a little shocked.

But Jim didn't seem to want to talk about that. "Yeah, so you're back from up north."

"I am."

"Put your books in the basket here. There's plenty of room."

"What are you doing up here?"

"I was delivering groceries to the Steeples family."

"In the old house near the columns?"

"Yes."

The Steeples were sort of second tier gentry after the Lawsons. They had sent their sons off each generation to serve in the Army or Navy and to go to some traditional college. Their daughters had generally married into other solid families even though everybody knew they didn't have any money and had sold off most of their land. Sometimes people would wonder aloud what they were living on. Aunt Ida Mae said old Mrs. Steeples probably got social security is all.

After I placed the books in the basket, we headed down the road together. "So how do you like being back?"

I laughed, "How can I like what happened today?"

"Must be very different up there?"

"Yes. I think so. But I don't remember a lot because of the accident."

"Yeah, I've heard. Real bad about Miss Ellen."

I didn't say anything, so we walked in silence a few yards. "You've certainly grown up," I said.

"Yeah. That happens."

"I remember you in the midget football team."

"You do," he seemed both delighted and surprised.

"I sneaked into the ballpark and watched you play not long before we left for Connecticut."

"How about that? Sneaked in, too. Do you remember knowing me before that?"

"What do you mean?"

"Like when you were real little. Out at the Ridge near our place."

"We played bottle stoppers at the creek."

"We sure did. I went looking for you. We had some fun."

To know that it had been important enough for Jim to remember made me feel shy. I looked away. He stopped and turned to me, still holding the bike, "Sport, what did I hear about you burning up the woods with your tennis up there in Connecticut? You were a champion, weren't you?"

"I was good," I admitted.

"Better than good. That's what I've heard. What about now? What you got planned?"

"I can't play tennis anymore. It's my right arm. Got it sort of wired together. Maybe in a couple of years."

"Oops. What's the problem?"

"Hurt in the accident."

"I'm sorry."

"It doesn't matter. I think I was burned out on tennis, anyway. Tennis was everything to Miss Ellen. We lived it day and night."

"Thought you said you didn't remember much."

"I remember that."

"Well, it's too bad. Maybe the arm will heal up."

"Not if somebody like Chandra gets hold of it, it won't!"

"I don't think she'll bother you now she knows I'm looking after you."

"You are?"

"Sure."

He started pushing the bike again. As we strolled, I said, "Why?"

"Why what?"

"Why are you looking after me?"

"Aw, it has to do with my father and your mother. I don't know as I ought to talk about it right now."

"Please!"

"Well, I knew that Pa was seeing a lot of your mama. I followed him out to your cabin many times." Jim walked a little without saying anything, like he was trying to figure out how to go on. Then he said, "You grow up on a farm and you know what that means. I figure you are my half sister."

"Half sister!"

"Sure. Your mama was Pa's favorite, I can tell you that. When I think about it, I don't blame him much, in a way. She was real pretty. My ma wasn't much to look at, and she hadn't looked after herself, either. She's always complaining, too."

No wonder his mother had hated Negroes so, I thought. It was understandable why she'd stand up out of her chair on the porch when any of us came to the edge of the woods and scream at us. "I'm sorry. I didn't know you thought that—"

I couldn't get the rest out of my mouth, for some reason. I couldn't pronounce the word 'sister.' After that we didn't talk much. It seemed like neither one of us could think of anything more to say.

The reason I was silent is that I was finding out how the news felt. In one way, I was glad that Jim thought I was his sister. It connected us. On the other hand, I was also sorry. The trouble either way was that it wasn't true.

Finally, I decided to tell him. I took a deep breath and said, "My mama was pregnant before she left Lawson Hall. She had to be. My aunt told me I was born right after she got out there."

"Your mama came from Lawson Hall?"

"Well, her sister is the cook there. Don't you know that? We'd been serving up there since I don't know when. Both my mama and my aunt were born up there. Mama had to leave, I guess, because she was pregnant."

"That don't mean nothing," Jim said firmly. "Think about it. Why would she go out there right next to our farm? I bet they'd already been meeting before that."

I could see that Jim was not a person to let go an idea he liked that easily. "A white man and a colored woman," I asked.

"I'm telling you, my pa don't believe there's no difference! You know why he got after me the day I run away?"

"No."

"I'd bought up old Mr. Esa White's clothes and stuff and went and sold it to the coloreds down at Mill's Creek. Pa found me counting the money. You should'a seen him. He was madder than hell." Jim put the bike down so he could act out the scene. "'Where you git that goddam money,' he screamed at me. Then he took the tray I was holding in my lap with all the money on it, and he threw it as far as he could throw, out in the yard."

"Wow," I said.

"Yeah, and he swiped at me, too, just as I jumped off the porch and went out and started picking it all back up. He was up on the porch yelling, 'You ain't no different than them!'" Jim waved his arms in such agitation I felt as scared as if I had been there. "'You ain't no different. Milking the poor and calling them niggers or white trash! What's the difference! That's the way they keep us all down, callin' us niggers, Jews!' Then he took a big stick he kept at the door and started down the steps. I just took off running and didn't stop till I got to town."

We stood there looking at each other. Jim's chest was rising and falling, and he was breathing heavily. "It was awful," he said quietly. "As far as I was concerned my pa wadn't gone whup me no more. I went to Sheriff Moore and told him my pa would be after me. I knew the townsmen all liked me because of football. The only one didn't think it was funny was Mr. Hendricks. He said I could take the room that was his office over the feed room, overlooking the whole store."

"They all came out to the Ridge," I interjected. "All the white men in town. During coon hunting. Your pa wasn't the only one."

"They're hypocrites," Jim spat. "In his way Pa is the only man in the county that ain't a hypocrite, the only one that tells the truth."

"White man, maybe," I agreed as I qualified. "Looks to me like you got mixed feelings about your pa?"

"Well, anyway, you know how people are. I was ashamed of myself, but I sure wasn't going to try to make up with Pa. He is about the hard-headedest man there is. He is no man for forgiving."

"Your Pa sure is an unusual man."

"Yes, he is," Jim said, pride creeping into his voice. "I know he was right, but I can't bring myself to go tell him. He was too mad, anyhow, when I hid behind Sheriff Moore and Mr. Hendricks. He felt like I'd gone against him. You done become like one of them is what he said; then he just walked off."

I reached over and touched Jim, "Don't worry. There'll come a day when you can make up. I bet it'll happen. A man can't stay mad the rest of his life at his own son."

"You don't know my pa," Jim sighed. He leaned over and picked the bike back up. We started walking. "They say Pa is like that because his daddy was a Jew. They say it's the old prophet in his blood coming out. You know how they come in from the desert telling people what they didn't want to hear?"

"Yeah, I know."

"Well, it's true, Pa sits out there reading the Bible at night and brooding over it like it's the only book around."

"But he doesn't go to church?"

"No way. He told me once that not a one of them had ever listened to what they was reading with their hearts."

"With their hearts," I repeated. It was a beautiful phrase, and it moved me strangely.

"Take me. I go to church, but I don't read the Bible. Pa says the Jews had the Bible before anybody ever thought of church. He's interested in his roots, I guess. I'm not. As far as I can tell, Israelites were just a tiny group of people in the middle of nowhere. They got beat every way they turned. They didn't amount to much in history. I'd rather have been an Assyrian any day."

"Why?"

"Assyrians were conquerors. They actually amounted to something."

It was at that juncture that our discussion came to an end. We had reached the path I usually took across a high ridge through the woods to Lawson Hall. "I guess you want your books," Jim said, pulling the bike to a stop.

"Yes, thanks." I reached in the basket and took my books. "Thank you again for helping me."

"I'm just glad I came by."

"You saved my skin. Goodbye."

VI

He smiled and waved. As I turned and went down the path into the woods, my heart was singing. Could it possibly be that I was Jim's sister? Could anything be more wonderful? And was it not the same thing as being real if he believed it? I thought it was. I was also relieved at myself for not just letting it go. I had told him I thought it wasn't true, and he'd just ignored it.

My joyous mood didn't last long. A cool shaft of air crept out of the woods and penetrated my clothing chilling me. My happiness dissipated, and I shivered involuntarily. Would I turn the next corner and find Chandra waiting? I didn't believe she'd give up that easily. And there was always tomorrow when she'd seek vengeance.

Without really commanding my legs, I found them running. The first few yards were easy enough, but I quickly ran up against the extent of my fitness (or the lack of it), for the long convalescence had taken its toll. Gasping and stumbling, my strength running out like an exhausted bank account, I had to stop and sit down on a log. I was so weak all my muscles were trembling like a leaf in a breeze.

I sat dreamily, tired, frightened yet happy, wondering about what Jim had told me. Then something in the woods flickered like a shadow from tree to tree. Something low and running, darting. The leaves rustled in its wake, and I thought it must be a squirrel. To my enormous surprise, a fox stopped just at the edge of the path, still half-hidden by a tree trunk, one of its paws lifted as if it were held up in mid-stride.

My first impulse was to scream and jump up on the log. Realizing how absurd that would be, I simply froze. The animal turned and looked directly at me. He was not at all shocked, but seemed to have expected to find me there. His coat was a deep, rich red, and his eyes were alert and intelligent. For a moment I thought he would speak, that he had come to tell me something.

Did I actually register his nodding slightly, as if to say good afternoon, before he turned and vanished back into the dark canopy as suddenly as he had appeared?

I remained quite still in my place upon the log, and I had the oddest feeling that the fox had used telepathy, that I now was in possession of some new, profound information I had not known before. Perhaps, it would emerge in my consciousness in the coming weeks or months.

Only when I felt the dampness from the log seep through the fabric of my clothes and into my buttocks did I stand up. I felt strangely refreshed; the run, however brief, had chased away my weariness and confusion. I began to step down the path in march-step, humming to myself and filled with an indescribable hope.

All too quickly I reached the pasture and looked across it to the stables and Lawson Hall. Sorry that my woodland walk was done, I lingered on the edge of the pasture a moment, still humming quietly some random tune.

"You have a pretty voice," some one spoke to my right. I whirled about and saw a ragged, unshaven man with a tuft of white hair standing up on an otherwise balding noggin. He was sitting on a tree stump and smiling broadly at me. At least two of his teeth were missing.

"You startled me," I said.

"Begging your pardon. Not intended, Missy. Do you belong in that place over yonder?"

"Yes, I do."

"Sorry to ask, Missy, but, begging your pardon, could you fetch a tired traveler a sandwich of some kind? Doesn't have to be much."

"I'll get you something from the kitchen," I said. "Come with me."

He sprang up with a vigor I hadn't expected and joined me. As we walked across the pasture, a horrid stench enveloped me. It took me a moment to realize that it was the man himself who reeked.

I stopped at the stables and turned to him. He had a round face, and the reddish-gray beard was tightly curled and plastered close to his cheeks; these were flushed red, rouge and blue veins running like a road map just under the pale skin and visible even through his beard.

The fellow had pale blue eyes that seemed to laugh. I guess it was the web of wrinkles that emanated out from the eyes that accentuated the effect. Here was a person one simply liked, not knowing him, not having any knowledge of his life. "You wait here. I'll get you something," I instructed.

"Would you be ashamed of me, Missy?"

"No," I said, taken aback. "No, if you want you can come along."

"I'll do that. I was just a hoping you might lend me a bar of soap and show me a spigot where I can wash myself."

He sat on the lowest step, and I mounted up to the back porch, opened the kitchen door and called, "Aunt Ida Mae?"

"You're mighty late," she bellowed back from the pantry. "I done started getting supper ready."

"I'm sorry. There's a man outside who's hungry."

"A man?" She backed her enormous bulk out of the pantry, head last. When she turned to me, her face broad and beautiful despite her corpulence, the whites of her eyes were the largest part of what I saw.

"He's a tramp, I think," I explained.

"A tramp! We don't want no tramps around here!"

"I asked him to come with me."

"You done what? Chile, what you been thinking?"

"He's a nice man."

"My foot!" She bustled past me to the door and peered out. I looked through the window and saw the cheerful tramp tip his hat at us.

"Can't I make him a sandwich?"

"I got some leftovers in the pantry. Get him some cornbread and whatever you find and make him a plate."

I did as I was told and prepared the man quite a feast. Taking a bar of soap from the washstand on the porch, I brought the food down to him.

"Thank you, Missy," he said. He began to devour the food, stuffing it into his mouth. Once he stopped and said apologetically, his mouth still full, "I'm powerful hungry, Missy. Begging your pardon."

The effect of his speaking with his mouth so full and him being so humble struck me as comic, and I had to cover my mouth to keep from laughing.

When he finished I handed him the soap. "I got this from upstairs. There's a spigot over by the stables where nobody can see you. I'll see if I can find a towel first, though."

When I came back with the towel, he was standing midway between the house and the stables. The tennis court was visible to the right of the stables, half hidden by a row of cedars trimmed into a hedge. "Here you are."

"God bless you, Missy."

"Who are you and where do you come from?"

"Lord, Missy, you wouldn't believe me if I told you."

"We used to have lots of tram—I mean, men coming through when I was little."

"They were hard times. Yes, they were hard times. My travels are my own fault."

"Why?"

"Well, I'll be plain with you, Missy. I was a respectable man until I took to drink."

"Do you still drink?"

"I'd be dead if I did. One night I found myself in the middle of a forest with my tongue dry as a bone, my clothes in rags. My family was gone, and I didn't know how to get back to them, anyway. I swore I'd never take another drink, and I haven't."

"You've kept your promise?"

"Didn't have much choice. Didn't even have food. So I've been wandering about ever since. There was no way to go home." He bent down close to me, winked, and bent his index finger, urging me to come closer. When I edged over within inches of his face, close enough to smell his odor, he whispered, "I don't like to tell anybody, but I don't remember where I lived. I couldn't go home if I wanted to. I don't even remember what my name was." He straightened up and I backed away quickly. "There it is. Don't even know my own name. Terrible thing, you know. Terrible thing not to know your own name."

"It is terrible," I agreed.

"You won't tell anybody, will you? I mean, that I don't remember where it was I lived or what I was called?"

"You should make up a name," I suggested.

He straightened up and smiled, "Now that's a good idea." Then his face clouded, "Only I have trouble remembering names. I think drink did it. Just wiped out my memory, you know. I'd forget it, if I gave myself a name. Forget it as surely as I'm standing here."

"Well, you could pick a name and write it on a piece of paper – or on your sleeve!"

"Now that's an idea. Let me wash up, and maybe you could fetch me paper and pencil. A pin, too. I could pin it to my shirt."

"Yes, I'll get the paper. When you're washed just come back and holler."

When I went inside to get the paper, Aunt Ida Mae met me at the door. "I'll get him some clothes. That man is in rags. He can't be seen like that. People be scared of him."

"Yes, m'aam," I agreed.

He decided to call himself Tom. I tested to see if he could read by writing "T O M" in big letters on the piece of paper, holding it up and asking him to tell me what it said.

"Tom," he said and cocked his head as proudly as if he had won the Nobel Prize.

"Tom is your name then," I pronounced, handing him the paper. "But won't you need a proper name, too."

"Now what do you mean, child?"

"Like Jones or Smith."

"I'd never be able to remember two names. I wouldn't, sure as I'm born."

"Okay, Tom then. That'll be enough," I declared with mock dignity.

And Tom it was. "Thank you, Missy," Tom said just before he went into the stables and changed into some of Uncle Cajus's old clothes. When he came back out, he looked downright respectable. Looking at him, I propped my hands on my hips and thought that Tom had been a doctor or a judge as sure as I was born. That's how respectable he looked.

Uncle Cajus's clothes were a little too big, but Aunt Ida Mae said they could be taken up without any trouble. Tom's stench was nearly gone, too, after his bath. Aunt Ida Mae said he ought to shave, but he said he'd just keep his beard, that it was less trouble, and he had no money to buy himself a razor.

Tom asked to sleep in the stables that one night. The next day he helped Uncle Cajus with the garden work down where he raised the vegetables and greens we used in the kitchen. After that he did other chores and showed himself to be not only very useful but enterprising. He would repair things without even asking.

Pretty soon a week had passed. Neither Aunt Ida Mae nor Uncle Cajus was anxious for him to go. Tom's little pallet in the stables was being transformed into a domestic arrangement complete with kerosene lamp and toilet utensils. He used the old outhouse for such purposes as it had been originally designed before indoor plumbing put it out of use.

All that was left for Tom to become a permanent fixture at Lawson Hall was some approval from Judge Lawson, and that followed three weeks later when Judge Lawson first noticed his presence and came out to see who he was. "Hulloh," the Judge said.

"Hulloh," Tom answered.

The two met in the gravel drive, and Tom cheerfully pumped the Judge's limp hand. "What brings you here," the Judge wondered.

"Business, sir. Business."

"And what is that business?"

"Growing things, sir. Growing things," Tom responded.

The Judge waited for further explanation and, receiving none, said, "Well, good luck then. See that you use your talents here. We have plenty of things to grow," at which point he nodded and strolled back to his library.

After that Judge Lawson and Tom seemed to have a kind of silent understanding. Tom was about as likable a man as there could be. He was all good will and cheerful helpfulness. He had a simple humility that made every person his equal concern. After a little conversation or two with Tom, Judge Lawson announced that we "ought to find a place for him to bed down. He'll be a useful addition to the staff."

The Judge even went so far as to add that, "As long as it doesn't get too cold, he could sleep in the stables. The feed room has a floor. All it needs is a little clean up. And he could use the old outhouse." When it was reported to the Judge that such arrangements had been made, he said, "Splendid!"

That is how Tom came to join our little family at Lawson Hall. A welcomed addition, I might add, whom even Aunt Ida Mae decided she liked. "Maybe," I said to Uncle Cajus one evening as I was washing the dishes and he was whittling at the kitchen table, "Everybody should drink too much like Tom for awhile if it would make them such kind and loving people!"

"What you talking about, girl," Aunt Ida Mae called from the back porch where she was peeling potatoes and listening to our conversation, "licker is the tool of the devil! Can't no good come of it. That's why poor Tom is simple."

"Well, he's simple in the best way possible," I retorted with feeling.

There was no use arguing with Aunt Ida Mae, of course, so I just winked at Uncle Cajus, and he smiled back. If there was one thing I knew that was certain in this world, it was that those two people loved me.

VII

All that happened next was in late 1957 and the first months of 1958 in my senior year at George Washington Carver Colored Consolidated High School. First of all, Judge Lawson kept teaching me German. We moved fairly quickly from basic grammar to reading stories.

The first story we read together was Ludwig Tieck's "Blond Eckbert." It took me a good while to get the hang of it because it was confusing in itself, though Judge Lawson really loved it. It was about this baron who was happily married until his wife fell ill and died, at which point he killed his best friend in the woods – but you couldn't be sure he killed him or that he really was his best friend.

After that, Eckbert went away to another town where his best friend showed up as different people until, finally, he found a cottage in the forest with a little bird that laid golden eggs and sang

Waldeinsamkeit

Which means something like "a delicious aloneness in the forest."

With all the confusion of identity and strange happenings, it was hard to know if I had translated it right. It turned out that I had, and Judge Lawson really liked that kind of story with lots of magic. He saw lots of significance in it. The stranger the story, the better he liked it. You wouldn't have thought that about him if you hadn't known him in the circumstances I came to know him. He was mostly just so dry, remote, and prosaic.

But let me get back to the story: Finally, in the end, Eckbert turns out to have been married to his sister. That seems to be the point of the story, according to Judge Lawson, who veritably gloated over it. Then the final twist at the end, according to Judge Lawson, is that Eckbert may even have been his own sister. That gets really weird because I guess it meant he was married to himself.

"But that's just it," Judge Lawson exclaimed, bouncing in his chair. I had never seen him so excited. "That's just it! His wife was his sister, the best friend he murdered was the old lady who had tended her in the forest. They were all the same people."

"But then was he Berta, too?" That was the one in the woods with the singing bird who laid golden eggs and such.

"Folly this is absolute subjectivism, don't you see?"

I looked up subjectivism in the dictionary later, and Webster seems to think it is a theory that stresses the subjective elements in experience. What that means, as I figured out for myself, is that the person thinks the world she spins in her mind is really the only reality, that everything is sort of an appendage of her imagination. I settled on Webster's third definition: "a doctrine that individual feeling or apprehension is the ultimate criterion of the good and the right."

All the stories we read in that year were more or less variations on that theme. Judge Lawson loved to go on about how the protagonist (his word for the main character) was so wrapped up in himself that the rest of the world was for him just a projection of his own delusions. Why this was such a big thing in Germany in the early nineteenth century is beyond me. I also never did quite understand why Judge Lawson got such a kick out of the whole, crazy business.

The next story we read was by E. T. A. Hoffmann and called "The Sandman." But it wasn't the sandman that children think comes to spray sand in their eyes and make them sleep. Hoffmann's Sandman was a terrifying figure who had something weird going on with his eyes. In the end the young man telling the story falls in love with a mechanical doll.

Now if you can imagine what sort of person would fall in love with a mechanical doll, you are a good few steps ahead of me. I couldn't for the life of me see why anybody would cook up a story like that. I decided in those months that I was not really cut out to go to college and waste my time reading and interpreting that kind of nut story. All it had done for Judge Lawson is make him like to sit there in his study reading.

What I liked was what I began during those days to call (to myself) Hard Reality. Now what I understand in the term Hard Reality is the here and now, life as everybody was living it around me. Lawson County, Lawsonville, Georgia, being white and colored. Circumstances.

Maybe some aristocrat like Judge Lawson could afford to stay in his library reading German romantic stories and philosophy. He was insulated from Hard Reality. I was Folly Steeples. My great-great grandaddy wasn't in a portrait in the Georgia history book. I wasn't born in the most ancient house in the county up on a hill overlooking the town one of my ancestors founded.

You can say that Judge Lawson taught me an important lesson about myself by way of contrast. He was who he was and liked German Romanticism. I am who I am and like Hard Reality. It is my natural element. It's not always comfortable, but it's what there is to deal with when I wake up every morning, Chandra included.

Another thing I learned from Judge Lawson was that, as the old saying goes, you can't tell a book by its cover. Whoever would have imagined that this oddly distanced, humorless individual lived in a universe and with a language that was so remote from his own. He only read the works of writers who were long dead and had, at any rate, lived in distant places across oceans.

Well, of course, I still had something pretty startling to learn about Judge Lawson. It had to do with sex. I had wondered about a man who had lost his wife right after his only daughter was born and who had not needed companionship or sex since.

When the Judge would get all excited about these German stories, you could tell that he had passion. It was just directed in odd ways and to odd places. Sometimes he could be downright explosive. So he was a man the world around him simply didn't know.

On the other hand, you have to say that the basic reason the world didn't know Judge Lawson is he chose to keep himself hidden from it. He didn't care what the world thought. In fact, I don't think he took much notice of the world at all, whether it was the world in Lawsonville or the larger world of, say, Washington, D. C. or New York. But there was a world that was real to him alone.

I'll give you an example. When we finished Hoffmann's Sandman, he took out a record, placed it on the victrola, took the heavy arm with the needle and let it down upon the spinning black surface. As the sounds began, he eased into his chair and closed his eyes.

When the piece was finished, his eyelids were drawn up like ancient curtains. He blinked, got up, went over and took the arm up and the slick disc off the turntable. "That was Beethoven," he said. "Now I want to go back to Mozart for you to hear what it was like before these ideas began to inhabit the skulls of these men."

First of all, I didn't realize when he said "ideas" he meant music. Nobody had ever told me that music consisted of "ideas." I thought music was just sounds strung together to give pleasure to somebody who was singing and the others who were listening. That music could also be historically determined idea almost exploded my mind.

Judge Lawson surprised me a lot while he was teaching me. Not many people can do this. His sister, Miss Ellen, had never surprised me in those years I lived with her. She had been privately exactly as she was publicly. There was no guile, nothing hidden, no unsuspected niches of character unknown to the world from the beginning. She didn't come up with anything as unexpected as music being "ideas."

Then one evening after our German session, I was mulling everything over in my room in the cottage behind Lawson Hall, and it hit me. Judge Lawson had chosen me alone out of all the world – so far as I knew – to reveal and share himself. It plain choked me up. What I felt is gratitude. And mainly I just couldn't understand why he would choose me, of all people, though I sure could see why he wouldn't have chosen Laura. And I guess Miss Ellen wouldn't have been too interested.

In spite of the great honor Judge Lawson showed me, I think I betrayed him. I wanted to be the book that neither fooled nor enchanted, a book whose substance was revealed in its cover. I wanted to be a book of hard facts that people could depend upon. I wanted there to be no difference between my public and my private self. I wanted to hold no surprises. I wanted to be more like Miss Ellen than her oddly complex brother.

Something happened that turned my mind to a new model for my life. Everybody has got to become something. It was easy for me to see in Lawsonville that those who didn't get a clear idea of what they wanted to be ended up being shiftless or just ordinary.

This is why my mind turned to Amos Hendricks, the solidly successful redneck who ran Hendricks Mercantile.

Now Amos Hendricks had come from poor white trash, as everybody knew, but he had made something of himself when he founded his store. If you think of the odds against a child wandering into town like I heard he'd done without a penny to his name and no kinfolks to help him along and then becoming the leading merchant in town – well, they're pretty long, is all I can say.

But I didn't decide easily which way I was going. My hair roots itched wildly as I tossed on my sheets somewhere in those dead moments of the morning before daybreak and thought of what I wanted to be. Yet, it wasn't a sad worrying business. I felt it all like it was something really big just waiting out there in the future for me. Sometimes I thought the fox I'd seen in the woods had known and wanted to tell me.

Jim had a definite idea about what he wanted to be and where he wanted to go. He had strong opinions, and once he got his mind's teeth into an idea, he just didn't let go. What I figured is that you don't need a lot of ideas, you just need one good, solid one. Then you have to latch on to it and follow it through. Jim preferred being an Assyrian prince than a Hebrew prophet. His dad was a kind of prophet, and he hadn't gotten anywhere with his life. He still had to work that poor grade farm of his.

At first I thought maybe I wanted to be like Harry Dale. Until I found out that he wasn't the kind of person you could envy much. Not to say that he didn't look the part because, as I've already mentioned, he was a dandy, elegant person. He had that special sense of the importance of making even lighting a cigarette a memorable event, something people could just enjoy because he was such a smooth fellow.

The trouble with Harry Dale was the darker side of his life. His wife had left town, and he didn't have the courage (or whatever) to go get her or to leave himself. He just sat in his office smoking cigarettes and writing letters to very important people about all kinds of issues. Looking back I think he was probably just what people today call 'depressed.'

Harry's dis-ease expressed itself in a steady stream of letters he dictated to the prominent of the world. It was a nuisance, and Miz Bargain sighed with relief when she realized that I could take Harry's dictation and transcribe his letters. "Miz Bargain," he would call, and she would look at me and nod, so I'd go in.

Harry dictated letters to the Pope, bishops, cardinals, intellectuals of the church; his epistolary audacity knew no bounds. He would address anybody about anything. The very notion that he might have something important to say to these people about the affairs they dealt with in their professions amazed me. I admired it at first. But only at first. Later I began to grow tired of his turgid style, the convoluted, almost crackpot character of the whole enterprise.

I would take the dictation into a small room where I would type it out. During the first weeks I honestly felt like what I was doing had weighty significance for the world. Gradually Miz Bargain's cynical weariness about her boss's habits infected me, too. I began to roll my eyes when he call for me to take dictation. What now, I'd groan to myself. Soon he'd be writing letters to Almighty God Himself.

And I don't mean that he never got any answer from these very important people. Oh no. He got answers, especially from politicians. He would often show me the letter. It usually began, "Dear Friend..." What he never got were real answers written by the people themselves to whom he had addressed his comments.

My contempt for Harry Dale grew. How could he think that a "dear friend" letter was in any fashion a real answer to the lengthy epistles he wrote? I figured some assistant to an assistant, sort of like me, actually wrote those answers. Or maybe they just had a file of form letters and somebody like me would go and select one and then write at the top, "dear friend." They probably called the file "Answers to Crackpots."

When I realized that Harry Dale was spending countless hours writing complex letters that were totally unheeded and utterly pointless, I understood two things. One of the things was personal and simple: I didn't want to end up doing something that dumb. The second thing was general and pertained to the nature of the world:

It was apparent to me that the high and mighty are not interested in the opinions, however well considered, of obscure citizens. If you think about it ten minutes, it makes sense, too. Why would they be? They invest enormous energy, their lives and careers, in getting ahead in a profession. They are experts in their own areas, had negotiated the tricky road to the top, know the people who run the country, see and talk to them every day. And then this letter comes from Lawsonville, Georgia from a person they never heard of. It is a long, complex letter. Would you read it if you were them?

Of course I knew that Harry Dale was not stupid. He was actually a very intelligent person. But he was running a colored high school in Lawson County Georgia. The highest people with whom he dealt were the members of the Board of Education. And I knew for almost a fact that not a single one of them had an idea of anything that ever was or would be real beyond the borders of the State of Georgia. These men were not only provincial, they were white and tolerated Harry Dale for one reason only – and it had nothing to do with their respect for his intelligence!

In other words, Harry Dale was an intelligent man with real limits to the circle of people he knew or could actually influence. You can't really blame him for writing those letters, even if he knew it really didn't do any good. When you get down to it, he felt sorry for himself, so he knew he was pitiful.

The short of it is, I knew pretty soon that I didn't want to be like Harry Dale, either. I didn't see any reason to go way up north to Columbia University to get an M.A. or any other degree. And why? Just so I could come back to Georgia and be a front for a bunch of local white men whose chief pleasures included coon hunting and having sex with mulatto women on the sly.

Amos Hendricks wasn't educated like Harry Dale. He wasn't elegant, and he sure wasn't handsome. He was as common as dirt and made no pretense to be anything else. But he was a good merchant. He ran the best store in town. His vegetables were the freshest, and everybody knew that, whatever the circumstances, you could count on him not to cheat anybody, no way. So I figured he was the best model on my horizon.

There were some extra obstacles to me becoming like Amos Hendricks, including the fact that I was colored and female. Otherwise, I was starting out about like he did: 1. I had no money, 2. No parents, 3. No advantages. As for being honest, I figured that I could fight the little tendency I had to tell an occasional lie when it was convenient. I had experimented and found that when the time came, I could usually summon up the courage, even if the people I was talking to had rather me not tell the truth.

But Harry Dale was far from being really contemptible, even if he was somewhat pathetic at the time. One day he said to me, "I have a novel I would like you to read."

"What kind of novel, sir?"

He opened a drawer and took it out. It was old and worn. He handed it to me, and I opened the cover and read that the author was John Weldon Johnson and the title *The Autobiography of an Ex-Colored Man.*

"Have you ever seen it?"

"No, sir," I said.

"Read it. But don't let anybody see you reading it, hear? I don't think the white community would be pleased to know I was giving students this kind of reading."

"Yes, sir."

"Don't show it to your aunt or uncle, either."

"I won't."

"They probably wouldn't understand."

"Yes, sir," I said. I didn't think a thing about Harry Dale's caution. It was necessary at the time and considering his peculiar place in the community.

"It was first published in 1912. This is the 1927 edition. I bought it many years ago. In Chicago."

"Yes, sir. I see it's old."

"That book changed my life," Harry Dale said.

"Sir?"

"My life," Harry Dale said, looking away, as if he were embarrassed.

"Oh," I said, for lack of anything else. Changed his life, to what, from what?

"Good," Harry Dale said in conclusion. He returned to his smoking, picked up a pen and dashed out his bold signature on each letter with a gold ink pen he kept for the purpose. He then handed me the letters with his usual instructions: "Get those mailed. They're very important."

I read the book in a single night. It was not very long. When I brought the book back to him, I shut the door to his office firmly behind me and handed it to him. "What did you think," he asked.

"It was short," I said.

"Yes, but what did you think?"

"I—" I tried to get my thoughts together and discovered feelings I didn't know I had in turmoil. Without any warning, I sobbed. I didn't know why. I had no control. The sobs were deep and racked my body. For the life of me I couldn't stop.

Harry Dale stood up, almost knocking his heavy chair over in the process. He was alarmed. "Folly," I heard his voice tense, felt him embrace me. Embarrassment spilled over the sobbing, my chest heaved. I couldn't stop it. "Miz Battle," I heard him cry through the door.

Before Miz Battle managed to get around her counter and down the hall to the office, I had mastered myself. "She seems to be all right," he told her. I noticed he jerked his arm away. "It's okay, Miz Battle."

"Yes, sir," she said, looking skeptically at me.

"I'm sorry," I babbled, "I don't know what happened to me."

"It's fine," Harry Dale said. "I understand." He took out a beautiful handkerchief, unfolded it and handed it to me. I held the lovely linen material out and looked at it. "Go ahead, use it," he urged. I hesitated again, and he smiled, "It's okay. That's what it's for."

Gratefully, I took the cloth and cleaned my face. Then I handed it back to him a little ashamed. Saying nothing, Harry Dale returned to his place behind the desk. Opening a drawer, he took out another book and looked across the desk at me. "Here is something else you can read now."

"Thank you, sir," I said as I looked at the title. *The Souls of Black Folk*, I read.

"Don't you hurry reading this one," Harry Dale cautioned as I was leaving.

"No, sir," I said.

It wasn't the last book he gave me, either. I read others by black writers like Thurston, too. The fall that year lingered. The view from the kitchen was bathed in autumn light one Saturday morning, and a cool, clarifying breeze swept in tiny gusts at the leaves already accumulating in brilliant oranges and reds under the maples and oaks.

I hadn't read DuBoise all the previous night so much as moved myself completely into his imagination. It was as if he had opened a curtain for me behind which was a new world I hadn't expected at all. Now I could see the South as a piece of history and not something absolute and final. I could feel that we weren't necessary relegated to being the dirt white people walked on because of some intrinsic inferiority we suffered from but because it was a temporary historical circumstance.

I was standing at the back window of the kitchen peeling potatoes and looking up occasionally at the glory of the morning when Jim pedaled into my view. He tapped the kick-stand down with his foot, stood back to measure the bike's stability and then called up, "Folly!"

I saw Uncle Cajus out near the pond raking leaves with two men he hired for the job. Tom was helping. Beyond them a third man was setting fire to an already large pile of leaves. "Who that," Aunt Ida Mae wanted to know behind me. "If that's Jim Hall, you can't go down."

I ignored her, threw down the peeling knife and ran out on the porch. "Good morning," I called down to him. He leaned back upon his hips and smiled broadly, and I ran down the steps and would have flown right past him with the momentum I gained if he hadn't reached out and grabbed my arm.

"Hey, where're you going, sport," he laughed.

"Out to see you," I laughed back, hoping he wouldn't let go my arm.

"Looked like to me you was headed out to the pasture."

I kicked at the gravel and smiled at him. "It must be the weather," I said. "I'm just about to bust wide open."

He let me go a little awkwardly, like he didn't really want to and said, "You're happy then?"

"I'm happy," I said. But it was only half what I wanted to say. If this had been a world where you could say exactly what you felt, I'd have said, of course I'm happy. You're here. Stay. Stay. Hold my arm again. Anything. Maybe hug me, too.

"I'm glad being back in Georgia makes you happy."

"Being back in Georgia makes me very happy right now."

"Well, I got an idea, Fol. Want to hear it?"

"Sure."

"You know I've got a paper route."

"Yes."

"And with this job at Mr. Hendricks, it's almost more than I can handle."

"I'll bet."

"So I was wondering if you can ride a bike?"

"Well, my arm is getting better. Maybe I can. But I don't have one that works. There's two old ones in the stables."

"I just bought one for two dollars in town."

"Why'd you do that?"

"Well, if you're gonna help me deliver papers, you'll have to have a bike," Jim said, like it was the most reasonable thing in the world.

"Help you deliver papers?"

"Sure. I'll start you at five dollars a week. When you get fast, I'll raise you."

"Oh, Jim! Five dollars. That's a lot of money."

"It'd be a great help to me. I got more'n I can do."

"Sure I'll do it," I said with no hesitation.

"Can you work it in?"

"I'll drop anything I need to."

"That's the spirit, sport. Thanks."

"When do I start?"

"I figure this Saturday I can kind of show you the route."

"What time?"

"Meet me behind the movie at four a.m. That's when the man brings the papers out of Atlanta."

"Four a.m.!"

"Hey, what did you think? Paperboys have to be up early on weekends. Four Saturday and Sunday."

"I bet it's dark then."

"It is dark. I'll bring you the bike up tomorrow."

So Jim got on his bike, waved goodbye and pedaled away. When I got back to the kitchen, Aunt Ida Mae was standing there with her hands on her hips. At least, I guessed it must have been her hips. Or it would have been her hips if she were not coated with layers and layers of flesh like a big tree with accumulated rings as it gets wider and wider.

"Now what I tell you," she said as she rolled her eyes. When she did that, it was all I could do to keep from telling her that she looked just like those colored women in the movies. They always rolled their eyes, too, so that the white was the most prominent thing you could see.

"What do you mean," I said assuming an innocence I didn't feel.

"I mean you ain't got no business out there flirting with that white boy! You gone get into trouble, honey. You gone get us into trouble. You gotta be careful. You back in Georgia now. It ain't something you do!"

"Oh, Jim thinks I'm his sister," I said a little impulsively, sorry I'd done it as soon as the words were off my tongue.

"You his sister! What kind of crazy talk is that?"

"His father was a regular visitor at Mama's when we lived out at the Ridge. His family owns the farm nearby. He thinks I'm his father's illegitimate daughter."

"Lord have mercy! Where did he cook that up, pray tell! Honey, there ain't no truth in it. No truth at all. Believe me."

"Well, how do you know, Aunt Ida Mae? And if you know, then tell me, who is my father?"

Aunt Ida Mae got the most peculiar look on her face. It spread all over her features. She was closing up. She just hummed loudly the way she did when she knew something really bad that somebody else wanted to know but she wasn't about to tell, and she turned back to her work.

I went up to her and tugged at her sleeve, "Come on, if you know I'm not his father's then you have to know who my real father is."

"I don't know nothing."

"Then I don't believe you about Jim. I believe he is my half-brother. It could be true. I'm virtually white. I'm lighter than you, and you're already pretty light." I leaned over and tried to look into her eyes, but she averted them. "Tell me, Aunt Ida Mae. It isn't fair to do me this way!"

"I ain't telling, but it ain't because I don't know."

"You're terrible. I hate you. I don't believe you." I stomped around the kitchen pretending to sulk. "I believe Jim. Why shouldn't I be his father's child."

"Old man Hall? You want Old Man Hall for a father, honey? He's white trash."

"I don't care. I want to be Jim's sister. As it is, I don't have a father, white trash or not."

"I don't know what you gone come to, baby. Wanting to be white. Talking like a white girl. Going off and playing tennis. I told Cajus it was a bad business. I told him not to let you go."

"What could he have done!" I stamped my foot on the linoleum. "Tell me, what could he have done if Miss Ellen wanted to take me? Do you think we have any rights? Do you think we have any control over what's done to us? We're treated like dogs here in Georgia, in our own country!"

"Hush now!"

"I won't hush. It's true. We're human, too. Why can't they treat us like humans?"

"Honey, please. The Judge is in the library. What if somebody hear you?"

"Shouldn't he know this? He's an educated man. What did they teach him at Harvard? How can you have the benefit of the best education in the country and still not understand that skin color doesn't change the fact that people are human beings no matter what, and you can't treat us like they do? Aunt Ida Mae, I'm going to work with Jim. You'll just have to get used to the idea."

She had closed the kitchen door and, by her face, would have knocked me on the head to silence me, if she could have. Now she looked at me with a new astonishment, "What do you mean, work with him?"

"He wants me to deliver papers."

"Deliver papers?"

"Yes, he has a bike for me and will pay me five dollars a week."

"Five dollars a week!"

"Why do you repeat what I'm saying, Aunt Ida Mae? That's what he says."

"You can't do that, baby!"

"Why not?"

"No colored person done ever deliver no newspapers here in this town."

At first I stared. I was surprised again at all the hidden rules about who could do what and how she knew. "Well, I'm going to be the first one."

"No!"

"Why not?"

"It ain't colored people work, that's why not."

"Why isn't it? What is colored people's work, anyway. Delivering papers is just work. It sure isn't anything high-faluting."

"I don't know why not."

"That's not good enough for me to turn Jim down. He'll protect me. You wait. He'll protect me."

"He gone protect you?" She stopped in the middle of the floor and frowned like a person considering some serious business. "Come to think of it, he might do that, honey. He might be able to do that. But what gone happen when he go away. He be finishing up high school soon. You know that. Next year you is gonna be here by yourself."

Next year seemed so very far away and today seemed so urgent, so real, so important. "Don't worry, Aunt Ida Mae. It'll work out."

"You don't know nothing, child. You didn't even grow up here. This'll make trouble, believe me. I know this will make trouble. Whenever colored people move into work they hadn't done, there's trouble ahead. Mark my word."

"I know why no colored person has delivered papers! I can tell you right now," I declared, caught in a wave of inspiration. "It's because it pays good money. When there's any money in it at all, they don't want us to get near it. Well, this time it won't really be a colored person doing it. I'll be working for Jim. That's different than me actually running the show."

"I'm gone see what Cajus think about this," Aunt Ida Mae said as she returned to her work.

"Please do. I want to hear, too."

She did, and he told us he thought it was a good idea. "Five dollars a week," he said. "That's a lot of money."

There were grown men in town that didn't earn five dollars a week on a regular basis. Grown men, mostly but not all colored men. Some white men, too.

"So you telling this child she can do it."

"I'm telling her she can if she want. She damn near being grown, anyhow."

"She would'a been grown and out working in my day," Aunt Ida Mae declared. "It's high time, I believe. If she stay around here, she gone be getting us into some bad trouble."

VIII

I began working with Jim every afternoon. We would meet behind the movie-theater where the papers were left in stacks. Then we'd roll and tie them, divide them between us, load up our baskets and take off.

I was a bad thrower at first, but I got better fast. I got so I could toss the paper right within a foot of any place I aimed. At first the main problem were the dogs along the route. The worst was the big German shepherd. He would maneuver into the attack mode as I approached, and he looked fanatically mean. I panicked the first day, turned around and skipped the street. Jim had to go back and do it himself.

"Sport," he told me, "let me tell you something. You can't look at a dog like he's a mean man. A dog is just an animal. He doesn't hate you or nothing. He just sees the wheels turning and wants to chase them."

"It's like a game to him," I suggested.

"Not really. To play a game you gotta be human. You're still reading human notions into dogs when you liken it to playing games. What did they teach you up there in Connecticut? Dogs do everything in the same way. It don't matter whether it's chasing wheels or tearing up cats. It isn't a game it's just how they are. It's just what you do to them."

"Okay, I get it. He's not really mad with me. He doesn't really just want to eat my leg up."

"Well, he might want to eat your leg up, and he'd enjoy doing it, too. But he's just as ready to do something more important to him if the opportunity comes up."

"Like what?"

"Like eat. I'll tell you what I do. I take these treats and toss them to them." He took the treats out of his shirt pocket. They were little meaty biscuits he got from the store.

I didn't have a lot of confidence in what Jim said, at first. As I approached him, the German shepherd still looked like he didn't like me personally. He trotted out into the middle of the street and looked every bit like he didn't want me to get by him. Forcing myself not to turn tail and run, I struggled to get a grip on myself. Then I took out a treat and tossed it.

The little biscuit landed to the left of the dog on the blacktop. The shepherd took note, veered off course and sniffed it. Then he snatched it into his snout and gobbled it up.

As I threw him another, I pushed off and pedaled in his direction. Aware that, if Jim were wrong, my leg would soon be in shreds, I took another treat and threw it far off in another driveway. For a long moment, the shepherd seemed to vacillate between the pleasure of another feed or frightening the life out of me. I gritted my teeth.

With a mighty bark tossed at me for good measure, he bolted to the treat. I threw the paper into the yard and stood up on the pedals, giving all the steam I had to put distance between that canine fiend and me. By the time he had gulped down the last treat, I was out of his territory. I looked back and saw him bolt out of the driveway and up the road after me. I pedaled harder.

Another thing I learned about dogs is that, if you can just get out of their territory fast enough, you'll be okay. Dogs recognize invisible borders. The shepherd's territory ended at a big oak about thirty yards from his front yard. I guess he had that oak well marked because when he reached it, he reared up on his hind legs and pulled himself to a stop just like he was about to run into a brick wall.

Later I discovered other, non-canine impediments like Miss Sally Sails. Miss Sally was an ex-missionary who lived a reclusive life in an unpainted house with a rusty tin roof that, according to town legend, had already belonged to her great-great grandfather and looked as if nobody had done any repairs since. She had served many years in China, people said, and it had left her a sour misanthrope. I don't know if she had liked the Chinese, but it didn't seem likely. Later on I thought that she probably did a great deal to assure that China would remain pagan.

In my second week of throwing papers, I approached the wilderness where she lived and saw her standing at the gate waiting for me. She was wearing a big, floppy straw hat that looked like she might have brought it back from China when she came home. "Stop," she called, waving her hand while I was still fifty or sixty feet away.

"Yes, m'aam," I said, bringing the bike to a stop and propping it with my left leg. When the basket was full of papers, the bike was a heavy thing to manage, and I didn't like to stop unless I just had to. I looked over at her, and I could swear she had slanted eyes, so you wondered if all those years with the natives hadn't somehow infected her looks, too.

"You're not throwing my paper right," Miss Sally said in a voice as bright as treble organ pipes. She was subjecting me to a scrutiny barren of compassion but full of contempt. "Thursday's edition landed under that weeping willow and took me two days to find it."

I knew it wasn't true. I threw my papers with accuracy. Most of them landed on the front porches of the houses on my route. "Maybe your dog dragged it under that tree," I suggested.

"Don't argue with me, gal!" Miss Sally burst out in a fury that took me aback. "And don't make excuses. I won't accept them. You're lucky to have this job, and if it happens again, I'm going to report you to the distributor! I won't tolerate carelessness, you hear!"

"Yes, m'aam," I said. I feigned regret and shame and hated myself simultaneously for doing it but knew it was the best and maybe only prudent course of action. It's the way all the colored handled such moments.

Miss Sally was, in any case, unmoved. She gave me another fierce, uncaring stare and looked for the world as if she'd like nothing better than to see me torn apart by wild dragons from China.

At that moment, one of those yelpy little lap dogs, a diminutive little bundle of white fur with two eyes and a black little nose, looked around from behind her legs and yapped. "Take care," Miss Sally warned me again with a grimace.

"Can I put the paper in your mailbox," I asked.

The way Miss Sally jumped at that, you'd have thought I'd told her I planned to bomb her house: "So I have to walk out here twice the same day," Miss Sally replied furiously. "Because you're too lazy to throw it to my porch?"

"No, m'aam, to make sure you get it."

The lap dog began to yap indignantly again, backing away from her mistress's legs and twisting his little, furry head. He was so little, I expect I could have squashed him with my foot. Miss

Sally looked down. "Don't you dare imply that Millie Bean has dragged the paper under that tree!"

"No, m'aam. Not Millie Bean," I agreed, unable to keep a certain tone of sarcasm out of my voice. I pushed my bike off as Miss Sally shook her fist at me,

"Don't you dare be insolent with me," she cried after me.

When I told Jim about the encounter back at the loading dock, he just laughed. "That old witch," he said. "Can't nobody do anything to suit her. Don't worry. Everybody has had his scene with her. Sure it was that stinky little dog she keeps that did it. Don't worry about things you can't help. Living in China all them years didn't do her much good. It don't matter how hard you try, there's always gone be somebody you can't satisfy, sport."

"She said she'd call the supervisor."

"She don't even have a telephone," he chuckled, "and she's too mean to pay the quarter to call from the only public phone booth in town. "Anyway, it'd be a long distance call to the supervisor, and she wouldn't know how to make a long distance call."

Jim and I always had a race to see who would get finished first. When we finished, we'd head straight for the loading dock in back of Mr. Hendricks' store. The first few weeks Jim was the first one back, of course, and he always had an RC cola opened and waiting for me as he sat dangling his legs off the dock. He liked to pretend he had just been there for ages, and he'd say stuff like: "Where you been all this time? Get into trouble with Miss Sally again?"

We would sit out sipping our RCs and talking. That's how I found out what Jim had been talking about when he came to my rescue with Chandra. It just goes to prove that you never know what's in another person, and, whatever it proves to be, it's likely to surprise you as not.

"Tell you what," he said with sudden passion, "you won't find me out there farming cotton on some worn-out one mule farm! I'm not gonna do it!"

I was so surprised at the intensity in his voice that I set my RC down on the boards of the loading dock and leaned around to look him in his face. "Who said you had to do it," I wondered, since he had announced it like it was a declaration of war against some known person.

"Ain't nobody told me I got to do it," he admitted.

"Well, then," I said and picked up my drink again.

"But it's what everybody expects."

"Not of you, Jim. Believe me. People in this town have a lot higher expectations of you than you think. Honest."

"You think they do?"

"Sure."

"They wouldn't be surprised, though. It's what my people have been doing for so long. Farming cotton when everybody knows it can be done cheaper in India and Egypt and God knows where else."

"What are you going to do then?"

"I'm going to college. I've got accepted by North Georgia College."

"Where is that?"

"Up in Dahlonega."

"Up in the mountains then?"

"Yeah. It's a military school. I can get a commission there."

"Oh yeah, this is about getting into history."

"Sure. I've told you all about that, haven't I?"

"Oh yes. I've heard all about it," I said.

"Well, we're gonna change things, Fol. We're gonna change things here in Georgia."

"What things are you talking about, Jim?"

"You know, this thing between colored and white, for one thing. It's a burden on this whole land. It's why my class of people are out there farming cotton and voting in monkeys to office. Everybody's so scared to upset the system they walk around on tiptoes. Don't want to upset the boat cause they're scared to death of what might come from the change."

I looked at Jim with a new respect, if that was possible. There was more to him than I had imagined. He was not just my ideal dream guy. "How can you do away with segregation, Jim?"

"It's coming, Fol. You know how they start yelling 'nigger' every time elections come up, don't you? It's so the people in power can stay there. My pa has said it a million times. They set us against each other so they can rule over us. Call me and my folks white trash or rednecks and your people nigras or worse. It breeds suspicion and hate and makes the white man vote for fear."

I thought I'd have to swallow my heart because it was beating in my throat. "Where'd you get these ideas," I tried to say, having trouble finding the air in my lungs to get the words out.

"I'm not the only one. I heard it from my pa first."

"How does you father have such ideas?"

"Maybe it's still the Jew in him?"

"Why would that have anything to do with it?"

Jim shrugged. "Like I said before, they're the people with the prophets, don't you know. Coming in to tell people things they don't want to hear."

"If your granddaddy was Jewish, does that make you Jewish? And if I'm your half sister, I must be, too."

Pa says not because his mother was a Gentile. He didn't learn nothing about being a Jew, either, so whatever he knows must have been in his blood."

"So you aren't Jewish?"

"No," Jim replied. He thought a minute and added, "and it's a good thing, too."

"Why?"

"Well, if I was Jewish, I expect I wouldn't have a chance of getting into history."

"You can't get into history if you're colored or Jewish?"

"Well, how many colored people or Jews do you know in history?"

I thought hard, then I said aloud, "I don't know who's Jewish and who isn't. Jews are white, so they can mix without any problem. They wouldn't have to pass for white to get into important jobs and positions. If you ask me about a colored person in history, though, I could say George Washington Carver. Our school is named after him, and he was an ex-slave."

"Come on, sport, George Washington Carver was just a scientist. He made stuff out of peanuts. He wasn't in history," Jim sneered. "Scientists aren't really in history even when they name a school after them."

I shrugged, "And it's just a colored school, I guess. I don't know any other names."

"There's Booker T. Washington, I think," Jim said as he rubbed his chin. "But he was just into selling insurance or something like that. Maybe he invented insurance. But that don't get you into history. That isn't what I mean about getting into history, anyhow."

"Wait a minute," I said, snapping my finger. "I know a Jew in history!"

"Who?"

"Franklin Roosevelt."

"Come on, Folly, he wasn't no Jew," Jim said.

"Are you sure?" I was a little disappointed.

"Naw, he was just another aristocratic blue blood like Laura Lawson."

"Laura Lawson?" I couldn't believe Jim would put her in the same sentence with Franklin Roosevelt. It seemed a sacrilege. "So you think she's an aristocrat?"

"Well, my pa says the Lawsons are the bluest blood in Georgia, for what it's worth."

"And Jews can't be aristocrats?"

"Well, Disraeli may have been, I'm not sure. I think maybe the Queen raised the Rothschilds up to be nobles, too," Jim mused.

"I know a couple of other Jews in history," I said, snapping my finger. "Heinrich Heine."

"Who is he?"

"He's a famous German poet."

"How do you know about a German poet? Well, a poet can't be in the kind of history I'm talking about, Fol."

"Your history is pretty narrow then. I guess there're only generals and politicians in there."

"That's about right. Statesmen, I call them."

"Yeah, okay, statesmen," I said, thoroughly disgusted with Jim's narrow scope. "But I think history is bigger than that. If it's not, it's not worth a lot. I sure wouldn't want to be in there with just generals and politicians. Oh, and I thought of somebody else, too."

"Who?"

"Felix Mendelssohn."

"Yeah, so what did he do?"

"He wrote music."

Jim slapped his forehead, "Poets and composers. Folly, this just isn't the kind of history that counts."

"Oh, Jim Hall! Your history is boring! You're just talking exclusively about political history."

"Whatever you say, that's the kind of history that matters. That's when somebody actually does something. You have to be a general or a governor. Poets and composers don't actually do anything that makes any difference. They just write."

"My music appreciation teacher would be furious if she heard you say that."

"Take General Grant," Jim said. "Or Abraham Lincoln. People around here don't like them, but they sure did a lot. They kept the Union from splitting up."

"The way I've heard it, that wasn't a good thing. I mean, most people around here think Robert E. Lee hung the moon, Jim."

"Well, whatever they think, the South lost," Jim mused. "Everybody around here is all het up on Robert E. Lee and Jefferson Davis, but they were losers. I don't mean they didn't put their hearts and souls into the war, but what difference did it make in the end. Just a lot of people died. It wasn't worth it. It'd have been better not to have done it."

"But they're in the right kind of history?"

"As the losers. So it's the wrong kind of history they made. The right kind of history is when you win."

"I thought the right kind of history ought to be when you stood up for the right thing. Doesn't it also depend on what you win or lose? You could win and it might be the wrong history, like the segregationists winning. Or the Chinese communists."

"Or the aristocrats winning," Jim added.

"But the aristocrats didn't win, did they?"

"That's what you read, but I'm not so sure. There're still plenty of them around everywhere you look."

"I guess, if Laura Lawson is one. I wouldn't want to be one, though."

"I don't guess you could be. I never heard of a mulatto aristocrat. But I tell you what, when I start getting into history, I'm gonna win."

He picked up his RC and took a swig, and we sat there saying nothing for awhile, just sipping. I would look over at him every now and then, and I felt a laugh welling up in my chest and pushing up my throat. When I finally laughed, though, Jim looked critically at me and asked, "What are you laughing about?"

"It's just so weird," I said, "us sitting here drinking RC cola and you talking about getting into history. That's all."

Jim grinned. "Pretty wild, huh."

"Yeah, pretty wild. And you called me a mulatto, but I'll tell you one thing."

"Yeah, what's that?"

"In Connecticut I was white. Honest to God I was."

"Yeah, I believe it. Sport, now I'm gonna tell you something."

"Tell me then."

"I want you to be with me when I get into history."

"Whoever heard of a woman in history," I mocked. "If coloreds and Jews can't get in, how do you think women can?"

"They will. I'm gonna see to it with you. Some of the presidents' wives got in, too, didn't they?"

I laughed again. "Now you're funny. Presidents' wives. What difference did they make? I hear they just keep the dresses they wore up in Washington."

"We're gonna do it together, sport, I gar-on-tee you!"

"How?"

"I need somebody to get me the colored vote."

"Vote?"

"More coloreds are voting every year."

"So I'll help you get their vote?"

"That's right."

"Okay. I'll do it." Then I laughed again. I couldn't help it. It was all so totally out of bounds. Nobody in Lawsonville would have even vaguely imagined what we were talking about. People passed up and down the street at a distance and saw us talking.

"We're in this together," Jim said, and he held out his hand. I took it firmly in mine,

"We're in this together," I confirmed.

IX

Amos Hendricks rubbed the front cowlick of his greasy hair down into a Hitler shaped wave of black covering half his forehead. "Now Jim thinks you ought to start getting trained so as you can take over his place when he goes on to college," he said to me. He pulled at his right earlobe and then rubbed the stubby beard on his receding chin. "Do you think you could get started, say this coming Saturday?"

I couldn't even speak for a minute. Jim hadn't warned me. I had beat him back to the loading dock that day not too long before Christmas. We were already in holidays.

Laura Lawson was expected home for Christmas, so I knew I'd have to look for another place to stay as long as she was there. It wasn't that I minded going. The last thing I wanted to do is help Laura have a grand Christmas by being around to bully and snub. "Where would you like me to start out, Mr. Hendricks?"

"Like Jim did, delivering groceries. You are pretty fast with that bike. You done beat Jim back here again." Mr. Amos grinned. "I can tell it irks him just a little. He don't like to lose."

Amos Hendricks was like the original redneck storekeeper. He used rustic grammar to his advantage. He also wore that wooden expression he shared with all the small farmers. When they cracked a smile, it had to be something really special that tickled them.

Mr. Amos had the trade of all the white farm folk who came into town on Saturday to provision. They'd come in wagons and old Fords. The men wore their brown hats square on the noggin, like they were uncomfortable. They'd be wearing overhauls, or bibbed denims, and their wives would be in squarely cut cotton dresses with some floral pattern.

Like I say, Mr. Hendricks had their trade wrapped up. They were a stubborn people. Utterly unlike us coloreds, they were dry and grim. They liked everything austere, including their jokes. When they got together to play their hillbilly music, you'd have thought they were all in pain for the pleasure it seemed to give them. They deadpanned their way through the liveliest tunes and never cracked a smile.

Now we coloreds knew that these small acre farmers hadn't lost any love for us. They kept us at arm's length and were as unfamiliar with us as their European ancestors had been before they came to the New World. As far as they were concerned, we were beasts from another planet, and they all wished we'd go home to wherever it was.

Now I'm going to say something that may shock you. I believe there was an integrity in their frank and open hostility to us. They didn't want to have anything to do with what they called us "nigras," and they made no bones about it. There wasn't any of this pretending they loved us or were going to take our part and look after us. If we inhabited the same country, they were too honest to act like it was okay with them.

What's good about that? Well, in the first place, it lets you know what the score is. You don't have any illusions. You know that, if you're gonna get ahead, it'll have to be your own doing. They're not going to help. That's Hard Reality. It's not a pretty story, but it's the way things are. If you accept it, you won't be disillusioned or disappointed because somebody doesn't live up to some fantasy you have of how they ought to act.

I don't have any use for America's fantasies about everybody getting along just fine. How can people like each other who're so different? It isn't possible. It runs against human nature. When it does that, you're headed for trouble. It's not worth the fifteen minutes it makes you feel good about yourself because you're so open-minded and accepting.

These small acre farmers had no reason to like us. We hadn't been their servants. They didn't have any servants. There were no circumstances in which we could have gotten to know one another enough to appreciate what made us different. As far as they were concerned, we were just a potential threat. We could easily get into competition with them. We could take their jobs, take their land. As far as they knew, we might be better at things than they were. There was no telling. Once Bossman lost control of us and segregation was gone. We might be superior to them.

If they knew anything at all about us, it was how we could do twice the work that a white man could out in the hot Georgia sun. That must have been a scary kind of half-knowledge. Think about our energy, our laughter, our exuberance. It must have scared the living hell out of them to watch it from a distance. What would happen if we were unshackled? They wouldn't have a chance.

More than once I caught some angular countrywoman staring at me, blatantly the way they did when they saw something strange and horrifying. They didn't have manners, you know. Nobody had taught them how to be courteous, and they wouldn't have been able to show any decency to a "nigra," anyway.

A lot of the staring came when I took Mr. Hendricks' offer to clerk in the store and take over Jim's place when he went off to college. It was my chance to learn how to be a merchant. In order to rise above the random, visionless ordinary, I had to do it, had to risk it. I had to endure the stares.

The good thing was, I could understand it. If I'd been in Connecticut, nobody would have known. I could have passed for white. I was light enough. I had blue eyes, for God's sake. My hair wasn't kinky or anything. Nobody would have known. Nobody did. But in Lawsonville, Georgia it was different. People were obsessed with connections, with relations, with community. In order to be understood, you had to be placed in a context. The context was real, but the context was also rumored. Rumors ran rampant. The rumor with me was that I was the first colored store clerk in the history of the world.

Reading DuBoise convinced me that the only true way to independence in America was money. Let's be honest: Money is what put Judge Lawson's family on top back when it was made in long staple cotton. It had put Mr. Hendricks on top more recently and in a more minor way because it wasn't as much.

The Lawsons had doctored it all up and made it really pretty and connected it to gentility, manners, and culture, but it was really just about money and the privileges that money could buy. The important thing was, it could be my turn next. All I had to do was keep my mouth shut, work hard, save every penny and play my cards right.

As I started working in the store, I realized there was another fantasy out there everybody was told to believe. It was the fantasy that people wanted you to get ahead. But it was as much a lie as the fantasy that different kinds of people can come to love one another given enough proper feeling.

The truth here is that people really don't want *you* to get ahead; they want to get ahead themselves. If you go around expecting them to be applauding your success, you'll be disappointed again. The reality is that people like to buy fresh vegetables and meat at reasonable prices. If you can provide them that, they'll be willing to grudgingly accept your success. They won't like it, but they'll accept it. Not just the small acre white farmers but everybody else, too, including the aristocrats and the colored folk.

So it stood to reason that the small acre white farmers weren't the only ones to shop with Mr. Hendricks. We coloreds did it, too. In fact, everybody did it except the town fools who cared more about their prejudices than getting good produce at reasonable prices. He was Mr. Amos to the colored, Amos to the small acre farmers, and either Mr. Hendricks or Amos to the blue bloods. We all trusted him. It was as simple as that. We trusted him within the narrowly circumscribed area he had staked out for himself. And that was enough to guarantee him success and to enable everybody to accept it, even though they were certain that success should be reserved for them personally and resisted and envied in anybody else.

"Tell us how you got started," Jim asked one afternoon after we had finished delivering papers. He was squatting by the drink cooler. Mr. Amos was standing nearby sipping his own soda.

"I just come in to town one day from nowhere, I reckon. My ma and pa and my sister had died out near Tupelo. They had took the fever. Don't know how I didn't get it. I watched 'em for four days. When they was dead, I buried 'em. We was sharecropping, so we didn't own the land I buried 'em in."

"When was it you come into town, Mr. Amos," Jim asked (young white people called him "Mr. Amos," too).

"In the Depression," Mr. Amos said. "I didn't want to wait around for the boss man to show up cause my pappy owed a lot of money. Seems like in spite of all the work he done, he never could scrape together enough to pay for the food we ate, much less anything else."

"So you just left? How old was you?"

"I must've been eleven or twelve. I don't even rightly know. Them was hard times. Folks didn't have no time to celebrate birthdays. They didn't know exactly when they was born, neither. You worked from sunup to sundown and still didn't know whether you was gonna starve to death come winter."

"How did you end up here," Jim asked, leading him as surely to a story as I was standing there listening. There's no doubt he had heard the story before, but he wanted me to know it, too. Then it would be part of our shared history.

"I just walked and walked, I reckon. I come through several towns. I don't know why I didn't just drop down somewhere and die. Don't know to this day what kept me going except the good Lord. I reckon I was pretty tough.

"You could tell when a town was gone be trouble or not. If I smelt trouble, I kept on walking. Sometimes a lady would send her colored maid out to give me a sandwich. I guess I looked pretty pitiful, but there was lots of pitiful folks out there on the road in them days."

"Yeah, but how did you get here to Lawsonville and settle down?"

"You don't remember him, but Mr. Lunsford had a little store in that building down yonder on the corner by the telephone exchange."

"Brick?"

"Yep. I stopped in there. I was so hungry and thirsty, I'd have eat slop from a hog's trough. Miz Lunsford come out and give me a biscuit and some buttermilk. I never will forget it, and I'll be beholden to her till the day I die. She saved my life out of the kindness of her heart."

Mr. Amos turned a little to the side and reached up with his right index finger. When I realized that he was dabbing a tear, I felt my chest retch and had to fight down a sob.

"Don't know how it happened, but I ended up staying on with the Lunsfords for years. Practically growed up in their house. Just did odd jobs for the Missus and worked in the store.

"Can't account for why she took me in of all the orphans wandering about in them days. I shore wasn't no pretty child. I was about as filthy as a ole swamp dog. Smelled as bad, too. Wadn't nothing to look at, neither."

Once again I had to fight down a sob. Mr. Amos's gratitude was still undiminished by the years and the death of his benefactors. "How long ago was that," I asked, more to keep from sobbing than really wanting to know.

"Oh, the Missus done been dead now thirty years, I reckon," Amos Hendricks said, his grating tenor voice breaking with emotion.

Thirty years, I thought; then, as I looked at Amos Hendricks, I realized he might be a lot older than I had assumed. He had that ageless quality of those born with solidly ugly but distinct features, the rednecks who looked old when they were still young but never got any older after that, at least until they were very old.

"So you come into town without nothing to your name," Jim said for emphasis, looking over to see if I had made a special note of Mr. Amos' humble origins.

I nodded because I knew Jim was saying to me: He's like us. It can be done. We can make it. We don't have to rot at the end of some little dirt road, living in some unpainted shack, doing backbreaking labor in fields for a pittance, starvation always sitting on the porch waiting.

It was clear to me that afternoon, standing there by the icebox where the soft drinks were kept, Jim understood. Amos Hendricks was our model.

If you wanted to live in Lawson County there were three possibilities. You could work at the sawmill. You could work on some hardscrabble farm you rented, or you could work in the stores in town. As a white male Jim could also have gotten a job on the highway or maybe gone into small town politics.

What Mr. Hendricks taught me with the story of his life is that anybody who wants half a start in life needs a benefactor and champion. He had found the Lunsfords. Kind, childless people who ran a small store during hard times.

Kids of the better classes had such ardent champions and advocates in their parents and other family members. I thought that my chance had now come. Maybe Mr. Hendricks was destined to be the same thing for me. That is, if I played my cards right and didn't step out of line or if he didn't get killed in some accident or die early another way.

It wasn't more than a couple of days after I started working that Miz Dubbie Happity showed up. She was God's wrath on the colored, as she had proven in the affair with Rhonda Dale.

"Mr. Hendricks," she screamed over my head when I went up and asked if I could help her. "Mr. Hendricks!"

"Yes, m'aam," Mr. Hendricks said as he came around a high shelving structure.

"If you want to keep my business, you gotta do better'n this," she screeched, nodding significantly at me.

I didn't know whether to come or go, stand or squat. What I did is ease back into the background, making myself as invisible as possible.

"Now, I don't know what you mean, Miz Happity," Mr. Amos said. He ignored her vigorous nodding.

"I mean," Miz Happity finally declared, "do you expect me to be served by a colored girl? We don't have colored help in stores in this town," she declared, as if it were a permanent principle of the universe. "It just ain't done, and I won't have it."

"Well, you can take care not to hire no coloreds for your store," Mr. Hendricks said.

"I don't have a store, Mr. Hendricks," she retorted.

"Well, in that case, I don't reckon you got a problem."

"Don't be a smart alec!"

Mr. Hendricks started using the cloth in his hand to dust around the shelves as he replied, "I always heard folks is smart alecs who take it on theirselves to tell somebody else how to run their business."

"That does it," Miz Happity cried, "I'm taking my business elsewhere, Mr. Hendricks. You have done lost a customer!"

As she huffed herself up, tucked in her chin and pinched her mouth, Mr. Hendricks said, "I reckon you'll find everything you need down at Tommy Turner's. It ain't more'n a block from here. Shouldn't be no problem,"

He said all that without actually looking at her. He was dusting around the shelves talking kind of absentmindedly. Miz Happity stormed out of the store and never shopped with us again, so far as I know.

Losing Miz Happity's trade was a great relief to me and did nothing to reduce Mr. Hendricks' business. I guess Tommy Turner gained a good bit of new business by me being there at Mr. Hendricks'. Only Tommy Turner wasn't a good merchant. He rarely had fresh produce and sometimes got the change wrong – always to his benefit, though.

The incident with Miz Happity shook me up a good bit in spite of all I could do. I tried not to let it, but it got under my skin. I worried about Mr. Hendricks keeping me on, though he never gave any sign that he was bothered one bit.

Jim set me straight one day on the issues at hand. He did it in his inimitably straightforward fashion: "Don't worry, Fol, Mr.

Hendricks won't pay no attention to that old bitty. She's a witch and everybody in town knows it."

"That's easy enough for you to say, Jim Hall, but she has influence," I replied. I heard my voice tight with worry and fear.

"Naw, not really."

"Didn't you hear how she ran off Mr. Harry Dale's wife?"

"Everybody knows that story, and it's part of why people lost all respect for her. People are still scared Harry Dale's gone pull up and leave for Washington D. C."

"Why would they care?"

"Well, because they done built this fine nigra school so that the federal government won't step in and end segregation altogether."

"Where did you hear that?"

"Aw, I don't know. Little pitchers have big ears," Jim grinned, as though that was explanation enough.

"Jim Hall, you're about the most maddening boy I've ever known."

"Come on, sport, don't take things so serious. Loosen up a little."

It was easy for Jim to say things like that. When the Baptist deacons showed up that Friday night, on the other hand, it was crystal clear that my worries hadn't been baseless.

Miz Happity was not one to give up racial supremacy easily. She knew that swaying public opinion was arduous, and she went to work on the Baptist deacons because her husband was one of them.

It was Friday night about ten o'clock, and I was sweeping the store. Mr. Amos was back at his desk adding up accounts. I was spreading out the oily sawdust and then sweeping it up, the way I always did, so as not to stir up much dust in the process that would get on the cans and other goods.

About that time the front door started rattling. I nearly jumped out of my skin. Throwing down the broom, I hurried to the end of the aisle and looked down the main aisle to the front door. What I saw was a strange scene.

First of all, it was cold out, and you could easily raise a condensation on a glass if you blew on it. What would you think if you looked down at the show window and the glass front door and saw gyrating creatures pressing their noses against the glass, blowing it full of steam?

They looked like a bunch of hungry fish pushing up against a fishbowl. For one moment my fear nearly dissolved into laughter. But then I got a catch in my throat and hurried back to Mr. Amos to tell him. Behind me I heard the men hollering, "Open up this here door!"

"Mr. Amos," I said as I got close to where he was sitting with a strong beam of light falling on the green billed cap he wore when he did the books. "Mr. Amos, there're a bunch of men out front wanting to get in."

He pushed the green visor back up off his forehead and scratched his head. "Now what could they be wanting at this time of night?"

"It's the Baptist deacons, I think," I pointed out.

"Lordy mercy," Mr. Amos said. He pushed back the chair and got up. I followed him down the aisle. He stopped at the front door and said, "Hoke, what do y'all want?"

"We need to get inside to talk to you."

"I'm closed and working on the books. It's durn near ten o'clock, boys."

"We need to get in," another voice piped up, stronger than Hoke Happity's.

"Lemme get the key then," Mr. Amos said. I turned and ran behind the first shelf of cans as he headed back to his desk to fetch the keys. When he got the door open, the men spilt in, sort of half stumbling and blinking like they'd lost their balance and weren't sure where they were.

"Awright," Mr. Amos said, "What's on your minds?"

"Amos, we done come to talk to you about a serious matter," Hoke Happity announced. As he spoke, he leaned back on his buddies. They had gathered in a sort of knot behind him and seemed to be both holding him up and pushing him forward at the same time while hiding themselves behind him.

"Yeah, well this ain't no respectable hour to be coming to talk serious to a man that's about worn out. I've had a long day, and I'm ready to quit."

"We worked all day, too," the smallest fellow piped up from the back. For a brief moment he emerged into individuality before melting back into the anonymous knot, and it was plain to see that he was Walter Taylor whom people called "bantam rooster."

"Let's have it. What's so important as to bring you out this time of night bothering an honest man," Mr. Amos said. If his poke-face revealed no emotion, there was an impatient edge in his voice.

"It's this way," Hoke Happity went on, "we have niggers working for us down at the mill. That's all right, don't you know, cause it's nigger work. But we ain't never heard about no niggers working in the stores in town. Folks don't think it's right."

"Folks don't think it's right," Mr. Amos repeated, as if the words were so ridiculous, he had to hear them again with his own voice to understand what Hoke was saying. "Well, I don't know what folks you're talking about, but I'll tell you one thing. If I tried to run my business according to what these folks or those folks thought, I'd have gone bankrupt long ago."

"You might yet," Bantam rooster piped up from the rear of the knotted beast.

"I got people never wanted me to do no business, in the first place," Mr. Amos went on, ignoring the jibe. "I got people out there now that'd love for me to start bending with the wind instead of providing good product at fair prices. I look for folks to do their work, keep their mouths shut, mind their business, and pay their bills. If they do that, I don't care what color they are."

Hoke Happity's face was beet red, but he cleared his throat and began in what to him was probably a reasonable tone: "Now, Amos, you know we're friends and only want the best for you."

"Hoke, my friends don't give me no stupid advice," Mr. Amos shot back.

"Now I don't take nicely to that," Hoke began.

"Neither do I," a voice boomed. And Frank Hollison stepped out of the tight knot. His face was red as a tomato, and his blood vessels were popping out in his forehead. He was a violent, quick-tempered man, and it was pretty evident he was about to explode again.

Everybody in town knew Frank Hollison couldn't speak beneath a bellow. As foreman at the sawmill, he had to shout orders above the sound of the saw and plainer. "It's this way," he bellowed, "We don't give a goddamn whether you think it's right or wrong! We ain't gone stand for no nigger working in a store here in town when there're good white people out their needing a job!"

"I ain't never heard a Baptist deacon cuss in public," Amos Hendricks said.

"He ain't no deacon," Hoke Happity corrected.

"What's he doing here, then?"

"Ain't nobody said we was Baptist deacons," Frank Hollison screamed. I saw his fists balling up, and I was scared.

"If you ain't deacons, then what you doing here. I don't open my door at night to get advice from whoever happens to be standing in the street!"

At that Frank Hollison began to hurl his arm like it was a ball and chain, the fist at the end being the ball. The knot unfolded into five men scrambling around to restrain him. Mr. Amos backed away to watch the struggle.

"Shit, I tole you not to let him come along," somebody said.

Arms and legs were thrust out here and there. Grunts were prolific. Mr. Amos edged around and opened the front door while the wrestling men moved out onto the sidewalk. Then he shut and locked it.

We both stood there watching them awhile. Finally they all untangled and began to stray away one by one into the night. In the end only Frank Hollison was left standing there. He leaned up against the glass and shouted, "You gone be sorry, Amos Hendricks."

When he had delivered himself of that threat, he stomped off into the darkness. Mr. Amos kept standing there awhile, and I stood by him. At last he said, "That man's dangerous. We'll have to watch out for him."

Up until then I knew very little of obsession. There had been Miss Ellen's tennis obsession, of course, but it was not malignant. Amos Hendricks' words echoed in my mind. He drove me home that night in the delivery truck where I'd ordinarily have ridden my bike.

X

I just seemed to know that I was supposed to keep quiet about the scene those men made, and I did. I didn't tell Aunt Ida Mae or Uncle Cajus. But when I got to school Monday morning, Harry Dale called me into the office and asked directly: "Did the Baptist deacons make a scene at Mr. Hendricks' store Friday night about you working there?"

I stood there a minute. Faced with either lying or telling the truth, I couldn't decide what to do. If I told, I felt I'd be betraying something, though I wasn't really clear about what. "Well, they weren't all Baptist deacons," I said finally.

"I heard they were."

"Not Frank Hollison," I said. "He isn't a deacon. They said so."

"That man is a member of the KKK. Do you realize that?"

"The KKK?"

"Yes. Come on, Folly, don't pretend you don't know what that is."

"I didn't think it existed any more," I said, playing innocent.

Harry Dale just let out one of his short, ironic laughs that blew smoke from his cigarette everywhere. "You know, you turn Negro obliqueness into a fine art," he said. "Now tell me about it."

"I can't."

He thought about that a moment. "Then just say yes or no when I speak." I didn't say anything in agreeing or disagreeing, but he went on, "So they asked Amos Hendricks to fire you?"

"Not exactly."

"Well, what exactly," Harry Dale snapped, his lip curling a little into impatience.

"They just said they wouldn't tolerate a..." I flinched as I spoke the word, "nigger working in a store here in town when good white people needed jobs."

"Well, that's about as plain as you can put the problem, isn't it, Folly. Now we see racism in its bare bones. Keep the Negro down so that white men can work."

I nodded. "That is about the size of it, isn't it," I agreed. "Why us, Mr. Dale?"

"Because we're handy, and it's wound into their traditions. It isn't just because they're white or European or whatever you want to call them. Every majority inclines to oppress a minority. In another country it could be blacks oppressing whites. And think about it: they try to keep each other from succeeding, too. It's called competition. They can just block us as a group. With each other they have to deal on an individual basis."

I looked at Harry Dale with something close to the respect I felt for him when I first came back to Lawsonville. "Is it awful that I would rather not stick it out in the minority, Mr. Dale?"

"The trouble with a lot of us is that we can't pass like you. If you're really black with African appearance, you're stuck, you're doomed, there's no way out. It's the category they've defined to shut you out. People like that are stuck in a land that should be home but isn't because the majority won't let it be."

I felt my heart thumping so hard I thought Harry Dale might see it through my blouse. "Gosh," I gasped, for lack of any other word handy that would express my palpitation.

Harry Dale hadn't noticed me. He was caught up in his own feelings, and he went on, "It's like hanging from a ledge of a forty story building by your finger tips. You look up and the people like Frank Hollison are about to stomp on your fingers. You look down. It's a long way down..."

I'd never heard Harry Dale discourse at all on what it felt like to be colored in America. I fell back into the chair as if he'd hit me with a boxing glove.

"I'm so selfish," I heard myself admit. "All I want to do is get out. It was wonderful up there in Connecticut when I wasn't colored."

"Don't let them fool you. Every one of us wants to get out. We'd be crazy if we didn't. If we could all be white, we'd do it. We only learn to be black gradually and with great effort. Being black is a learned experience and, for those of us who survive, it builds patience and fortitude, Folly."

The words sounded noble, but I blurted, "What's the reason to want to be black?"

Harry Dale looked at me a long time. His eyes drooped there mournfully beneath the heavy eyelids that made him seem so sophisticated and aristocratic. "Right now I can't think of a single reason except that you know people just like you are caught and can't get away. You want to stand with them."

"Is that why you came back to Georgia?" He took a long draw on his cigarette and let the smoke out in a vertical column of air. Then he made little spitting noises with his tongue against his lips like smokers sometimes do. After that, Harry Dale said this: "Yes. And, believe me, to answer your next question, there have been times I deeply regretted what I've done. Deeply regretted. I'm far from sure it's the right thing to do. It's...it's downright..." he sought the word, "paralyzing."

"Why do you stay?"

"It wouldn't be right to leave now that I've made up my mind," he concluded.

But what possible good was he doing here, I wondered, as I pushed myself back onto my feet. For a moment I hesitated, wondering if in this moment of self-revelation, I should tell Harry Dale what some people said of him, that he was an accommodating Uncle Tom helping to perpetuate segregation? I decided not to say anything because I couldn't think how it could help, and it wouldn't matter to him, anyway.

Now Harry Dale and Judge Lawson were, so you might think, as different as night and day. But they were both men who had secret lives. Maybe a lot of men do, I don't know. It's just that those two pulled the curtain back a little for me to look in.

It was not too long after I talked with Harry Dale that I heard Judge Lawson cough as I came around the stables from my shortcut. When I looked around, expecting him to be standing somewhere half hidden behind a bush, I couldn't find him. Curious, I peeped around corners, looked through the mesh fence at the tennis court. He wasn't there, either.

Then he coughed again, and I whirled around and stared at the side of Lawson Hall, waiting. All the long windows of the first floor were shut, but as my eyes wandered up, I realized that one of the series of little round windows above the library was open. Smoke was drifting out. I could see him move as he cleared his throat.

Judge Lawson was in a room above the library! But I hadn't realized there was anything at all above the library. I could visualize the bookshelves stretching up just short of the ceiling. Any room above that would have to be small and cramped.

I remembered the narrow circular, movable staircase the Judge used to fetch books from the highest bookshelves. The contraption was made of maple and mahogany and was built on a carriage with wheels. The entry into the attic room might well be simply a trap door in the ceiling. The Judge could push the stairs over, mount up, open it and climb in.

Since I was not scheduled for a German lesson and dusting wasn't until Saturday, I had to wait a couple of days to get into the library. When I finally made it, I saw immediately why I had never noticed a trap door leading into a space above the library. The whole ceiling was covered by a large Rococo painting complete with clouds and angels and hordes of figures draped in Roman garb.

It turned out that the trap door was concealed as a gate into some kind of garden in the painting. As soon as I looked carefully and knew what I was looking for, it was fairly easy to spot. It was in the back of the library, the last aisle.

I pushed the stairs over to it and climbed up. Once I mounted the steps, I was close enough to inspect the door. When I pushed it, it opened up. I was able to step up and look into the space. In the semi-darkness, I saw a table with papers in disarray or some kind of chaotic order scattered there and on the floor, large schematic drawings of something I couldn't quite make out.

There was no way I could risk climbing up into the room. Aunt Ida Mae was in the kitchen and might have looked in to see how I was doing with my chores any minute. Uncle Cajus was whistling out in the back yard, and I heard Tom singing in the front. Tom usually sang and sometimes words emerged and took striking form. I heard him singing: *Day time, night time, it's the right time...* and I knew he was just enjoying rhyming the words,

I almost panicked when I couldn't get the door to come down at first. Then, on closer investigation, I found a catch that reversed the system of weights, and it closed automatically, sighing down until it was fully shut.

I came down the ladder and pushed it along the aisle so there'd be no chance of anybody connecting me with the trapdoor. In spite of all I could do during the next few days, all I could think of was that room and the secrets it held. I wondered what great scheme Judge Lawson was working on to need so many large sheets of paper spread out.

The imminence of Laura Lawson's return home for Christmas finally did call my mind to other tasks. The main problem for me was to find a place to stay during the holidays. That was the only way to avoid Laura and the inevitable unpleasantness she would cause if she found me at Lawson Hall.

What I didn't want to do was stay again for two weeks with Reverend Smothers' widow. It was not that she wasn't a kind woman, it was just that she had become so infirm. Naturally, I was being selfish, knowing that I could be a great help to the pastor's widow now that she was half blind and half deaf, bent with a widow's hump weighing her down, and almost without real teeth.

I was tormented, on the one hand, with guilt about not wanting to stay with Widow Smothers; while, on the other, I was tormented with the idea that I had no choice but to spend the time at her little home on the edge of the colored part of town.

Then my friend Lila came to the rescue. I had confided my need to be away from Lawson Hall during Laura's visit to her. Lila listened with sympathetic interest, but I didn't expect the invitation she finally offered.

At first, Lila had been a rival rather than a friend. I didn't so much notice her; rather, she noticed me. I was the only real threat to her academic supremacy in our class. Lila wanted to be valedictorian of our class. Until my arrival, she was easily the single choice for the honor. It was not so much that I really cared about being better than Lila. I was much too preoccupied with my own life to think much about her at all.

Lila was not a particularly attractive or noticeable person. She was a dark-skinned girl with decidedly African features. She was also quiet, polite, and otherwise the sort of person one might overlook, except that she always had the right answers in class. She was like the teacher's pet in a play, not altogether real she played the role with such unconscious perfection. I guess if I felt anything about her, it was a kind of bemused pity.

The truth is, Lila courted me. At recess she started hanging around me. She would follow me in the halls. My first reaction was mild irritation, but then – I suppose it was her unassuming manner – it flattered me to have such a blatant admirer. Lila seemed genuinely interested in my life. Her attention bordered at times on worship. She especially asked me a lot about my life in Connecticut, Miss Ellen, the school I attended, and tennis. She couldn't get enough of that. Her most burning curiosity had to do with life as a white person.

By December of that year, our friendship had progressed to the point that I could confide things to her about my feelings. I suppose she encouraged such confidences. It was just natural to tell her about my fear of being around when Laura Lawson came home for Christmas.

"Why do you have to leave?"

"Laura hates me," I said.

"Why?"

"I don't know. She just always did. The first time I came to Lawson Hall, she hated me." I proceeded to tell her about the tricks Laura used to play on me.

"That's awful," Lila sympathized.

The more I knew her, the more I found Lila likable, though I guess I liked her like you'd like a pliant little puppy. I realized that it pleased me to find that people of very dark skin and decided African appearance could also be ambitious and intelligent instead of shiftless, lazy and stupid. It was then that I realized just how much I had shared in the prejudices and presuppositions of my racist world.

Then one day Lila just up and asked me if I could maybe stay at her house during the time Laura was home. I thought there might be a problem because I'd have to work at Mr. Hendricks' store every day except Sunday. That meant I'd have to get into town and back each day. Lila assured me it didn't matter. I told her I'd ride my bike. It was only five miles, she said, out to their place. That really wasn't too much on a bike.

When I told Aunt Ida Mae, she looked around at me with her heavy, suspicious frown. "What you up to now, Folly Steeples?"

"I'm not up to anything," I said as innocently as I could manage. In spite of all I could do, Aunt Ida Mae could make me feel invariably guilty. I never did understand why.

"Why would Mr. Ralph Walborough want you to his house for Christmas? They don't even go to our church."

"Well, where do they go to church, Aunt Ida Mae," I asked, thinking to deflect her suspicion with a question.

"They go out to Big Sandy Baptist is where they go. Near where they live. Near where they got a BIG farm."

"That big?"

Her eyes widened, as they always did when she was about to tell you about something that to her mind was profoundly impressive. "Yes, that big. He the richest colored man in five counties."

"Five?" Five counties for Aunt Ida Mae was like saying "the whole wide world."

"Yes, five counties," she affirmed. "Now why he want to take a no account girl like you in for Christmas? Can you tell me that?"

"Probably because I'm friends with his daughter."

"He got a daughter your age?"

"He sure has, and she's in my class."

I told Ida Mae about our friendship. When I had finished my little tale, she said, "You beat all I ever seen. You and Ralph Wallborough's daughter. How you always manage to get picked up by quality?"

"Because I'm quality," I queried facetiously.

"You quality," Aunt Ida Mae chuckled (this was rhetorical on her part), "now, chile, I don't know what's happened to your head. You was born with the big head, and it ain't gotten no smaller as you growed up. I said nothing good would come of you going up north with Miss Ellen."

"Why are you so impressed with the Walboroughs, Aunt Ida Mae?"

"Because everybody knows that Mr. Ralph Walborough is the biggest farmer around here. He pay cash for everything he buy. I bet he got a thousand acres if he got fifteen. And they own a mill and a store, too. That man come into town and paid cash down for a brand new Chrysler!" Her voice soared up into the highest registers on this last remark. When she stopped, her lips pert, she was just daring me to deny a word of it.

"He drives a Chrysler," I said, trying to deflect again.

"Does he drive a Chrysler? What you talking about, child. He drive a Chrysler, but he has him a truck and a tractor, too."

"Wow," I said.

"He's richer than most white men, that's for sure."

I can tell you that I was really curious and glad when that Chrysler drove down the gravel drive and stopped in back of Lawson Hall because I wanted to see what this impressively endowed farmer who could pay cash for Chryslers might look like.

Both the front doors opened like the Chrysler was spreading wings. On one side Lila jumped out screeching my name with delight, "Fooolly!" Out the other stepped her papa, a stout man in a vested suit, a tie and a hat like any white man in town.

Ralph Walborough was coal black with a broad nose, heavy lips and what I later came to think of as a West African noggin. His face was impenetrable, though he habitually wore a jolly smile. The smile was empty. No moods were reflected in it. You couldn't tell what he thought, but his eyes seemed penetrating and shrewd.

Ralph Walborough was a man against all odds, a man of parts, a Negro man who had not merely survived but triumphed in a world dominated by his enemies, by forces sworn like Mrs. Happity to keep him down. I was deeply moved to see him in the flesh, and I wanted terribly to understand his character.

"I never been here," Lila said looking around breathlessly at Lawson Hall, the stables, the tennis courts. She was so excited, she didn't notice my preoccupation with her father.

On the way out in the country, we knelt on the back seat and looked out the back window at the billows of dust the Chrysler stirred up as it sped along the dirt road. It had been unusually dry during the fall.

When we arrived at Walborough Farm, Lila hopped around to the front and pressed the palm of her hands against the door window. "That's the mill and the store," she said proudly.

"Look," I cried, "the water wheel's moving!"

"Ben is grinding something this morning," Mr. Ralph Walborough intoned from the front seat. His voice was deep and authoritative.

"Ben helps us," Lila explained.

A colored family with help, I thought. Now it was my turn to be impressed and a little confused. Before I could formulate a question, we pulled up into the yard in front of the long, low, unpainted clapboard farmhouse. Several chickens took flight, breaking out of dust billows around us and clucking madly.

We waited a moment for the dust to blow away in the morning breeze before we opened the doors of the Chrysler to jump out. Mrs. Walborough was waiting at the top of the stairs on the porch just in front of the front door. "Welcome to our place," she said as I came up the steps holding hands with Lila. She took my hands from Lila into her own and said, "Why you're even prettier than Lila said."

"Thank you, m'aam," I said. There was an insincere edge to her compliment that didn't escape me but which I chose simply to file away for future reference. I had known such compliments from those I defeated in tennis.

I couldn't wait to see the inside of the house, and it didn't disappoint. Walborough House wasn't at all like the suburban ranches the tiny Lawsonville white middle class had built at the foot of Lawson Hall's park where I had been waylaid with the sugar that day many years before. It was a farmhouse that didn't apologize and didn't pretend to be anything else, big, rambling, with wooden interior walls made out of planks that were painted pale blue and yellow. Each room had its own color.

When we walked through its many rooms, Walborough House seemed to embrace us with its pleasant odors and its cleanliness. A picture of Jesus hung over the living room sofa. Everything had been scrubbed and polished clean on a regular basis over generations. Aunt Ida Mae would have loved it. I noted that it would have met all her expectations about how the richest Negro in five counties should live.

Most impressive were the assortment of genuine family photographs that hung in the hall to the kitchen. The portraits bespoke generations of prosperous colored farmers. Well-dressed people looked confidently into the camera's eye. Some of them broke into a grin. Others were serious. It was just like the family photographs I had seen when delivering groceries to the white homes.

I went to the piano in the living room and tapped a key or two. "Do you play," Mrs. Walborough asked behind me, her voice still somehow vaguely disconcerting, on edge. It was as if she expected me to say something threatening at any moment, as if she were resenting it in advance.

"No," I said. "I wish I could."

"Mama plays," Lila gloated. "Play something, Mama!"

"First we'll wash up and have dinner," Mrs. Walborough instructed. "Follow me, girls, I've got things about ready, but there are a few things left to do."

The table was set, and, when we finished the last preparation, we all sat down to a country feast of hot biscuits, cornbread, okra, corn, peas, gravy, potatoes, and beef.

Lila sat across the table on one side, and I sat across on the other. Mr. and Mrs. Walborough sat at each end. When the blessing was said, Mr. Walborough tucked his napkin into the collar of his shirt. Uncle Cajus did that, too, but Judge Lawson didn't. Uncle Cajus said he needed to protect his white shirt. He was really protecting Ida Mae from having to wash one more shirt.

"Mr. Walborough," I heard Lila's mother say, "our visitor thinks that is a strange custom."

"What, my dear?"

"Tucking your napkin in your collar."

"Keeps me from ruining a good shirt," he said in perfect good humor.

"No m'aam," I said. "I don't think it's strange at all. My uncle does it, too."

"Your uncle?"

"I live with my uncle and aunt," I explained.

"Up at Lawson Hall," Mr. Ralph Walborough explained to his wife. "That's where we went to get her."

"Your folks work for the Lawsons," she said.

"Yes m'aam," I said. I'd have thought Lila had told her that.

"What do they do," Mrs. Walborough asked. Her voice was full of condescension.

"Cajus drives the Judge," Mr. Ralph Walborough explained to his wife as he cut a piece of porkchop.

"Oh," said Mrs. Walborough, turning to her food. She sounded like that was unexpected and about the lowest thing she could imagine. As she raised her fork to her mouth, just before she stuck it in, she said, "These light-skinned colored folk is always working for the planter families. It's a funny thing."

I didn't see why it was a funny thing. I'd never thought of it, either, for that matter, and I didn't really think it was true. The colored school was full of light-skinned folk who were teaching, for instance. But I didn't point that out. My digestion wasn't too good, though, that day. It was apparent that Mrs. Walborough actually had something against me, though I didn't know what it could be. She didn't know me at all. So why would she have let her daughter invite me if she didn't like my kind?

Plenty is what this family was blessed with, and I had two weeks to see it all in its endless supply. As I was treated to a review of everything, including Lila's large closet full of clothes, I wondered why so many farmers in Lawson County were so poor.

I was willing to endure Mrs. Walborough's contempt just to understand how Mr. Walborough had acquired the magic touch to draw from a poor land such bounty? This was a study I wanted to pursue. What was it that enabled him to succeed where so many failed? I determined to use the time there to find out. It obviously had nothing to do with race.

My first opportunity to get to the bottom of the puzzle came when Mr. Walborough showed up to drive me back to his place the first afternoon I worked.

"But my bicycle," I said.

"Just leave it here. I need to come into town tomorrow, and I can drive you in."

On the drive, I asked bluntly (having been unable to devise a more subtle approach and fearing to lose my opportunity), "Why is it, Mr. Ralph, that you're so successful?

Since I was sitting on the front seat beside him, I could get a good look at his face. This was important to gauge his answer.

Mr. Ralph was smiling, of course, in his usual fixed way, but there was also a new, kind of inward, self-contained pleasure visible in his dense features. "Folly, my daddy taught me that you don't never spend beyond what you got."

"Yes, sir?"

"Yes, that whatever you have or take in, you try to lay some of it aside for later. The more, the better. It'll grow faster'n most people think. The trouble with most people is they spend more'n they take in. See what I mean? It don't matter how much you earn, it matter how much you save."

"I see," I said. "Is that what you've done?"

"Not just me. My daddy save, too. And my granddaddy when he got out of slavery. It take more than one generation, honey, to pile up enough to have a really good stock."

"I don't have a granddaddy," I said. Then I added on consideration, "And I don't have a daddy."

"Well, you might not be able to pile up too much, but you'd be surprised what a person can do. Live on as little as you can. Put most everything you take in aside. Pretty soon it'll make a difference."

Is that all there is to it, I wondered. My first reaction was disappointment. "But what else do you do," I persisted after a spell of sitting silently while dust almost encapsulated us as we drove along.

"You work hard," he said, understanding the nature of my question, "and you work smart."

"What's working smart?"

"I guess that's the key. Lemme give you a example. You try to estimate the markets. If they ain't good for cotton, then you plant corn. If too many folks is planting corn, plant tomatoes and beans. People always has to eat. Don't get hung up on one crop, honey. That's the secret. If you see a possibility, go to it where the market's good."

"Yes, sir," I said. I understood exactly what he meant, and it was to change my life. It was one of those moments I was always expecting to happen, like a convergence of heavenly bodies and the cry: Got it! "Flexibility," I suggested.

"Yeah, das it! Flexibility." Mr. Walborough really liked the word. He said it twice more as we sped along. "Ain't everybody got it," he concluded.

At the farmhouse Mrs. Walborough began to interrogate me. She asked lots of questions, especially about my life with Miss Ellen in Connecticut. When I answered she made little "ummm-hmmm" noises that implied she didn't really believe everything I was saying.

"So you lived the whole time with Miss Ellen Lawson?"

"Yes," I said forthrightly.

"You sound unsure."

"No, of course I did, but, you know, the accident wiped out so much of my memory of things. I was no more than seven when we left and sixteen going on seventeen when I got back."

"And you lived the whole time with Miss Ellen Lawson. In her home?"

"I said I did. Yes."

"Did you do the chores? Dust, things like that?"

"No, Miss Ellen hired somebody to come in to do that. We spent all our time at the club playing tennis. That is, when I wasn't in school."

"My, my," was all Mrs. Walborough would say to that, and there was a whole universe of envy in those two syllables. By that time, I was aware that Mrs. Walborough was jealous of me and my life. It seemed crazy, but there it was. She had everything. I had nothing. Yet, she was jealous, and I figured it was just a matter of time till that jealousy congealed into real poison. I only hoped the holidays would go by faster than her animosity grew.

Then another time she would come at it from another angle: "You said you were always playing tennis."

"It's a game," I said.

"Yes, I've heard about it."

"Two people stand across a net from each other," Lila said, "and bat a ball back and forth."

She had that from me.

"Yes, I know that," Mrs. Walborough said, "but what else did you do. You lived in the same house with Miss Ellen? All the time?"

"Well, all the time I lived anywhere," I said.

The thing that was beginning to strike me about all this interrogating was that Lila didn't seem impatient or upset that her mother was digging in. She took it all as pretty natural, or seemed to, though I'd have thought she'd have gotten irritated. After all, they'd invited me. Lila had invited me. I was supposed to be the guest, but I guess she believed her mother hung the moon. She wanted to please that woman more than Aunt Ida Mae wanted to follow the Bible. So Lila became a sort of silent partner to the gradual buildup of persecution that was going on with me being the victim.

"And there weren't any colored children in your school?"

"Not a one," I said, thinking I'd already told her that half a dozen times.

"Where were all the colored children?"

"I never saw any," I said. "Well, actually, when Uncle Cajus took me out of the hospital, we stayed a night in a colored boarding house before catching the train to Georgia. That was the first time I knew there were any colored people in Connecticut."

I looked at Mrs. Walborough and saw that she just didn't believe me. She not only didn't believe me, what I said made her angry. She was so mad she was about to bust. It was written all over her face. She wouldn't last too much longer until she did blow up totally. If I could have gone home then, I would've. But Laura was still there.

One night after I'd finished washing up, I must have come out of the bathroom too quietly. When I got about halfway across the hall and was headed to the kitchen where they stayed because it was warm in that room, I heard Mrs. Walborough say, "You don't think I believe that about her passing for white, do you? That child can tell a lie and never blink! She didn't see no colored people in Connek-tu-kit! Pshaw!"

"Mama," Lila whined, "she can't help it that she's so light. Everybody says she lived just like a white girl up there and went to a white school and everything. Everybody says it."

"You can't believe these high-yellers, Lila. They don't have no character. Papa has said it himself many a time. Mixed blood is bad blood. That's what I always say."

I tiptoed back to the bedroom I shared with Lila and got under the covers and cried. I felt awfully sorry for myself and turned my back on Lila and wouldn't turn around when she came to bed. Every once in a while I felt a big, delicious sob work it's way up my chest.

Lila kept saying, "What's wrong, Folly," but I didn't answer. I think she knew, anyway, that I must have heard something.

I would have loved to leave and go home that next morning, but I couldn't because I didn't have anywhere to go. Laura Lawson was going to be at Lawson Hall until Sunday, and it was only Thursday. So I had to tough it out through the weekend.

Saturday night when I got back late from the store, Mrs. Walborough was waiting up for me. "I kept you some supper," she said with feigned friendliness. By this time I saw right through her and hated her hypocrisy as much as I was afraid of it. Mr. Ralph had gone on to bed, so there were no witnesses. I think she had staged the whole thing as one of those little showdowns some people enjoy so much and feel the need of, too.

"Thank you, m'aam," I said.

"Just sit down here," she said, and I did. She sat down across the table and watched me. Pretty soon, she said, "Lila says you're Miss Ellen Lawson's natural daughter. Is that true?"

I almost spat the food out when I heard that: "I am not Miss Ellen Lawson's daughter," I declared indignantly, "and I never told anybody I was!"

"Well, Lila says everybody in town thinks so. Now we do most of our shopping in Washington," she added primly, "so I don't really know what people in Lawsonville are saying." She patted her hair for emphasis to show she was too good to shop in Lawsonville and all Lawson County gossip was beneath her.

"I don't know what people are saying, and I don't see why they'd be saying that because it's not true. I've never pretended to be anything I'm not," I said. Even as I said it, I felt the edges of the statement crumbling into a void.

"Well," Mrs. Walborough said reasonably, "if you haven't ever pretended to be what you're not, how did you pass for white all those years?"

I put down the fork. "That's not how I looked at it. I simply did what Miss Ellen said. She never used those words."

"People must have known. Everybody here knows you're colored, I expect."

"Well, either people didn't, or it didn't make any difference."

"Don't tell me that," she snorted. "It's gonna make a difference anywhere you go. You'd have to pretend to be white to live with a Lawson and go to her clubs and play tennis there."

"You really don't like me, do you, Mrs. Walborough," I said dead level. "I haven't wanted to do anything to make you not like me, and I wish you'd say what it was I've done. I certainly don't like having this kind of relationship with you, and I thought I was a guest here."

That took her by surprise. Her mouth moved but nothing came out at first. Then she managed to say, "I don't like liars, and that's a fact." Her face twisted up so I thought she might spit on me. "High yeller like yourself is always going out pretending to be white and passing," she said. "Putting on airs," she added for good measure, almost breathless.

"And it's something impossible for you to do, isn't it," I said pointedly, "as black as you are."

I don't know why I said that. It was mean. What happened once I'd done it was more than I'd have thought possible. Mrs. Walborough jumped up from the table. She turned over her chair in the process, and it made such a racket, I jumped in my seat. "I won't be insulted in my own house," she cried. "We are proud to be black!" She drew herself up into a scornful superiority and piped, "We're not bastards. Not a one of us, and that's a fact."

It was like I was stuck to my chair. I couldn't seem to move. I wanted to say, 'and well you should be,' but I couldn't utter a sound. And there was Lila coming through one door and Mr. Walborough coming through the other. Then, pretty quickly, I was being hustled out of the house, pushed by Lila.

"Don't ever speak to me again," she hissed as I climbed into the Chrysler that Mr. Walborough had paid cash for.

All the way to Lawson Hall he didn't say a word. I sat there trying to keep myself under control so I wouldn't start bawling. I wanted to explain how it had happened, but I was scared to start. I knew Aunt Ida Mae would be furious when I came home early. She would feel I'd disgraced her with the richest Negro in five counties. Besides, so far as I knew, Laura Lawson was still at the Hall, and I'd have no choice but to hide out in the cottage until Sunday evening after she'd gone.

Under cover of darkness the Chrysler came to a stop, then Mr. Ralph turned the lights out. I got out on one side, Mr. Walborough on the other. Soon he and Uncle Cajus huddled outside the door. My clothes were brought in. I went to my room.

When the Chrysler was gone, the door to my room opened. Aunt Ida Mae appeared with her funeral mien. "What you gone do next? Huh? What you gone do next?"

I sat up in bed, "Can I explain?"

"What you got to explain. You go and insult folks in they own house, call them niggers."

"I didn't call them niggers," I moaned.

"Let her explain," Uncle Cajus said, coming up behind her. So I did.

"So she don't like high yellers, huh," Aunt Ida Mae concluded. "Stuck up nigger!"

XI

The New Year had to be an improvement on Christmas, but it wasn't because Jim was gearing up to leave and go off to college. That's all I heard from him the whole time until he graduated and was gone. Nothing but how college was going to get him in a position to get into history and so forth.

I got so irritated with how happy he was about his future opening up that I wanted to puncture his balloon more than once. "Don't you know there won't be a major war for a long time, Jim," I told him. "Then how'll you get into history just by being an officer in the Army?"

"There'll be little wars."

"Whoever got into history in a little war?"

"Zachary Scott. He was a hero of the Mexican War. He was elected President. Lots of people got into Congress and what not on that war."

"Oh, gee whiz, Jim."

"Look at Korea."

"Yeah, Douglas MacArthur got out of history in that one. But I don't know that that was a LITTLE war, Jim."

"Maybe. But maybe not. But MacArthur's still respected."

"I read that he's living in a hotel in New York. Is that history? Living in a hotel?"

"Hey, and there was Theodore Roosevelt!"

"What about him?"

Jim began to gesticulate excitedly, "Yeah, he got his rough riders together in the Spanish-American War, remember? Now, that was a little war, wasn't it. You can't deny that."

"Yes. I think it was a very little war."

"Boy, he got into history good. How about that?"

I knew when I was defeated. It was true about Roosevelt. "You shot my argument all to hell," I said, risking cussing for the humor it injected. It wouldn't be right to be cross when Jim went away. He should have been thrilled about the opportunity he had to go to college and get a commission. We laughed after I said that. I guess I could have got away with most anything around Jim.

One thing I do remember about the last month when warm weather came and Jim started going without his shirt a lot. He wanted to show off his manly physique because he'd developed fully by that time and had some hair on his chest, too. I really enjoyed seeing him without his shirt on. Sometimes it made me feel a little dizzy.

Then suddenly he was gone. It was like something had happened you really never did believe could. You kept thinking something would come up. Jim would get a really good job offer to stay around Lawson County. But who would have given him such a job? They didn't exist. Any young man who wanted to become something had to leave. It just goes to show how unrealistic I still was.

Another thing Jim's going away made me do is think about my own future. I didn't have the foggiest notion what I wanted to do with myself. If anything I thought dimly about going back to Connecticut and coaching tennis. The idea wasn't serious enough for me to have even thought about finding out if you need certification to coach tennis or to really plan. On the other hand, I had a fairly good grasp of the kind of person I wanted to be (and probably was already, to some extent).

There was no doubt, though, that I had to start planning. I couldn't live there in the cottage behind Lawson Hall with Uncle Cajus and Aunt Ida Mae forever. I didn't want to end up like all the random lives around town. It wasn't terribly encouraging for me to note that, where Jim had developed a solid, muscular body, I had sprouted wobbly breasts that really got in the way. What good were they, anyway, I wondered.

These breasts and stuff not only slowed me down when I ran long-distance – something Harry Dale had encouraged me to take up – but they attracted the undesirable attention of drooling, beastly boys. I hated them both: My breasts and those boys. I just wished they would go away. But they didn't. They became another part of Hard Reality I had to deal with. I won't even mention that other business females have to put up with every month.

Boys don't know how lucky they are is what I thought. They don't even have to take down their pants and squat to pee. Nature has conspired to make a female vulnerable every way she turns. The worst of it is, in order to propagate the human race, she has to carry the baby inside her for nine months. Nine months is a long time, and, as far as I could tell, carrying a developing baby stretches everything inside in the worst kind of way. Plus a lot of women got sick and were otherwise unable to work or stand tall.

If you think having breasts isn't a big deal and that my concern was misplaced, you don't know how it is to be colored in segregated Georgia. And you sure as hell don't know what it's like to have all this female stuff laid on you just about the time you're going to be forced out to face the world on your own.

But before I get busy and tell you about Mr. Violence and his Demon Company Triumphant Testosterone, I must tell you just how I discovered more about the secret attic where Judge Lawson had spent so much time working on his project. It happened one afternoon when I came into the library expecting to sit down with him to my usual German lesson.

The thing is, Judge Lawson wasn't in the library. I saw right away that the stairs had been moved over and the trap door was open. Judge Lawson was still up in the attic. For a moment I couldn't decide what to do. Perhaps if I waited, and the Judge realized I knew, he'd simply invited me up and include me in whatever it was he was doing. I had a sense that, whatever it was, it was scholarly in nature.

I saw his legs emerge out of the ceiling. He began to feel about for the ladder with his feet. That's when I left the library and waited, giving him enough time to get down and get everything out of the way. He was getting careless. Or maybe he just was getting to the stage where he wasn't so concerned with hiding the attic room from me.

The more I thought about it later, the more I was certain that the latter was true, that what the Judge was working on he'd finally share with me. Of course, things don't always happen the way you expect them, too. That summer got hotter and hotter. Judge Lawson had stopped going up there himself, but I didn't want to wait until fall to find out what he had been doing in secret.

One evening as we both were sitting there in the steaming heat with an electric fan blowing and Judge Lawson sipping punch with ice in it, it happened. We were working over a poem by Hugo von Hoffmannsthal who Judge Lawson said had been the librettist for Richard Strauss. He had an album of Strauss's *The Woman without a Shadow* in German we'd heard several times together.

The poem began, "Kinder wachsen auf mit grossen Augen, wachsen auf und sterben…"

"Can you translate that," he asked me, interrupting my reading in German.

"Well, 'children grow up with large eyes, grow up and die,'" I said reasonably.

"And everybody goes their own way," he added, completing the line. "What does it mean?"

"They don't care. They are indifferent to the suffering," I said.

"No, they don't. Does that strike you as a little too pessimistic?"

"No. Not really," I said. "People have things to do. They can't sit around grieving. Not that I've seen any of that stuff around here."

"No, I suppose they can't," the Judge said. Then he smiled a moment, "Yes, you haven't seen any of that stuff around—" Then his face folded up on itself. I stood up out of my seat in alarm. He gripped desperately at his chest and grunted, started to stand up only to fall back down as a dark green bile issued forth from his mouth like a waterfall, coursing and splashing all over his shirt front and the desk. He lurched forward, pitched down, head first, into his own vomit and lay there, his eyes sort of rolled up in his head.

I ran from the room screaming for Aunt Ida Mae. She came from one direction, and I caught sight through the window of Uncle Cajus and Tom running from one of the sheds as best they could in their old man, bowlegged gait. But there was nothing anybody could do. Judge Lawson was dead.

He had died of a massive stroke right in front of me on a hot, summer evening while discussing Hugo von Hofmannsthal. It was as simple as that. Since it had been a Friday night, I had to get up the next morning at four a.m., go down to the alley behind the picture show like I had done every morning since Jim hired me to help him with the newspapers.

The paper had been thrown out of the truck in bundles, and I had to sit under the little lean-to, take each paper, roll and tie it for tossing. That took nearly an hour. There were moments while I was doing this that it just seemed absurd. Judge Lawson was dead, and I was rolling papers. At around five I'd start out on my bike, the basket full of papers, to throw them.

I had kept the route divided out of habit, and that morning I especially did things out of habit. It wasn't exactly that my mind was on Judge Lawson. Not exactly. One side had been Jim's route. I always did my route first, as if Jim was still there with me, just like I'd probably do things from now on and have the feeling that Judge Lawson was there. When I finished my side, I came to a dead end that backed up to the pasture behind the stables of Lawson Hall. It was about six a.m., and the sun was already coming up fairly strong. At that point, after I threw the last paper, I usually went back to the back of the picture show and got the second load of papers.

As I took out a handkerchief to wipe off the sweat, three men stepped out of the little wood of the empty lot to my right. It was the lot that hadn't ever had a house built on it. Pine trees had been allowed to seed and grow. They weren't big trees but fairly dense, so that anybody could hide in there. I thought it was odd to have these men come out, but I wasn't scared. I hardly paid them any attention at first. I'd just tossed my last paper, dismounted and was turning the bike around to head back to the picture show.

It didn't occur to me that the men had anything to do with me, though I recognized Frank Hollison as one of them. It had been a long time since the scene at Mr. Hendricks' store. Hollison had never showed up to threaten us again. I suppose both Mr. Hendricks and I had just forgotten about him. When I recognized him, I was, of course, a bit surprised. But even then I wasn't afraid.

Out of the corner of my eye, though, I could see that they seemed to be coming my way. Then I realized that they were focused on me, too, though it didn't make any sense to me. For a crazy moment I thought they might want to buy a newspaper from me, so I said, "I'm sorry, I've thrown all the papers. You'll have to get one later."

The young one laughed at that. It was a short, mean laugh. Something about what I said must have solidified their determination because they started off at a kind of slow trot, sort of fanning out around me. Frank Hollison pointed at me and said something I didn't hear clearly. It was still kind of like something you don't understand, confusing somehow. But that's also when I moved the bike around so it was pointing at Frank Hollison who was coming dead on. When he was close enough, I shoved the bike at him. It rolled his way, and, against all odds, caught and tripped him. He went down cussing.

Now I was scared and dodging. The young man played with me. He was grinning as he dodged back and forth trying to out-anticipate my next move. He looked like he was having fun. I was worried that I might totally panic. If I let panic flood in, it would smother my thinking. When you're trying to dodge three people, you've got to keep your head clear.

Well, we dodged each other back and forth while I knew Frank Hollison was getting up behind me. The second man was a little younger than Hollison, but he was slow and clumsy. He wouldn't be much trouble because he was already panting. I had to concentrate to keep just out of the grasp of the young one, though. I was easy to see that he and the other one were trying to box me up against the fence. That's when I had the idea that I'd fool them. I'd let them box me up, then I'd get over the fence and head up the hill to Lawson Hall. I'd scream as loud as I could for help, too. It'd be risky because they might be able to catch me on the fence.

The other alternative was to run down the street. I knew I could outrun Hollison and the other man, but the young man was fast and powerful. On a straightaway, if he had the breath, he might catch me. Maybe if I screamed somebody would come out of one of the houses, but I didn't think I could depend upon it.

The way the dodging game was going, my choice of running down the road was closed off, anyway. Once I had to turn on my heels and run right between them. They ended up getting tangled in each other. The young one dived for me and missed. Hollison ran into the third man, and they both cursed again loudly. That was my chance to get to the fence and get over.

I leapt off the fence and into the pasture just as the young one made a grab for my leg. He cut his hand on the barbed wire, too, and started cussing. I was in the pasture running for all I was worth. I could see the stables at Lawson Hall at the top of a long incline of grassland. It looked so terribly far away, but I knew the terrain in between really well because I'd picked blackberries on bushes scattered around the pastures as long as I could remember. The bushes had grown in the eroded gulleys.

Then I heard the young one breathing behind me, which meant he was very close. I didn't dare look back. Lawson Hall was still three football fields away. It didn't seem to be getting any closer. I could virtually feel the young one reaching out, about to grab me. I dodged and, sure enough, he lurched to one side and stumbled. I veered back to the left and headed for the blackberry thicket.

I knew my way through the thicket. When I got through I looked back and saw the young one in the middle of it. He was throwing his arms at the thorny vines and cursing. This time I thought I could make it safely home, but then I realized that Hollison and the other man had gotten over the fence and moved up the short way to cut me off. They were watching me as they huffed their way in front.

Why would a grown, middle-aged man act like that, I thought to myself, chasing a young girl like me. Did he hate me so much? What would he do when he caught me, only a couple of hundred yards from my own safe haven? My heart was sinking fast when I heard Tom cry, "Hold on, honey, I'm coming!"

I looked up the incline and saw a rotund juggernaut hurdling down from the stables. It was Tom, and he was wielding a pitchfork, shaking it high over his head and hollering, "I'm coming! Leave her alone!" The only thing I could figure is he had woken up early and had been washing himself at the spigot outside the stables.

"Who the hell is that," Hollison said, digging in his heels and coming to a dead stop not thirty feet from me as he stared up at Tom.

The other man turned tail and started down the gentle hill. He looked back nervously, tripped on something, tumbled along through the grass, got up and ran again. "That's that crazy man," the young one called as he was extracting himself from the last thorns, "It's just that crazy man that works up there."

I used the moment to get around them. The young one was free of the briar patch and was now screaming at Hollison, "Hey, don't let the bitch get away! She's coming right by you!"

There was a long moment, I think, when they couldn't quite decide what to do. I stopped and looked back now, then I started screaming as loud as I could with my chest heaving for air: "Uncle Cajus! Help! Help!"

Everybody was surprised when Uncle Cajus thundered in his great bass, "Stand still, honey." I looked up and he was aiming his rifle, had it braced against the side of the stable. The report of the rifle cracked across the morning. "The sonovbitch has a gun,"

Hollison cried. Then he broke and ran behind the other man. By that time Tom reached the young one who had ignored the rifle report and had lunged to get me.

Tom thrust with the pitchfork. The young one sidestepped him. He grabbed the tool. They wrestled briefly. The young one flourished the pitchfork. Uncle Cajus was now hurrying down the hill. He had the rifle in hand. The young one raised the pitchfork. Tom had been brought to his knees and was trying to shield himself with his hands. "No," I screamed. The young one brought the pitchfork down on him. He looked over at me. I had picked up a rock, and I flung it at him and missed.

Uncle Cajus came up to Tom, put down the rifle and pulled out the pitchfork. Tom had been holding it steady. He picked up the rifle, leveled it and fired at the retreating figures. Hollison and the other older man were on the fence. "Christ," one of them screamed. I couldn't tell which one. He began to scream, and Hollison turned to help him. The younger one came up behind and gave him a boost. Uncle Cajus fired again.

"Don't kill them, Uncle Cajus," I called. "Let them go. You'll just get into trouble."

"I done hit one," he said. He looked like he was about to fire again, but then he lifted the rifle, laid it down. "Come on, honey, we got to get Tom to the doctor."

XII

Tom didn't die, but he had some bad punctures and had to be taken to the hospital in Thomson where they kept him at least a week. People said Frank Hollison didn't come in to his job at the planing mill Monday. Two weeks later he still hadn't showed up, and nobody seemed to know what had happened to him. Not that anybody seemed to be very sorry. He didn't have any friends.

Judge Lawson's funeral was the biggest anybody had seen in their lifetime in the county. Bigwigs came from all over. Laura Lawson flew back down and took the train from Atlanta. The sheriff and his deputies stopped traffic everywhere, and the line of Cadillacs was long. At the cemetery everybody moved along, men in expensive suits who were too important to notice the townspeople, their wives in jewels and furs.

It was the last time I saw Laura for a long time. She didn't notice me at all, so I was okay staying there. She had that same distant look that all the important people wore at the funeral. They just kind of looked straight through you like you weren't even there. I wondered what it'd be like to live in such ethereal realms immune to human feeling, where most of the people around you were hardly more than scenery in a play, except where you needed them to do something for you.

Laura stayed a couple of days longer after her father was in the ground, and then she left. None of us mortals had the slightest inkling about her plans. She didn't share anything with us. Even Uncle Cajus and Aunt Ida Mae, who had virtually raised her, were strangers, so far as she was concerned. She addressed them with such authentic absent-mindedness that you couldn't be sure she even remembered their names or knew who they were.

I knew because I heard them whispering at night that Aunt Ida Mae and Uncle Cajus were worried that Laura would sell the Hall and leave them without a place to live. When she went away, we lived for months in suspense, waiting for the ax to fall, for the agent to arrive who would tell us to pack up and leave. I don't remember exactly when we started relaxing, but it was at least six or seven months. In all that time, my aunt and uncle didn't hear a word. I started thinking that maybe Laura had simply forgotten about Lawson Hall altogether. Which was okay with us.

After a year we got used to being without a master at the Hall. Uncle Cajus no longer had to drive the Buick, but he kept it polished and full of gas, just like he thought the Judge might be resurrected and want to drive to Augusta. Aunt Ida Mae cooked, and I helped her keep the house clean. There was a lawyer in nearby Washington who kept paying the utilities, taxes, and Uncle Cajus's salary.

I don't know what made me do it except that I just longed to hear some of the music that the Judge had played for me in conjunction with our discussions of German literature and philosophy. It must have been more than a year after he had died that I went back into the library. Aunt Ida Mae was gone to her missionary society down at the church. So I took out Mozart's *Magic Flute* and played it. I got so involved I forgot to listen for Aunt Ida Mae to return, so she came in and found me there.

When I saw her standing in the door of the library, I jumped up like I'd just sat down on a pin. But she just nodded, turned and left. After that I would play a lot of music in the library. I was careful with Judge Lawson's music library. Aunt Ida Mae knew she could trust me to keep everything clean and dusted and in its proper place.

After that two years passed before Civil Rights came to Lawsonville. It was unseasonably cold that year, and we were wearing woolens in November. It had already snowed twice, though the snow didn't stick more than a day or two. I was wearing rubber boots and slopping through the mud in the back lot behind the store when somebody called out: "Hey, wait a minute."

"Yes," I asked, pulling my bike to a stop.

A tall, nutbrown young man was approaching. He wore a wild haircut that looked like a gigantic headdress or a helmet. He was approaching in a sort of goose step. You could see the sole of each shoe as he hoofed it. He couldn't have been dressed more outlandishly. He wore fashionable college style black slacks and a button-down pink shirt.

Nobody dressed like that in Lawsonville, of course, though I knew the fashions from the advertisements in the magazines on the rack at the drugstore. Everybody would have known immediately that he was from out of town and maybe even from out of state.

"You're in a hurry," he grinned. His teeth were even and very white, his nose had a narrow bridge, so that he looked more like what you'd expect an Indian to look like than a Negro of African background. Still he was plenty dark to be colored, and his crazy hairdo wanted everybody to notice that it was colored African style.

"Well, yes, I am."

"You work in the grocery store, don't you?"

"It's general merchandise," I corrected.

"General merchandise. You work there?"

"Yes, I do. And who are you?"

He ignored my question and asked, "Aren't you Afro-American?"

It was the first time I had heard the word. I was two years out of high school. Jim was halfway through college. It was 1961, and I was now a full time employee with Mr. Hendricks earning forty dollars a week.

"Afro-American," I asked. But I knew what it meant though I'd never heard anything but "colored" all my life.

"Yes, Afro-American."

"You mean 'colored'."

"No, I don't mean colored," he shook his head. His smile had a touch of mockery in it.

"Yes you do," I said, making myself smile back at him in the same way.

"No, I don't. Nobody says that anymore."

"Everybody does around here," I insisted. "Why wouldn't you say it?"

He shook his head again like he couldn't believe he was hearing that. "Well, 'around here' isn't the world, you know. Anyway, 'colored" is just what whites would call us. Would we think of ourselves as colored? I mean, we'd be just people to ourselves, wouldn't we? And if the whites say that to your face, what do you really think they call you behind your back?" I pursed my mouth and looked away. I realized that he was one of those troublemakers from somewhere else. We'd been dreading their arrival in town. "Aha," he went on, "I perceive you catch my meaning!"

"Does saying 'Afro-American' change anything," I asked. "Do you think it'll be any different when we call ourselves that?"

"Well, look, it's at least our term for ourselves and not theirs."

"So what," I said impatiently. "Who cares?"

"You may one day find that you care," he said, suddenly smiling warmly at me, like he was enjoying the argument.

"How is saying 'Afro-American' going to change anything?"

"I thought you'd already asked that – and answered your own question. If you're so determined to believe it doesn't matter, what's the point of arguing about it?"

I thought a minute, "That's supposed to be my argument."

He grinned. "You have a sense of humor. Look, I'll give you an example of why what you allow yourself to be called can make a difference. I have a friend who studied anthropology. He studied the Choctaws in Mississippi. The Choctaws were able to maintain a social and economic position above the Afro-Americans in that area for one reason. You want to guess what it was?"

"They're Indians," I said.

He laughed, "Not quite the reason. They refused to call white men something like Mr. George or Mr. Ed."

"And white women?"

"Yeah, stuff like 'Miz Cindy'. You know, like 'Miz Cindy, can I take out the trash for you?'"

"What did they call them?"

"Mr. Smith and Mrs. Smith."

"Aw, come on," I ridiculed, "that couldn't have made any difference."

"Oh yes it did. The whites were never able to address them by their first names. They called them things like Mr. Birdsong and Mrs. Tombstone – or whatever Indian surnames are."

"And so what?"

"They were treated with more respect than Afro-Americans."

I sniffed like I didn't really believe it. "Well, it's been nice talking to you," I said and started to go.

"Wait a minute."

"Yeah," I said, slowing down.

"They also refused to be called 'Indians' and got called 'Choctaw.'"

"Good grief," I said.

"See. If you let the oppressor name you, then you've lost half the battle."

"Well..."

He held out his hand, "I'm Walt Cross," he said.

"I looked a little skeptically at his hand a moment and then very slowly reached out and took it. He grasped my hand so firmly it hurt a little as he gave it a vigorous shake. "I'm Folly Steeples," I said.

"I'm from Chicago," Walt Cross said.

"I figured you were from out of state," I told him. "What are you doing here?"

"I'm with the Southern Christian Conference."

"Uh-oh," I said. "That's bad. That's that Civil Rights organization, isn't it?"

"Yes."

"Well, Walt Cross, I wish I could say 'welcome to Lawsonville,' but I can't."

"Why not, Folly?"

"Because you're probably here to start trouble."

"What you call trouble isn't always bad. Sometimes the kind of trouble we bring is less evil than continuing the status quo. It's trouble for the people who deserve trouble."

"It would be trouble for me, Walt."

"Without our kind of trouble, you might just all keep on like you're doing."

"Is that bad?"

Walt crinkled his nose, "Is that bad, the lady asks. Well, do you know any Afro-Americans around here who have a business?"

"There's a couple have a store."

"Yeah, sure. Down on nigger street," Walt retorted.

"I'm working on that myself, Walt, but I don't need your help," I replied. "In fact, your kind of help would spoil what I've accomplished thus far."

Walt frowned, "You're pretty sure of yourself if you can handle your own emancipation, MISS Folly Steeples."

"Well, I can tell you how I'm going to do it," I said, suddenly far too sure of myself and sassy. "I'm gone get rich. I've got a job in a store, and a boss who is willing to back me up. One day."

"One day what," Walt said, smiling broadly at me. I could see in his smile that I'd stretched that one a little far and probably looked pretty ridiculous in his eyes. "You are mighty sure of yourself, Miss. You've got a job in that little store there," he nodded at Mr. Amos's store, "and you're already rich and powerful. Man oh man. That's the trouble with us Afro-Americans. We are powerful dreamers. We can imagine up more success than five hundred white people thinking hard together. The trouble comes in the executing. And while we're lying around imagining everything, the white man is working hard to see that he doesn't have to share anything with us."

"Listen, you may be from Chicago, but I don't expect you know everything, Mr. Cross," I said.

"No, you're right about that," he admitted.

"I know you think we're a bunch of bumpkins. Well, maybe you're wrong."

"You don't talk like a bumpkin," Walt Cross said.

I looked at him suspiciously. "What do you mean?"

"I just mean your accent. You're not really from here, are you?"

"Yes, I'm from here. Can't you believe that you can be from here and not a complete moron?"

"Look, I know you're not a moron. That's not fair. But I also know that it's easier for somebody to come from the outside and see things in perspective than it is for the people who live right in the middle of it."

"Which means you, doesn't it," I said as snidely as I could. "You're the guy with perspective. We're the dunces who can't see the nose on our face. It's the same thing as you thinking you're superior, isn't it. Even though you put it that way, that's what it really means."

"Not really."

"Why?"

"Because, if I thought I was really better and you were really a dunce, I wouldn't bother to leave my home and come down here to help give you some perspective."

"I understand, Walt. You're here to educate us."

"That's sort of the idea."

"You're here to educate us and to give the white man trouble."

"No, I'm not here to just give anybody trouble. But, if we're demanding rights that Afro-Americans ought to have, and if the white man causes trouble, well then it's him that's doing it and not us. We're just asking for what should be rightfully ours. Aren't we Americans? Isn't this supposed to be our country, too?"

"So if trouble comes, it's not your fault?"

"That's right. But it'll help our cause."

"How is that?"

Walt pointed at a man stepping out of a car on the courthouse square. "You see him?"

"Yes."

"Do you know who he is?"

"He's a stranger, as far as I can tell."

"He's a newspaperman. If the white man causes trouble, that white man is gonna be happy to write it up in his newspaper."

"And what good is that?"

Walt shook his head slowly, "What good is that? Simple. People around the country will read it and get mad. They'll say, it isn't right not letting those people down there have their rights and causing trouble when they try to take what's rightfully theirs."

"Hmmm," I said. "That's cause the rest of the country are Yankees and think people down here are either mean or dumb."

Walt twisted around and said, "Goodness, Miss Steeples, you talk like a white person. You don't understand a thing, do you?"

I did understand for the first time, but I wasn't about to let him know it. "You're just too too smart," I said.

"We need your help, anyway," Walt Cross went on, his voice taking on a patient tone.

"You know what I don't like about this conversation," I said.

"No, what?"

"It sounds rehearsed. I believe you've done this before, Mr. Cross."

"Many times," he said. "Sometimes I wish there'd be a variation."

"I'm sorry we're not original enough for you."

"But it's the situation, Folly. I understand that. The situation determines the conversation."

"Our conversations are the creatures of our situations. Is that what you're saying?"

He was smiling again, enjoying it, "Well, now this is new. This is new."

"So I'm measuring up to your standards," I said with heavy irony.

"You show promise. You really do," he said.

"What is it you want to persuade me to do?"

"You won't do it," he said.

"I see. You know my type so well, you can predict how I'll react?"

"I didn't mean that."

"Just cut all the predictable stuff in between and tell me what you hope you can persuade me to do and why."

"Well, I figure you have influence."

"You're wrong. I don't have any influence with anybody."

"I can't believe that. Maybe you just aren't aware of it."

"Do I act like a person who could have influence and not know it?"

Walt Cross seemed to consider that a moment. Levity fought with fun in his face, "No, you don't."

"Then believe me. You're wasting your time with me."

"Who should I talk to? I need somebody to get out the young people for the demonstration Monday."

I shrugged, "I'm the wrong person to ask. I never go down on Saturday night to cut up on – what did you call it? – 'nigger street.'"

Walt Cross winced. "Did I call it that. I was trying to make a point."

"Oh, I know. But I tell you what. If you want to find who influences the young," I gathered up my most acerbic tone, "*Afro-Americans*, then just go down to both the juke joints this Saturday. They'll all be there."

"Why don't you go?"

"I've got my own program," I said.

"I can believe it. Well, thanks for the advice. Remember the name: Walt Cross."

"Oh, I haven't forgotten your name, Walt Cross."

He was one of the advance scouts for the Movement. That Sunday when we walked into AME Zion Church, I saw Walt sitting to the right toward the back. Up front there was a fleshy man ensconced in the throne chair to the right of the pulpit where the preacher usually sat. He wore a dark silk suit already half drenched in patterns of sweat though it was not exactly warm in the building. He raised an arm to scratch his graying noggin.

"We got a visiting preacher," Aunt Ida Mae whispered loudly as we slid into our usual places on the third pew from the front. When the choir got through with an introductory number, Harry Dale stood up, got out of his pew and came up to the pulpit to introduce the guest preacher.

First, Harry Dale surveyed the congregation. He did it slowly, and I thought he must have practiced in front of the mirror at home because he looked important, calm, and collected. It was his public face. "We are honored," he began. When he finished, he turned to the stranger and held out his hand.

The man pushed himself up with some effort and very heavily made his way to the pulpit. You wouldn't have thought he could talk about anything because he looked so awkward, overweight, and clumsy. But you'd have been wrong.

"Brothers and sisters," he called out as he assumed the speaker's dignity, "I bring greetings from all your brothers and sisters everywhere in this great country! From the Atlantic to the Pacific. From Florida to Maine. From the whole span of God's BLESSED globe!" And that was only the beginning! Within ten minutes he had the whole congregation on their feet crying, praising God, chanting their amens, in short, transposed.

All of that didn't surprise me much. I had seen other visiting preachers at work dancing back and forth across the raised platform, moving out into the aisles, exhorting, crying, moving everybody under the roof of the church. But I was worried this time because I knew he had a purpose. He wanted to get us all out there Monday morning to march.

The way I kept my head during his antics is to concentrate on the substance of what he was saying. That was the guiding principle of my sessions in German with Judge Lawson, too. The Judge would remind us both at the beginning of each lesson that we were to keep our minds on the substance of the passages we were reading. Otherwise, I'd have been rocking and singing with everybody else.

Actually, his sermon was fairly predictable. He started by likening the colored in America to the Jews in Egypt. He cited a man named Martin Luther King as our Moses. In the end it all came down to his exhorting us to join his organization that next week in back of the courthouse to march. He finished up with half the congregation on their feet allelujahing.

The whole business threw me in an awful conflict because part of me wanted everybody to spill out into the streets crying to high heaven about how unfair it all really is. The other part of me – and this was by far the dominant part – knew that I had an opportunity I didn't want to lose in my job with Amos Hendricks. I didn't want to see anybody rocking the boat because, once that boat capsizes, you don't know what's coming next. and whatever it is might not be good.

Outside the church, in the clarity of an early fall Sunday afternoon, a soberer frame of mind began to assert itself, especially among the older people. "I ain't no Afro-American," old Widow Smothers protested. "I don't know nothing about Africa, and they ain't gone send me back. I ain't going back to no Africa! I'm an American just like everybody else."

"It's alright now," the other women crooned, trying to soothe her. "Ain't nobody gone send you back to Africa."

"I'm too old to be going no place," Widow Smothers wailed. "They don't wear no clothes in Africa."

"Now, nobody gone send you to Africa, Miz Smothers. It's gone be alright."

But Widow Smothers was not to be consoled: "He be wantin' to get us into trouble. Gone rile everybody up. My grandmammy told me they's gone try to send everybody back to Africa after slavery. We get white folk riled up, and they pack us off, you mark what I say. They just be lookin' for a excuse all along."

It worried Aunt Ida Mae. She asked me when we were washing the dishes after our late Sunday dinner, "You ain't gone be going to that demonstration?"

"Of course not," I said. "I've got to work on a weekday, anyway."

"Have you read in any of them books that they wanted to send us back to Africa?"

"I never read any such thing," I said.

Aunt Ida Mae ruminated as she washed the dishes. Then she said, "I bet you they'd like to pack us all off, just like Widow Smothers say. Pack us off to Africa."

"That's nonsense," I said. But once I'd said it, it didn't seem so farfetched.

When we went back to the church Sunday night there was a big controversy going on. People were arguing about the significance of the designation 'Afro-American.' Some thought it was the first step in repatriating us back to Africa. This party kept insisting that we were "American." Wynona Acre was the most outspoken on this point. "We as American as any white person in the whole State of Georgia. My people been here longer than any of them. We was brought over to Virginny back when they first come. Half these whites' granddaddies was foreigners."

The more politic camp kept trying to explain, as Harry Dale put it himself, that "Afro-American is merely a new word for 'colored.'" Whenever Harry or anybody else would start explaining,

Widow Smothers would go ballistic again, wailing: "I ain't no Afro-American. I be a colored American. I ain't letting no out of town nigger brand me and get me sent back to Africa!"

"How I gone go march," Miss Sadie Turpine wailed. "I gone go march and then you think Miz Veazey gonna keep me on to work for her? If my daughter get out there and march, she get somebody else to iron her laundry, and that's a fact."

"Talk about caught betwixt a rock and a hard place," Uncle Cajus lamented, "if you go out to march, you be out of work. You stay here and don't march, and you done failed to follow Moses across the Red Sea."

"Moses can go," Widow Smothers declared, "I be gone stay in Egypt."

I didn't point out to her that Egypt is in Africa, the very place she didn't want to go.

Finally, I told them that I had met Walt Cross and that he was from Chicago. "See what I say," Sadie Turpine cried, "these is out-of-town, city folk! It won't be no skin off they noses onc't they gone if we don't have no work."

"See what I say," Aunt Ida Mae exclaimed, joining in the fray, "no way we can trust nobody that come in here from Atlanta, much less Chicago, to tell us what to do. They just meddling. They make a holy mess here and clear out."

Opinion in the colored community was generally against participating in the demonstration, except for a few hot heads. Harry Dale said he was going to stay home, which he did. I guess he had the most to lose of any of us at the time.

The morning after Lawsonville was crawling with strangers from out of town. Some of them had cameras. Buses began to arrive in the late morning and unloaded what seemed like hundreds of people, black and white, people were saying, near the state park at the white school.

The march began at one o'clock. The people came up the steep hill, underneath the railroad overpass. The AT&T building was to the left of the crowd as they topped the hill. Several of the white-shirted employees were standing on the roof to get a good look at the proceedings. The courthouse steps and lawn teemed with white people out to see what would happen. Some of them began jeering. A few Confederate flags were waved. Some of the meanest boys and men scowled as they began to shout epithets at the marchers. I could see it all from the window of the store until Mr. Amos came up and put his hand on my shoulder, "I spect you better go back to the back for awhile."

"Yes, sir," I said, though I hated to miss the rest.

Shortly after noon Catfish Wallace stumbled into the store drunk out of his mind and shouting, "Niggers and white nigger lovers done come in by the thousands on them buses, Amos! The state police is out waiting at the city limits on the Augusta highway. They's gone be hell to pay!"

Mr. Amos hustled him out of the store with Catfish protesting every step of the way. Men outside restrained Catfish and moved him in a big huddle down the street out of sight. The marchers reached the red light at juncture of Justice and Main Streets. There they hovered and didn't seem to know quite which way to go. If they turned left from our vantage point, they'd be headed down the Atlanta Highway. If they turned right, they'd soon be on what we thought of as the Augusta Highway.

Finally, they turned right because most of Main street was lined up that way, so that they had to pass by Mr. Huddle's gas station, the hotel, Purina store, and Cheeley Furniture on one side, the Liberty Café, Goodfellows, and the People's Bank on the other. The post office was the last building on the left before the houses began.

I went out on the loading dock where I could get at least a partial view of them as they moved along the street between our store and the picture show. After that they disappeared behind the solid phalanx of Main Street businesses and only the stragglers were visible. These last marchers were the halt, the lame, and the hesitant, and they offered the mean bullies a chance to move out into the street behind them.

The meanest boys first threw rocks. When they encountered no resistance, they were emboldened. Some of them started running. A couple reached the stragglers before they disappeared from view behind the picture show. I saw one of them kick a man hobbling along with a cane.

"Get on back in here," Mr. Amos called from the door.

"Yes, sir."

"I don't want you to be seen," he said. "We gone just lay low for the time being till this is over."

"Yes, sir."

"You stay back here but don't go out there no more."

"Yes, sir."

I heard Mr. Amos walk up front and lock the front doors. I figured he'd put up a closed sign for a little white, until he saw what was going to happen. There was nothing left for me to do but clean up and straighten up in the back and keep myself busy.

"Will it be over by three," I asked Mr. Amos.

"Maybe. Depends on the Ku Klux Klan and the Sheriff, I expect."

"The Ku Klux Klan," I said, the very words spoken standing my hair up on the back of my neck.

I locked the door and strained to look up and down the street for signs of white cloaks and steepled white hoods. There were none to be seen. "If you're looking for them," Mr. Amos said behind me, "you won't find them out there right now. They tell me they're all gathering out at the city limits." I must have sucked in my breath and looked pretty alarmed because Mr. Amos added, "Don't worry. Just stay down until this is over. I got some things in the back for you to do."

All I know about what happened is what I heard after that because I didn't have access to a television in those days. That night I listened to the radio with Aunt Ida Mae and Uncle Cajus. We sat there in the little sitting room of the cottage huddled together, our ears close to the radio, staring emptily into the darkness that seemed to press in upon us and against the weak light from the lamp.

The marchers had moved down Main Street as planned. Whites stood along the sidewalks and hooted. Some threw rocks, but the locals were pretty confused by the presence of a number of whites. Nobody knew the count for certain, but it was plain they were marching with the Afro-Americans. Coming through the little brown wooden box, it sounded like what you'd expect in a war. There was shouting and the sounds of combat.

When the march approached the city limits the Ku Klux Klaners came out of ambush and fell upon the marchers with clubs and other weapons. An anemic line of Georgia State Patrol was present, but they pulled their single rank back and didn't interfere during the first moments of the melee.

Nobody was sure how long it went on, but some marchers were badly beaten up. The odd thing the radio announcer kept telling us was that the marchers didn't offer any resistance. He was calling the action like a sportscaster until something happened and the sound went dead.

We stared at each other. I could see something in Uncle Cajus I'd never seen before. His powerful frame trembled slightly. Then another voice came through: "John Corrigan was hit by a rock and had to be moved to the back for safety, ladies and gentlemen."

Nothing could have been more dramatic. After permitting the beating for several minutes, the State Patrol had moved in and backed the Ku Klux Klaners off. Those beaten were taken in waiting ambulances to hospitals in the vicinity.

The next day the sidewalks and Main Street were littered with debris, rocks, even hats and articles of clothing. Nobody cleaned up. Reporters patrolled the streets looking for any story they could find. Among other things, Catfish Wallace got on national television for beating up a reporter who tried to photograph him. He was, as usual, drunk.

Nobody was sure how the fight got started, but Catfish was arrested and taken away, it was said, by the GBI. Then there was Tommy Turner giving an interview for WSB in which he said he wouldn't serve any coloreds who had participated in the march. Talk about stupidity. It made you wonder.

It wasn't until Friday that I heard Walt Cross was in the hospital in Thomson. Thomson was sixteen miles down the road. That was a pretty long bike ride, but there weren't any big hills that I could remember, and I had no other choice. I set out after work on my bike.

It was already getting dark by the time I got the store swept up, but I had a bike light and, in those days, there was little traffic in the evening, even on the main highways. I kept my head down and just pedaled until my mind was numb. The hospital was on the outskirts of town towards Lawsonville.

I guess I didn't think about anything much, but I was surprised when the lady at the front desk looked up and answered my question with a very impersonal: "He's in the colored wing, honey." I don't know what I'd expected. Maybe she thought I was white.

When I knocked on the door, Walt said, "Come in." Then he said "Folly!" when he saw me like he was really totally bowled over and shocked to see me.

I was pretty startled myself to see him all bandaged up with one arm held up by wires and stuff. "What happened to your arm?"

"Got broken," he said.

"I'm sorry."

"Sit down." I went over to the chair right by the bed and sat down.

"Will you be okay, Walt?"

He had a little trouble smiling because of the bandages, "Oh sure. I'm pretty tough. How did you find out about me being here?"

"A girl came in the store and told me."

"Oh, no. I promise I didn't tell her to bother you. After what you said out there behind—"

I winced, "Don't mention it. I'm so sorry. I'm just…" I searched for the right word, "dumb sometimes."

"Come on, Folly, you aren't dumb. You were talking a kind of sense."

"It's awful that this had to happen."

"No, baby," he said, the sudden turn to endearment not sounding out of place at all for some reason, "it couldn't have been better. This is exactly what we hoped would happen."

"You hoped the Ku Klux Klan would come out and beat you up," I said in amazement.

"We were counting on their stupidity. What do you think that's going to do to public opinion?"

"Outrage," I guessed.

"Of course," Walt said, so pleased with the results that it came through his discomfort.

That was the main thing I learned that night. Anything else we said was hardly more than just my telling him I thought he had been very brave. You can imagine how awkward that was for me.

I thought all the way back to Lawsonville how he seemed to appreciate my visit and my support. That was all. No recriminations. After that I knew that things would change. It was just a matter of time. That is, if people like Walt didn't lose their nerve – and I didn't think they would.

I didn't tell him I had biked all the way. It was a long way back, and I really dreaded it. My legs were sore, and within a couple of miles I was in pain. I kept telling myself that it was good to push myself a little physically. I had not done enough training since getting out of high school. I kept going by sheer will power.

About five or six miles out of Lawsonville the battery in my light ran out. I had to reach home in pitch black. What I did is watch the centerline on the pavement. It was a new highway, and the paint was fresh, white and almost luminous. I kept my mind staight ahead so the woods, night movements and sounds couldn't scare me too much.

My legs and upper arms were sore for days after that ride, but it made me think about my physical condition. Instead of whining about it, I squeezed in an early run each morning. As far as I was concerned, the soreness was a warning signal that I had let myself go too much. You can't afford that when you don't know what kind of challenge you'll be facing next.

XIII

I saw the paper trembling as I held the letter up to Mr. Hendricks, and I realized that it was my hand that was trembling. He took the letter without saying a word, pulled his reading glasses out of his shirt pocket, placed them on the bridge of his long nose and began to read.

When he finished he folded the letter along the three creases and handed it back to me. "Where is Vietnam," he asked, looking away.

"I'm not sure," I said. "I'll look it up in the Atlas in the library. But I think it's in Southeast Asia."

"Why would they send him there?"

Neither one of us had much time or inclination to listen to the news. Even if you listened regularly, you could hear a lot of local news without ever hearing a single report on international affairs. It was like Georgia had been all there was until young men like Jim started getting sent off to Vietnam.

"I think I heard or read somewhere that we're sending advisors to teach them how to fight Communists," I said.

Later I stopped by the library and checked the Atlas. Mrs. Vickery adjusted her thick, black-rimmed glasses and snorted frostily when she saw me. Coloreds now had access to the library, so I no longer had to sneak in the back and stand waiting to see if she'd let me tiptoe in and get what I wanted. It was better for me, but Mrs. Vickery resented my convenience.

Vietnam turned out to be in Southeast Asia, just as I had thought. The old maps had Siam written all over the area. Newer ones had French Indochina. I went back outside and stood a little back in the hedge so nobody could see me. There I opened Jim's letter. It was dated August 5, 1962 and read:

"Dear Sport, now that I'm through all my training, it looks like my orders are to go to Vietnam. That's likely the little war we talked about. They say you can get promotions fast over there. Keep your nose clean and wish me luck. When I get back, we'll go into politics if I haven't already made history in the army. Is that okay? Love, Jim."

Jim didn't come home before he left because he was out in Missouri and hadn't made up with his father, anyway, so he didn't have family to visit or anything. As far as I know he wasn't given any time to go anywhere.

After Jim wrote that letter, Mr. Amos and I took a more active interest in listening to international news and reading the Atlanta Journal. It seemed to us like he had just been by to show us his new uniforms and bars after he graduated from college and got his commission. He had been so proud and handsome. You couldn't help but be proud with him.

"Well, Folly," Jim had said standing in the back of the store at the drink cooler, "looks like history is about to begin."

I had always been pretty suspicious of this history business Jim talked about, but now I hated the idea. His history turned out to be a vicious war in jungles nobody had ever heard of. Nobody really understood why we were there.

None of that mattered to the patriots, of course, who were mostly older white men who had fought either in World War I or

II. They didn't care where the government decided to send the troops. Once the boys were there, it was our duty, according to them, to support the war.

Actually, a split developed between those who didn't like the war and those who were patriotic. In Lawson County the split seemed to be drawn along colored versus white lines with a few exceptions. If white people were against it, they kept their mouths shut because of the outspoken confidence of the veterans in town.

Then young Mason Biggs even went off to Canada to escape the draft and got a lot of people pretty confused because he was a good boy from a good, white family. People debated whether he was the lowest kind of coward or nothing more than a young man determined not to do something he didn't believe in.

Eventually most of the white community was forced to choose the former notion, especially after it became clear that the colored community tended to support Mason though he was white. That made him by implication not only a coward but a nigger-lover. Word was out that he had been for integration, but I can't say I know anything first-hand. I'd seen Mason around. He was the dentist's oldest son and just a little on the fat side with the self-indulgent tits and pink color in their cheeks that you see in boys who spent most of their time inside reading and playing with their chemistry sets.

Dubbie Happity was foremost among the outspoken, as usual, in the anti-Mason camp. She didn't care if he was Dr. Simon's son. As far as she was concerned, that made it worse. Just because Simon had gone to college and then to dental school and so forth. His wife wouldn't even buy her clothes in Lawsonville. She had to go to Atlanta for her dresses, so you can just see. That was Miz Happity's reasoning, and she went about in her shrill fashion declaring that Mason had always been a spoiled kid at heart, it was just that she was the only one that had noticed it until now.

Now if you ask me, I'd say that most Afro-Americans (we had taken to calling ourselves that) sensed that war would draw national attention away from our problems. With a war going on, any opposition to the existing system would be perceived as unpatriotic. So we were naturally prone to be against the war. What business did we have going way off to some place nobody had ever heard of to fight other colored people?

One thing happened for the good, though (I guess), when I got a chance to get into the attic and see what Judge Lawson had been working on when he died. I don't even know exactly how it happened, but it just goes to show that everything has its time and place. I had waited a long time, and the first thing I knew, I was pushing that rolling staircase over to the trap door in the ceiling.

Once in the attic, I picked up the long, wide sheets of paper that Judge Lawson had left all laid out over the desk and spilling down to the floor. Long, wide sheets of paper that made you wonder where he got them. I began to study them in the dim light. It was a half an hour before I saw the light switch and turned on a light. Then I decided to turn it off again because I knew Tom might still be poking around in his moronic manner, see the light and mention it inadvertently later to Aunt Ida Mae. Not that he'd want to give me away, but just because he didn't know any better and was always trying to do the right thing.

I took the papers over closer to the windows. What they were is a family tree. So far as I could tell with my first glance, the paper I was looking at began with Randolph Lawson I in 1780 in Charleston. Randolph was the man in the large portrait I knew so well in the grand foyer of Lawson Hall. His hair was blowing in an imaginary wind, and he was wearing tight pants with his penis hanging down one leg. I guess that was the style then. It wasn't until later when I started doing all my research that I realized it was Regency period fashions he was wearing.

It always struck me as an odd thing that his portrait figured in our Georgia history textbook what with the penis so plainly in view. Generations of students had giggled about that with the nasty boys and girls making wise cracks. After we'd had ample time to thumb through the new history book, Chandra had been unable to get her mind off Randolph's penis. It was the standing joke among her clique for weeks until all somebody had to do was say "Randolph" to get them all snickering in their fists.

Randolph Lawson had been more or less not only the founder of the Lawson dynasty in Georgia but also a founder of the state. In our textbook he was presented as a kind of father of our country. One of his public offices, I recalled, had been as American plenipotentiary to German courts. I remembered that because I saw the portrait every day I dusted hanging there in Lawson Hall. I also liked the antiquarian sound of that title, though I wasn't at all clear about what the duties of a plentipotentiary might have entailed.

In the meantime, I had discovered that Judge Lawson had created a kind of two track genealogical table up and down those big sheets of paper in his elegant hand. To the right the legitimate line was printed in black ink with strong, decisive, even florid lines. It was visually indisputable that the legitimate line was firmly scratched into the paper by the Judge himself.

To the left of the legitimate line were penciled insubstantial connections with a much less certain hand. The relatives to the left of the legitimate line were connected at crucial junctures by broken pencil lines that stammered across the page. The questionable line began with a certain Miriam Steeples who was connected in a coughing pencil line to Randolph The Original of the Penis.

Out of the union between Randolph and Miriam emerged a certain Charles who perched – in name, at least—upon a precariously penciled pedestal above his mother, Miriam. Underneath his name

Judge Lawson had written pertinent information concerning Charles' birth and death. Born "near Stuttgart...murdered in Lawson County, 1868."

Before getting murdered in 1868, Charles had married a certain "Ethel" of whom nothing was noted. Out of their union issued two daughters, one whom I recognized (by the name) as one of my great-aunts. She died at Lawsonville, Georgia on July 24, 1925.

I stopped and looked out the round porthole window at the autumn sky and wondered about this Destiny business that had seen Charles born in Germany, murdered in Lawson County, descended of a certain Miriam and Randolph Lawson. And there were so many questions.

I went back to the paper with an effort, for I felt a lethargy, a reluctance, almost a fear to go on with the genealogy. Miriam Anne was in Lawsonville; at least, she had died there. Her father had been murdered somewhere in Lawson County after coming from England. What for? What was it all about?

I traced up the net of interconnections with my index finger. Miriam Anne was connected to Vandiver Lawson by a faint pencil line. The lead dots on the white paper were almost broken as they linked the violent man to this child from Europe. Vandiver was, of course, Judge Lawson's father, still remembered in these parts as a fierce and brutal man who whipped and raped his Negroes and shot down white trash in the streets. In his life he had earned the privilege of being universally loathed long after he was gone.

A single name issued from the union and poised upon its own penciled pedestal. It was my grandmother, Ida, born February 22, 1871. Judge Lawson entered in his most delicate hand, "Ran away—," doubtless to avoid having her own father beget another generation upon her.

That was not the end of it, though I looked away from the paper a long time before I let my index finger wander back across its expanse following the tell-tale lines upwards from my grandmother to my mother and Ida Mae. How they came back to Lawson Hall was not explained in the terse notes in parenthesis that Judge Lawson had deigned to place below most of the names as basic explanation.

It seemed nearly an after-thought, if the reluctant pencil could have spoken, that linked my mother, Baby, to Judge Lawson himself. At the end of my searching, I found my index finger frozen just below my own name, being the issue of that union.

I fixed my gaze upon his full name, which I had not known until then: Colson Randolph Lawson. I had seen the C. L. Lawson engraved on a gold plate and fixed to his briefcase, but it had never occurred to me that the initials might actually stand for two Christian names.

He had been a young man in 1939. A very young man. Somehow he had not been drafted into the Army. But he had had time and inclination to father me upon a young woman. Perhaps it had been in the stables. I recalled my mother's sensuality. The lusting expressions on the white hunters' faces as they stood there in the yard in front of our cabin came back to me in vivid procession. Mother would be preening herself on the porch. I could suddenly hear her rich contralto speaking: "Come on up here on the porch now."

There had still been horses in the stables in 1939. A vivid scene filled my mind of young Randy or Colson and Baby wrestling around between the horses' legs. I had to rub my eyes and blink hard to erase the scene. A twenty-year-old young man/child and a fifteen-year-old girl who must have had sex on her mind very early.

If Judge Lawson had been my father, then what? My mind balked at considering the consequences; yet, when I did it, I realized there had been very few. His sister had taken me with her to

Connecticut. I had enjoyed a good education, learned the ways of the tennis classes, and then been fetched back to Georgia when it was over. Here the Judge had taught me German, something about serious music, literature, and philosophy.

Many other fathers, I thought, had done less. So this was my heritage. And Miss Ellen had really been Aunt Ellen, though she had never told me, did not even encourage me to call her that in private. Had she known? Surely she must have known.

No, I couldn't be sure of anything. The Judge worked it all out in the privacy of his secret, attic compartment. So when I realized it was almost dark, I hurried down the staircase and shut the trap door. Uncle Cajus would be driving up any minute. He should have already gotten home. He had gone to Covington to pick up Laura Lawson from the train station because she was coming back home. We didn't know why, and she brought fear and anxiety with her again.

It was not until the next afternoon that Laura summoned me to the library. She was sitting in the Judge's chair, in the very place I had seen him die. Aunt Ida Mae and I had cleaned it all up, washing the upholstery, scrubbing the table. You couldn't smell the vomit any more.

As I stopped at the door, Laura gave me a signal, saying, "You can come in, Folly." I stepped over the threshold. "Sit there," she instructed, indicating the chair where I'd always sat for our German lessons.

Not only did my long experience in hiding my feelings help me in facing Laura that day. I had developed a fearless persona that often acted upon my potential enemy as an impediment to bold action. I would stare straight into her face, as unblinking as possible, as if I were studying every flicker of movement.

I will have to give her credit for not being affected by my bold stare. She was in command without being strident. There was a sparkle in her large eyes, an amusement in the suggestion of a smile she wore. "Well, I hear you've finished up at the colored school," she began.

"Yes. It's actually been awhile," I said.

"And what are you doing now?"

I knew she would despise me more for what I would tell her, but I kept remembering to watch her closely as I said, "I'm working at Hendricks' store."

"How nice," she said, packing vast tons of contempt into those two words. "I'm sure its nice to be the first Negro to work in a store in town." She waited for me to answer, but I couldn't bring myself to give her the pleasure. So she went on: "I thought you'd be ready to leave Lawson Hall. And I see you are. I would suggest you move out by the weekend."

"Yes, m'aam," I said, trying not to have my voice choked in my throat.

"I remember when they first brought you in from the country. I must have been about eight." All I could do is nod, a slight consent, hardly visible. "And my aunt took you up north with her. You had quite a tennis talent. Done anything with it since?"

"The accident," I said, "I—"

"I remember," she said, waving me into silence, "your right arm was broken several times. Never healed entirely, did it? Left you too handicapped to take the game back up? Well, it's too bad. I hear that coloreds are now beginning to appear on some courts, you know. What is that young man's name? Never mind."

I felt demolished. I felt as if Laura had dismantled my vital organs, made a surgical incision in my gut and ripped them out one by one. And I could think of nothing to say and was afraid to say anything lest I should do no more than gag. "That will give you a couple of days to pack. You probably don't have much."

She watched me with eyes both detached and, yet, somehow potentially murderous. Of course she was doing the best she could to murder me. "No," I heard myself say, "I can easily be out by the weekend."

"If it's that easy, maybe you can get out a little earlier."

"Do you plan to rent my room in the cottage or something?"

Laura's upper lip twitched, and then she said, "By the way, I have something for you." She looked down, opened the right-hand drawer of Judge Lawson's desk and extracted an envelope. She held it out to me.

"What is it," I asked.

"Just a little for you and the work you've done here."

"But whatever I did here, I was never paid," I said.

Laura dangled the envelope. "Take it," she said. Her gesture, her dismissive expression conveyed the real message: Get lost. Get out. Don't let me see you again.

"No thank you," I managed. My chest was heaving. Surely she could see, I thought.

"Oh," she said, shaking her head like I disgusted her ever so slightly. "Okay then. Whatever."

Later on I thought of so many things I should have said. Only I couldn't think of them there in the library. I had to find a place to stay, and I was surprised at how much it grieved me to think of leaving Lawson Hall. It shouldn't, I told myself again and again; it shouldn't matter. But it did no good; I would just have to work my way through it

My favorite imaginary scenario with Laura came to me three days after the actual event. I imagined it so intensely that it became for me what really happened. Laura held out the envelope, and I said, "What's in it," and she said, "fifty dollars," and I said, "Your father gave me free German lessons. Keep the money to pay for that."

Mr. Hendricks gave me the room Jim had occupied over the feed department. It was dirty and had neither toilet nor running water, but I cleaned it up and made curtains for it. Laura surprised us by not firing Uncle Cajus and Aunt Ida Mae. I guess she still thought she needed somebody around who could keep things running and knew how to treat her deferentially. She didn't stay long in Lawsonville that time, either. She was said to be involved in a hot romance in Boston.

On November twenty-second of that year, nineteen-hundred-and-sixty-three, President Kennedy was shot in Dallas. Word spread along Main Street from one store to the next. People ran to turn on radios. Lots of people hurried home. Nobody knew why they hurried home, but that just seemed the thing to do.

XIV

Now if you go back to 1962, I can tell you something about Jim's father. Mr. Amos and I were closing up the store, and I was going out on a last minute errand. Mr. Amos called me over to his desk. He was wearing his green visor, and the strong light darkened the shadows of his face and made him look more haggard than ever.

"Folly," Mr. Amos said.

"Yes, sir?"

He pushed the visor up and leaned back in the swivel chair out of the light. "I've been thinking."

"Yes, sir?"

"There's a lot of building going on in this area."

"Yes, sir?"

"You see old Mr. Stewart's got more than he can do, and folks has to go as far as Augusta to get materials. So I think you and me ought to put together a building supply depot."

"Yes, sir." It was fine with me. That would be more experience, and experience is what I needed to know how business worked.

"Now Shamon Conyers bought that building Mr. Jim built down by the railroad track. It's just been setting there. Ain't nobody used it yet. But it's got a loading dock right there, and we could have lots of the stuff we need shipped in by rail." I nodded to show him I was listening and in general agreement. "I figure it's gone cost a good twenty thousand dollars to get the thing going," he continued, pausing at last to study me, putting his hands flat together like he was about to pray. Then he asked, "How much money you got?"

"Me?"

"Yep, that's who I mean. Ain't nobody here but us two."

"I got pretty near ten thousand dollars," I said.

"Would you like to put it in something like this?"

At first I couldn't get my mind in gear. My thoughts scattered, and I duhed: "Put my money into the building business?"

"In my judgment we could make some good money off this, maybe – who knows? – we could put up a place in Washington and Thomson in the next couple of years."

"Yes, sir, I'd like to put my money into it," I said, coming back into focus. "It's just sitting in the bank right now."

Mr. Amos pushed the chair back and began to stand up, "You want to shake on it?"

"Oh, yes, Mr. Amos. I do."

He held out his huge hand, and it swallowed mine. "We're partners then," he said.

There was no doubt in my mind then and there isn't now that it was one of the most important moments in my life. I was to become a full partner with Mr. Amos Hendricks in the building supply business.

Jim could have history and the army and his war, and Laura could have her fancy schools and aristocratic name. Things like that paled in comparison to the chance Mr. Hendricks was giving me.

But Jim stayed on our minds, and we weren't alone. It wasn't long into that year that his father stopped me in his brusk fashion with: "Wait a minute there, gal!"

"Yes, sir?"

Henry Hall had never approached me before that, never gotten within fifty feet of me. I had seen him only from a distance. Now he was bearing down upon me, and I found myself almost ready to run, my feet itching to move.

He came right up to me and didn't stop there. He bent down until his face was right in front of mine. I could see that his right eye was bloodshot, a web of clotting half covering the pale blue of the iris. His breath smelt like onions and buttermilk.

"You heard from my boy, gal?" I must have hesitated because he reached out and grabbed my shoulder and shook me. It was only slightly, but it scared the living hell out of me. "You got a letter, didn't you?"

"Yes, sir."

He straightened up and relaxed, "Well, where is he? Tell me what he said."

"He's going to a place called Vietnam," I said.

"Vietnam? They sent him to Vietnam?"

"Yes, Mr. Hall," I said.

Henry Hall's lip curled underneath his long nose. His bottom lip was too full and oddly damp. I saw a mole under his chin. "You got the letter, gal?"

"Yes, sir."

"Can you get it?"

"Sure. It's up in my room."

I was just out front straightening some of the seed bins we'd put out for the season. When I brought him the letter down from my room, Henry Hall read it carefully. "They gone put him in one of their filthy little wars," he grumbled as he handed the letter back to me.

"Do you know where Vietnam is," I asked him.

"Indo-China, child, don't you know? The French got kicked out at Dien-ben-pooh. It's one of them colonial places where they suck the blood out of Chinamen. Now the Chinamen are tired of it, and they kicked the French out. Then we go in next like the fools that we are!"

"Henry Hall, what are you talking about out here on the street," Shanon Conyers demanded. He was shaking the stump of his left arm as he spoke, and the scar on his left cheek was blushing red and blue. It was the arm he lost in the Ardennes when he was hardly sixteen, so people said.

"Nothing that would interest you, Conyers," Henry Hall answered with disdain.

Shanon Conyers spat a ball of yellowish liquid out into the street. He had a way of swirling his stump every time he spoke, and it gave him a kind of frenetic air. He had to be every bit of seventy, if not more, though he hadn't noticed it himself. "Well, if you're talking about Vietnam, you better clean out your mouth," he hissed. "We been going in there to advise the South Vietnamese against them Commies up north."

"I am talking about Vietnam," Henry Hall answered simply, "But I don't know why I should clean out my mouth."

"And you call it a filthy war? It ain't no filthy war. Them South Vietnamese is fighting for freedom."

"How do you know all about it? Can you tell me that? Have they done put you into the Pentagon, too. I said it's gonna be ANOTHER filthy little war, and that's what I meant," Henry Hall corrected.

I slipped away fast and left them disputing whether Vietnam was another filthy war, just a filthy war, or a patriotic cause.

When I came back out thirty minutes later both men were gone. Later in the afternoon Vince O'Doole walked into the store. He looked around for Mr. Amos and found him in the back.

As he took a soda out of the icebox drink cooler, Vince said, "Amos, you should've been over at the warehouse this afternoon."

"Yeah, Vince, what happened?"

"Well, Henry Hall and Shannon Conyers came in. We thought they was coming to get into the game, but they was arguing about this here war they're getting drummed up. Have you ever seen a one-armed man get into a fight?"

"Nope."

Vince was laughing and talking at the same time, "I'm telling you, it was a sight. I wouldn't have give nothing to have missed it. First thing we knew they was swinging at each other. Ole Shannon and Henry Hall. Shannon swinging that stump. Then he piled into Henry. You know there ain't no two meaner men in the county."

"They started fighting?"

"Fighting? What you talking about! I never seen such a scrap. You ever seen two weasels fight? That's what it was like."

"What was it they didn't agree on," Amos Hendricks wanted to know.

"This Vietnam business. You ever heard of it? Henry's son is getting sent over there to advise the South Vietnamese. As far as I could tell Henry didn't think it was worth getting our boys involved. Ole Shannon said he was a dirty traitor. He sez it's our patriotic duty, and Henry's boy ought to be proud he's going. We're fighting the Commies, don't you know."

"Who won?"

"Didn't nobody win. Shannon lost his glasses finally, and that was the end of it. He couldn't see nothing without 'em. So we all had to look for them."

"Did you find them?"

"They was pretty bent up," Vince chuckled.

Vince took a swig of his soda, swallowed and started all over again, "You sure should'a seen that, Amos. It was a sight to see!"

Two days later Henry Hall waved me down from his black, 1949 Chevrolet pickup truck. I wheeled the delivery bike over to the side and kicked the kickstand down. He waited in the cab of the truck for me to approach.

"Yes, sir, Mr. Hall?"

"You got my boy's address, you say?"

"Not where he really is. Just an APO address."

"Can you give it to me then?"

"Sure I can," I said. This time I had it memorized, so I told him on the spot. He scribbled the address down on something inside the cab of the truck, thanked me and drove off with me still standing right there. I had to jump back to keep from having my feet run over by the wheels. I'm telling you, you could see why Henry Hall wasn't the most popular man in the county.

I remember when it happened because it was the same afternoon Mr. Hendricks called me back to his office and said, "You better start using the pickup for deliveries."

"Yes, sir."

He looked up at me. "You're gonna be my partner now, so you gotta learn to drive."

"Yes, sir."

"We gone be delivering bigger things than a bunch of groceries soon."

I smiled, "That's right, isn't it, Mr. Amos."

"Now go get you a learner's license. I done called the sheriff and told him you was coming."

It was a proud moment for me. I went across the street to the courthouse and got a learner's license that day. It wasn't every colored person who had the opportunity to learn to drive. Mr. Amos took me out that night to practice after we closed up.

It took about two weeks for me to get the hang of changing gears and coordinating the clutch, the accelerator, and the brakes. Getting a license was no problem since they knew at the courthouse that Mr. Amos wanted me to drive, but I had to wait for the Georgia State Patrol officer to come in and administer the test.

What I hadn't calculated is how far out into unknown and dangerous territory being able to drive was going to take me. It seemed as if the building supply business required a lot of long distance deliveries.

Since we found Shannon Conyers impossible to deal with, we had decided not to use the warehouse he had built right by the railroad track. We just cleared a few of the trees out on the back lot behind the store. Then we built sheds to cover the woods and other materials. The brick and masonry stone and such just sat out exposed to the elements. The warehouse Amos Hendricks had down by the tracks was enough for getting stuff by train.

I was sure there'd never be a prouder moment in my life than when I drove up to Lawson Hall to see Uncle Cajus and Aunt Ida Mae. They both came outside to see who it was. "Honey, is that you," Aunt Ida Mae asked.

"Yes, m'aam, it's me," I said, climbing out of the truck. "I'm driving the delivery truck now."

"You done learned to drive?"

"Yes, m'aam."

"What's gone happen next. A colored girl learning to drive," Aunt Ida Mae wondered aloud.

Uncle Cajus strolled on up from the garden. Tom was trotting behind. "Hello, missy," Tom called, waving both hands in greeting. He had fully recovered long ago from the pitchfork wounds.

"Hello, Tom."

"But I've come specially to ask Uncle Cajus and Tom if they want a job in our building supply business," I said, turning to them.

"What kind of job you talking about," Aunt Ida Mae demanded behind me. I turned around and saw her brow furrowed suspiciously. She was rolling her eyes.

I had to laugh, "Aunt Ida Mae, you look like Aunt Jemima when you roll your eyes like that. It's okay, it'll be with me and Mr. Hendricks."

"Doing what," she wanted to know. "How much they gone make?"

I laughed, "It's okay. You probably heard that we're starting a building supply business. We need Uncle Cajus to drive the delivery truck and stuff. Tom can help in the yard."

"Will I be mowing grass," Tom wondered innocently. "I can mow grass. I can push the mower, missy. I do a good job, too. I'm a hard worker, aren't I, Cajus?"

"No, Tom," I explained. "It'll be lumber and stuff."

"He ain't strong enough to do no heavy work now," Aunt Ida Mae cautioned. "You forgetting that we ain't getting no younger, chile. While you growing up, we getting old."

"Oh, Aunt Ida Mae, I'm not going to have them doing more than they can do. I'm gonna get somebody younger to help them. I just know I can trust you both," I said, turning to them. "I can trust you better than anybody. That's why I want you working with me. I want you share in my good fortune, Uncle Cajus and Tom." I reached and grabbed Uncle Cajus's hands and squeezed them. "I want you to be there with me."

"Honey, that's mighty sweet of you. You wants me to drive the delivery truck," Uncle Cajus asked.

"That'll mean loading and unloading," Aunt Ida Mae noted accusingly.

"Yes, it will mean that. But we'll get help," I said. "I told you, I'm getting somebody younger to help with the heavy stuff."

"How much is that gone pay us, honey?"

"Thirty-five a week, Uncle Cajus" I said. It was more than he had ever earned working with Judge Lawson.

Uncle Cajus grew goggle-eyed. He could only whisper, "Thirty-five a week! Can you pay that much, honey?"

"We sure can. And Tom will get twenty."

"Missy, twenty dollars? What will I do with so much money? I don't think I should be paid that much now, missy, don't you know. I can't be trusted with money. I might forget what I did with it. Somebody will rob me. I can't remember everything, Missy. You know that."

"I'll give it to Uncle Cajus to keep for you, then, Tom. We can open a bank account for you or something."

"A bank account," Tom cried. "An account in the bank!" He began to jump up and down, and that was a sight. He clapped his hands and then began to scratch his nearly bald pate. Then I realized he was wiping a tear from the side of his eye. "I haven't had a bank account since drink ruined me," he said, choking with joy.

Our first big job was to supply the materials for a wing they were building on Licksplit Creek Baptist Church. It was to be called the Preacher Brown Sunday School Annex in honor of old Preacher Brown who was going to be a hundred at the end of the year. His granddaughter would roll him out in the wheelchair to watch the structure going up.

It was no time at all until we had so much business we had no time to keep up with either the war in Vietnam or the continuing upheavals of the Civil Rights Movement. We worked from early to late every day, six days a week. On Sunday we rested. That was a rule both Amos Hendricks and Uncle Cajus would have enforced, in any case. At the end of the first quarter, I gave Tom and Uncle Cajus a bonus.

In the meantime, we went through several hands in the yard. If they were strong, then they lacked something else. Some of them were not smart enough to fill orders without being under constant supervision. The worst of them sassed Uncle Cajus, who was at first the de facto and then the official foreman. Others overlooked items, omitted things, failed to fill certain orders. All of them were trifling and kept irregular hours at best.

I tried white and black workers. Neither race proved dependable. Work discipline among the hands in Lawson County needed to be improved, but we had no time to start a program of general education. One particularly powerful young man who was the best of the lot liked to work only when he was in the mood. More than once he just walked off the yard in the middle of the day, leaving the truck half-loaded for an order we had to deliver by three. Uncle Cajus, Tom, and I had to finish the loading together.

After six months of dealing with unpredictable labor, I was at my wit's end. "What can we do," I asked Mr. Amos.

"You see, getting dependable help is one of the biggest problems when you have a business," he explained. "That's why I was happy when I found you and Jim."

I was standing out back on the loading dock watching Tom struggle with lumber that was far beyond his capacity. "Stop that, Tom. That's too much. Put it down."

He stopped and scratched the strands of white hair still sticking out of his reddish scalp. Then, in his precise English, he said, "Missy, we must get these things up on the truck."

"Miss Folly," somebody said behind me. I turned around and found myself facing Chandra. You can bet I started. She was bigger and more powerfully built than the last time I had seen her, a veritable giant of a woman, an Amazon.

The worst of it was that Chandra had seen my discomfort, for she said, "Don't be scared. I know you don't have no reason to like me, but I heard you was having trouble getting somebody who could do the heavy work out here."

"Yes," I said cautiously. "Whom do you have in mind?"

"Me," she said.

"But you're— a..." I searched desperately for the term, "a woman!"

"That's right, and so are you. Anyway, I'm stronger than most men. I can do it, Miss Folly. I tell you, just give me a chance. Give me a week. Honest to God, I'll prove it to you. I can do the work better than any man in the county. I'm different than when you knew me in school. I was mad at the whole world then. I've changed."

"What changed you, Chandra?"

"I found the Lord."

"Where are you working now?"

Chandra looked about as devastated as a person could and shook her head, "That's just it. Nobody's give me no chance to be steady. A black woman like me can't get nothing. A little job here and a little job there and part time stuff. Nobody will let me work enough to make a living, and my mama is sick, Miss Folly."

"Don't call me Miss Folly, Chandra. What about house work?"

Chandra held out her arms and looked down at herself, "Look at me. The white women say I scares them. You jumped yourself when you saw me. Miss Folly, I can't help it I'm so big. God done made me this way. It was the same ever since I can remember, and I was mad about it a long time. I'm so big the mens don't like me. Now all I wants is a chance. I'll show you I can do the work. Anything you got to do. Honest! I come to think that God made me this big for a purpose."

"And that purpose is to work for me? How do I know that's true?"

"Ask around town. I ain't been in no trouble. Can't nobody find nothing to say against me. You ask. Ask Reverent Butts at Holly Mill Baptist. That's where I go, but give me a chance. I'll prove it. The first time I don't report to work, you can fire me."

I studied Chandra a long moment. She certainly looked as strong as any man, and she was at least six feet tall. No telling how much she weighed, but there didn't seem to be a lot of excess fat there. Her bosom was fairly large and might get in the way, but otherwise I saw nothing negative.

As I turned back to the yard I saw Tom standing there with a long board in his arms, one side of it dragging the ground. "You got work clothes?"

"I got 'em on," Chandra said.

"Tom," I called, "have we got another pair of gloves?"

"No, Missy, but you have a rack of gloves in the store."

"Come on in, Chandra, and pick out your gloves. You can start now. I'll check with Reverend Butts this week for a recommendation."

"Yes, m'aam! Thank you!" And Chandra smiled.

Hiring Chandra was a good lesson in the benefits of giving people a second chance. She could do the work of two of the hands we'd had before, and she was always on time and as dependable as the clock. I never did check with Reverend Butts for that recommendation.

I guess it makes for boring writing telling how well a business is growing, but when you're in the middle of it and it's yours, there's nothing more fun. We were so busy that we knew little of the world outside Lawson County, almost nothing of the growing ferocity of the Civil Rights struggle or the budding national dissension over Vietnam. That probably seems pretty callous to lots of people, but running a growing business is a full time proposition. You hardly have time to notice anything, and when you get through at the end of the day, you're too tired to read any serious newspapers or periodicals. You don't even keep up with who comes through town. And that's not always good.

Take me. I was coming back after dark from a delivery out at the Walborough farm where Ralph Walborough was adding to the mill store. I had been glad to get his order because I figured it was a sign that he hadn't held the incident at his home that December against me. Maybe he had known or heard somehow from his wife or daughter what had really happened. Maybe he had forgiven me. Maybe he never held anything against me in the first place. Men can't always be responsible for the way their wives behave and vice versa.

I had no idea who was coming and going in the county. I didn't know that Frank Hollison and that young one were back. I was not coming straight back from the Walborough place, however, because I'd driven a few miles in another direction to bring a few odds and ends to a farmer working on his barn. So I was on a relatively unfamiliar road a good ten miles from town.

The thing is – and I've had reason to think about it a lot! – people who are working hard and minding their own business don't know that there are some sorts out there who have nothing better to do than to plot mischief and meanness. People might laugh at all those old sayings like "idleness is the devil's workshop," but they're often true enough. I also know there're a lot of people out there who simply refuse to believe in evil because maybe they don't know how it feels to be the prey of evil.

I don't know what you can do about those people. What happened to me that night might convince them; on the other hand, it might not. If everything that's happened in the twentieth century hasn't been enough to convince everybody that the devil is out there stomping around like a roaring lion looking for who he can devour next, there's not much hope that one more incident will do the job.

Anyway, it had been later than usual when I started back to town. The weather was fair, but there had been a cloud cover moving over as it got dark. Though winter was approaching, we had had neither ice nor any sign of snow. Not that it was warm because it wasn't. Still, there was no apparent reason to worry about anything.

In spite of the seeming normality of things, I was glad to have a .38 revolver in the glove compartment of the pickup. The road was no different than many other country roads: Lonely, dirt, poorly graded, miles from any other farmstead with washboard stretches that had been poorly banked to start with and had washed out with the last heavy rain.

When you're in an automobile, these distances don't matter much: five, ten miles. That's nothing for the internal combustion engine on four good wheels. But then something happens that gets you out of your car or something. Like that evening my bladder finally forced me to stop and take to the bushes. When I finished peeing, I came out of the bushes with a feeling of physical relief. There was also an odd, new anxiety mixing in my mind that made me hurry and climb back up into the truck cabin. The anxiety was still with me a few minutes later when I first noticed the headlights behind me.

The first thing I thought was how far I was from any other living person. In those days Georgia may have had a population of less than Atlanta today. In fact, the larger part of that population was concentrated in Atlanta, so that the rest of the Empire State was only sparsely inhabited. If something happened out where I was, you could have screamed your lungs out. It'd have made no difference. There was nobody to hear.

That evening darkness had fallen earlier than usual. I reached down and pulled out the headlight switch, and two thin poles of light probed the threatening emptiness, swallowed up after fifty or sixty feet. The moon was diving in and out of a heavy cloud cover, so that the faint dashboard lights of my truck seemed very weak company to me.

As I topped a hill and began a descent to one of those narrow, meandering Georgia rivers, hardly bigger than an Alabama creek, I saw the bridge ahead. It was one of those rusty old steel superstructures that still spanned some rivers, and it was hardly more than one lane wide.

Without any warning a set of headlights appeared blinking in my rearview mirror as the vehicle behind me bobbed over the hill. I reached up and adjusted the mirror. As I made the adjustment, I couldn't help but notice how fast the headlights grew. The vehicle behind was coming on at high speed.

Within moments it was riding the bumper of my truck. Since the road was so narrow, I thought I probably needed to get over as far as possible to let them by. So, as I started over, holding the steering wheel as the wheels bounced along the washboard edge of the road, the vehicle began to pass.

The road was not only narrow, it was steeply banked on either side. Worse, we were approaching the narrow, one-lane bridge. As I wrestled with the steering wheel, I saw out of the corner of my eye how the car was pulling up beside me.

The car was actually a good bit lower than my truck, but I caught a glimpse of a hooded head thrust out the window. Ku Klux Klan were the three words that poured into my brain like hot lead. I felt my pulse race out of sight. Looking up ahead I realized that, if they reached the bridge first, they could stop me by simply blocking the lane. More likely, they could block it at the other side, stopping me on the bridge where I had only one direction to run – backwards.

What happened next could have taken no more than seconds. I swerved into their path and actually struck the car. I heard the men beginning to shout at me, but I rammed them again. The only thing I knew was that I would take the bridge first, no matter what. I wasn't letting them get there first.

When the car began to roll over the steep incline on the left side of the road, I was surprised. "Ooops," I said aloud. The hooded figure riding shotgun disappeared. I actually saw all four wheels, the gas tank, axle, and other parts clearly as the car went belly up. I guess the moon must have come out and drenched the scene.

The odd thing was that, in tapping them over the edge, I had sort of lost control of the truck. Dreamily I watched it sliding sideways into the bridge. There was nothing I could do, though I began to turn the wheel wildly this way and that. The vehicle straightened enough to enter the bridge, but it struck first one side and then the other, raising enough sparks to make a fireworks show as it careened along the metal chute.

When my truck finally came to a stop at the other end of the bridge, I was on the floor. It seemed to be leaning over heavily to one side but balancing somehow so as not to topple. The motor coughed a couple of times and died. At first there was nothing but silence. Then the whole frame groaned something awful, like the inside of a submarine with the whole weight of the ocean on it. It creaked and groaned and then wham! It went back down and sat there upright.

I jumped into the driver's seat and tried the ignition. Something had come loose because all I got was a click or two. No motor springing into life. Nothing. The moon dived behind the clouds, and I was engulfed in darkness. Only then did I become conscious of the screaming and hollering going on across the creek, on the other side where the car had turned over. Male voices were cursing, threatening.

I reached over the glove compartment, but there was so much jagged metal. It was impossible to get it the compartment open. I rattled it until the handle came off in my hand. Then I really felt stupid. I tried to sort out my options. Without a weapon and with a carload of KKK warriors about as mad as wasps, all I could figure is that I needed to clear out and head across country as fast as I could. Otherwise, I would join my ancestor Charles in being the victim of a lynching.

I couldn't get the door open, but I was able to roll down the window and climb out of it onto the running board. When I jumped down onto the road, I hit it running. I tried to remember exactly where the moon was, so that I wouldn't lose my bearings. About then the cloud cover grew thinner so that I could see it.

After about a hundred yards, I left the road and found myself up against a fence. I felt along it until I came to the barbs. As I held the wire up very daintily, I slipped through it, lifting one leg through and then passing my body and neatly bringing my left leg through last. It was gingerly done, and I was proud of myself. I had done the same thing thousands of times as a child.

Once on the other side of that fence, I wasted no time in starting into the forest. It sounded like at least one of the men was on the bridge. I could hear the metal reverberations as he clopped along on its surface. "Come back here, Frank!"

"I'm on get that bitch first!"

Frank, I thought, trying to keep from burping my heart into my mouth. Frank Hollison? Christ, have mercy! Then I was certain that my only safety lay in running as fast and as far as I could in the dark. Which is what I did, ignoring the briars and switches that bruised and ripped at me.

Had they planned it? Had they been following me on those deliveries, maybe trailing me for days? Had they known about the bridge being there? Was that where the showdown was supposed to have taken place? He said "bitch," so he knew it was a woman. It was likely then that he knew it was me. I was actually the one they were after.

"Alright, bitch," a disembodied voice screamed from somewhere behind me, sounding much closer than I thought it might be. "We're coming to get you now! You ain't getting away this time!"

I began to run blindly. I don't know how long I did this before I was able to get myself under control again. Even when I stopped a moment, I could feel the icy sweat pouring down over my face. I had to wipe it away with my arms, and they were wet, too. My mind was like an arctic blizzard. I couldn't see anything but spots.

As I started again, I tried to set a more measured pace, focusing on the feel of the ground beneath my feet. I had to watch it so I didn't fall and break a leg. I fell more than once. It was important not to fall against a tree or do anything that would stop me there where they could come upon me.

Then I came to the edge of the woods again just as the moon broke through the clouds. Standing there, my chest heaving, I thought there wasn't enough oxygen in the air and I'd die on the spot. No matter how deeply my lungs drew breath, it was like all that air had no nourishing value whatever. My knees were giving way, and I collapsed upon them, kneeling like a pilgrim having arrived at a place of worship.

"Lord, save me," I whispered through my fear and the sweat. "Save me from these men. I'll do anything you say."

I couldn't have stayed in that position more than a couple of minutes, but when I started up, I felt refreshed. That's when I heard the dogs. Just as they struck up their howl, the moon tore itself perfectly free of the cloud canopy and bathed the field in front of me in a silvery, luminous light.

Across the field that lay before me there was a long rank of hardwoods profiled in shadow and moonlight marching in a kind of winding line across the middle distance. I thought they must mark the meandering course of creek or river. The howl of the hounds filled the air. I'd heard the sound often enough. They were rabbit dogs.

I had no time to debate with myself whether rabbit dogs would be efficient in tracking down a person. I doubted it. As I ran across the field, I prayed that I wouldn't step in a hole along the way. When I reached the creek, I threw myself into it and began to wade upstream, stretching my muscles to lift my legs so that I could run in the water. After about two hundred yards, I came out again on the other side. When I got up on the bank, I collapsed prone and lay there panting for another couple of minutes. Then I got up and jogged on across into the forest beyond.

Once I was in the trees again, I stopped a moment to listen. The dogs seemed closer. I just hoped that either rabbit dogs couldn't track people or that my ruse had worked in wading downstream to throw them off. That's what they always did in the old movies.

I was soaked, of course. My clothes clung and weighed me down, but then they began to dry surprisingly quickly. My body temperature was raging. I was like a moving figment of steam. My feet in my shoes sloshed awhile, then felt damp, then felt dry.

It was like doing a ten-mile run. After awhile your brain goes dead. I still would tumble occasionally but mostly into the soft forest humus. It wasn't pleasant, but I didn't break anything.

When I finally stopped again, the sound of the dogs was very faint. My ruse had apparently worked. They were thrown off my scent and had continued in another direction. Lest I regain confidence, however, a new danger appeared in the form of a man moving along the line of trees not too far from where I stood.

I tried to orient myself. I tried to think in terms of where the road had been, where the bridge, where the creek. North of town. And I had left the truck and proceeded south, across the creek, southwest. Was it possible that I was in the vicinity of the Coosa National Forest and the Hall farm? I thought it possible.

As I waited, the light bobbed and swang along the man was carrying. He was making his way over the uneven furrows, but I realized he was approaching a lot faster than I had at first imagined. I had just enough time to back into the forest and to get down flat under some underbrush before he reached the place where I had just watched him.

He cleared his throat as he came up and set the lantern down. I thought he was about to get down on his knees and look for me, and vomit welled up in my mouth that I had to hold in. I could have reached out and touched his feet where he stood, facing away from me. He didn't turn around. Rather, he struck a match and lit a cigarette. If he'd looked back of him while he held that match lit, he'd have seen me for certain. He cleared his throat again and then took a long drag, coughed and leaned heavily on what I thought was a rifle.

Even a murderer needs a break.

For a moment a little devil peeped around the corner of my mind and pointed out that I didn't really know this person belonged to the gang hunting me. He is probably, the devil suggested, just an everyday kind of farmer. Reach out and touch him and then tell him who you are, he urged me. It'll be all right. Soon you'll be sitting by a warm fire holding a warm cup of cocoa and all this will be a bad dream.

It wasn't easy, but I rejected the devil's advice and pushed him back into a cell I shut and locked. He didn't like it and told me that I was fantasizing, that I'd be so embarrassed and ashamed when I realized. Etc. I paid no attention and waited. The man coughed again, picked up the lantern, heaved the rifle into swinging position and resumed his progress along the forest edge.

It really was a rifle he was carrying. I leaned away from my position and let the vomit out of my mouth. No more than a hundred feet or so beyond, he swerved away from the tree line and cut across the field to a fence that I realized ran along the road.

As I crawled out of the underbrush to get a better look, I saw him set the lantern and rifle down, climb through the fence, and approach a hulking automobile that I had totally overlooked. I did a double take and wondered how that had happened. It was scary to think I might have overlooked the automobile's presence and just blundered out into the field a few moments earlier.

He bent over the car. His words were crystal clear all the way to my ears. His crisp Irish tenor voice carried across the field: "I don't see nothing. She didn't come this way." The voice from inside the car was muffled; then the man with the tenor voice said, "Naw, hell, she could've gone anywhere. We ain't gone find her here. Let's move on down the road a little and have a look down there."

He reached back through the fence and got the rifle and the lantern, turned off the lantern, opened the car door and climbed in. The car lights came on, the motor cranked, and the dark silhouette of the vehicle lumbered slowly off, the motor growling.

Since they had now eliminated the field where I was, it stood to reason that it'd be safest just to stay put for the night. That was, at least, the first thing that occurred to me. They would be looking elsewhere for me. On the other hand, who knows where the dogs would lead them?

Spending the night freezing on the edge of the field was not very appealing. My clothes had not completely dried as I ran. Inactivity would exacerbate the chill in my bones. Hypothermia was the secret killer most people hadn't ever heard of. Since the only remedy was to keep moving, I decided to keep moving.

Instead of going out into the road, I moved along the edge of the forest. After crossing several fences, I caught sight of lights in what looked like a low-slung farmhouse. When I got closer, I could tell it was the Hall place.

The chill air had dried the perspiration on my face and shrunk the skin around my eyes. It felt like my forehead was tight as a drum. As I stood there looking at the lights and trying to decide for sure if it was the home of Henry Hall, I pushed my tongue against my teeth and popped my lips. It was my ruminating tick and the way I told myself I was thinking when I wasn't really thinking very good at all.

Next I heard a motor and backed into the woods only to watch headlights appear and a sheriff patrol car speed by. It left a huge wall of billowed dust in its wake which looked in the moonlight like some magic smoke exploding upward out of the earth. I thought of magicians and wished I could do magic now. Maybe somebody had told them about the wreck. But was that the right road and the right direction? I didn't think so.

Hope awakened in my heart, but I discouraged it from raising its head too much. I stood a few more minutes, decided that Henry Hall's house would have the usual pack of hounds and thought it wiser to give the house wide berth. If I didn't get close enough for the dogs to catch my scent, maybe they wouldn't set up a howl.

XV

I was making good time and very near halfway past the house when one of the beasts struck up his howl and then fell into a fit of barking. He couldn't have seen me, so I figured he must have caught my scent. Several other hounds joined him and broke the night silence with a veritable canine chorus. It was probably music to a dog's ears, but it set off every alarm in my body. I knew it was just this kind of dog racket that would carry several miles, and I might be just what they were out there listening for.

I came back out into the open. Since they were most likely coon dogs, they would stop barking as soon as they recognized me as a person instead of some varmit. Hounds were notoriously friendly once they got within sight of a human being. They were known to fawn about obsequiously on any passing stranger.

The furrows under the grass of the field made the ground much too rugged for real running. I waited as the dogs gathered, reached some kind of agreement on common action and headed across the field toward me. Then the front door of the house opened. A shaft of light fell across the expanse, and a man stepped out. A mighty whistle followed, and the dogs drew to a stop, turned and ran back to the house as in one accord.

The man stepped out further into the darkness and called, "Who's there?"

"Mr. Hall," I called back, "it's me, Folly Steeples."

"What you doing out here in the middle of the night, gal?"

"I had a wreck," I hollered.

"Well, come on up here."

"Is your wife there?"

"No, she ain't here. She's visiting relatives."

That was a relief. I knew that with her and her nigger-hating there, I didn't have a chance. If I got too close, she'd come out throwing rocks.

I climbed the fence and hurried across the field until I came into the pool of light from the front door. "Say you've had a wreck," Henry Hall asked.

"Yes, sir," I said, waiting there at the bottom of the steps.

"Yeah, well, come on up here," he said, peering into the darkness.

"Thank you, sir. But it's worse than just a wreck," I said, stepping up the stairs to the porch. "Some men ran me into the bridge and they've been chasing me with dogs."

"Gal, you are a mess. You look like you been wallowing in a hog trough. You're bloody, too," he said, moving instinctively to hold me up.

"I'm okay," I said.

"Come on in the house."

"Thank you, Mr. Hall."

He shut the door and locked it. "You say some men been chasing you?"

"Yes, sir," I said. The living room was warm. A stove was humming away, and I edged up close to it and began to rub my hands. "They're still out there looking for me."

"They run you into the bridge?"

"They did. But I ran them off the road, too."

Henry Hall looked down at the floor and frowned. He was actually a taller man than I remembered, long-legged and lean, though his head was nicely proportioned. His bottom lip was fatter than the top and was working as he thought. There was nothing of Jim in his features.

"Any reason they was chasing you?"

"I don't know. I was coming back from a delivery. They came up behind and started passing me. They were wearing hoods. One is called Frank, though, and I think of Frank Hollison."

"How'd you know that?"

"Well, one of them started across the bridge after me. Called out 'bitch,' and then somebody behind him called him Frank."

"What'd you do?"

"I thought that they were going to cut me off at that bridge—..."

"You talking about the Hood Creek Bridge? Steel?"

"Yessir, I think that's it. I bumped their car. I didn't mean to do it, but the car turned over and rolled over in the ditch, I guess."

"What happened then?"

"My truck hit the bridge, too. And then the men were hollering that they'd get me, so I started running. When I was in the woods good, another car came, I think, and they had dogs."

"Child, that bridge must be six to eight miles across country from here. Is that the way you come?"

"Across country. Yes, sir. I didn't have much choice."

Henry Hall looked at me. "Gal, you need to wash up a little. I'll get you a towel. We got hot water here in this house now. I had a bathroom put in two year ago. Come on."

"Could we call the state patrol or something, Mr. Hall?"

"I don't have no telephone. I wish't I did."

"What if they come here?"

"Don't you worry about that right now. Come on with me." I followed him down a hall. He got a towel out of a cabinet and opened a door to the new bathroom. "Take your time."

"Mr. Hall, I'm scared they'll come here."

"Don't worry. If they do, they won't find you."

"They have guns."

"Go ahead and wash yourself. It's times like these I wish I'd got myself a telephone."

He handed me some clothes through the door. When I finished I called quietly, "Mr. Hall. Where are you?"

"In the kitchen. Come on in here."

He was loading a rifle as he sat at the kitchen table. He got up and propped the rifle against the wall. "I'll get you one of Jessie Lee's bathrobes now and you'll be all right."

He came back with a warm robe I thankfully put over the clothes he'd given me. Then he got a plate full of food out of the oven. "Been warming this up for you. You ain't had no supper, I guess."

"No, sir."

"You know it's nearly eleven o'clock?"

I sort of laughed at myself and showed him the watch on my arm. "I haven't thought to look."

"What time was it this happened."

"Couldn't have been later than seven. I was running late."

"So you been running since seven. There's another bridge near Sandy Point. Maybe it was that one."

"I'm not sure, sir. Sandy Point could be right. I delivered at the Coots farm last."

Henry Hall puzzled a moment. "Don't know that I know the Coots. But that's near twelve miles from here by the road. I guess it ain't quite that far across country."

"Some of the time I was wading through the river to throw the dogs off," I said.

"You said there was dogs, too?"

"Yes, sir."

"You sure they was?"

"I'm sure. But I got them off my trail by wading in that river, I think."

"You say they were right back over that'a'way," he nodded in the direction from which I'd come.

"Yessir, they were just up the road from here, too, when I came out of those woods. I came up to the edge of the field and saw a man with a lantern. I crawled into some underbrush, and he stopped right in front of me and lit a cigarette."

"Could'a been anybody."

"He had a gun. Then he went down and joined a man who was waiting in the car. I heard every word he said. They were looking for me."

"That's the danggumbdest thing I ever heard. Why would they be wanting to hurt you, gal?"

I was eating by this time and just shook my head because my mouth was full.

"Can you shoot?"

I nodded. He got up and left the room. When he came back, I had about half cleaned the plate. He laid a Smith and Wesson .38 down on the table by me. "Know this?"

"Yes, sir," I said through a mouthful of potatoes. "I have one of them myself. Just couldn't get it out of the glove compartment of the truck before I ran."

He set a box of cartridges down beside it. "When you finish you better load it."

"Yes, sir."

He went over and stood at the window above the kitchen sink looking down the drive to the road. When I finished he showed me a ladder. "I'll get you some blankets. I want you to climb up in the attic. There's a window above the front porch. You can set up there. Stay out of sight, though. If you look out that little window, you can see right down to where somebody would park out front, you hear?"

"Mr. Hall," I said, looking into his big, faded gray eyes, "I feel better now. I'll just get on out there and get on back to town."

He put his hand very gently on my shoulder, "Child, you gone stay right up there. It ain't the most comfortable spot in the house, but it's about the safest. When I push that ladder up into the attic after you and shut this door, nobody is gonna think to look for you up there. In the morning we'll go straight into town and get the Sheriff. Now go on and do like I say."

So I climbed up into the attic. There was a window in the front gable and one in the back, and the light that poured in was enough for me to see where to step. I got a chair and pulled it over to the window, wrapped the blankets around me and sat down where I could see the yard. After I loaded it, I laid the .38 in my lap and then thrust the box of cartridges into the pocket of the robe.

I was nodding off to sleep when I heard the sound of pneumatic rubber crunching gravel. It was like an electric shock worked its way up my back and into my scalp as I listened. A big, dark-colored sedan pulled slowly up in front of the house and stopped.

Below me I heard the scrape of the screen door opening, and I prayed: "Don't go outside, Mr. Hall. Stay inside."

I couldn't be sure, but I thought he did step out onto the porch. A face thrust out of the front seat window of the car. It was the young one who had tried to catch me when I was finished with delivering half the newspapers that Sunday morning at the dead end.

I remembered again how he had thrust the pitchfork into Tom and then watched curiously as my friend sank to the ground. Then he spoke: "We looking for a nigger gal, bud." It looked like he'd lost one of his front teeth since I'd seen him last. But he was still wearing the same snide grin he had worn as I dodged him back and forth on the spare lot before getting over the fence.

Henry Hall's hounds prowled around the car growling. A couple stood back and barked at random. One by the barn howled. Mr. Hall below said, "Ain't seen nobody tonight."

"Your dogs bite," the face in the window asked casually.

"Can't vouch for them," Henry Hall answered. "The old one is real bad with strangers."

"We want to get out."

"No need. It's past bedtime, and my wife's already asleep. You boys'll have to come back tomorrow."

"What you doing up so late then?"

"Yeah," somebody in the back seat sneered, "and standing out here with a loaded gun?" So Henry Hall had his gun with him, I thought. That was good and may have inhibited these killers.

"A doe come through the yard. I seen her from the bedroom. Happens sometimes."

"Hey, that's good. Shoot your meat from the front porch," the back seat voice sneered.

"You can't shoot no doe," the skeptic countered, "and we shore ain't no deer. You don't need to be aiming that thing at us."

"Oh, beg your pardon. I ain't aiming it at you. Goodnight now, boys."

"Who said we was going," the back seat voice bristled.

"I did," Henry Hall said sort of low and calm.

"Why you—"

"Shut up Case," the young one commanded. "Okay, partner. You go get some sleep now. Don't be letting no nigger gals in your house, you hear?"

"My wife don't like niggers," Henry Hall said. "By the way, what you after this gal for?"

"She's one of them civil rights niggers," the man said. "We want to teach her some respect." He drew back into the car and the motor sprang into life. The sedan backed around, turned and started out.

"We'll be back," somebody called. It sounded like the same voice in the back of the car, the sort of voice you wouldn't like to hear in your worst dreams. Utterly without any human regard for anything.

I heard Henry Hall open the screen door and edge back into the living room a little. I heard him lock the door and then proceed around from room to room checking the window latches and, finally, the back door.

Soon I heard him unlock the closet door. "Gal," he whispered loudly, "can you let that ladder down or just poke your head over here." I took the covers off me and crawled over to the trap door, opened it to look down. He was standing there looking up at me. "Just leave the ladder where it is. You're right about them," he said, the stress evident in his raspy voice, "Them is mean customers. You better stay up here. No matter what happens, don't come down. We can't drive into town tonight no way with them out there waiting around."

"Mr. Hendricks, I better move on. You're in danger while I'm here," I said.

"Naw, you stay put. Good night," Henry Hall answered.

"Good night, sir. And thanks." Neither of us knew just how generous Henry Hall was being.

As strange as it seems, I had no trouble getting to sleep. I dozed off bundled up right there in that hardback chair. Sometime during the night I woke up. Something was going on below. It sounded like furniture turning over and a herd of cattle running through the house. I rolled over carefully and pointed the Smith and Wesson at the only place you could come up into the attic.

There were two sharp reports from a gun, maybe more than one. "You dirty sonovbitch," somebody screamed. The struggle continued into the kitchen area, and then the backdoor slammed. "Come on, goddamn it," somebody yelled outside. "Let's get out of here."

"Don't give me no shit, cocksucker," was the answer. It sounded like the young one's voice. "I'm on kill me some dogs first."

The curses went back and forth.

"I told you not to hurt the man, you bastard!"

"Fuck you!"

"She wasn't even there, you bastard!"

"Fuck you," came the violent but monotonous reply in the young one's voice.

Somebody must have kicked a dog because one began to yelp and move off around the house. There were other dog sounds I couldn't make out, like they were gasping for air or couldn't breathe. The voices receded down the drive, swearing and cursing each other. The low-toned grumble of an internal combustion engine without much of a muffler sounded down by the road. Car doors slammed. The engine whined into life as the vehicle moved off.

I listened a long time to nothing but absolute silence. Still, I was afraid to move. I kept expecting Henry Hall's head to pop up through the hole or something. It may have been fifteen or twenty minutes, maybe more, before I finally decided to crawl slowly on my hands and knees out of the blanket, still trying not to make any noise. As I crawled I realized my whole body was trembling and shivering from bottom to top.

I got to the ladder and looked down. The shaft was dark. Mr. Hendricks had shut the closet door. I don't know how long I waited before I laid the revolver down and then began to work the ladder slowly across the rafters and then down the shaft and into the closet space. Finally it rested firmly on the floor. I took the revolver and then eased from one wrung to the next so as not to make any noise. I had my hand on the trigger, and I calculated how I might swing around if anybody jerked the door open.

When I found the knob on the closet door, I turned it as slowly as if I were winding an expensive watch. The door creaked a little as I pushed it open. First I hesitated; then I stepped out into the house, holding the pistol up ready to fire. That's when I heard the groan.

Losing all sense of caution, I followed the sound into the kitchen and found Henry Hall sprawled on the linoleum, his head forced up against the cabinet. There was a dark pool around him. When I understood that it was blood, my trembling somehow stopped. I ran to him and knelt. His denim clothing was soaked in a sticky liquid, and he was breathing in tiny gasps.

"Mr. Henry," I whispered.

"Stab...in gut. If you can...get me into town..."

"Where are the keys to the car?"

"No truck. Put me in...flatbed."

"Keys?"

"Pocket."

I fished the keys out of his pocket and ran out into the yard to the barn where I somehow knew Henry Hall kept the truck parked. I stumbled over something soft and yielding. Later I realized it was a dog's carcass. The men had somehow slit the throats of most of the hounds. That's how they'd been able to surprise Henry Hall. Don't ask me how they did it. Hounds have a keen sense of smell.

As I slipped into the front seat and under the wheel, I inserted the key into the ignition and prayed that the motor would start quickly. It didn't. It ground and ground the way old Chevrolets usually do, with its own distinctive sound.

I had to stop and gather my wits before I was able to crank the truck by using the manual choke and pumping the accelerator with my foot. That's how Amos Hendricks had taught me to start the delivery truck on a cold day. He'd say, "Tromp on it!" So I tromped, and the motor sprang into life.

How I got Henry Hall into the flatbed of the truck I do not know. He was a lightly built man but still weighed a lot more than I could ordinarily have managed. When I went into the kitchen and looked at him, I guess I panicked and that triggered the release of the adrenaline I needed for the job.

Dr. Veazey lived on that side of town, so he was the closest. The gasoline tank registered a quarter full. When I hit the road, I shifted into third and pressed the pedal to the floor. "Please, Lord," I prayed as I negotiated the road, "don't let them come back yet."

When the headlights appeared in the outside rearview mirror attached to my door, I braced myself. I had not forgotten the revolver. It lay on the seat beside me. If this is it, I told myself, I hoped my many hours of target practice would pay off. It may not be Christian, but I decided I would take as many of them with me as I could for what they did to Jim's father. If I lived to see the next day, I'd debate the justice of what I did by daylight.

When the headlights pulled up behind me, a blue and red light began to flash. It was the sheriff patrol car I'd seen earlier coming back to town. Great, I thought. Timely, as always. I pulled over and jumped out calling out, "Mr. Hall is here in the back bleeding to death. I'm trying to get him to Dr. Veazey's."

Marlon Frazier stuck his round head out, "How'd it happen?"

"Some men came in his house and stabbed him."

"Let's get going," he said.

"Let me go first. I don't want him breathing your dust," I instructed.

"All right," he agreed.

Once we pulled up into Dr. Veazey's yard and got him to the front door, Marlon helped get Henry Hall in and onto the operating table in Dr. Veazey's office. Mrs. Veazey joined us. She was a competent nurse. We could hear Marlon's police radio crackling in the hall as he contacted Sheriff Moore.

XVI

"So Papa was protecting you," Jim said as he held both my hands.

"Yes. He was protecting me, Jim." I looked away.

Jim squeezed my hands, "I knew he was that kind of guy, Fol. I knew it all along. Pa always knew what was right."

"He saved my life. Oh, Jim, I'm so sorry. If I'd just gone on instead of staying there—"

He squeezed my hands again. "It's not your fault, Fol. It's not your fault," he crooned. "Pa would have wanted it this way. This is how he'd have liked to go. Protecting somebody like you. That guy was a killer. He'd have killed him whether you were there or not. He just took it in his head when Pa stood at the front door with that rifle, like you said."

"What about your mother?"

"She'll manage."

He let go my hands and sort of rolled around and leaned back against the wall sighing. "It's funny, sport. If this hadn't happened, I don't think I'd be alive. Getting this emergency leave saved my life, too. So Pa saved both your life and mine."

"Are you serious, Jim? Why do you say that?"

He shook his head slowly, reached up and rubbed his eyes. I'd seen Jim look cool, triumphant, happy, but I'd never seen him look so bone weary. "Oh yeah, I'm serious, all right," he said with his voice so awfully tired, "You said awhile ago that you couldn't understand the bloodlust of those men coming back and stabbing Pa. I understand it. I've seen a lot of that the past few months, Fol. More'n I ever wanted to see or want to see again. 'Nam is full of it. You don't know whose got a gun or a hand grenade and who doesn't. Little kids come up and stuff a grenade in your pocket."

"No, Jim. Is that true?"

He nodded and rubbed his hand through his hair, "When they came to get me for this, they found me waiting to be run over by ten thousand of them. Say what you will. They all look alike, just like I guess we do to them. They could carry an atom bomb in those clothes they wear. I figured that my time had come, and they got through with the helicopter to get me. I couldn't believe it. It was like God Almighty had come down and grabbed me right out of the mouth of hell. I ain't shitting you, sport."

I could see the way Jim looked that the rest was too terrible to put into words. "I'm glad the helicopter got through to get you, Jim," I said softly.

Jim looked at me, but his eyes were filled with something else that was right there for him but way out of my reach. "Look," he said, "you know what—I could use a drink."

"A drink?"

"Sure, whiskey or something like that."

"This is a dry county," I said.

Jim laughed. "Let's drive over to Thomson and get something."

"I don't drink, Jim."

"She don't drink and she don't chew and she'd don't play with boys who do," he mocked. "Then you need to start, sport."

He began to turn around and get his knees under him, so he could get up. We were lying on the floor near the drink cooler in the back of the store. "No, wait, Jim. If you want a drink, we've got a cabinet full of whiskey."

"Naw. You're kidding me."

"No, we do. Salesmen give the bottles to us. Neither Mr. Hendricks nor I drink, and you can't sell it. Mr. Hendricks won't throw anything away—"

Jim stretched and laughed, "Of course he wouldn't. That'd be wasteful, wouldn't it. Even wasteful throwing away something he disapproves of."

"Yes," I agreed while missing the humor. After what Jim said, I figured he needed a drink. The funeral had been trying, too. Dr. Veazey had sedated his mother after she went into hysterics. Of course she would have made a spectacle of herself. It had been as though she thought that's what the county expected of her. Died to save a nigger gal, she'd howled. I fully had expected her to have a stroke on the spot. The very idea that Henry Hall had given his life to save a Negro had been more than she could stand.

Later, when his mother had seen me outside the church, she had lurched towards me screaming. I had jumped out of the way, and Jim just barely kept her reigned in. Other men came to help. I didn't feel too popular at that point. After that she had just lost it.

Jim strolled along, hands in pocket, with me to look at the contents of the storage cabinet. The bottles had really accumulated lately after we went into the building supply business. The stakes were higher than in the grocery and software business, so the gifts were more frequent and more expensive.

"Geez, Fol, you've got a regular bar here! You could go on a two month drunk."

"If there was any point to it," I managed to counter in my driest tone. "What would you like?"

"The Jim Beam looks good. Black label. We could get a couple of cokes to chase it with."

"Chase it?"

He laughed, "Don't tell me now that you don't know what chasing a whiskey is, Fol. You know, first a swig of whiskey and then a swig of coke."

"Oh. What for?"

"Well, you'll see."

I had come back to my room after the funeral and just sort of hidden myself up there, taken off my clothes and gotten under the covers. That's what I did to recoup when something really embarrassing and shameful happened. Jessie Lee Hall had made a huge scene right in full view of the whole town: Folly Steeples, responsible for the murder of Henry Hall! I was mortified.

After dark Jim had come and thrown rocks up at the window until I woke up. I jumped out of bed, got my .38, put on my robe and went to the window to look down. There he was standing below on the loading deck looking up. "Hey, sport, open up."

"Just a minute. Gotta get something on."

I pulled on my jeans, put on a blouse and ran down the narrow steps, through the feed room to the large, sliding door to the dock. When I unlatched and opened it, Jim stepped in quipping, "Hey, what's up, sport? You look plumb wore out!"

"Oh," I said. I stood there, but Jim always knew what to do. He reached over and drew me to him and hugged me tight.

"It's okay, sport. It really is. Don't you worry about it. Nobody in his right mind could possibly blame you."

"Oh, Jim," I groaned, a sob wrenching its way out of my throat.

"Fol, I'm sorry about Ma. You know how she is, though."

He sort of unfolded us but kept his arm around me. "We need to close this door," I said.

When that was done we walked over to our old spot near the drink machine. "Jim, I could understand what tore your mother up," I began, by way of explaining. "When I was there that night, I asked your father if I shouldn't just go on back to town on my own. He didn't want me to. Your mom wasn't there—"

"Sure, if she'd been there, she wouldn't have let you in the door," he said.

"You father urged me to come in and to stay."

"Yeah, I know."

"Jim, I didn't know he'd be –" I choked, "killed, though, or I wouldn't have stayed. I really wouldn't have, Jim."

"Aw, sport, sure you shouldn't have gone on walking into town. Are you nuts. Pa wouldn't have let you, anyway. He knew what was right. Look, I'm sorry. I really am. I wish my ma wasn't like she is. She's a redneck bigot."

I pressed three fingers against his mouth, "Shhh," I whispered. "Don't ever think you need to say things about your mother."

He pulled me up against him again, and we hugged, this time a little longer than we should have. "You know I've always been crazy about you, Fol. When I was out there in the jungle, I thought of you."

"Oh, Jim," I said, "thanks."

"Thanks for what," he said, nearly laughing.

We were curled up around the whiskey bottle and two cokes then and had the three objects standing on the floor between us. Jim reached over and picked up the whiskey, lifted it to his mouth and gulped a swig. "Whoooeee," he yelped. "Powerful stuff."

"Ummm," I mumbled.

"Come on, take a swig. Then you chase it with Coke. It's great. You'll see."

"No thanks."

"Just one swig, sport. Sure enough, it's good."

"Okay, one swig," I said. When I tried it, it tasted awful. I coughed and Jim laughed. Then I drank the Coke to soothe my mouth and throat.

"The next swig will taste a lot better," Jim chuckled.

Soon I did take another swig, anyway, and Jim was right. It tasted better. It wasn't the taste of the liquid so much as a sense of relief that came over me. I felt relaxed for the first time in a long time. Suddenly we were sitting on the floor there curled around the bottles, and anything seemed fun to talk and laugh about.

"So you thought of me in Vietnam," I ventured. The words came out like they were greased and cost me no effort at all. Whiskey was a wonderful conversational lubricant.

"I did. I didn't expect to, that's the weird thing. I thought of you when I didn't expect to think of anything but when and who was going to break out of nowhere next and blow us to bloody hell."

What the whiskey was doing is making me coy. Instead of focusing on the horror of Jim's war experience, I thought of myself. "How did you think of me," I heard myself asking in a voice full of frivolity. I couldn't believe what I was doing. I didn't even bother to chase it with the Coke the next time I picked up the bottle and swigged.

"Ummm," Jim said as he thought. "Well, as a woman."

"I am a woman," I said archly.

"Nobody around here would know it the way you act and dress."

I sat up. My laugh died in my throat, "What do you mean?"

Jim was grinning at me. It was the old careless, carefree grin, the grin of the football hero, the young man who did everything right, whom nobody could whip. The whiskey had done that, and I was grateful. "Well, look at you now. You've got on shapeless jeans and a denim shirt. And you aren't even wearing a bra."

I put my hands up to cover myself, "How do you know?"

He laughed again, "Yeah, right."

Embarrassment spilled over me dark and muddy. I felt almost naked, exposed. "I'm not interested in being attractive," I countered.

"No, I know. But you are, anyway. If we weren't sister and brother…"

"What? What then," I asked. My muscles tightened and I sat up alert and waiting.

"I just feel like our destinies are linked. It's stupid. But I can't help it. I've felt that way for years. I don't know why. You can't explain stuff like that, sport."

That's when I said, "Jim, what if I told you that I found out I'm not your sister."

"Yeah? Where'd you find that out." I explained about discovering the attic above the library at Lawson Hall with the genealogical tables. Jim listened while he took an occasional gentle sip of the whiskey. "You're kidding me," he said finally when I finished. Then he said it again: "Come on, you're kidding?"

"No, I swear it on the Bible," I said. I held up my right hand as if I was ready to swear an oath for good measure.

"No horse manure! You're telling me that you're Judge Lawson's daughter?"

"That's what was there in the family tree the Judge had drawn up himself."

"It wasn't Pa after all?"

"Not according to Judge Lawson."

"Does anybody else know?"

"Judge Lawson is dead. Aunt Ida Mae probably does, and Uncle Cajus. Maybe even Laura knows. I'm not sure about that. Maybe that's why she hates me so much. Otherwise, it's just you and me. Miss Ellen may have known, but she sure never said anything to me."

"And he let you live there like a beggar in his house? He never gave you a red cent?"

"I wasn't exactly a beggar, Jim."

"What were you then? The maid? You cleaned up for him?" He exploded into movement, jumped to his feet and cried, "Great God Almighty!"

"Keep your voice down, Jim."

"Wasn't Pa right about the rich? A white man wouldn't acknowledge his own daughter and used her as a servant? Rich as Croesus and wouldn't give her a dime?" He stormed around in a circle, swinging and pumping his arms for emphasis.

"No, he did give me some money when we first started to learn German," I protested.

He stopped and demanded, "Yeah, how much?"

"I think it was a dime a lesson. Maybe it was a quarter. I'm not sure."

"Sure. Open handed guy. A real gem."

"Jim, don't get so upset. Judge Lawson is dead."

"Your father. Your father is dead."

I shrugged, "Well, I mean I can't really feel that he was my father. I mean, I don't feel anything about that. I know it's probably true, but what difference does it make?"

"Yeah, none to him, obviously. You don't resent hell out of it?"

"You've learned some rough language in the Army!"

"This is nothing, baby. You ought to hear them cuss. Soldiers are geniuses at cussing."

He calmed a little and then sat back down really close to me. "You lived with the rich all your life until Laura kicked you off the place, didn't you?"

"I guess...I guess I did."

"What do you think about them?"

"What do I think about them?" I could feel his breath against my cheek. It confused me. I couldn't think about his question.

"What are you an echo? Come on, sport. You should know them better than anybody else. You've been closer to them for longer than anybody else in town among all us rednecks and Negroes."

"Yes, but I really lived with Uncle Cajus and Aunt Ida Mae in the cottage. They were all just—people."

"No, you lived with his sister up in Yankeeland. You lived with her in the same house. You told me so yourself. She was your aunt, wasn't she!"

"Yes," I admitted. "That's true."

"So, are they really that way?"

"What way?"

"You know, the way they act in public."

"What do you mean, Jim?"

"I mean," he began. And the way he was turned, his lips were so close to my skin. In the next moment he was kissing my neck.

"Jim," I said.

"Wanted – to – do this," he stammered through his kisses, "a – long – time."

Somehow I turned to meet him. It's hard to say how it happened, but I certainly didn't want to stop once it began, though it seemed as if I couldn't breathe deeply enough, couldn't get enough oxygen into my lungs to keep me going.

When I remember that moment, I know it is something that has been repeated as many times as the world has turned and in as many places. The absolutely mind-boggling thing about it to me was that so much pleasure, so much sheer joy could be compressed into touching lips to skin and lips to lips, that something so utterly commonplace could seem to me so rare, so precious. I'd never guessed that before. Never had.

Then Jim stood up abruptly, almost falling backwards like he was in a terrific hurry. He virtually threw me off him, shedding me like a bad skin as he rose up: "Damn, sport, this won't work! Gotta get hold of myself. Sorry."

"It's all right, Jim," I said. Why was he apologizing? Hadn't I shown myself perfectly willing?

"No. I'm sorry. I sort of lost it. Haven't had it together lately, sport. I—" To my utter amazement, in the middle of a sentence, Jim burst into wild sobs, covered his face with both hands and, collapsing onto his knees, he wept, wept bitterly, drew deep, deep gasps from somewhere within him and sobbed. His shoulders shook. Every fiber of him trembled.

At first I simply sat there petrified, astonished; then I moved to him, folded my arms around him and rocked him as he wept, pressing my head against his as best I could. When it was impossible, I simply held him.

I had never seen a man weep like that. The word "weep" could never have meant anything to me before it happened. People didn't weep in Lawson County Georgia. They dabbed their eyes a little. They squared their jaws. They pulled in their chins. A stray tear could be seen here and there at times of grief or comfort, but not weeping, not unrestrained weeping.

As I held him and felt the mighty sobs reverberating through his ribcage, rattling his shoulders, I knew somehow that we had entered a new country beyond the hard reality we had both known until then. Jim was already there. He had been propelled to that new country on the battlefields of Vietnam. But I was utterly baffled at the time. Jim had always seemed so completely in control of life.

It was he who had rescued me twice, once from white children, then from black adolescents. It was his smile I remembered; it stood square in the middle of anything that mattered to me. It was a smile that was all the more charming for that little twinkle of mischief and recklessness that was always present. Jim was never afraid. Jim was never in doubt. Jim never lacked to know exactly what to do.

I think I grew frightened as I realized just how much I had depended upon the idea that Jim would come and help me. Jim would defend me. Jim would protect me. It had given me courage where I might not have had so much courage otherwise. And now he was bent over and huddled in a pool of vulnerability on the floor.

Sometimes after midnight he simply gave out. The weeping turned to wimpers and then to an occasional sigh. I was perfectly content sitting there, holding him. I could have sat there a thousand years and never grown tired. We didn't speak. I could have sat like that forever.

When it was all over I knew what women mean when they say they love a man. I knew from inside the fierce love and affection Aunt Ida Mae felt for Uncle Cajus. It was entirely new to me, fallen upon me when I least expected it.

I loved Jim that way, too: In spite of whatever it might be in him that was not perfect, in spite of whatever it was that grieved him so deeply, in spite of anything and everything that had ever happened or ever would happen. I loved the man.

It must have been near midnight when Jim whispered weakly, "You okay?"

"Ummmhmmm," I answered.

"Your legs not gone to sleep?"

"I don't think so."

"Better be getting up."

"I guess we'd better," I agreed.

"Better let me out."

"Yes," I said.

When I opened the door, we stepped out onto the loading dock and staggered backwards as the brilliant, star-filled night exploded across the sky. "Wow," Jim said. We stood there holding hands a long time. Finally, he squeezed my hand and let it fall. "Goodnight, Fol." He walked to the edge of the loading dock and hesitated, "and thanks."

Then he jumped down and hurried off.

I watched him out of sight before I turned back into the store and locked the door behind me. I hurried up the stairs, took off my clothes and slid under my sheets so that I could spend the night remembering every moment, the feel of how it was to hold him, to have him kissing my neck and shoulders.

"It's a good idea," Mr. Amos said the next morning when I presented the idea of hiring Jim to join us. "We'll be able to open that store in Augusta sooner than we think if we can get him to join us. But I didn't know he was finished with the Army yet?"

"Jim says it's possible now that he's lost his father, he can get an early release."

"I'll talk to him about it. We can get in touch with Representative Calhoun."

Representative Calhoun was on the Armed Services Committee in Washington and was, by virtue of the seniority system, a very influential man. That much I knew. "You think that'll help," I heard myself asking with more eagerness (and a good bit of fear) than I really cared to show.

"I reckon it might," Mr. Amos allowed. He also gave me what amounted to a pretty penetrating glance. "Depending upon the rules and all. If it's just a case of the Army needing a little nudge, it'll help."

That afternoon Mr. Amos sent me out to find Jim. I was supposed to bring him in to discuss the business and see what his intentions really were. Would he really quit the Army if he had the chance?

I drove out to his father's farm with some trepidation. I wouldn't have taken that same road again for any reason except to find Jim. As the farmhouse came into view, I saw Jim walking across the field alone. All that had happened in that night came back upon me, and I thought I might lose consciousness. But I didn't. Jim reached the yard by the time I pulled up in the new delivery truck. I bent down so I could see up to the porch hoping his mother wasn't there.

"Finally got all those dogs buried," he said, thrusting the spade down in the ground and leaning forward on it. "They slit their throats. I don't know why Pa didn't hear it. They had to make some noise."

"I didn't hear anything, either, Jim," I said.

"Yeah, but you were worn out from the wreck and all that running."

I sort of hung out the window and propped on my elbows, "Mr. Hendricks wants you to come in and talk business with us."

"What about?"

"Working with us. That is, if you can get out of the Army."

"Hey, how did you know I was thinking about that?"

"You mentioned it."

"I didn't do it."

"Sure you did. You said this had kept you from getting killed. I figured if you said that, you might figure you'd done your share already. No reason to push your luck."

"Yeah, but I'm not really sure it'll work."

"Mr. Amos knows Representative Calhoun. He's very important in Congress and all."

"It's worth a try. I've done enough, and there isn't any history to be made in Vietnam, believe me."

Jim left the spade sticking up and walked around the front of the truck. His movement was slow and weary. I reached over and unlocked the door for him. He opened it and slid into the seat. "Hey, Fol," he said simply and then righted himself in the seat – almost primly.

I surprised myself by being disappointed. What I had expected was a kiss. But I acted as if I hadn't noticed, put the truck in gear, and we lurched forward, barely missing a tree. "Hey, you always drive this fast," he said as he grabbed to hold on to something.

"What fast?"

"This fast."

We were bumping down the drive to the road. At the gate I slammed on the brakes, throwing us both forward. He had to stretch out both arms to stop himself banging against the dashboard. "Whoa," he said. Then the motor wailed as I turned out into the road. Jim just held on.

When I pulled around in back of the store and stopped, Jim said, "What's ailing you, sport? You want to get the son killed, too?"

I ignored that and said, "Nothing is wrong. Why do you think anything's ailing me?" I pulled up the emergency brake with a violent jerk.

"You're driving like a maniac. I guess I have to assume you're' mad about something."

"No, there's nothing."

Just as I was about to open the door and jump out, Jim grabbed my arm and stopped me. I turned back all ready to be mad; then I stopped. He was frowning like he was in pain, "Fol, it won't work. It can't work."

"What won't work?"

"Us. It would've been better if we'd stayed sister and brother."

"We aren't sister and brother. We've never been brother or sister."

"Help me here. We've been friends a long time. I love you dearly, but it can't work."

"Okay, now you tell me what can't work."

Jim looked around desperately and then whispered, "You know, a romantic thing."

"Jim, you said you thought about me in Vietnam even when you didn't expect it – and all the time."

"I was wrong to do that, Fol. That's what I'm telling you. I was totally worn out, and then the whiskey... It just – I don't know. I haven't had it together. Things get away from me before I know it."

"Jim, look, I didn't expect it. Honestly. But I didn't mind."

He released my arm, "I noticed, sport. I guess that's the real problem."

"The real problem?"

"Right." He pressed himself against the seat and looked up at the top of the cab, "but there's no way, sport. I've been thinking all day."

"You said you thought of me in the worst places, when you didn't want to. Remember? That has to mean something."

"Sure I did. I didn't expect to and...and I couldn't help it. But we can't talk about it."

"You said you've known our destiny is tied together. Jim, you said that, didn't you?"

"Look, I said our destinies are tied together, and I believe that." He grimaced, shifting in his seat, "Folly, honest, can you see me getting anywhere in Georgia politics with a colored wife?"

"A colored wife?"

"Well, what do you think? Let's talk plain. This is reality, Fol. If I said I thought of you all the time without wanting to, you know what that can mean and where it leads. Let's face it."

I was really dumbfounded because I hadn't thought that far ahead. I was still hung up on the kisses and the touching and the hugs of the previous night. The morning collapsed around me and fell into a black hole. My vision narrowed, just like somebody was closing up the lenses of my eyes or putting blinders on me. It was like I was speaking out of a hollow tube when I said, "Yes, I see what you mean now. I really do."

"You're hurt now, aren't you."

"No. No, I'm not."

"See what I'm talking about, Fol? Don't get hurt, look at it as realistically as you can."

"Sure. Sure, I'm looking. Laura Lawson would be more useful as a wife wouldn't she? Georgia aristocrat and all that."

"Yeah," Jim laughed sardonically, "people would like that. A redneck farmer's boy like me married to the original, genuine aristocrat of Georgia."

"That'd be just great," I said, fighting back the tears.

"I can see we can't talk about it right now, can we?"

"Sure, that's it. We've talked about it. I know exactly what you mean, Jim. We'll just forget about it.

"Don't say it like that, Fol. Say it like you believe it. We're still going to be partners in history."

"Well, actually, right now we just want you to join us in the building supply business, Jim. Is that asking too much of reality? It has nothing to do with history." And you know where history can go, I thought. But I didn't say it.

"No. I think it's a great idea."

Jim had his role all figured out before Mr. Hendricks and I were finished talking. It took him no time at all to begin to develop the sales department. Within a couple of years he had twenty salesmen and had quadrupled our gross.

Later, when it did happen, when Jim met Laura again, I could have shoved my foot in my mouth for having had that last scene with him. That must have been when he got the idea that a farmboy and an aristocrat could capture the imagination of state voters.

XVII

"Miss Steeples," somebody called from across the sidewalk.

The crowd was thick and milling in front of the courthouse. Reporters were weaving in and out with pencils in hand. "Miss Steeples," the voice persisted. I braced myself. I thought it must be another reporter. The case had exploded onto the front pages of the Atlanta papers and was being picked up by the wire services.

"Miss Steeples, excuse me," as I turned to meet him, he pushed through the crowd.

"Walt Cross?"

He beamed with pleasure, "Well, I'm amazed that you remember me. You look surprised, too?"

"Well, I am surprised, and of course I remember you, Walt. I've wondered about you a lot. What are you doing in town?"

He jerked his head awkwardly to one side like a singer being caught singing slightly off key. "It's your trial."

"My trial? I'm not on trial," I said, "yet."

"Oh, I don't mean that. Can I call you Folly?"

"Sure. I'd hope so."

"This trial is important to us."

"By us you mean your organization."

"Yes, that's right."

"That may be bad news for me."

"Why would you say that? We're here to protect Afro-Americans."

"Getting many of them in trouble in the process."

"There's a transition period."

"For a lot of people it's very long, too," I said, bulging my eyes to make my point and, yet, keep my sense of humor.

"Could we go somewhere to talk privately?"

"Where?"

"Back to your place of business, for instance?"

I looked around. Nobody seemed to be watching us. Nobody would think anything about two colored people going off to talk. I looked at my watch and said: "Yes, I think court's in recess for the rest of the morning, anyway."

We had built an office out at the backside of our lumberyard, so I took him around there. Uncle Cajus was just finishing up preparing an order at the desk. He pretty much ran the yard. "Uncle Cajus, this is Walt Cross. Walt, this is my uncle, Cajus Horning."

"Pleased to meet you, Mr. Horning," Walt said, extending his hand.

Uncle Cajus looked at the extended hand a split second; then he took it and shook it firmly. Colored men in Lawson County didn't always shake hands when they met. "Likewise, Mr. Cross."

"Walt was here back during the trouble. He was hurt in the march and put in the hospital in Thomson."

"Yes, and your niece pedaled all the way from here to visit me in the hospital," Walt said, beaming.

I saw the surprise in Uncle Cajus's face. I hadn't told him about that episode. "Oh," he said. "On her bike?"

"Yes, sir, Mr. Horning. On her bike."

Uncle Cajus looked at me almost as if he were expecting me to say it was a lie. I nodded, and then he said, "Well, I guess y'all have something to talk over. Me and Chandra's got to get this order out."

"Bye now, Uncle Cajus. Where are you going?"

"Just over to Sandy Springs. They're adding on to the church there. We've got a load of two by fours for them."

"Good to meet you, Mr. Horning."

"Yeah. Likewise, son, likewise," Uncle Cajus said tipping his cap as he left.

"Nice man," Walt said conversationally.

"How did you know I came on my bike?"

"Did you think you could do that without anybody noticing? The nurse told me."

"Aw, come on."

"No, really. She came in after you left. She'd watched you go." Walt assumed the nurse's persona and a high-pitched voice: "You know how that gal got here?"

"And you said?"

"I said I didn't. She said she figured I didn't but I ought to. Could I tell her where she was going because she was on a bike and looked pretty tired out. You know what she said?"

"No."

"She said: That girl must really like you a lot."

"Can't keep anything secret," I admitted.

"So you grew up with Mr. Horning and his wife?"

"Yes. They're my uncle and aunt. My mother's sister," I said. "My mother skipped town."

"Do you know where she went? Is she in touch?"

I looked sharply at Walt. The questions were not just academic. "Nope, haven't heard since she left. I think I can do without knowing where she is, too."

A crease appeared between his eyebrows and showed his concern. "I bet I can find her."

"Don't bother."

"Well, anyway, that's not why I'm here."

"It's good to see you," I said, meaning it.

"Thanks. You know, I really like the sound of that," Walt said.

"Why are you here, Walt?"

"First all, we don't want Frank Hollison getting off scot-free, and we think he might."

"You think he might?"

"'Fraid so, Folly."

"Then what?"

"Well, we want to try something new. Would you cooperate if it were your civil rights that had been violated?"

"I wouldn't mind getting that man behind bars any way I could. He was in on the murder of Henry Hall."

"Good."

Walt stayed around for the next two weeks of the trial. In the end, Frank Hollison wasn't let off scot-free. He and one of the accomplices were sent to prison for a long time – or, at least, until the first parole came through.

The worst of it was that the young one wasn't caught. He was still at large, and I was almost sure that he had been the homicidal maniac who knifed Henry Hall that night while I hid in the attic.

When I left the courthouse after sentencing, Walt was waiting at our building supply office. "So there you are," I said.

"Your uncle let me in. He just left to make a delivery. I told him I'd man the office till you got back."

"Looks like there's no need to go on to a test case."

"You look too relieved. I don't like that. But congratulations on getting two of those murderers in jail."

I pressed his arm, "Walt, I've been glad you were here."

Encouraged he stepped up close to me, reached out and gripped both my arms. "I hope we meet again, soon," he said.

"If you would just trim that hedge you have up there, I wouldn't mind being seen with you. Atlanta isn't that far from here, is it? I know you'll be poking around looking for trouble, stop by any old time."

"I intend to. It's high time you stopped living an ascetic life. You're not a monk."

"Or a nun?"

"Whichever." He leaned over and kissed me on the cheek. Then he walked around me to the door.

"Walt," I said.

"Yes?"

"Thanks for being here. Honestly, it made me feel a lot better seeing you in the crowd and knowing I could count on you."

"No problem, partner."

"Believe me, though, as long as you keep that hairdo you've got, you're not going to be able to fade into any crowd."

"Naw, for most white people I'm still invisible. Doesn't matter what I wear or how my hair is."

Walt went off to Atlanta and other places for awhile. Lawsonville was off the agenda of the big organizations. It was too small a place for the big fish, but it was big enough for us. Especially now that Laura Lawson was apparently gone for good.

We had all followed Laura's post-college career in the society sections of the Atlanta papers. She had married some Brahmin from Boston after she asked Uncle Cajus and Aunt Ida Mae to clear out of Lawson Hall. We thought she'd sell the hall. When she didn't, we didn't understand. It was only much later that we'd discover why.

We built Uncle Cajus and Aunt Ida Mae a house on the county road that made up the main street of colored town. It was brick veneer and about fourteen hundred square feet. The kitchen was the newest kind of linoleum complete with a Maytag dishwasher.

"Honey, I can't believe this kitchen," was what she kept saying when we got them moved in. Uncle Cajus just stood back looking very satisfied with the way things turned out.

The first time we ever heard of the foreign service is when word spread that Laura's Boston Brahmin husband was in it. People speculated that the foreign service meant he was a salesman of some big company in South America. Later it became clearer to everybody when we heard that he had been posted to an embassy in Singapore. It's the diplomatic corps, somebody said. When did they start calling it the foreign service? Sounds like the french foreign legion!

That was about the time Chandra came to me in the office during lunch break. "I got something I gotta ask you," she said.

I put my pen down, pushed my glasses up on my forehead. "Yes?"

"You done built a mighty fine home for your uncle and aunt."

"Thanks, Chandra. I think so, too."

She cleared her throat. She was a big-boned, awkward woman with fat, pouting lips and a tendency to avoid looking you in the eye when she was nervous. "Well, I was wondering if I could maybe ask..." She started coughing.

"Come on, Chandra. Get it out. Neither of us have all day."

"Well, do you think we could build me and my mother something, too. I don't mean brick or nothing, and it could be a lot smaller."

"I've been thinking about that myself," I said. "What I decided was..." I couldn't help smiling then, "that's exactly what we need to do. It'll be the next project on the side for our company."

Chandra's look was enough to make anybody feel they had done a good deed. Tears began to stream down her cheeks. She tried to speak but then turned and hurried away. I guess that our company's policy of getting every employee into his or her own house started about then.

We built Chandra's house on the lot next door to Aunt Ida Mae's. She had proved herself, as far as I was concerned. I already thought she was good enough to take over from Uncle Cajus when he got too infirm to foreman the yard.

I heard about Harry Dale just by accident when I came into the store after my weekly two days at the Madison store. I had come in through the feed room, and it was after hours, so I was surprised when I heard men talking. I stopped at the double-doors that led from the feed room into the main store.

"I just thought you ought to know what they are saying out there, Mr. Amos."

"I done always maintained that I don't take kindly to people trying to mind my business, Marlon. But I appreciate you coming in here to tell me."

"Well, I don't have nothing against *her*. You know I helped her get Henry Hall in that night when he was murdered?"

"I remember."

"You might just take a look. She's got nothing but Negroes out there helping her in the lumberyard. It's just that everybody'd feel better about it if there was a couple of white men working, too. White men need jobs, too, Mr. Amos. You know that."

"Yes, I know that."

"And now Harry Dale's done gone off and got hisself a job in Atlanta and left everybody in the lurch down here." Marlon's voice was plaintive, "And when you think about all this town's done for him. It just goes to show you that the nigger ain't grateful. You can't do enough for him."

"I don't see we done too much for him, Marlon."

"He had the best job in the county! But, anyway, ain't nobody rich around here, and everybody has to fend for hisself, Mr. Amos.

You know that. You done well yourself without no help from nobody."

"You say he had the best job in the county, Marlon, but that was because he was qualified for it. They went out and hired him to come here. If anything he was doing us a favor. But lemme tell you, I ain't helping any of them out there working for us neither. They earn their keep, believe me."

"They're just saying looks like since you get lots of your business from whites, you'd have at least one white working."

I stepped in at that juncture. "Oh, good evening, Sheriff."

"Good evening, Folly," he said, tipping his hat and then looking a little sheepish, like the boy discovered with his hand in the cookie jar. "Well, I was just going. I guess you been out working the stores or something?"

"Yes, I sure have, Sheriff. I'll let you out," I said. When I got back Mr. Amos was deep in thought. "I heard what he said about needing to hire a white person," I said.

"Oh," Mr. Amos said like he was just waking up from a long nap. "Yes." He stretched and yawned. "How'd it look?"

"We're on schedule in Madison. Jim's got two men working that territory already. The problem's just keeping the organization ahead of demand, that's all. Getting people isn't easy. I fired the second assistant manager yesterday."

"What was wrong?"

"Not dependable. Hal just can't depend upon him to pitch in when he's needed. You have to tell him everything."

"Anybody in mind?"

I shook my head. "We're interviewing next week. I guess I'll have to use an extra day there. Say Monday or Tuesday?"

"That's fine. We got things covered here and in Thomson."

"I thought I'd hire a white guy. Just haven't found any who'd take orders from a nigra woman," I said.

"It's okay. I understand. Don't pay no 'tention to them, you hear. They gotta admit that whites is about as sorry as any colored you can find. Maybe worse."

"Yes, when it rains, they call in and say they can't come to work cause the roads are too muddy. But we really do need to find somebody. It just isn't easy. Nobody wants to work for a Negro foreman and a female Negro boss here in Lawsonville. They're making noises about us hiring, but then they rag anybody who'll stoop to work for us."

"I know somebody," Mr. Amos said. I could tell that, even with his poker face set, he had something new up his sleeve.

"Yeah, who?"

"Judy Anne Fitts."

"Judy Anne Fitts," I said. The freckled face tomboy who belonged to Miss Sarah Fitts who worked at the café. Her younger sister was twice as smart and four times as fat, but Judy Anne was one of those outdoor types who break track records in high school, have a clear, clean, toothy smile that exudes good humor and don't know what to do with themselves.

"She's just been hanging around since graduation last year."

"What's she doing?"

"They said she went off to college in August and then came home. Nobody knows why. She was lifeguard at the Little Lake this past summer."

"Can you call her in and we'll talk to her?"

"Why don't you go talk to her?"

"Is she prejudiced?"

"Let's see."

So, not wanting to let anything slide (my motto is do it now if it can be done), I biked over to Judy Anne's mother's trailer the next morning after I knew Miss Sarah had gone to serve breakfast at the café.

Judy Anne came out rubbing her eyes. I had never taken much notice of her. She was about nineteen, I guessed, and she looked more like a man than most men do. She was wearing blue jeans and a checkered shirt. Her hair was short and, when she stopped rubbing her eyes, you could see they were hazel.

She looked at me with undisguised surprise, then looked at my bike. "Hey. What you doing over here this early?"

"It's not early," I said.

"Oh, I guess I overslept," Judy Anne said as she took a quick glimpse at her watch.

"Overslept? You got anywhere to go this morning?"

She looked surprised again. "No."

"Not working anywhere?"

"No," Judy Anne answered. "Not working, ain't got no money."

"I got a job for you if you aren't scared of what the town says about you working for a nigger gal."

"Who's the nigger gal?"

"Me."

Judy Anne blinked twice and then started laughing. "You're Folly Steeples. I know you. You're making all that money with them stores and building stuff and such."

"That's me."

"So you want me to work for you?"

"Mr. Hendricks and me. We do. We need to get a white person trained who'll work with us coloreds. We hear people are talking about us not having any whites in the lumber yard."

Judy Anne's eyes brightened. She tucked her thumbs in the pockets of her jeans. "Hey, that'd be working outside."

"Yes," I said. "There be physical labor involved. You'd get to learn to drive the delivery truck, too."

"Hey, you got Chandra working for you, don't you?"

"That's right."

"Sounds like a good idea to me. I know Chandra. Me and her is friends."

"You'll give it a try, Judy Anne?"

"When do I start?"

"Now."

She didn't even ask how much we'd pay. Neither did she comb her hair. She just ran her fingers through her short, black hair, shut the trailer up and walked back to the store with me pushing my bike.

Harry Dale, I was told, had landed a job with the State Department of Education in Atlanta. Shortly after he got settled, Rhonda Dale saw fit to join him. February had been a cold month that year, but March was unseasonably hot.

At the end of her second week, I asked Judy Anne if anybody in town had harassed her about working for a colored female. "You mean because you're a woman or because you're colored," she asked.

"Either."

"Listen, do you think I give a fart what anybody says. I been ragged since I can remember by everybody and his brother."

Now I was surprised. "You have?"

"You didn't know?"

"No, I'm sorry. What's the problem? You seem fine to me."

"Yeah, well I didn't know what it was till I went off to college. I mean, I knew it was because I look and walk so much like a boy and all. You've seen me. That's what everybody says."

"Mr. Amos said you were a tomboy."

"Yeah, well it's more'n that. I'm like a boy, Fol. I've always wanted to be a boy, too, I guess. I'm queer that way. Can't help it."

"So people picked on you?"

"Well, I get ragged. The men rag me, and the girls – well, it depends. Some of them don't like me at all. Others don't mind."

"I'm sorry, Judy Anne."

"Aw, I tell you, it ain't bothered me so terribly much, I guess. I can't do nothing about it. Anyway, I like working here, Folly. Me and Chandra, we're good friends."

"Well, Judy Anne, you're doing fine. You been with us two weeks, and we're mighty happy to have you in the family."

"Thanks, Folly." She looked down a little shyly at her feet. Her freckles stood out like a constellation of brown against the pale of her skin. "I 'preciate you thinking of me when you needed help. I couldn't make up my mind to do anything, and then you just come and knocked on the door that morning. Thanks."

So everything seemed to be going really well and then the state representative killed himself by chopping a tree down that fell on him. The next thing we knew, Jim came to tell us he wanted to run for the seat. That was March the thirtieth. "Why'd you want to do a damn fool thing like that," Mr. Hendricks asked more vehemently than we were used to.

"I been planning to do something like this a long time," Jim explained.

"What? Get into politics?" Mr. Amos looked for the world like somebody had just told him the world was really flat. "I can't figure why anybody in his right mind would do that. Especially when business is going so good."

"Folly, you tell him," Jim said, looking over at me.

I decided not to make it easy on him. I just shrugged. "What should I say? I agree with Mr. Hendricks. Seems like a damned fool thing to me, too."

"Come on, Fol! Don't do this to me. Of course you know. We talked about it lots. Don't you remember? Sure you do! Anyway, it won't take much away from the business. Being a state legislator isn't a full time job. I can keep on running sales, and I intend to." He looked at us and added, "If it's okay with y'all, of course."

Mr. Amos shook his head. "What's the point, boy?"

"Well, it can't hurt our business if I'm up in Atlanta some of the year. Have you both thought of that? I'll be making contacts that can't hurt as we grow."

"Wait a minute. Are you saying that politicians can help us run our business? No, sir. We don't need no help from politicians. I ain't never had no help from nobody. I've always run my business the way I saw fit."

"Mr. Amos," Jim pleaded.

"Son, the only folks that go into politics is them that's too lazy to do anything else or them that wants to meddle in other folks' business. There's also them that wants a free handout."

"Folly, tell him that's not entirely true."

I shook my head. "As far as I can tell, it comes pretty close to the truth, Jim."

"Aw, hell, you're no help, sport. Well, you both can just get used to the idea," he concluded.

Jim was right, of course. Ultimately, the decision was his and not ours. There was no way to stop him from running, no matter what we said. I knew he'd been programming himself for something like this since he was a boy. Maybe even since he was born.

On April the fourth at 6:01 p.m. somebody gunned down Reverend Martin Luther King in Memphis. Those are the bare facts. There's hardly any way to clothe them in the emotional truth of what happened.

There was a glint in the eyes of some white people as the news was spread. They had thought of him as a nuisance and troublemaker. Some gunman had done the thing many of them had hoped for and swept him from the scene.

Us coloreds felt like it had happened again. Once again they had pulled the rug out from under us, brought down our champion. There's no way I can put it into words, and it wasn't just that one man was dead, just another imperfect man, even with all his courage and determination. It was so much more than that that the whole world couldn't contain everything you'd have to write about it to get it right.

None of this phased Jim very much, and we had to keep on working, of course. A few weeks later he strode in on me at my weekly working stop at the Madison store. He was his old jaunty self, graceful without trying, handsome without seeming aware of it. "Hey, sport!" he hailed me.

I was checking the books as he came walking in accompanied by our manager. "Jim," I said, laying the pen down. I couldn't help but be glad to see him, no matter what, no matter where, and he knew it.

He came over and mussed my hair like I was his pet dog or something. "You're looking good, you know that."

"Okay, what do you want," I laughed.

"Come on, I'm glad to see you."

"I'll accept that as sincere, but there's some other reason you planned to intercept me on the day you knew I'd be here —without telling me in advance."

He slid down on the desk so close I could breathe on him. "Well, you remember how we used to talk, and I'd say we'd do it together."

"Do what together?"

"The political thing."

"I don't remember."

"Oh yes you do. And now I'm asking you."

"Asking me what?"

"I need you to be my liaison with the colored community."

"Well, the first thing you've got to learn is that people don't call themselves colored any more," I shot back.

"Negro then?"

"No. Maybe a few old folks. The word is Afro-American now, Jim. Pay attention."

"Aw, come on. I intend to. You're my intermediary, my contact, my way in."

"That's putting a heavy burden on me."

"Not really, sport. It's just a little legislative campaign. It's not like I'm running for governor – yet!"

I looked up and, sure enough, he was grinning from ear to ear. A big chessy cat grin. And he looked so handsome it would have melted iron.

"Why do you need the Afro-American vote?"

"Come on, kid. Count the heads in this district. If I have the colored vote, and the community is really mobilized, I can win hands down. Because I'm getting the white vote, anyway."

"Will you have opposition?"

"Probably, but I don't know yet for sure."

"You'll get the Afro-American vote, anyway, if some racist cracker runs against you. I won't even have to work to mobilize it for you."

"May be true. May not. Can't take any chances. This is too important."

"Why is it so important?"

"Fol, this is the first step. Anyway, I don't like to start something unless I know I can finish it."

I could understand that. In that way, Jim and I were exactly alike. "The first step where?"

"Into history."

I almost groaned, but I stopped myself. It wasn't like it was the first time I'd heard it, and I wanted to be loyal to Jim. I wanted very much to be loyal, though I can't tell you why.

XVIII

"Guess who I saw in town yesterday," Walt Cross's voice came crisply through the wire.

"I can't guess. But you're phoning long distance from Atlanta, aren't you, so something must be going on. How did you know you'd find me here?"

"I tried the other stores. Mr. Hendricks said you'd be in Madison this morning."

"And you went to all this trouble to tell me you saw somebody in town we both know?" I pulled a leaf off my daily calendar. It was the middle of a relatively mild May, nineteen hundred and sixty-eight.

"Oh, no. I was going to call you, anyway."

"Who was it?"

"Who was what?"

"Don't play with me, Walt. The person you saw in Atlanta."

"Laura Lawson."

"Laura," I said. "Laura Lawson. How do you know her?"

"I thought that might interest you. She was your former mistress, wasn't she?"

"I don't think I'd have called her that, Walt. Why do you think she was my mistress, anyway?"

"Well, your aunt and uncle were house servants at Lawson Hall."

I forgot that Walt had spent a lot of time in Lawsonville and that he had both an ear trained to pick up lots of information about a place and a keen mind to put it all together. "Okay. Conceded. So you saw Laura Lawson in Atlanta. Is that supposed to be some kind of news worth phoning me long distance about when I haven't heard from you in how long?"

"Well, it's also an excuse for calling you."

"I'm flattered."

"You should be. I'd be a great catch."

"My heart is fluttering madly."

"Word is that Laura is getting a divorce."

"You call her 'Laura'? Do you have designs on her, Walt?"

"Silly girl. Remember I'm a racialist. I only date Afro-Americans. Just thought you might want to know. I got the feeling you didn't like her and were pretty glad to have her out of the state."

"Your perspicacity is impressive. Someday I'm going to ask you to explain this new coinage of yours."

"What?"

"Racialist."

"Yeah, we need to talk about that – some other time, Fol." I could tell the real reason for the call was about to be revealed to me. Walt had assumed such a casual, by-the-way tone, "What is this I hear about you stumping for Jim Hall?"

I picked the pen back up and began to doodle in the margins of the paper I was working on. "Do you know Jim?"

"Not really. I understand he's working for you?"

"He's an old, old friend, Walt."

"Old friend. Is that what he is? And a business partner, too, I hear. I've wondered about that. He's working with you now, isn't he? White guy, of course."

"Well, if you want to know his ethnicity, I think he might be one part Jewish, the rest is sharecropper, white trash, and redneck."

"Not a happy mix, Fol."

"It doesn't sound like you like Jim, Walt."

"I don't know him, but I've already got more than one reason not to like him, don't I. First, he works with you, and you admit that he is a good friend. The thing is, we are thinking about running our own man. It's a real opportunity to get a black man in. Especially now, in the wake of Dr. King's murder. It'd be good for black morale, Folly."

"You may as well forget it, Walt. Jim is going to win."

"Folly, this is just what we'd been waiting for. A seat in the legislature is vacated in a district in which the white and black vote is split fairly even."

"What about a district in which the black vote is a majority. Then you'd really have it in the bag."

"Tell me where there's such a district. There are no such districts, Folly."

"Why not. Lawson County is sixty percent colored. Maybe more."

"Yes, but those districts are conveniently arranged to provide a slim white majority. This is the only one where the odds would be good for us."

"Let me tell you something, Walt Cross," I heard myself saying.

"Yeeees," he said with heavy dignity.

"You won't beat Jim Hall."

"Why not?"

"Demographics. There isn't an Afro-American majority, as you say, and lots of black people don't vote. Plus, when I get through telling them what Jim believes and what he plans, those that vote will be voting for him."

"What do you mean?"

"I've known Jim for years, and he's one of three white people I've ever known who are totally colorblind."

"Who are the other two?"

"My partner, Amos Hendricks, for one. Then there's Judy Anne who works for me."

"Okay. So he's colorblind. That makes him an unusual white guy for Georgia. But what will he do for us?"

"Jim told me years ago that he wanted to get into politics so he could do away with discriminatory institutions."

"Years ago? You're talking about a very young guy, Folly."

"I've known him since I was a child. He rescued me more than once. Once from black girls beating me up, by the way."

"All right. I'll admit it. Some black people are pains in the ass, too. So he's had this plan that long, huh?"

"His father was a kind of maverick here in Lawson County. My mother was his lover."

"Good grief. Things run deep in Georgia, don't they!"

"So don't think you're talking me into anything, Walt. I'm on Jim's side."

"Are you in love with him, then?"

"God, Walt, you know how to be blunt, don't you. Is that the Yankee way?"

"No, but when a man needs to know something, it doesn't pay to waste time being politic. Well...?"

"It's none of your business – but no," I lied. "Jim wants to represent the Afro-American community, too. He's on our side, Walt. He protected me as a little girl. He's against segregation."

"That's hard to believe. I'm not saying I don't believe you, but I'm just wondering what your real relationship to this guy is?"

"We're in business together. We've been long term friends."

"Yeah, I know. Your mother was his father's lover and so forth. This is one of those Southern novels. What's the Gothic angle, Folly? Is this all straightforward and naturalistic?"

"You can forget putting anybody up. I'm already started."

"Yeah, I know. We've heard about your work. Look, I'll be up front with you, Fol, you're highly respected in the black community. No doubt. You're the big success. People look up to you. More than you probably know."

"If it's at all it's more than I know," I said.

"Now why hasn't this Jim fellow made any public pronouncements about his views on segregation?"

"You'd like that, wouldn't you, Walt? That'd be political death, wouldn't it? Then Jim would be out of the way."

There was a long silence. I looked at the receiver and frowned. Then I heard Walt speaking, "I've got to think about this."

"Sure, think it over. Let me suggest something."

"Okay."

"Arrange a meeting with Jim. You'll be satisfied."

"That's a good idea. Let me see what I can do."

"It all has to be off the record."

"I'm a realist, Folly. I know that Jim Hall can be elected, especially with the pride and joy of the black community backing him. Your support is an endorsement everybody would trust. If he works for us, that's something we've gained. It's not the same as getting the first black in office, but it's important. I wouldn't tell this to anybody else."

"Let me know when and where," I said.

"I'll get back to you." Walt hesitated, "Folly, do you love him?"

"Walt, I said it's none of your business but no."

"I heard the words, but that's not the way it all looks. This is important to me."

"So important I haven't seen you in months, right? Goodbye, Walt."

Click. Laura Lawson was back in Georgia. Why couldn't she stay in Boston or in Southeast Asia? Knowing Lawson Hall was sitting up on its hill above the town like a collapsing dowager, abandoned and empty, had freed me from a lot of private ghosts.

Now she was back. Back on the scene. But what was I afraid of? What could she do to me? That was just it. I didn't know. What I knew is, if there was any way to hurt me, Laura would find it.

I seesawed back and forth like that over the next couple of weeks. My rational mind told me that Laura was impotent to hurt me. My increasing success was based on a business totally beyond any sphere of influence she could possibly command. My fortune was growing not merely steadily but by leaps and bounds, and it depended upon abilities I myself brought to bear and could continue to bring to bear to complex tasks. There was nothing she could do.

Still, whoever thought that fear or dread had anything to do with reason? No matter how clearly I thought the whole business out and made it clear to myself that Laura was harmless, that she could never more put nails in my way or stretch a wire across the path in front of me, well, the more I worried. Her presence in Atlanta disestablished the fundament of a life I had been constructing a long time.

I was present at the meeting two weeks later when Jim went secretly to Atlanta. Being incognito is still easy when you are an obscure candidate for a rural legislative seat. We had, nevertheless, to be very careful. Georgia was a small place in those days.

Sometimes you were very surprised to discover who knew whom. News circulated very rapidly by word of mouth.

We looked for an address in an older building just off Auburn Avenue not a quarter of a mile from downtown. When we found it, we had trouble finding a parking space. Jim and I were still true children of the country and found the traffic and noise of Atlanta disorienting.

We passed several parking lots because the price on the signs seemed too high. Finally, we found ourselves circling around and coming back to a lot that lay about two blocks from the meeting place.

Once we had parked we had trouble figuring out the system to pay. There were no attendants. All that we found was a sort of big metal box with little slots and numbers attached to them. It looked like people stuffed the money for the parking into the slots.

I couldn't believe they were using a system that primitive in Atlanta, but we finally had to admit that was the way it worked. Jim took his pocketknife and pushed in the three one-dollar bills. Then we started out walking.

It was early July, and the two blocks along baking pavement laid wide open to the sun left us soaked in sweat by the time we reached the lobby. Lobby is, perhaps, too dignified a word for the dirty space just inside the building. There was no directory posted, the air was utterly sultry, dripping moisture. The elevator creaked and groaned as it lifted us up to the third story.

When we stepped out, we entered a large room crowded with people absorbed in frenzied activity. The clickety-clack of typewriters and buzz of conversation welled up towards us like a heat wave, almost driving us back into the shelter of the elevator. We resisted the temptation to turn tail and leave. Despite it all, we stood our ground and valiantly surveyed the bustling scene before us.

These were mostly young people, typing, running back and forth with papers in their hands. Engaged in intense conversation, some speaking loudly into telephones. Their faces had that high seriousness that young people get when they feel they're doing something important to history.

"Folly!" Walt spotted us and maneuvered between the aisles, dodging young women who were dashing about with papers in their hands.

"Walt Cross, this is Jim Hall," I said too eagerly as he approached. All jittery nerves, I stood to the side and watched the two men measure each other as they shook hands.

"Come on back," Walt said, turning to me. "I'll get the others in. We're glad you came. Pretty hot, isn't it?"

Remember that this was pre-air conditioning. Big fans were blowing hard from every side of the room, yet the air still hung thick and sultry, drawing sweat oozing out of places you didn't even know had glands.

We followed Walt down a hall to a conference room. He then went out, excusing himself. Not long after a very shapely woman just this side of plump moved into the room. She had straightened her hair and parted it just to the right of center, and she wore a very bright lipstick.

"Hi, y'all," she said. She went straight to Jim and took his hand, "I'm just so glad to meet you. I'm Krishina."

"Hi, I'm Jim," Jim said.

She was very top-heavy with buttocks that thrust out behind far enough to make a shelf on her rear at the base of her spine. "Krishina," I said, "could you check to see where Walt has gone." I tapped my watch. "We don't have a lot of time."

I couldn't tell whether she smiled or sneered, "Yes, honey. Be right back."

Just as Krishina left, the same burly man I saw preach in Lawsonville before the big civil rights march strode in. "Folly Steeples," he boomed. As he smiled, his mouth pushed back great fat rolls in both cheeks that gathered up and nearly hid his eyes. He advanced on me and I stood up. Without warning he grabbed my hand and began to pump. He gripped my arm hard with his other hand and said, "We've been hearing so much about you, sister."

Since I hadn't been to church regularly for the last five years, I felt a little uncomfortable with the 'sister' thing. I decided to let it pass, though. "And you are," I said looking him over carefully.

He seemed genuinely taken aback at my not recognizing him. "Why, honey, I'm Reverend Washington. Dr. King's right-hand man."

"Oh, of course," I said. He was a fairly big lieutenant in Walt's organization, maybe a brigadier general. "I should have known."

He actually wrinkled his nose and strutted around me, "That's fine, my girl, we're all so proud of you."

"What have I done?"

"Why," he boomed, "you're blazing pioneering trails of entrepreneurial achievement, sister. Trails of pioneering entrepreneurial achievement. We need more models like you: Afro-American women who are successful in business."

Reverend Washington went to the head of the conference table and started to take his seat. He moved jauntily for his size and weight. Catching sight of Jim, he said, "Why you must be the young man who's running for representative."

His studied condescension was put on a bit thick, I thought, but Jim rose as graciously as ever, "Yes, sir, I am." He took the necessary steps over to shake Reverend Washington's fat hand. They exchanged a few remarks that were markedly less than sincere on the good Reverend's part.

About that time Walt came back with a tray of lemonade. "Something for the heat," he announced.

Krishina was behind him, and she gave a little girl clap and beamed about the room like she had committed magic and created the lemonades right before our eyes. Then she helped Walt hand the glasses and napkins around. She spent a lot of time giving Jim his.

I took a sip of the fruity liquid, and it did my soul good. The nearly two hour drive from Lawson County in the heat had taken its toll. Then we'd walked from the parking lot, as well. That wasn't easy in hundred-degree weather when the humidity was as thick as a Turkish bath.

We settled down to business fast as Reverend Washington leaned over toward Jim and said, "You know we had planned to place a candidate, too."

"I don't think that's necessary, sir" Jim said deferentially but also with confidence.

"Now," Reverend Washington wondered, a chuckle percolating somewhere beneath the surface of his mighty bass, "why wouldn't that be necessary?"

Jim leaned over the table toward him, just as he had done us: "I ask myself why you'd want to have a candidate when you've got me. You and I are agreed on what we believe, so Folly tells me."

"Is that so," Reverend Washington said, nodding and casting a benign glance my way. "Now that's what we want to hear. That's what we want to hear."

"Well, I am determined to represent all the citizens in my district, black or white. And I know, as any sane man ought, that black citizens need a lot of representing!"

"That is so. That is so," Reverend Washington intoned. Then he cleared his throat and asked, "How do you understand that, Mr. Hall?"

"I mean it from the bottom of my heart," Jim said. "Whatever it takes to move this state forward, we have to change things. And the first thing we have to change is the inequality between our citizens because of the color of their skin."

"Like what," Walt interjected.

Jim turned to Walt. "I think we all know what we're talking about. The legal status quo is being forced by federal intervention to change. Dr. King's martyrdom assures that it'll happen sooner rather than later, gentlemen. Still, there's lots to be done. And I hope to work my way into a place where I can help the process along."

"And how do you propose to do that?"

"It's not something you can just answer in a sentence," Jim said, "There are more policies and issues than we can discuss in one day, and we can't predict how the agenda will be worked out. At this point it's intent that's at issue. My intent is the same as yours."

"How do you propose to serve us and your white constituency. Isn't there a contradiction there?"

"I'll tell you frankly that there are things that can't yet be discussed. I want to avoid somebody pulling out the race card on either side of the fence. I want to work to unify and not divide. But it doesn't matter what public office I achieve, I won't tolerate racism. Period. It isn't in the interest of either whites or blacks."

The meeting went on in that vein for some time. It got hotter and hotter in the room. The fans churned away, but they were just stirring the thick, sultry air. We opened the doors. That didn't help. Finally, when everybody was close to exhaustion, we decided we understood each other.

Jim waited until we were nearly to Covington before he jumped up and down in the car seat and hollered, "Yahoo! We did it, sport! We wrapped up the colored vote."

"Don't count your chickens yet," I warned. "All we did there is make sure they wouldn't provide opposition."

"Oh, I know. You still need to go around to all the churches and talk to the folks. But it's sewn up now. You can do it, too, sport." He leaned over and kissed my cheek.

"We still have to be careful. Word on this meeting can't get out."

"It won't. They knew what I was talking about. They won't let it happen. And you," he said, turning to me, "are the heart of discretion, my dear, beloved friend."

Jim was right, too. I met a lot of people. I found my reception much warmer and more supportive after that meeting in Atlanta than before; yet, there was not the tiniest suspicion among white voters.

The whites loved Jim as their candidate, their native son. He was a farmer's son, one after their own hearts. He held barbeques and moved among the crowds like people expected of the son of a local farmer. He spoke their language, knew how to swap stories, laugh, kiss babies, encourage people. They loved him.

We had expected the cracker candidate to announce in late July. When nothing happened we knew we had the election in the bag. It was a cinch. All we could figure is that the old segregationist hard-liners decided Jim was one of them, or wasn't a threat and that there was no need to run against him.

It was all going according to plan. Jim blossomed. He loved campaigning. He was a natural, in his element. Watching him I knew where his real devotion lay. He wouldn't stop at the legislature. He was in it for the long haul to as near as he could get to the top. Luck and circumstance would see how far that would be.

XIX

"Congratulations, good-looking," Walt said.

"You came all the way from Atlanta to congratulate me," I smiled.

"Well, I heard you were opening the biggest store yet," he said. He made a display of looking around, "Very impressive, too."

"This is the fourth. Lawsonville, Madison, Thomson, and now Augusta. Let me introduce you to my manager. She's over here. Judy Anne!"

Walt turned to me. His tone changed from fun to serious. He took my hands in his, "You're really remarkable, Folly. Do you know that?"

"Is this where you propose," I laughed.

"Yes m'aam," Judy Anne called, coming around some corner.

"Come over here and meet Mr. Cross."

Judy Anne hustled over. She wore our trademark apron in purple with a big H&S emblazoned in white across the front. "How do," she said, thrusting out her hand in her manly fashion.

Walt stepped back slightly, but he took her hand. "Good to meet you, Miz…"

"This is Judy Anne Fitts," I said.

"Miz Fitts."

"It's Miss, sir. Just plain miss," Judy Anne said.

"Nice store," Walt said.

"Oh, it's a humdinger. It's the best yet," Judy Anne agreed.

Without any further ado, Walt turned back to me, "Look, can I ask you to take me seriously for a minute."

"Judy Anne, how is that going back there in garden supplies," I asked. His summary dismissal of Judy Anne angered me.

"Oh, got that under control," Judy Anne beamed.

"Okay. I'll be with you shortly," I said.

"Sure thing," Judy Anne said, and then she bustled off.

"I thought you were hiring Afro-Americans," Walt accused.

"Hey, white people get a chance here, too. Don't forget that. I'm color blind."

"Don't be too color blind."

"You run your show, and I'll run mine," I snapped.

"Not the right tone for a guy who did you a big favor."

"You mean—" For a minute I tried to think of his meaning. I was not accustomed to owing anybody for favors. "Sure." I got my face straight and looked up at him. His expression had turned tender. I had seen intelligence, combativeness, eagerness, concern written in his distinct features before, but never tenderness. Not like in that moment. It got to me somewhere. I'm not sure where.

"Okay. Jim is going to win, Folly," Walt said. Like: hey, look what I've done for you.

"He doesn't have any opposition. Does he?"

"That's right."

"Thanks, Walt."

"No, there's nothing to thank me for. We have a deal."

"And Jim won't forget it."

"I don't believe he will. Because he wants to go further than just the state legislature."

"You think so?"

"Come on, Folly, of course I do. Your friend is a very ambitious man." He cleared his throat, "Fol, there's no future for you with him."

"I know that."

"Maybe you do. Maybe you do. But I don't think so. The woman's heart is a –"

I turned as if I would leave him standing there, "Don't start condescending to me, Walt Cross," I said.

"Let's go back to your office," he suggested as he looked around at my employees. Some of them had stopped and were watching us. I was for them a definite point of interest. That's the way it is being the boss of a growing operation. There is that sense of admiration, envy and dependence employees often feel towards you.

"Okay," I agreed.

So we went back to my office. "Fol, can I ask you out to dinner tonight?"

"Do you know that's the first time you've asked me out?"

"We've both been very busy. And we've lived in different places."

"We still do."

"Sit down over here," Walt said.

"You're giving the orders?"

"Please, Fol, be sweet. Don't be so on your guard."

"Maybe it isn't a bad idea to be on my guard," I said, but I followed him over and sat on the sofa. He sat facing me. I tried to look straight ahead, but that felt contrived, so I hiked my right leg up on the cushion and faced Walt as casually as I could.

"Now," he began, "this is promising. Where would you like to go to dinner?"

"Let's just make sure it's either completely integrated or black. I don't want us to go anywhere on our first date and get the treatment. I could pass, but you couldn't." I stared deliberately at his hair.

Walt laughed. "Okay, I know a place. It won't have the most elegant ambience, but the food is good, and we'll be safe."

"Tell me this, Walt."

"Yes?"

"Is this all preliminary to something more?"

"I hope so."

"I thought it might be."

He squeezed my hands gently in his. "I'm proud of you, Fol. Wait..." he held up his hand to stop me, "Let me just say simply and sincerely what I feel, okay."

"Is that ever a good idea," I asked. I decided to relax and play by his rules just to see where it led. I was tired of so much. "Okay," I agreed. "Be sincere and simple, Walt. I'll slack up a little, too."

We had supper in Augusta. The food was good. It was a black restaurant. Walt was the perfect gentleman. I was sleeping in my office, as usual; had my sleeping bag there. He was surprised when I told him where to drive me.

"You sleep in the office?"

"I always sleep in the offices of my stores. I have a little washbasin and everything right there. Toilet."

"Shower?"

"I built one in the Madison store, but I forgot to do that here."

"How will you shower?"

"Oh, I'll wash up. Right out of the basin."

Walt thought about that. "That must take a lot of time. Isn't it a lot of trouble?"

"Not really. I'm already at work, anyway."

"Jim is out of your system?"

"Jim? Why do you keep bringing him up?"

"Did he invite you to the Milledgeville shindig for all the white supporters?" I hesitated replying. I was irritated with myself for letting Walt know so plainly that I had not been. "I thought not. Well, it's all part of politics, of course. You couldn't expect him to invite any of his black supporters, no matter how important they were to the effort."

The evening was spoiled after that. I was angry with Walt for letting me know, and I wasn't sure how I felt about Jim for not inviting me. I stewed about it for a couple of days.

Look, I told myself, Jim has never pretended. What did he say about us? What could a person do with a colored wife? It was a good question, a question for Hard Reality. He had been right, too. That question had to be answered before anything could happen between us.

Result: Nothing happened, and nothing ever would.

How did Walt sense how I felt about Jim? Was it so obvious? Yet, it was important to him, if he was really interested in me. I could see that. He'd have to know before he started getting involved with me – for his sake, if nothing else.

Still, I came back to a churning in my stomach about the upcoming Milledgeville festivities. Especially since I talked to Jim often about business. It was unavoidable. He worked for me and ran an important part of my business.

That Monday I read in the Augusta paper about the Milledgeville fete. It was planned for the coming Saturday evening. Wednesday Jim was supposed to meet me back in Lawsonville for our weekly powwow early in the afternoon.

Driving over from Augusta took me a little more than an hour. I wasn't at all sure Jim would show up. It would be easier for him just to make some excuse and telephone. When I saw his company car parked out front of the store, I wasn't sure how I felt, but I knew my blood started pumping.

I drove around back, parked in my old space near the office of the supply depot and walked to the loading dock of the old store. I heard Jim talking inside. He was jawing with other men.

First I hesitated; then I put my right foot on the bottom step and started up. When I swung around the corner, Jim and three other masculine faces turned my way. "Hey, sport," he said.

The other two men nodded, mumbled less articulate greetings of their own and then shuffled away. "How about this! How did our first week in the big store go?"

"Fine," I said, trying to sound bright and cheerful.

We strolled in to the drink cooler and got ourselves an RC just like we'd always done. Our business meetings were routine. We'd been working together for a long time. Jim knew exactly what to tell me. I didn't even have to ask any questions. He was a wizard of organization and motivating his salesmen.

The meeting took us about thirty-eight minutes. I timed it, as I always had. "Are we on time," he said, grinning.

"Yes."

"Precision is your middle name, isn't it, Fol."

"Time is money," I agreed.

"There's gonna be a shindig in Milledgeville Saturday. Bunch of women, wives of my supporters, are putting it together. But I can bring somebody. Want to come along?"

Hope springs ever fresh in the human heart, I thought as I felt my whole being begin to soar. Cool it, Folly, I urged myself. "What time is it," I asked.

"We're supposed to get there about seven. It's formal. Got anything formal?"

I laughed at the deadpan expression with which he posed the question. "What do you think," I said.

"Yeah, me neither. I'm buying a used tux in Athens. Costing me a hundred and fifty bucks. But I figure I may be needing it again."

"I'll get something. How are you billing me?"

"My aide-de-camp," Jim said.

"Isn't it a little dangerous being seen with a colored girl?"

"Nobody can tell."

"You have a blind side you definitely will have to work on if you want to go far in politics," I said.

It was Jim all over again: One side cautious and shrewd, the other side wildly reckless. Still, I was thrilled. There's no other way to put it. The old cliché will do.

I got myself a three-hundred-dollar gown. That seemed a lot of money to me in 1969. I had practically nothing but casual wear and work clothes, and I was worth roughly three hundred thousand, so I figured I could afford it.

The party took place in one of those Corinthian-columned showplaces from the big cotton days in the 1850s, everything on the outside dazzling white with Cadillacs parked all around. Cadillacs were the luxury auto of choice in those days.

In the meantime, I had found out that these were Jim's core supporters who had also bankrolled his campaign. It was a dual celebration for another win in another district, so that put the importance of Jim's victory into perspective.

We wended our way to the front door and were greeted by a committee of Junior League types who peeped and screeched over us. "We've been just dying to meet you, Folly," the lead screech told me.

It seems Jim had been bold enough to tell them about me. I was not only the person who delivered the black vote (for which they were all bubbling with gratitude), but I was an up-and-coming entrepreneur and, being of the colored variety, something, I took it, of a new phenomenon.

These were "progressive" young people. Many of them, it turned out, had gone to school in the Nawth, and they had returned home anxious to get on with modernizing Georgia. Jim suited them to a "t" because he had qualifications which they did not (he was a child of the people) and, yet, he shared their progressivist views on everything from economics to civil rights.

I found myself being a little bit lionized along with Jim. We had to talk a journalist from Atlanta out of doing a feature on us. "No yet," Jim told him. "Not yet, Don. Wait until I run for governor." He patted the man on the shoulder, "hey, you're the first who heard it, too."

"Okay," Don said. "I know what you mean. Too early, huh?"

How many vain politicians did the man have to humor to do his job? He was good at it, and it gave me a little mini-interview for future reference, he said. He thought I'd figure in a future issue of the business news. He had a friend on the editorial staff.

When Don was finishing up our interview, he suddenly said, "Excuse me, Miss Steeples, I see Laura Lawson over there. I'll have to try to speak to her. Thanks a million, and I'll keep in touch, all right?"

"Sure," I said.

It didn't matter what I said, Don was gone. I followed him with my eyes as he moved through the crowd. At the far end near the front door a knot of people –chiefly men – had gathered. I couldn't see Laura Lawson, but somehow I could feel her presence.

When I located Jim talking to a couple of balding, corpulent chairmen-of-the-board types with cigars (people smoked at parties then), I scurried over. "Gentlemen, let me introduce the brains of my campaign, Miss Folly Steeples."

"Ah, partner in Hendricks-Steeples Building Supplies," the largest of the two men said, heaving back and thrusting his belly out toward me in a friendly gesture.

"Folly, this is Mr. George Greer. He runs Ivy-Lane."

We got through the usual exchange of basic information about each other, and then I got to tell Jim that Laura was there.

"Laura Lawson," Jim said. He was already all but standing on tiptoe to look around the room.

"She's over by the front door," I said, wondering why I was telling him anything about her whereabouts.

"Hey, okay. Thanks, sport." He shook one of the fat men's hands and was gone.

I had a little trouble disengaging from George Greer and finally had to say I needed to go to the restroom. I found a staircase and got up to about the third or fourth stair before I could see over the room and locate Jim.

Jim was moving through the crowd into Laura's vicinity. I could see her, too, regaling a circle of men with what appeared to be hilarious stories. Occasionally the men would open their mouths really wide, lean backwards and let out what people refer to as "gales of laughter."

Jim proceeded to elbow his way in. He was saying something. Laura turned to him. You could see that a couple of the men didn't like the way he had broken in. Then it became clear to everybody that Jim was one of the people being celebrated. That moment the tight knot of the crowd broke into fragments. These fragments began to float out and become absorbed in the generality.

Laura and Jim were left standing there together. They were talking like two people who'd known each other all their lives and were really pleased to meet again.

Laura opened her mouth and Jim nodded. She placed a hand on his arm. She leaned just ever so slightly toward him, just enough to make it look intimate. She had learned a lot in those Yankee schools.

I wondered where her Brahmin husband was. Probably at some diplomatic post in some awful, obscure little tropical place somewhere in Southeast Asia. He was probably busy doing things important to the national security.

Naturally, Laura Lawson wouldn't want to stay too long in places like that. Why should she when she could come back to Georgia and get into any respectable party anywhere from the Atlantic Ocean to the Alabama border? She was, after all, one of the very few aristocrats Georgia had.

I hurried back down the steps and meandered without really any particular destination in mind to the terrace. As I wandered on the terrace a chill, early autumn breeze penetrated my gown. I rubbed my upper-arms and felt hundreds of little chill-bumps raised.

"May I help you, m'aam," a gray-headed waiter asked. He was holding a tray.

"No, I don't care for anything, thanks," I answered.

"Gone get a little chilly tonight," he said.

"I'm afraid you're right. And I didn't bring a jacket."

"Well, that gentleman down there in that car," he pointed down into the jumble of cars. I saw the red taillights blazing. "He say he got a jacket for you, if you need it."

I looked at the waiter in alarm, "Who?"

"He say he know you." The waiter had one of those very wise African faces, and he was nodding gently. "He say you know him, too."

"Is his hair all puffy and sticking out," I asked.

"Oh, yes, m'aam. He have an Afro."

"Did he tip you to find me?"

The chuckle came percolating up, "He don't need to tip me. We all know him well around here. Yes, we shore do," he said, nodding.

"Thank you," I said. I hurried to the end of the terrace, stopped at the bottom of the steps and wondered if I was insane to be leaving a party to hurry to a waiting car of an unidentified man. As I ran along the grass, the car door opened. Walt hurried around to meet me.

All I had to do was run into his arms. As he picked me up, he said, "Have you had enough now?"

"How did you know I was here?"

"I figured. Wasn't sure but didn't want to take any chances."

"I'm chilly."

"I figured you might be. Somebody said that dress you bought was pretty thin material. I figured somebody who never wore anything but jeans wouldn't know how to pick out the right thing for the season."

"Where are we going?"

"I know a place where we can get some of the best fried catfish in Georgia."

XX

"Let's go," Walt said, and we both got into his car. It smelt new inside. When Walt turned on the headlights, the panel lights came on automatically and seemed as good as a warm fire to me.

I didn't ask any questions. I shut my eyes and leaned as close to him as I could, trusting him. After seeing how Jim Hall honed into Laura Lawson, it was nothing but salve to find Walt cared. Only when he stopped did I open my eyes again. There was nothing to see but darkness. As the motor died into the evening, a huge wave of silence washed over us. We both sat, staring sightlessly out the window a moment, comfortably together, and then we turned and embraced.

I had been so busy surviving during my twenty-eight odd years that I'd had no time for love. I guess there had been no men other than Jim I'd have been interested in, anyway. I just shut off my mind and was basking in the warmth of another desirable body against mine, arms that felt solid and strong wrapped around me. It was what I needed. I felt the tension draining out, down through my arms in little electrical currents, out my fingers, dissipating and leaving me rising into a great arc of relief.

"This is better than I'd ever thought it'd be," I whispered, a gurgle of joyous laughter coming from somewhere inside. How I was surprising myself, I thought.

"Yes," he sort of panted. I didn't like that. It didn't sound like Walt.

Walt seemed busier than I wanted him to be running his hands around me. I withheld the urge to tell him to stop and just sit still.

Then I felt a little jolt when I felt his hand edging towards my crotch. That meant he was under my evening dress. Or did it? I couldn't be sure. It was an odd thing.

I reached down and grabbed his hand (which was outside the dress) firmly, moving it away. It was with a sinking feeling when I realized my gesture had only made his frenzy worse. Walt was breathing heavily by that time. He was pressing me back against the passenger door. The metal handles thrust into my back and side, and it hurt. "Walt, this isn't comfortable," I whispered. It seemed to me he should know. I wasn't some sort of rag doll to be shoved about and squashed.

"We could get in the back," he said.

That was the first moment I wished I could see his face. I made the mistake of following him over the seat. I think we laughed as I fell into his arms, but humor vanished quickly from my heart as Walt's hands found their way back into my secret places. "No, Walt," I said. But he had somehow managed to loosen my bra. When his hands touched my breasts, he dropped all pretense. Our caressing became a wrestling match.

I tried to sit up more than once, but Walt pushed me back down. "Walt, let me up," I said.

"Sweet, sweet," he began in a low chant, "lovely woman. You don't know how much I need you, etc. etc."

"This hurts my back," I complained.

My rational statements were answered by a chanting: "Baby, you don't know how much I've been waiting for this. Baby, baby, ummm." I was a body in the dark for him, a desirable Any Woman or Every Woman.

Just as I was gathering my strength and anger was beginning to crescendo in my chest, Walt penetrated me. How he got that far was beyond me. I let out a startled cry, and then I sucked air like a person drowning. Walt was pumping me, but it didn't feel good at all. He was more like a piston than a person, and all he could do is grunt, "Good, good, good!" His orgasm came before my surprise had dissipated. He wretched over me, grunting like a pig. When he had finished, he simply rolled off me, half onto the floor of the car.

I lay there with every one of my nerve endings tingling with fury. Feeling carefully with my hands, I realized he had come in from the side, ripping my underpants. I felt them around my waist. He had never even taken them off, and I was sheer astonished that I could be so vulnerable, that I could be raped so quickly. As my astonishment began to boil into anger, Walt opened the backdoor and climbed out into the night. As he did that something jangled to the floor.

What was he about to do? I was totally baffled until I heard him off in the grass somewhere urinating. As the trickling sound of water reached me across the chill evening, my fingers touched the car keys lying on the floor carpet. They had fallen out of his pants pocket as he rolled over. Snatching them up, I was over the seat and under the wheel before I could think. A key thrust into the ignition, me stretching to shut the back door and to lock all the other doors, then the engine cranking smoothly, just like you'd expect a new car to do.

"What the hell," I heard Walt cry. By that time the car was rolling forward. When I pulled out the headlights, the beams thrust shafts of pale illumination into the dense evening. The grass was exposed before me but looked white, like an odd, dead turf. Walt was walking alongside the car, pressing his face against the window of my door, knocking on the metal. I ignored him, wondering where the road was. He began to rattle the door, so I pressed the accelerator. The car bumped over old furrows under the grass cover. Walt began to jog to keep up. "What are you doing," he kept screaming. His voice had that wail of helplessness mixed with anger.

"Where is the road," I asked myself aloud as I bent over the steering wheel, squinching my eyes to see over the hood and into the illuminated shafts. Things bumped into the parameters of my headlights, and I swerved to miss a tree stump. Some kind of animal sprang out of the grass and loped off into the darkness. It bounced and loped sort of like a cat, but I thought it was too big to be a cat, though I wasn't sure.

"Open the door," Walt kept screaming at me as he jogged along. He tried the back door again, then he leaned over to strike the door with his hand. It must have hurt.

"Go to hell," I said.

Then I hit the packed dirt of the field road and really stepped down on the gas. "Hey," Walt screamed one last time. "Wait a minute! Where are you going!"

The engine surged. Walt vanished out of the circle of light. A hundred yards of so, and the wheels of his new car rattled over a cattle trap and hit pavement. The entire vehicle leaned heavily as I turned hard to the left on the county road. I didn't know where we were, but it couldn't have been more than fifteen minutes out of Milledgeville.

There was a junction not five miles from the spot where Walt had raped me. The signs were clear enough, and I took the one that would carry me to Lawsonville. My heart longed to get to the store, back to the familiar town, back to Uncle Cajus and Aunt Ida Mae.

I thought of Mr. Hendricks and the trust he had placed in me. I thought of the night he had stood by me against the Baptist deacons. I thought of Miss Ellen's thin smile, of her sturdy presence until that night on the coastal highway. I resolved to think only of those people and those moments that might comfort me while the dash lights illuminated the padded and upholstered interior of the metal contraption that was hurdling me forward, farther and farther away from treachery and betrayal.

I can't even remember how or when I got from the car into the store and upstairs to my old room, but, as I was passing Mr. Hendricks' office, the telephone rang. I answered it catatonically: "Hello."

"Hey, sport, where the heck are you? You just disappeared? How'd you get to Lawsonville." It was Jim. I don't remember what I said to him. I only know that at some point I must have passed over that threshold from shock to sleep. When I woke up it was to the noise of Tom and the others throwing lumber out in the yard. I washed up with whatever I could find of my old stores at the basin and then walked downstairs.

I managed to get outside without Mr. Amos seeing me, and I found Uncle Cajus in the lumberyard supervising the loading of the truck. "What the..." he said, just like you read it in books. "Where you come from girl?"

"I need you to follow me in the pickup."

"What we gone do."

"I've got an automobile to dispose of."

"That new Chevy? You done bought you a new car?"

I shook my head, "No."

He followed me obediently, recognizing that I was in no mood to explain. I drove Walt's new car out to Sandy Creek. Stopping on the edge of the steep incline that ended below in a shallow, stony rapids, I put the gearshift in neutral. I walked around to the back, stopped and leaned into the car hard. It groaned a little but hardly budged. "Can you help me," I said to Uncle Cajus.

"Honey, you must be mighty mad with somebody. I don't want to get in no trouble myself."

"Okay," I said. I understood. I went back and cranked the engine, put it in gear and drove it down the incline myself. When I hit the creek the water sprayed the windshield. The car rocked a little, hit a big stone and came to rest. I opened the door, stepped out on a rock, picked my way from rock to rock until I was back on the bank. I scrambled up through the tall grass until I reached the edge of the road where Uncle Cajus was standing. He looked drained.

"The county ought to get out here and trim the sides of these roads," I said.

"They will."

"You see how high that grass is?"

"You just gone leave that car there," he asked.

"Yes," I said. "But I'll leave the keys with you. When the owner comes, if he does, you can give them to him and tell him where to find the car. Don't help him, though. Don't offer him a ride or anything. Let him get it himself, if he wants it."

"Who am I gonna look for?"

"You'll know when he tells you."

"What if he ain't really the owner."

"It doesn't matter," I said.

"It's a brand new car," Uncle Cajus noted again.

"It smelled new," I said.

"I thought you was supposed to go to that big shindig down in Milledgeville for Mr. Jim."

"Not *Mr.* Jim, Uncle Cajus. Just Jim."

"That ain't his car, is it?"

I laughed with relief. "Has he ever bought a new car," I asked. Then I said, "If I can get hold of his keys, though, I might roll his car down into the creek, too, when I see him next time."

Jim was waiting when we got back to the store. He was standing on the loading dock with Mr. Amos. "Hey, sport, I came by to see how you are. You sounded weird on the phone last night. How did you get back here?"

"I don't want to talk about it," I said grimly, walking by both of them. I saw Jim glance over at Uncle Cajus. I didn't care. I didn't even care if he told them or what. Men could suck wind, for all I cared. I wasn't going to dance to their tune trying to look good for them any more.

I missed my period before I saw Walt again. I'm not going to panic, I told myself. If I'm pregnant, I thought, I'll rip open my own belly and tear out the usurper he planted there. I wondered how you could do that.

For a month I lived in a kind of expectant dread that Walt would appear. I wasn't even aware of it all the time, but it never left me. It was just there, sort of in the background, like nausea. One moment I was anxious to see him, so that I could hit him hard with whatever weapon I could find. Then I'd find myself trembling at the thought of seeing the monstrous hypocrisy I knew would be written all over his face.

Again and again I just had to choke when the words came up as bitter in my mouth as cheap vinegar: "How could he do that to me? What have I ever done to him?" I was angry with God for having made somebody that duplicitous and not warned me ahead of time.

When Walt did come, however, it was nothing like I had imagined. First of all, it was at the end of a very long day. I had just finished going over the books with the manager of our newest store.

I didn't even know that Walt would know we had opened a store in that town, but then I suppose it wasn't too hard for him to find out, and it was very close to Atlanta, so it'd have been convenient for him.

I had left the manager in the office with the intention of watching the employees shut down the shop for the day. Closing down a business is a crucial moment in the day, and you can tell a lot about employee attitudes just watching them finish up. I was sort of trailing behind a fairly big woman wearing a work apron with our company logo emblazoned across it when I came around a corner and almost ran into Walt.

For a moment we both stopped, gyrated like two people who really do not want to bump into each other. I think I caught myself first and settled into a watchful stance. He still looked ambivalent, like a beggar not completely confident that I wouldn't shout for the police if he tried to panhandle me.

I said nothing, but I backed up against the shelf and gripped it for support. "Why did you do it," Walt blurted. He looked like a desperate man who, not knowing really what to do, had decided to take a wild plunge into snaky waters. His voice was, on the other hand, caked with puzzlement and self-pity.

I was afraid to speak. I had no idea what my voice would do, but I knew it couldn't put together a rational sentence. So I said nothing. Walt rocked a little back and forth like a man caught in a slight, dizzy spell. Embarrassment crept into his expression. "It was a brand new car," he said. The edges of his voice skirted a soft wail, and my own confusion was pushed away by a new ferocious anger that made my chest pump.

"Your *new* car," I said like I wasn't sure I had heard right. The syllables came out so tight and bent, my words were hardly articulate. Walt shifted from one foot to the other, cocked his head and frowned. For a moment I imagined that he was expecting me to apologize.

"I had to hire somebody to pull it out of that creek," he said, probing the air. Then he seemed content to stand there and wait for my response until he blurted: "That car cost me a lot!"

I felt my chest heaving unreasonably. Why can't I control myself, I wondered. I'm not the one who has violated another human being. I'm not the one who has done anything wrong. My eye fell on the trowels. They were lying within reach on the shelf, with sharp points and a handle you could really hold firmly.

"You could have at least left me my pants," Walt said suddenly.

I guess I did a double take. The idiocy of his words drove a wedge through my anger and laid a funny spot in my brain bare. Laughter spilled down through the nerve tunnels, leaping over circuits and dancing into my vocal chords. I heard my own voice gurgling. It began as a chuckle, then a snicker. My first impulse was to hold it back. When I tried it sputtered out between my clamped jaws. I guffawed, caught my mouth with my hands like I could catch the laughter and hold it.

It was as if I had hit him with something huge and invisible, swung it out and caught him alongside the head. Walt reeled backward as my guffaws rolled over him. They were then joined into a procession of laughs interrupted by snickers, then bursting out again as guffaws. They sketched a ragged seismograph of ridicule that ripped Walt's self-esteem, while I was like a kid taken in church by a fit of comedy. I couldn't stop.

The large woman I had been trailing came back into the main aisle to see what I was laughing at. Walt turned sideways, saw her, then whirled away from us and started to flee. He hurried towards the front doors. He bent over like a man shielding himself from a heavy downpour. I couldn't stop laughing. I had left Walt without pants there in the middle of that field.

The big woman turned to watch Walt go. When the front door closed behind him, she looked over her shoulder at me and winked: "He don't like being laughed at."

"Probably not," I agreed.

"Can I lock up now?"

"Go right ahead."

When I missed my second period is also the time I heard about Jim and Laura's goings-on. The rumor had it that they were seeing each other. Seeing each other then meant they were having an affair. Having an affair meant they were doing it together. Laura was married, of course, so this was not the kind of rumor that made Jim a prime candidate for the next decency award in Georgia.

I had other things on my mind. I didn't want to wait until I missed another period before doing anything about it. My general sense (though I really knew virtually nothing and had no access to any information) was that the sooner you caught it, the easier it was to get rid of.

There were a number of days when I just tried to puzzle out what to do. I couldn't ask anybody I trusted because I didn't trust anybody that far. It was a pretty lonely problem to have. Finally, I just decided to take the plunge. I looked in the phone book and selected a doctor who advertised as specializing in women's problems. I called his office, made an appointment and drove in to Atlanta two days later.

In those days doctors were just beginning to change from the small town practitioners who knew your family and made house calls to businessmen who supervised an assembly-line medical office. The one I got was a member of the new breed. These were the automatons that had programmed themselves from childhood to make the 99 averages it required to get into medical school. They went from programmed A-students to health care robots.

What few moral principles they held on to boiled down to unreasoned cant and arrogant bluster.

"I'm Dr. Spotchfield," the relatively young man announced as he came into the little room where I had been sitting thirty minutes waiting in my underwear. "You are," he took a cursory look at the clipboard he held, "needing...?" He looked up at me with gray, neutral eyes. I am an important professional, he seemed to be signaling, and you are a pawn I need to move about in order to collect a fee.

"I was raped," I said, assuming an impersonal tone of voice I didn't feel. In fact, my stomach was churning, saliva was welling up into my mouth. "I think I'm pregnant, and I want an abortion."

As Dr. Spotchfield's color drained from his face, I grew alarmed. He stood there like my words had been nails that I hammered into his feet, pinning him to the floor. I was tempted to reach out and give him a push to see if I could get his little motor started again. It was unnecessary, though, because I had already pushed the buttons that would send him into an over-animated tizzy.

"Young lady," he began. It was all down hill from there. There are certain things that when said are a prelude to somebody's tirade. "Young lady" tops the list in this category. Whenever anybody started to address me with "young lady," I knew it was time to start packing my things.

I might sketch Doctor Spotchfield's argument, rudimentary as it was, in three theses: 1. Doctors are trained to save lives and indeed swear an oath to that effect, 2. Some people are immoral and have no respect for oaths or life, 3. I was a prime example of the immoral person with the gall to ask him to violate all the holy vows he had taken when he entered the medical profession.

As Spotchfield made these points, his face went from drained pale to hot red. He literally talked himself into high moral indignation. I wasn't even a person. I was just an excuse to make him feel high and self-righteous.

I was, in the meantime, doing my best to get on my clothes before he turned literally violent. By the time I got my second shoe on, he was screaming. "Get out! Get out of my office!"

"If you'll get out of the doorway, I'll leave," I said.

I got my pocketbook and started by. About the time I got into the door, Dr. Spotchfield was calling to his nurse, "Do not make another appointment for this woman," he declared to everybody within earshot. About that time I opened the second door to the waiting room and saw every eye in the room zeroed in on me, faces agog. Getting across the expanse to the front door I felt my legs turn to lead and the clock stand still.

In terms of sheer psychological time, I guess it took me thirty years to wend my way to the sidewalk. Once on the pavement, I remembered that I didn't know the people in the waiting room. That was a blessing. It didn't really matter what they thought. Dr. Spotchfield could yell his head off. I didn't care.

Right in that moment I conceived the idea of moving to Atlanta. Having people out there who didn't know and, therefore, couldn't care a lot who you were might be fun. Anonymity is a privilege the city conveys upon its inhabitants. If it had a downside, I wasn't concerned with that at the moment. All I could think of was the great relief I might feel that nobody knows who you are.

As I headed for my car, I suddenly knew what course of action I would take. I would go to Jim. He would help me. His mind would not shut down when I told him what had happened. He would listen. He would be concerned. And that's exactly what happened.

I caught up with Jim in Augusta, in the biggest store we had that was also growing by leaps and bounds. The growth was due to Jim's peculiar talent for organization. He was gifted. He could make things work the same way he used to dominate a football field as a boy. I could imagine he had been a good officer in Vietnam, too.

"Hey, Fol," he said, genuinely please as always to see me. "Give me a hug. Where you been?"

"Looking for you at least part of the time."

"Yeah, I'm hard to find sometimes. I hear they're developing phones you can keep in your car that'll be better than any two-way radio. Keeping up with me ought to be easier then. It'd sure simplify my job to have something like that."

"Yours and mine, too," I agreed. "But I've got something I need to talk about with you – in private."

"Yeah, sure."

"Right now."

"Okay, let's go to the back. I'll let the bookkeeper take a break."

That's what happened. The office was always in the back, and Jim told the lady at the desk to take a thirty-minute break. She was delighted. "Thirty minutes," she said, just to make sure he meant what he said.

"Make it an hour," I said.

"She's the boss," Jim verified.

The lady grabbed her pocketbook and left in a big hurry. She was probably afraid we might change out minds. When she was gone, Jim leaned back, half sitting on the desktop. "What's up, sport," he asked, smiling his lazy smile.

I paced back and forth in front of him as I told the story of Walt picking me up that night. He listened quietly, shaking his head and making a face at crucial point like somebody swallowing a horrible medicine. I didn't spare him many details and, when I was finished, he asked, "Why did you get in his car that night?"

I shrugged. "I was just so glad there was somebody who cared. When I saw you hugging Laura Lawson like you were old friends, I..." I searched for the right word and couldn't find it, "just felt awful. I went outside, and Walt was waiting. He had always been so decent. I had a feeling he really cared about me. I don't know."

"Decent? He's a rabble-rouser and trouble maker, Folly. He's the worst kind of opportunist. You had to find that out the hard way."

"Well, you certainly treated him with interest and respect when you needed them to get out of your way in the election."

"Good grief! That doesn't mean I approve of his methods or him, for God's sake. He goes into a place, sets up a confrontation, risks everybody's welfare, and then leaves. Okay for him. What about the good people who have to stay behind and live in a place. He doesn't care about them."

"Well, he thinks he does, anyway. He thinks he's working for a cause that will help them, Jim."

"Like he thought you were ready to have sex? Are you taking up for the bastard?"

"I know enough about white Southerners to know that, If it weren't for trouble-makers like him," I enunciated carefully, "we'd still be in slavery."

"Well, he's a royal son of a bitch. If I see him, I'll smash his face in."

"You wouldn't be the first person who wants to do that, Jim. But that's not what I'm here for. Adolescent posturing won't help me, Jim. I'm tired of men who act like they haven't grown up. That's why I'm in this jam I'm in. I need a doctor who can give me an abortion without risking my life. And soon, too, before it gets too complicated!"

Jim lowered his chin into his hand. He cupped the elbow in his other hand. For a moment I was afraid he was going to moralize about my wanting an abortion, but instead he looked up after a moment or two and said, "Don't worry, sport. I'll take care of it."

"Okay." When I started to leave, I couldn't help but stop and look seriously at Jim. "You won't get into trouble if you run into Walt, will you, Jim?"

"He ought to be guilty of some criminal offense."

"What about rape? Isn't that bad enough?"

"You gonna press charges?"

"No. Do you think I'd get anywhere with that? Everybody assumes the woman provokes it. They'd say I went willingly with him out into the woods. What did I expect, to play a game of checkers? You asked me yourself."

"It was a reasonable question."

"A reasonable question? Oh, God! He seemed like a decent person, Jim. Did I know he was going to take me out in the woods and rape me?"

"What did you think he had in mind, Fol? You said you swapped some fairly heavy embraces before you got in the car. What do men and women do after that?"

"Well, I didn't know they had sex right away, quite frankly!" I actually stamped my foot and thrust my hands against my hips. "That's not fair. Is that what you do every time you kiss a girl? No, don't tell me. I don't want to know. Just help me, that's all, and shut up."

"Folly, men can be like that. Honest to God. It's like saying 'okay, let's get on with it.'"

"I don't want to hear this!"

"You can't change human nature, Fol. Be careful next time."

"Oh, thanks. Thanks a lot for the advice."

He stood up, reached over and tried to pull me up into a big hug. I pushed away and stepped far back. "I'll take care of it," was all he said. And he did it, too. I went to a place one Saturday morning, and when they finished with me, the nurse handed me a garbage bag with something in it. She said I'd have to get rid of it.

I took the bag from her without even thinking what it was. It wasn't until I'd put it in the trunk and was driving back to where I was sleeping at the Monroe store when it really occurred to me what sort of freight I had. When I realized, I drove twenty miles farther between a defunct town once known as Salem and another one called Sparta. I kept hoping nobody would be around, and they weren't.

There was a dump there where we contracted to get rid of our lumber or whatever we had left over from jobs. I managed to tuck the bag down pretty far in the refuse. Later I kept telling myself that it probably wasn't recognizably human, anyway, even if somebody had found it. I don't know myself. I didn't look.

XXI

How do you say that two years passed and just leave it at that. Of course lots can happen in two years, but when I think back on the period between late 1969 when I planted that bag and 1971, I can't think of anything. It was one of those periods where days, weeks, and months pass and there's nothing but the usual to show for it. If lots happened, you can't think of anything in particular of note.

Of course, life doesn't wait around until we absorb the lessons of a previous episode before something else happens. The year was 1971. I had, as the nasty boys said back then, lost my cherry, but it was my thirtieth year as a person of ambiguous race, and I wasn't thinking about that any more.

Spring had arrived. It was late April by that time, maybe into May. School was still in session because you didn't see children rambling around during the day. That's when it happened. I was standing in front of Mr. Amos's desk. The time was seven p.m., Friday. The side windows with screens were propped open. The old rotating fans hanging from the metal ceiling were drawing in the outside air and circulating it, so that the store odors of old vegetables and spoiled fruit were being moved gradually toward an exhaust fan in the feed room. You could smell the new evening freshness gradually permeating the store.

"So that's that," Mr. Amos said. It was usually his final pronouncement and meant that we had finished our meeting. Income tax was very much on our minds. We had met to consider the advice our CPA firm had given us. There were decisions to make. Mr. Amos had gone over them, brought them up item by item, and we had decided. It was our usual method. In the end, I always had the certainty that he knew before he asked me what the best course of action for us was. I started to go, but he said, "Wait a minute. There's one more thing."

I turned back around. "Yes, sir?"

"Pull up that chair and sit back down, gal."

I reached over and rolled the old oak chair over to a place where we could talk quietly together if necessary. Mr. Amos rubbed his chin, then he pushed back his green visor from his forehead, and his face emerged more clearly from the shadows. "The building trade is good," he said.

"Yes, sir," I agreed.

"We've been doing right well with lumber and supplies."

"We sure have," I nodded. It may very well be, I thought, that I'm rich. I was certainly rich in any relative terms, though it was hard to calculate exactly what I was worth at that point, and I had no time really to add it all up. There was well over a couple of hundred thousand dollars in various bank accounts in my name. That much I knew, and that was cash money.

"There's still gone be lots of money to make in the trade."

"Looks like it," I said.

"But there's gone be bigger money made in Atlanta in real estate."

I looked at Mr. Hendricks carefully. Such a pronouncement heralded a shift in our strategy. Mr. Amos's face was impassive, as usual. Sometimes I wondered if he actually knew how to wear any kind of expression upon his haggard features. I suspected that he had been practicing restraint for so long maybe he'd forgotten how to be expressive at all. His tone was even and revealed nothing about how important what he said might be for our future plans.

"You think so," I ventured after a long moment elapsed.

"No doubt about it. I'm talking big money, gal."

"Big money," I said, trying to get the feel of those two words on my tongue. "How big?" Mr. Amos was not a man to exaggerate for effect.

"Well, I don't want to make no projections. I ain't no prophet, and we need to know the market. But I been watching things, and I figure we're in for a good ten years or more of growth. The big growth will be in Atlanta. We've been taking the leftovers, and that's been good for us. But there really ain't no reason for us not to move into the center of things. I figure we might as well move in and help ourselves to the big times."

"The center of things?"

"Yeah. Atlanta. We got the capital now."

"We do?" I waited again, but Mr. Hendricks sat there inscrutably. Finally, I said, "How do we get into real estate in Atlanta, Mr. Amos?"

"Oh, I 'spect it won't be that hard. I got a good lawyer I been knowing a long time up there."

"You mean old man Hawson?" We had used him as our legal help in opening the stores in Madison and Covington. Somehow I'd never met him in person, but I certainly knew him through the paper work and correspondence that had been necessary. He took care of the legal side of our business.

"Yeah. He knows the markets and everything that's going and coming."

"He must be smart," I agreed.

"Oh yeah, he's smart enough. And I can trust him. With a lawyer, that's the first thing you gotta be sure about. Smart comes next."

After that conclusive statement a pause set in. Mr. Hendricks seemed to be mulling over the grand picture he was painting of our prospects. "I think Hawson will help us get started," he began again. "He don't just do tax stuff and helping you get started and such. He's been in business sixty years. He knows Atlanta. He thinks it's the right time."

"How much capital will we need?"

"We'll start small. You gotta feel your way in. But you can do it."

"What kind of real estate?"

"Well, I don't hardly think it matters at this point. We can start with apartments because they're the safest. Just take too much work. You gotta know the city. Then I figure we'll do some commercial. Owning a warehouse or two wouldn't be bad, either."

I marveled at my partner. Here was a man who had a high school education at best in a little rural town, a man who had wandered into town after his parents had died somewhere in nowhere land, sharecroppers nobody cared about. Here was a man whose imaginative reach had yet to be really tested, a man with infinite patience and wisdom.

"Well, I'm ready when you are," I said.

Mr. Amos looked up at me, and I'll swear he smiled. His mouth stretched out on both sides. "I knew you'd be ready," he said. "And it's time you got yourself an apartment. You don't have no where to live, do you? Just been sleeping in the stores."

It was the truth. I was still taking my pallet around from store to store and sleeping in the office wherever I was working. I had kept my room in the Lawsonville store, the one above the feed room, but that was the only permanent domicile I had. "An apartment," I said.

"Yeah, get you an apartment in Atlanta."

"It'd have to be in the colored section?"

"Naw, gal, you can pass for white. You gone need to pass for white in Atlanta, and there's gone come the time real soon when it won't matter no way. You can use your apartment looking to get acquainted with the apartment market. I 'spect a nice apartment complex would be a good starting place for us. Old Hawson thinks that everything you buy right now will double in five years."

"Wow!"

"Just need to find the right location and get some cash flow out of, in the meantime. Location is the thing in real estate."

It was the last strategy session we had, but it was good advice. Like I said, that was Friday, and Tuesday Uncle Cajus phoned me and told me Mr. Amos had "passed."

"No," I said.

"Yes, baby, it's the truth," he said, his voice soothing. "He done had a stroke. Happened this morning before we opened the store."

I couldn't get my mind around the idea. Mr. Hendricks gone. I kept turning the notion around and around, trying to look at it from a perspective that made any sense. He acted like he had all the time in the world. He was cooking up plans to move into Atlanta real estate. He wasn't in a hurry. And yet he was always on time with everything he did – except die.

It was the pity of it that got me worse than the grief at first. That Mr. Hendricks should have to leave things unfinished when he was just beginning to hit his stride. He was just moving into a level of business that would challenge him. Why would God want to snatch him out of it like that. Why would the Creator have put

Amos Hendricks together with genes that were programmed to bring everything to a stop so early? He was not even sixty. There were such plans.

The whole town of Lawsonville was left sharing my own feeling that we had been robbed. Old Miz West was downright offended with The Lord when she said, "How does he expect us to get fresh vegetables now that he's called Mr. Hendricks home? Nobody else has ever been able to get the kind of fresh fruits and vegetables that man got for us."

Mr. Hendricks just wasn't the type to die. He was a fixture that you could not imagine out of the general picture without bringing things into an imbalance. Without him milk would go bad in the refrigerator days after you bought it. Salad would wilt on the plate. Everybody would have to pay higher prices for eggs and feed and lots of other items that he somehow, magically managed to get at bargain basement prices.

Even I didn't really know exactly how he did it, though I had apprenticed myself carefully to him. I knew the wholesalers. Yet, they didn't bring me the same kind of produce and not at the same prices.

Amos Hendricks had suffered a massive stroke. A major artery had popped and flooded his brain with blood. In fragments of a second all the synapses had shut down the vital power that made him tick. It was like a house blowing a permanent fuse that you couldn't do anything about. Then there was nothing left to do but get used to the idea that he was gone.

It was just another normal Sunday when they buried him. The sun shone. Nature didn't even give a nod by providing us with lightening or thunder. I guess the death of even a good, honest merchant doesn't count for much in the whole scheme of the cosmos. Our kind must be fairly low down in the great chain of being, may down about the twelfth or thirteenth level where they have a sign that reads: "All deceased merchants report here for processing."

All of Lawson County came to the funeral, black and white. They walked in hushed lines to the graveyard to bid him farewell. Their loss was etched in their faces. Amos Hendricks hadn't been a personable man. He hadn't been warm or kindly. He had never tried to endear himself to anybody. Nobody much really knew him.

"We'll miss Brother Amos," the preacher said. "We'll miss knowing that his store will be open when we need him, that there'll be good, fresh produce available, milk that won't spoil, feed when our animals need it. Brother Amos was a decent man. He didn't have a family – except to say that he served this town like it was his family. He served this church, too. He was a deacon. He never missed a Sunday service." He pointed to one of the pews, "He'd sit right there. I knew he'd be there. He'd be listening. He wouldn't nap off in the middle of my sermon." The preacher looked around the sanctuary. "He was a decent man," he said quietly. "The kind of man we'll all miss quietly, for a long time, not knowing how we'll ever replace him."

It was just the right kind of eulogy, I thought, as we left the church. Outside our lawyer showed up. His long, black Cadillac was waiting as I came down the steps. I had never seen him, but I knew whom that black Cadillac belonged to right away. I headed toward it. A blocky man in a gray suit, wearing dark glasses, unfolded himself from the driver's seat and went around to open the door and help the attorney out. When he emerged, the driver literally having to pull him up by sheer force, I knew why Mr. Amos had referred to him as "Old Man" Hawson.

You couldn't say that Bill Hawson had been ravaged by time. He looked more like an ancient, animated mummy. He moved in jerky movements, like he was having to concentrate on getting his limbs to respond. As I approached him, I saw a man with muscular ears flapping from a bald noggin. He raised a moon face dominated by a bulbous nose. His cheeks had a faint, funeral parlor rouge coloring the dead white. Widely spaced on either side of the large nose were two little pig eyes blinking hard like the light was a little too bright. Underneath the nose was a mouth fixed in a permanent expression of ironic bemusement.

Bill Hawson was "somewhere around ninety-five." Nobody knew exactly. He had been on the Atlanta scene longer than anybody could remember. His generation had long since vanished from the scene. None of Bill's contemporaries remained as witnesses to who he was. Any knowledge of him was purely historical.

"You are Mr. Hawson," I said, stepping forward. "I'm Folly Steeples."

Bill Hawson seized my hand, having first to let the arm of his driver go. I stumbled back, thrown by his shifting his weight upon me. Finally, I got my footing and held him up. He leaned into me as he spoke: "I knew who you were the minute I saw you, darling." His voice was surprisingly high-pitched and squeaky, the taut-stringed instrument of a very old person. "You're as beautiful as Amos told me you'd be," he said. He began shaking my right hand with his claw-like fingers (I wasn't sure it was voluntary) as he spoke, "I've wanted to meet you for years!" Then he farted.

"We've depended upon you, sir, and I've really appreciated all you've done to help us in our business" I said, trying hard to strain away from smelling the rotten egg odor rising up around me from his fart.

Bill Hawson continued to shake my hand, and I determined that I would not think of him merely as an extremely old person, leaving myself either to pity, condescension or impatience. As I led him along with the rest of the people to the cemetery, he farted twice more loudly than before but seemed oblivious to it.

Somebody in the group began to hum a gospel as they loaded the coffin onto the little wagon they pulled down into the cemetery that was next door to the church. Everybody took up the tune, and the song soared around us.

"Everybody was there," Jim said later as we gathered in the store for Bill Hawson to read the will.

"Everybody," Aunt Ida Mae agreed. "Coloured and white. Everybody was there. They knowed Mr. Amos was a good man."

"He was a good man," Uncle Cajus intoned, taking up the refrain.

"Amen," I said with feeling.

"He sure was a good man," Jim agreed. At which point Mr. Hawson farted loudly and then began to clear his throat.

I saw Aunt Ida Mae and Uncle Cajus look at each other. They didn't know Mr. Hawson and were surprised at a white man giving vent like that in public, especially a lawyer who wore a suit and rode in a big car. Since Mr. Hendricks had no relatives, we were the only ones present.

The driver (whose name was Melville) brought Mr. Hawson's attache case into the store and opened it for him after he and I had helped the venerable attorney into Mr. Amos's swivel chair. Bill Hawson unbuttoned his vest and loosened the stiff collar he wore. He rustled with the papers a bit, put on very thick glasses, held the paper very close to his little pig eyes and began to read.

There were legacies for the Baptist Church, the Lawsonville Library, the local Boy Scouts, and then something for his faithful employees. Uncle Cajus got twenty-five hundred dollars, by far the largest chunk of any employee – but I wasn't mentioned.

Next came Jim. He received the six percent interest in the business he had been promised when he joined us out of Vietnam. I was surprised because that meant it came out of Mr. Hendrick's portion and not mine. There was still no mention of me, but the vast bulk of the estate had still not been accounted for.

Jim got up. Made the customary noises. He had to go. Things to do, that kind of stuff. Business. You know. The fact is, he now had what he had been expecting, and he didn't want to fool around. I watched him go through these motions. He had filled out and squared off a little, looked more mature, more like a man of responsibility and business. But he was also a step removed from me now. I no longer felt that connection in the same way.

When Jim was gone, the next thing was that Uncle Cajus began to stir. "I reckon we can go, too," Uncle Cajus said, and he and Aunt Ida Mae started into motion. I knew that even then it might take them eight minutes or more to get out of the store. They were old time folk and could take longer moving in a straight line than I could have done on a bet.

"Well, there's no reason to hurry off," Bill Hawson said, turning his pig eyes at me. "The simple fact is that Folly Steeples is Amos Hendricks' sole heir. The estate goes to her." Having pronounced this with all the gusto of a merry oracle, he farted again loudly.

Aunt Ida Mae started fanning herself frantically. They had stopped again a few feet down the aisle. At first I thought she might be warding off the stench from the air Mr. Hawson had so obliviously let go. The fan was the one handed out in the AME Episcopal Methodist meeting the previous Sunday. It had a picture of Mary and baby Jesus on it in color. Except for the swishing of her fan, there was perfect silence in the store.

At first I couldn't quite focus. Everything around me seemed indistinct. I blinked my eyes, trying to recall something of what I was hearing and seeing. It was as if I were sinking into a coma. I began to look around the room like a submarine captain swiveling his periscope. I scanned Aunt Ida Mae's great bulk. The switching fan crackled against the dead air. My eyes fell on Uncle Cajus's face. He was standing at attention. His right eyelid began to twitch slightly. His coal black complexion glistened in reflected light from the show windows of the store. It was like everybody had suddenly just frozen on the spot.

What brought me back was the odor of Mr. Hawson's fart. It was putrid, once again the quality of rotten eggs. As it penetrated my nostrils, I wretched back into consciousness, but only to hear the high-pitched vocal chords of the aged barrister, calling across space to me: "Miss Steeples? Miss Steeples?"

"Yessir,." I answered.

He blinked his little piggy eyes. Age had given him a bleary look, his lids heavy over the eyeballs, like he was straining to get himself awake and couldn't quite make it. Each eye was encompassed in multiple sacks that endowed them with autonomy. "Hello," he said, his mouth mirthful, one arthritic claw held up. I saw he was waving at me. "Are you with us again?"

I moved in my chair and then stood up and paced away, trying to escape the stench. "Yes, I heard you, sir," I spoke backwards, over my shoulder. Uncle Cajus grinned.

"I 'spect we be going, too, now. You won't be needing us no more, will you, sir?"

Still oblivious to the sounds and odors of his bowels, Bill Hawson rubbed his hands together. "There'll be a lot of work tallying up what you've inherited you know. That's part of my job, too, but you have to help me, darling. I'm looking forward to that," he said. "Getting to see lots of you next week, if that can be arranged." Uncle Cajus cleared his throat loudly. Bill Hawson looked over at him, "Yes, you two can go. Thank you. That's all."

"Bye, honey," they said, speaking in unison. Aunt Ida Mae reached out and squeezed my arm as she passed. I smiled at her.

"Of course it can be arranged," I said. Why ever not? Was I a fool?

When everybody had left the store but me, Bill Hawson, and his driver, Melville, Bill blinked his sleepy little eyes and summed up what had happened: "You're rich, now, you know, darling."

"That's what it looks like," I admitted.

"Nothing wrong with that," he continued.

"No. I guess not. But," I said, struggling to find the words, "it doesn't feel exactly right, either."

"Give it time. You'll get used to it," was Bill Hawson's caustic retort. Then he added, "That's the way Amos wanted it."

Of course I knew that Mr. Amos had accumulated some money quite aside from the business we had built together. He had never had a family, never spent anything on himself. Yet, he'd run a successful, small town business. There had to be money there. Personal expenses virtually nil; it stood to reason. Everybody had assumed as much.

How much he was worth nobody would have guessed. It took us the next week to complete the audit. I was much in the presence of Bill Hawson, and he looked at me and nodded his congratulations, "Looks like about three million, more or less."

"Yes, sir. It does." It was 1971. Three million dollars was a lot of money then.

"Who would have thought that old Amos had managed to do that," Bill Hawson eulogized, blinking his tiny eyes and rubbing his bulbous nose.

"Well," I said.

"You've got your own money, too, I'm sure. Frugality is your middle name, young lady. Is it not?"

"Yes," I said. "I do have my money, too."

Bill Hawson farted. I couldn't ignore it, but I had become accustomed to his punctuating our meetings that way, and I developed a strategy. When he let go, I got up and paced away to the other side of the room. Once he said, "You're mighty restless." This time I stopped and opened a window. Then I went over and turned on a fan. He didn't seem to notice.

"I can't wait to see how your story goes on, sweetpea," he said.

I had also become used to the various terms of endearment he used when addressing me. "My story?"

"Yes, darling," Bill Hawson chirped, "your story. Fascinating story it's been thus far."

I shook my head the way I'd come to do in response to his most outrageous comments and questions. "What story are you talking about?"

"Everybody has a story, darling," he said. "There are two kinds of people: those who know it, and those who don't. You need to join the ones who do."

I shook my head again and smiled in disbelief and pleasure, "I'm ready. Can you give me some hints?"

"Well, at my age, darling, the only thing that holds my attention is a person's story. Take Jim Hall. There's a fellow with a story, and I'll bet he knows it, too. You wait and see. He'll take his story and turn it into political hay. He's a smart lad, but he's got a flaw."

I was trying to disguise just how much the mention of Jim's name alerted me. "Jim has a flaw? What is it?"

"Well, it's the same flaw that most politicians have. Most everybody, in fact, but politicians in particular," Bill Hawson concluded, and then he began to chuckle to himself, and the chuckle pumped him up and down in his chair and made the bulb at the end of his nose bleed into a bright pink. "I've known lots of politicians in my life, darling. Lots of them. They all work and live for the story's conclusion. It's that great moment when they arrive at the office they long for with all their heart." He sat a little in an attitude of mulling over what he had said, and I paced again about the room. We were alone in his office. He had sent the secretary into the outer office thirty minutes earlier. "Yes, most everybody has that flaw, darling."

I was thinking about Jim and Laura. I knew my blood was beginning to boil. He was risking everything – and for what? In order to get my mind off him, I spun around, faced Bill and asked, "What is it, Bill? What is this flaw you're talking about?"

"Conceit, sweetpea. Conceit."

"What do you mean by that? Speak English."

His smile widened. I had discovered in being with him day after day that he enjoyed nothing more than a bit of a verbal set-to, a debate, so to speak, especially when his opponent truly felt her position. "English? Nobody speaks it anymore, darling. Everybody who tried to speak English is dead – except me. It's a dying tongue."

"Well, whatever it is we speak, then," I snapped.

I saw him hesitate, and I knew he was considering launching into an extended little excursion about the deterioration of the English language and the general decline in people caring about anything. It was one of his favorite themes. He admitted it and had said it suited him, at his age, to bewail the decline of civilization. It's what the world expects, he added.

Now he decided, however, to stick to Jim. "Let's take Jim Hall," he went on, "I hear he's dallying about with Laura Lawson. My goodness, that's what I hear, and she's a married woman. I wouldn't be at all surprised if he hadn't left the store last Saturday and gone directly to meet her. And she being married to a rich fella from up in Boston. Can't remember the name of the family, but it's an old one. Old money. Now that's conceit. It flatters him to think that he can have her."

I shook my head and gave him the full frontal assault of my condescension, I all but said, be clear, old man. Nobody can understand you now. "Why is that conceit? What does conceit have to do with adultery?"

"Everything. Why does a woman who is married run after other men? Is she hungry for love? No, it's conceit. Why does a single man, who has access to every single woman in Georgia, run after a married woman? Certainly not for sex or love, darling. Conceit, pure and simple."

I opened my mouth to say something, closed it, opened it again, thought better of it and then simply laughed. "You love to argue," I said, still laughing. "You state everything in a kind of counterpoint."

Bill Hawson laughed with me. "I'm a lawyer, darling. People here in Georgia need a bit of argument. There's too much they don't like to say outright. The things people don't say outright, to your face, they'll say behind your back. It breeds hypocrisy, and hypocrisy breeds treachery."

"I promise not to talk behind your back," I said, still half-laughing.

"I don't think you will, darling. I don't think you will."

"I'm still not entirely convinced that everybody of your generation was so much more superior to my own."

"That's alright, darling. I love you, anyway. It's good we'll be working together. But Mr. Jim Hall might be hurting himself with this little dalliance." At that Bill Hawson fell into one of his vacancies. It was as if his brain shifted abruptly into neutral. Maybe it was a kind of mild seizure, but he simply sat there idling for a couple of minutes until his little pig eyes began to blink again. "You still there," he asked, stirring again.

"Yes, sir. I'm still here."

"Now how about your story, sweetpea. Before you go I want to hear more about it."

"Oh," I said, flapping my hand dismissively, "My story is boring!"

He sat back up and regarded me with interest. "Maybe you haven't quite decided on the plot yet, you pretty thing. But I don't like to hear you say it's boring."

"Why?"

"Well, there's vanity in that, surely. Your story's not boring at all. Why would you say it was?"

"I don't know."

"Well, darling, let me tell you something. You're very special. Amos Hendricks thought so, and I think so, too."

"Thank you, Bill," I said.

"Let's agree always to be honest with one another, darling."

"Yes. Let's do."

"That's how it was with Amos and me. Good. By the way, did you know that Lawson Hall was going up for auction?"

It sounded like an aside, but my whole body went into a state of alarm. "No! Lawson Hall?"

"The place is mortgaged to the hilt. Now that Laura is dallying with the Hall boy, I suppose we can't count on her rich Boston husband getting her out of hock. She's in debt up to her ears, I hear."

"Bill, is there anything you don't know?"

He looked up at me, blinking his little eyes, his long mouth upturned like a quarter moon lying down, "If you are actively engaged in practice sixty years or more like I've been, you develop your networks, darling. Everybody in Georgia knows about the Lawson fortunes in decline. It's been news for a generation. There was a lot to lose. It takes awhile to ruin one of the oldest and biggest fortunes in the state."

"What would it take to buy the place," I wondered cautiously.

"The whole estate or just the house and appendages?"

"How much land is there?"

"Several thousand acres. I thought you might have a better idea than I do."

"Is the land worth much as an investment?"

"Well, eventually, but there'll be plenty of time to buy piedmont land at bargain prices. I imagine you could get the house and everything with it for sixty thousand or so."

"Then can you do what needs to be done for me to get it?"

"That's one of my jobs, darling. Now we're in business."

"Yes. We are."

"Your hand on it," Bill Hawson said, holding up his claw for me to shake.

Miriam's Story

I moved Jim into a new CEO position in the business and began to do the things necessary to sell. My oldest and most loyal employees were housed, and I'd set up a good retirement program for them. Without Mr. Amos, I was ready to move on, and especially now that I had Lawson Hall. Besides, Atlanta would be beckoning once I got that one last thing settled in Lawsonville about who I come from.

When I first crawled into the attic over Judge Lawson's library and found everything intact, Henricks and Steeples began to fade for me. Judy Anne Fitts was proving her mettle at the Augusta store. Uncle Cajus was handling the yard in Lawsonville, but I had a stroke of luck when Mason Biggs came back from Canada. In spite of the bitter feelings when he left, white Lawsonville usually took its children back. They did it with Mason, too. There might have been a few holdouts who wouldn't speak to him for awhile, but they soon got over it. Soon it was clear to me that he was perfect to run the store Mr. Amos founded.

Another good thing about Mason I should mention: he was the son of Emily Conyers by her first husband. You remember. The store owner who refused to cooperate in the plot against Rhonda

Dale. So after watching him for a couple of months, I decided to set up an interview with him.

Mason was a stringy, long-legged young man. He had a ponytail and unkempt whiskers, and you figured if he took off his shirt, you'd be able to count every one of his ribs. His eyes had that characteristic of so who, during those years had taken on the role of the hippy – they were both soft-hearted and keen in turns. It made you wonder which was the real guy, the soft-spoken hippy or the shrewd trader. I decided that underneath Mason's hippy persona there was a shrewd, Lawson County, Georgia cracker style tradesman hiding. "Somebody said you are looking for a job," I suggested.

"Yes," he said, speaking in his soft-spoken hippy manner but with an educated voice that belied his homely, unkempt appearance, "yes, I am."

"Would you mind cleaning up a bit for a good job?"

He blinked as he searched my face for any impertinence. When he saw that I was both serious and wished him well, he nodded, "Of course. What do you mean, though?"

"Well, maybe shave. If a merchant offers fresh goods at reasonable prices, people don't necessarily expect him to look like a movie star, but it's always a good feeling to know that a guy who sells groceries as well as hardware is sanitary, if you know what I mean."

Mason joined me in laughing a little. "Sure, I can buy that. I grew up in a merchant family. I worked in Mother's store. Even during college I'd come back in the summer."

"I know."

"Yes," Mason said. He looked down at his shirt. "I guess I do look a little ragged. Didn't have any money up there in the far north."

"It's okay. I don't mean that you have to look spit and shined or anything."

"Sure."

Chandra missed Judy Anne, and I knew I couldn't keep them permanently separated, so that was another thing I had to take care of first. So I drove to Augusta and put it straight to Judy Anne: "Look, I'll let Chandra transfer up here to work in the yard. But only if you two can keep your personal and business lives separate."

Judy Anne gave me her tomboy grin. She looked more and more like what I'd imagined Huck Finn might have turned out as if he'd grown up in the story. "Hey, it's fine. No problem. Look, Fol, we're just friends. What do you think?"

I shrugged and decided to risk it. What the hell. I wanted to tie up the loose ends before I put the whole show into some stranger's hands. I would also take Bill Hawson's advice. "Don't try to rush selling a business this successful, darling. Just let the word get out and let them come to you. That's the way to get the best price. You've got a money machine going. There's no hurry."

I told Bill Hawson I also wanted to do what Amos Hendricks had told me before he died. "You mean get into Atlanta real estate," his voice piped over the telephone.

"Yes. He said you knew something about the market."

"Darling, you can get into Atlanta real estate right away. You don't have to sell your business. I've got a couple of wonderful deals you can participate in right now. No problem at all."

I knew that Jim was already working hard to position himself for the governor's race, but it didn't matter as long as he did his work running Hendricks and Steeples Hardware and Building Supplies. Somehow the two tasks he'd set for himself complemented one another because Jim ran hard for office and kept working hard to expand our sales.

I thought about Bill Hawson out there still working deals, not because he needed the money because he was filthy rich, but just for the love of the trade. It's funny in an age when everybody is scrambling to retire early when you find somebody really pledged to her calling like that. If you can do it well and are enjoying it, why stop?

We had six stores by that time spread over Northeast Georgia. Jim's sales force was ahead of us, though, covering territories where we hadn't yet planted a store. Our brick and mortar outlets couldn't keep up with his work. He was a genius at building successful sales territories. We'd had only to follow where he led to keep expanding.

But I'm getting off the subject. Let me go back to my acquiring Lawson Hall. At first I'd had a little trouble getting possession of the old place, though I found out later that Laura had fought auctioning it off with tooth and nail. She had gone to see people. She had tried to use connections. "Did she know it was me who was buying it," I asked Bill Hawson.

"No idea," he said. "We kept the identity of the buyer confidential. There was still some good will left, but she had backed herself into a corner. Saul Spiegel called the mortgage. His people came from Minsk a generation ago. He didn't owe the Lawsons anything and had no reason to give a damn about Georgia bluebloods. That cinched it for us." I liked the way Bill Hawson viewed my interests as "us."

Once I got into the place, the first thing I did was check the attic above the library. Judge Lawson's genealogical researches were still just as he had left them. Either Laura didn't know or didn't care. The handmade table was still covered with the large sheets upon which he had traced with pen and pencil his entire family tree. My branch of the family was covered in pencil.

Starting from the top, I checked it all out again. It was the way I'd remembered it after my fairly cursory examination several years earlier. Judge Lawson had himself connected by a thin pencil line to Baby, my mother. I sprang out of that liaison. As I looked at it again, I wondered if the uneven lead line was a sign of regret. I studied the line itself with a magnifying glass, engrossed in the jagged brokenness of the thing when enlarged. Then I answered my own question: Of course he had regretted siring me upon one of the servant girls. What was I thinking? I'm sure he must have considered it something like a youthful "indiscretion."

Youthful indiscretion. The sort of thing you'd rather forget. Except that a person was the consequence. I guess that getting somebody pregnant is the only time you can do an indiscretion that has the kind of consequence you simply can't forget. Not if the person you happened to have made during this indiscretion shows up again, which I did. Judge Lawson didn't have to let Uncle Cajus bring me in to live at the Hall. My constant presence would have been a reminder – unless he could just block it out. Or maybe he decided that he wanted me close by. He wanted to be able to keep an eye on me? I don't know. I would never know.

Maybe he didn't care. Maybe he didn't even think about my being the fruit of his youthful indiscretion. Maybe he was totally indifferent to the fact that I was his daughter. Maybe he didn't somehow know it. Or maybe he did. Maybe that's why he fetched me back from Connecticut after his sister was killed and taught me German. Maybe that was his way of showing paternal interest in me?

When you remember that Judge Lawson's father had been the notorious Vandiver – well, that changes the complexion of the whole business somewhat. Vandiver was remembered as the Lawson who rampaged about the countryside doing violence to black and white alike. I guess Judge Lawson didn't really have much of a chance to know what affection felt like, and my mother probably gave him a big hunk of it in the stables. Who could blame him? My mother, Baby, was about as sensual as the good Lord will permit a woman to be within the bounds of nature.

There were other penciled lines connecting Vandiver to my grandmother. My mother sprang out of that, drawn in Judge Lawson's unrevealing iconographic lead symbols, scratched upon the page, hardly visible in places without the help of the magnifying glass, as if he were both trying to make something transparent and opaque at the same time.

The meaning of all these lead scratches upon paper stupefied me. Until then I had simply assumed Laura Lawson was my half sister. I was the bastard side. Oh yes. The bastard side – an assumption I certainly had no need to back off of for the moment, which, in fact, all the information I was now taking in confirmed and quadrupled. Laura's grandfather was mine, too, three-fold. Her father was both my father and my uncle. What a curious mix of genes I must carry in my person! Laura was my half-sister but also my cousin several times over.

Incest plays havoc with the usual degrees of kinship. As I worked down the family tree, I realized that Vandiver had begot my mother upon Charles' daughter. Charles was Randolph Lawson's son, or so it seemed – unless there had been a Charles senior and Charles Junior, which, unless I could line up the dates properly, seemed likely. I couldn't yet be sure.

The whole thing had started back with Randolph the First, that noble figure standing in the portrait in the entrance hall, the portrait reproduced in our Georgia history books. Judge Lawson had entered neat citations to support the entries in pencil on the family tree. These entries cited some source. I read: "Diary, XII, p. 236."

Diary? My eyes wandered about the attic room. It had never been finished with plaster walls. The ceiling was the wood that held up the roof. The floor was only semi-finished planking. Like ancient ribs there were heavy beams supporting the roof, unclothed and bare.

If I leaned back and reached as far as I could, it was possible for me to take out one of the volumes lining the shelf. These volumes had leather spines upon which somebody had written the volume numbers in a kind of ink. These were tall, slender, elegant volumes. They were inviting, so I pulled one out of its rank and opened it.

I thumbed through to page 236 and read: "Today Miriam bore a male child. There was no trace of the African upon him except rather tightly curled hair. The grade was, however, of our race..."

The quality of the paper distracted me. I rubbed the paper between thumb and index finger. It was not at all brittle. I examined the binding. The thread used to sew it in was still firm. It was in better condition than some ledgers I'd found at Mr. Hendricks' store that dated back only thirty or forty years. Yet, this volume had been manufactured, perhaps hand manufactured, during the first three decades of the nineteenth century a century and a half earlier.

How is it, I wondered, that a product can be produced of such quality that it comes through more than a hundred and fifty years in better shape than a product made in 1939? Why would they have done such a great job putting such a product together in 1825, then again in 1935 it wasn't necessary. They could sell it without the added value? Was there something fundamentally different about people's expectations in 1825? Did they simply expect that kind of quality as a matter of course? Were the materials at hand simply superior to those available to the manufacturers in 1935?

These diaries were actually plantation journals. They contained a narrative describing the daily goings-on in a commercial agricultural operation, including accounts, expenses and income. Since person things were mixed in, and the personal dimension seemed to grow as the author married and had a family, it stood to reason that he didn't separate his commercial life as strictly from his domestic life as we do now.

There was no way I wanted to rush my exploration of my Lawson past. I wanted to relish it. I didn't think this strategy out. It just seemed like the right way to go about my exploration of the past. I knew so little about the world at the turn of the eighteenth to the nineteenth centuries. Little steps were advised.

First of all, I was enjoying the triumph of possession, squeezing out every ounce of joy I could find in it walking through the rooms and examining all the furniture, the portraits, the accumulations of generations of Lawsons. Laura had been unable to remove a single stick of furniture. The Sheriff had actually barred her from visiting after the foreclosure. It was decreed that the house would be sold lock, stock, and barrel.

Gradually, I began to read the diaries. First I searched out the places in the diaries that Judge Lawson cited to support his genealogical assumptions. Then I simply began reading cover to cover, starting with the early diaries. The saga began with Randolph the First. After reading awhile, I would climb back down into the library and stroll up to the front to look at Randolph's grand portrait.

He was captured gloriously in oils. It was a full-length portrait. Randy (which is what I started calling him) wore short curls framing his bright, pale face but also in an elegant disorder. The disarray of his hair suggested that it was being blown by some invisible breeze long since faded.

Randy had strikingly liquid blue eyes, wide but not surprised, rather confident, a little arrogant, but also with a touch of kindness and humor playing there. He was looking out at a friendly prospect because there was a Rococo smile playing across his features that complemented his eyes. I detected also just a suggestion of supporting haughtiness in the tilt of his chin.

Randy was highborn and self-assured. His equivalent today would be the son of a successful millionaire who had gone to all the right schools and gotten started with the best Wall Street law firm. He was successful but also inclined to magnanimity. This is, at least, what I began to imagine he had been like. What I knew is, the diaries would soon tell the tale.

More enigmatic to me was the portrait of Randy's wife, Clarissa, which stopped just below her cleavage and then again barely above her fluent locks. The frame squeezed her chubby, bare shoulders, and she looked a little piqued about it, too, as if she was ever so slightly irritated with the painter for doing that to her. She had a puffy little flower-mouth and innocuous or even somewhat stupid grey eyes. Compared to Randy, her portrait looked like the painter was trying to save money on materials, though it was still nicely rendered if not at all flattering.

Written in a flowery hand on the back of the frame was the legend: "Clarissa Symington Randolph, born in Charleston on May 6th, 1790, died Lawson County, Georgia 1838."

It was easy to like Randy, which might have been the intent of the painter who had been paid handsomely for his work. It was easy not to like Clarissa – and that might admittedly be because Randy had skimped on the fee for his wife's sitting. It might also just have well have been that she was portrayed accurately. But, if the latter were true, then the question was unavoidable: Why would a handsome, successful man like Randy marry a commonplace, perhaps somewhat peevish woman?

I anticipated finding answers to my questions as I began to read the diaries. In the meantime, I will remind you that Lawson Hall was nothing like the grand, colonnaded structures built by rich planters in the eighteen forties and fifties. Its peculiar charm, to my mind, was that it did not look like those mansions.

As I strolled around the park and thought about what I might do to restore it to a certain glory, as I stood down by the pond and looked across the expanse to the building itself, I knew that it was the Hall's unprepossessing aplomb I liked most. It was the difference between ostentation and solid and useful quality.

I think it must have been well into the second month of my ownership that it occurred to me as I stood in the drive looking back at the Hall that it was my ancestral home as well as that of Laura. It was *my* ancestral home, too, and my owning it somehow canceled for me the ancient shame of our illegitimacy.

Was I was not the real and, therefore, legitimate owner and mistress with a pedigree every bit as real as Laura's? Yes, I was. I had the deed and the genealogy to prove it. I would go into the national historical register as the owner of Lawson Hall. In the end, I had won. *We* had won. Our side had won. We owned the tradition and the heritage and the visible artifacts that make up the Lawson family history.

~

"March 15, 1803. We have found the highest promontory on the estate from which we can easily observe the fields for several miles to the south. We have set up a brick oven and have begun to cure some of the timbers. I intend to build a stables and other appendages around the central house, all in brick or stone for permanence and in order to facilitate a cooler interior for both myself and the animals."

There were some sketches of the house plans on the next few pages. A month later Randy wrote that "the four brick masons I have assigned to the task are energetic fellows and worth every penny I paid for them. I have assigned ten laborers to work with them in baking the brick and mixing the mortar. The two carpenters are making good progress putting up the framing of the main house. I have decided to build the west wing first, so that they can get the mill done and the stables before we continue with our living quarters. We will do the public rooms and the library later."

Randy's life was also dangerous: "Last night I was sitting in my favorite chair and had lit a pipe when I heard a noise behind me. I took my pistol and slipped outside through the back door. I came upon two men. One of them leapt up and ran. The other turned upon me before I could fire. He seized my right arm, and we turmbled upon the ground. He tried to gouge my eyes, but I believe I managed to break his arm. I felt the bone crack. He then detached himself and ran off into the darkness. I was relieved to have him go.

"Once I was certain he was gone, I examined the wall of my cabin and saw that the men had inserted a long rifle in a chink between the logs. They had intended to murder me as I sat smoking my pipe. I decided to station my brick layers and carpenters as guards and rotate them through the night. It will be a comfort when I finish the stone house and build it high enough so that one cannot simply fire at me through a window!"

A week later Randy recorded a conversation with the Methodist circuit rider that explained the episode: "Preacher Watson stopped by today. He told me that the two men who attempted to kill me were squatters who lived down near Nancy Creek in the settlement there. He told me that it would behoove me to provide some assistance to him in building the church he has been working on with his man. On considering the matter, I agreed that he has a point. If we can establish a Christian meeting place where the people of the area can gather and come to know each other, it might diffuse the violence and murder that comes from the suspicion and fear he squatters feel for us who have bought our property with solid cash."

The Methodist church was built by Preacher Watson and his slave with some assistance from Randy and his workers. The meeting house was open for Christmas services and word was spread through the district that everybody, squatter and landowner, was invited, that it was indeed their Christian duty to come join in the services:

"It was astonishing to see the squatter families arrive Christmas Day. They were at first wary and suspicious, and they are generally not a loquacious people. They are, however, proud and often handsome. Several of the older men made it clear to me and Mr. Steeples that we are the interlopers, though we might have legal title to our lands. Since they arrived here several years ago and have been living side by side and marrying among the Cherokees, they feel they have precedence.

"While they obviously resent our having legal title to such large tracts of land they feel is their own by right of prior settlement, I expressed some sympathy with their position without actually committing myself. I implied that I was open to negotiation where issues were passionately felt. Both Steeples and I pointed out that we had had no idea when purchasing our holdings that we were intruding upon prior settlers.

"Since Steeples and I were sponsoring the barbeque, we harvested a certain amount of goodwill, at least for the day, and, as the whiskey made the rounds (though not too much), tempers moderated. I think that, if we can promote church going here, the practice will mitigate the tension. Certainly it will enable us to get to know these people and to establish personal relations that may be useful in alleviating a fear they feel from simply not knowing us. Steeples and I both agreed with Preacher Watson that we would provide in future refreshments and edibles for church holidays. In this manner we may well establish a more Christian society in the long run – or at least until it is possible to organize an effective policing of the law."

Lawson Hall had grown, one wing being complete in 1804, with the kitchen in a building at some distance from the house to avoid fires and to save the inhabitants of the house from the heat generated in the kitchen. Randy was very conscious of maximizing the natural situation and structure to ensure interior coolness in the hot summers and warmth in the fairly severe though brief winters.

The roof was extended in order to cool the draughts that were drawn through the floor-length windows into the high-ceilinged rooms of the interior of the house. The supporting walls of brick and stone were thick. Each room was equipped with a fireplace. The second-story bedrooms had low ceilings for winter warmth. In summer the men would take their pallets and sleep on the downstairs sleeping porch, while the women slept on the second story porch.

Since there were no screens, they waged a constant battle against flies and mosquitoes. There was netting imported from the coastal ports, for there were few women and none with much skill at contriving finely woven material like netting. Randolph had one of the younger men fan him and his overseers as they sat at table in the evening "to blow away the insects as much as possible and to stir a refreshing breeze."

During those early months of my being the sole owner and inhabitant of Lawson Hall, I had arranged a hot plate, cups, and tea, so that I could make myself a drink without having to climb back downstairs. I worked at least an hour a day on the diaries and connections. The remainder of the day was given over to business, for we still had by now eight stores to manage and much work to do between Jim and myself.

Late in the afternoon I tried to find time to take long, woodland jogs, and I would also practice firing my pistol in the range I had set up behind the stable. I rarely went down into town except to go to the store once a day. Naturally I had my people deliver anything I needed to the Hall. I suppose I had assumed a lifestyle of somewhat isolated splendor as the new mistress of Lawson Hall.

I liked being in the house by myself among all the possessions Laura had once so jealously protected. Occasionally I would have the odd feeling that Ida Mae had just called me, as she used to do, or that Judge Lawson had just gone around the corner of the hall on his way to his desk in the library. A noise, the creak of a board in the old house would make me start. At night before I slept, as I lay in bed waiting to pass into unconsciousness, the house seemed alive with movement and sound. Sometimes I lay awake listening, and my imagination would run away with me. Then I would take my pistol and walk through the house to reassure myself that I was alone. It is easy to imagine some people in old houses beginning to believe in ghosts.

Lawson Hall meant so much more to me than it ever could have meant to any stranger. But there is no question. I don't believe in ghosts. Once as I was reading the diary, I imagined the hand that had held the pen, dipping into the ink at intervals and busily making passes across the paper. The hand, the pen that left these lines of meaningful symbols clustered as they are into paragraphs, scribbles that – for one who can read them – tell a story – that hand had long since crumbled into dust.

This is, I thought, a story of events and relations past, vanished, the very people who made them substantial long since changed from animate flesh and blood to dead bones – and finally dust. It was in that moment that I felt myself careening down into a great dark chasm that appeared before me, as if the earth had opened up along an enormous fault-line to swallow up the very breath one dares to draw.

My heart was beating wildly, my pulse accelerating. I could feel the pressure of the blood flow at my temples. It was just a matter of time until some random contraction in a remote part of my system would erupt, releasing fluids upon tissues, smothering and drowning the circuits that made up the total organism – and then what? Death? Cessation of bodily function, my consciousness swallowed up in a vast, dark stillness; my only hope of resuscitation being that some one might stray upon some artifact of what my own life? There would be an article of clothing, perhaps a record of my career in business, even a letter I had left?

How would my resuscitation proceed? The hand of that future curiosity might take up the letter, just as I was taking up these diaries, read it, thereby recalling something of my person in that particular article, for a moment, in their own consciousness. Was that all I could hope for? Was that all anybody could look forward to? Were we really nullities, as we suspect, spat out of some primordial gullet to splash about momentarily in oozing fluids only to be swallowed up again into the vacuum from which we had come?

This found me sitting in the very early hours of morning, before sunrise, exhausted, desolate, wondering why I should lack the solace Aunt Ida Mae and Uncle Cajus felt and the comfort they could exude as naturally as breath. I tried to think of somebody to talk to, but there was none. I got a Bible and tried to read. The print resisted my attempts to decipher it, like a jar too tight to open. I knelt and tried to pray, but it didn't seem to work. My mind wandered in the very act, leaping skittishly from one cracked notion to the next.

When this happened to me, as it did more than once during those months, I simply had to endure until morning. The light of a new day brought back Hard Reality with all its prosaic stoicism. This is the everyday, it whispered. There is no real joy, only perseverance. Folly, it spoke to me, you must simply get through it, from one day to the next. There will never be any Enormous Arrival. You will never find any other person who cherishes you for no other reason but that you are yourself, some lover who longs to know you for who you are alone, no mitigating circumstance, no ulterior motive – pure and simple love.

In the light of Hard Reality, I could recognize the sense of desolation for what it was, I thought. Was it simple depression, hardly more than a matter chemical imbalance? Or was I missing something that was real, that both could and should be a part of my life? And if I were missing it, what had I done wrong? Which step took me away from that proper destiny?

One side of me was clear about what I should do. It chided me. Brace up, it said. Be an adult. Stop pouting. This is the way it is. There is nobody out there waiting on you. There is no destiny. Still, I couldn't escape it. I wandered the house with a single assurance: Something was missing.

I jogged to the cemetery late one afternoon and walked among the tombstones. I found the Lawson plot again and saw them all gathered. Inadvertently, I stumbled across a tombstone far in the corner, a small thing, with the simple legend upon it, "Charles Steeples." There was nothing else; no dates, not even his wife's name.

There was, at some point, a moment when I just emerged from the depression. It was not that I had found the answer. It was not that at all. I had simply exhausted my grief. But Tom was an instrument in my momentary cure, for he came up to me one day in the lumber yard, put his hand on my shoulder and said sadly, "Missy, what is the matter? You have been so far down now for so long. I'm sorry for you, Missy. What is it?"

"Oh, Tom," I said, and I felt the tears welling up and filling my eyes.

Tom hugged me. We were alone there that afternoon. Uncle Cajus and the new man were out on a delivery. "Missy, you have me and Cajus. You have Ida Mae. We love you, Missy. Honest we do."

"I know, Tom." I clung to him a moment and whispered, "But how do you bear it?"

"Because you were kind to me, Missy, when I was low down. You came and saved me. That made all the difference."

"Is that enough?"

"It's like Cajus says when he's preaching, too. 'Jesus loves us,' he says."

"But where is Jesus when you need him," I moaned.

Tom turned me toward him. His face was flushed bright red, as usual, his pale, blue eyes bulging in fixed innocence, his expression earnest, "Missy, he's waiting, that's all. He's waiting on you to invite him in."

"If only that made sense to me," I said, the old desolation rising up inside me like a desert storm, hot and dry, enough to wilt any green thing in sight.

Those were the days when I began to realize that Lawson Hall was not merely an artifact but a living and breathing container for the aggregate experience of the Lawsons over time. I was separated from them only in time, though I am not sure I would ever want to erase that barrier. If I were suddenly face to face with them, would I also be face to face with their hauteur, their social superiority?

The first thing I did each late afternoon was to lock the gates at the bottom of the hill, so that nobody could disturb me. Opening the diaries I saw Randolph's legible, flowing handwriting. There was ease and elegance in the writing. Such script was not the product of an awkward person. The strokes were sure, firm, in command of the line they created as they moved from left to right across the page. I worked my way forward to volume 22, page 118. I thought that the romance between Miriam and Randy might have begun, more or less, in what followed:

"Munich. On returning from an interview with the *Staatsminister*, I found Prince Zukovsky seated in the lobby across from Miriam. Naturally, I was quite surprised and felt obliged to interrupt them. In our apartments upstairs I confronted Miriam for violating my instructions. It should have been understood, I told her, that she was not to make voluntary social contacts among the gentry visiting the place.

"To my considerable surprise, she responded with a most vigorous defense of her behavior. Her eloquence took me aback. Her person is quite developed in every womanly aspect, and the total effect is unusually powerful. That which makes any encounter with her memorable is not only her physical gifts but her prodigious mental capacity, unusual in a woman. The density of her thought, its scope, the subtlety and deftness of mind she displays is the mark of high intelligence. There is grace, too, in the effortless and assured manner in which she demonstrates her powers without seeming to try. I am reluctant to say so, but I stand amazed that this creature has grown up in my household with my being only dimly aware of her exceptional powers."

Judge Lawson had marked the place on his chart with number 1, and I saw that he must have considered this the beginning, as well, when Randolph first looked at Miriam not as a slave but as a person. Yet, I couldn't yet be sure. The only thing to do was to begin at the beginning. In order to do that, I went all the way back to 1809 when he purchased her. A relevant entry on page 10 of volume 4 told the story:

"Gamed with Nigel Steeples. He is a hopeless dipsomaniac and was deep in his cups. He had brought back a young girl, a very light mulatto of seven or eight and of exceptional beauty, from Jamaica and told me he was looking forward to the moment when he thought she was ripe for the harvesting. Liquor has made a savage of Steeples. I was frankly horrified at what he said, but I disguised my feelings. I was moved to pity for the fate that awaited the child. Her beauty is of an almost unworldly quality. He paraded her past us. Publicly displayed as she was, she exuded an air of angelic modesty. She has the most beautiful eyes and is quite as white in feature and aspect as any proper Charlestonian. I will admit that a certain outrage took hold of me, though I troubled to keep it hidden. I decided in that moment to save the child by winning her at cards."

Which is precisely what Randy Lawson did. He won my ancestress at cards in order to save her from the sexual abuse Steeples had in mind when he bought her, in the first place. After reading this episode, I scanned the next few years without finding Miriam mentioned again. In the meantime, Randolph married Clarissa Symington of Charleston and began to spawn a family of his own.

So far as I could tell, he kept the young Jamaican among the house staff. His marriage was largely a matter of building his network and gaining access to the considerable capital the Symington family made available. Randy made no comment because he took it for granted that marriage was a worldly alliance and not a conjoining of affinity and affection.

Though he kept his accounts in the same diaries, I couldn't make much sense of the equivalencies until I contacted Dalton Chambers at the State Archives. Dalton was very excited at the prospect of working with me on such a historical document. He became so excited when I described the diaries to him, that it was all I could do to keep him from driving down to Lawson Hall and examining them that very moment. In fact, the only thing that kept him away was my determination not to invite him.

When he saw that I would guard my treasure and keep it to myself, I think he decided to cooperate in the hope eventually of gaining access. After that, I could phone him whenever I had a question. Whatever he was doing, he would drop it and permit himself to be hailed to the telephone by one of the archival assistants. If there was something more important, I would take it with me when I went to Atlanta on business. In the meantime, with his guidance, my own library grew, as did my learning.

One thing I could measure in the accounts and descriptions of Randy's business dealings was his capacity as a businessman. It was nothing like the romantic images of fiction like *Gone with the Wind*. Randolph Lawson was an actively engaged, shrewd businessman. His products were agricultural, but he dealt with the same complex of problems as I. Not only did the product have to be produced and a system set up to that purpose. Randy also had to get his product to market.

Randy was resourceful, tireless, a good negotiator, frugal and demanding. He not only strove to produce the best quality cotton, he was determined to maximize the price he got for it at market. To that end he was constantly in motion, constantly busy, building networks, tying knots, making deals. His was a very busy life.

As I suspected from studying her portrait, Randy's wife, Clarissa, was a difficult, spoiled and moody woman. She was often "unwell" or "faint" or had "taken to her bed." She bore him three children, one son, Randy Junior, but childbirth sent her into convalescence for months and months. The babies were given over to Negro wet nurses who either gave enough milk for both their own baby and the new Lawson offspring or who had lost a baby.

I spent a number of months working out just what Randy's rise in wealth from 1803 until 1818 meant in current values. His combined plantations in Georgia and South Carolina produced an annual gross income in today's values of twelve million dollars in 1814. His labor costs had clearly been much higher than anything I could conceive, for he had to acquire and maintain a large force of slaves.

Dealing with slaves had a personal cost, as well, not only for the slaves (which I could only surmise, since they couldn't write their own records) but for Randy. He had to deal with the white overseers, some of them men who had either been attracted to the business because of a brutal streak, or who had fallen into violent and cruel ways after being corrupted by their jobs. He was frequently embroiled in arguments and even fist fights. Occasionally there were gun battles.

"May 12, 1812. No word of Napoleon's Russian venture. He has presumably drained the Germanies of its male population to create a force large enough to deliver Russia a debilitating blow. The blockade continues, but a privateer recently breeched the lines long enough to deliver a cargo south of Brest on the Normandy coast. The profits should be considerable, making it worth the risk.

"Had an altercation with Mordicai Pitt yesterday near Augusta. The man is pitiless. His hate is beyond bounds, and I came upon him whipping a woman. He knows nothing of dignity and cares nothing for the approbation of decent society. I must find a way to replace him for the sake of my poor field workers. When I first hired him he was not so obsessed, indeed a most useful overseer whom I promoted, I fear, to chief steward. Getting rid of him will be no easy task. And, yet, if I do not, I fear there will be open mutiny among my hands– and what will come of that is easy enough to predict. Ultimately, it can only harm them and me."

In order to check his overseers in their brutality, Randy lived much of the year in the saddle riding back between his various plantations. He described the prosperous growth of Washington, Georgia and other settlements. His arrival at one of the plantations brought a cessation of brutality and often even amnesty for those who were lined up to be punished with a number of lashes.

Though Randy was obviously responsible for the system he maintained, it was easy to see that the slaves must have seen him as their only hope for any mercy in a violent, unjust world. He made his surprise visits even more potent by sponsoring a big barbeque and giving the slaves a holiday wherever he went.

Randy had bought Georgia land long before it was clear that the Cherokees would be removed from the area. A new kind of long-staple cotton had been developed that made it profitable to grow the crops in the Deep South. The success of the crop gave the economy in frontier regions like Georgia and Alabama great energy and verve, provided a compelling reason for increased settlement and, consequently, put pressure on both the Indian inhabitants and the white squatter class.

There emerged in Randy's descriptions a sense of excitement, of men hurrying about, anxious to make their fortunes as quickly as possible. There was also a palpable aura of anxiety hovering in the background as the specter of slave revolts seemed ever present. There was also the constant danger in the early days that either the white squatters or the Indians might lay an ambush to murder the thin planter class one by one. Finally, Randy was surely not the only planter who worried that the land would quickly become exhausted as it had in Virginia and North Carolina, forcing him to look for more fertile soil.

In spite of all the hazards, Randy continued to work and expand his enterprises until 1821, amassing a considerable fortune in the process. In that year he began to consider the requests from high-placed political allies that he engage himself in the affairs of the nation. He wrote that "Clarissa has urged me to think about the offer young Carville made to me of taking five years to act as plentipotentiary in south Germany. There are two kings and one grand duke there created by Napoleon. It seems the United States needs representation for a number of reasons at the present."

I imagined that Clarissa, who had been bred in Charleston society, was attracted by the prestige of a diplomatic appointment. What her husband had written about her over a period of several years of their marriage had not made me like her much. She seemed weak, spoiled, petulant, and moody. That she had not considered carefully what it might really mean to accept a diplomatic post abroad would not surprise me.

By 1821 Randy's affairs had reached a zenith of success. His income was enormous. His plantations extended over thousands of acres. He had several dozen plantations, but I had as yet been unable to calculate just how many acres or slaves he commanded. Dalton told me that I could hire a researcher to do the hard work, but I thought I'd put it off for the present.

One of the difficulties of knowing the exact extent of Randy's holdings was that there were no income tax at the time, thus a person had no need to keep an exact account of things. Figures were written down for the planter's convenience, not for the purpose of reporting exact profits and losses to the government. There was much that Randy simply carried about, I imagined, in his own head. It might even have been advisable not to write everything down.

His position as planter was dangerous. He wrote, "Tim Wheeler was with me when they fired out of ambush last evening at about seven p.m. We were coming back from the Patton Place after tending to three sick women and our best gang-leader in the west fields. We managed to dismount with our rifles in hand. We had sufficient ammunition on our persons. We soon realized that the squatters were using old long rifles and a poor grade of powder. I believe the Almighty had a hand in providing them such inferior supplies, as it saved us both, though Tim received a bad wound in the hand at the end. I have instructed Tim to hire men to clear these people out of the area."

Before he left for Europe, Randy reported that "the family of squatters near the Patton Place, their names being Taylor, were cleared out with the cooperation of the sheriff after they killed one of my best men a week ago this Sunday. The slaves are terribly grief stricken at the loss of their own headman and hardly able to work. The squatters despise the Negroes. Their hate is murderous."

Once he had made arrangements, Randy packed the household and took passage with Clarissa and the children to England. He set sail in late summer of 1821. They put in first at Portsmouth, England and then sailed on to Le Havre. When they came into the Portsmouth harbor, Clarissa made an awful scene about wanting to go on land and visit England. Randy was able to resist, but it was the worst moment to date in their marriage and did not bode well for the European sojourn.

When they started overland to Paris, Clarissa's moods became more erratic. She vacillated between sulking depression and petulant scenes she pitched about nothing. In France her behavior grew worse. As they passed through Epernay, Randy could do nothing to appease her. She ran after his "man" (read: valet), Cassius, whom they'd brought with them, with a stick, and all for something she imagined he had neglected to do. Randy had, he wrote "forcibly wrenched the stick from her".

"What has happened to Clarissa I cannot say. I hardly recognize in her a rational being. The children are kept in constant anxiety at what she will do next. Cassius is pouting and angry. Only Miriam remains serene. I believe it must be something in the liquids we are drinking that has a unique effect upon her spiritual constitution."

...Only Miriam, I read. Only Miriam – this was the young Jamaican child he had won at cards from his neighbor, Nigel Steeples. Here she was reappearing on the journey to Europe. Randy (or Clarissa) had decided to take her along. When I told Dalton about this new development, he nodded genially and explained that, "having the servants along to take care of them was so much part and parcel of their lives that they couldn't imagine going off without taking some of them along. It would have been taken for granted. Nobody would have thought about it."

It turned out that Randy was actually accredited at three German courts at once, as he had earlier suggested might be the need of his government. One of these courts was the in Karlsruhe and belonged to the Grand Duke of Baden in Karlsruhe. That is where Randy was instructed to rent a house and settle for the duration. The other courts included the royal court of the King of Wurttemberg in Stuttgart. Then there was also the King of Bavaria in Munich.

In order to get accreditation, he had to present himself in turn at each of these places, giving the family many opportunities to travel about the countryside.

Randy's accounts showed me that he paid everything out of his own pocket the first year; yet, he seemed to think nothing of it. Dalton said we must assume it was what was usually expected of those who took on diplomatic appointments. Later, when we were able to ask some knowledgeable historian of the period, we would know for certain, but I thought it likely that Randy considered it routine and part of the cost of serving his country.

It took more than a year before the consular fees began to offset the family's expenses. Randy applied all fees to his own expenses. He made no distinction between public and private expenses. There was no Congressional watchdog committee waiting back home for his accounts. He was free to do what he chose.

Serving as a diplomat still continued to cost Randy plenty throughout the sojourn. "I have spent a total of twenty thousand dollars since my arrival," he wrote several months into his job. "My brother-in-law has written me that receipts at home have declined by twenty percent this year. He blames the markets and the weather. Whatever the cause, it is clear to me that this work is damaging to my fortune!"

Randy had left the operation of his enterprises in the hands of Clarissa's brother, Stuart, who had proven a good businessman, planter, and merchant. As time passed, however, Randy became less and less satisfied with his performance and more suspicious that he was not doing his job honestly. "I cannot help suspecting Stuart of pocketing more than his share of the income this year. How else could so much go missing? I do not believe his complaints about the weather. I hear about it from other sources, too, after all. Can he not know that, or does he simply not care, knowing me to be so far away?"

I was soon fairly lost in the intricacies of European life, the Society of the three capital cities in which Randolph moved as plentipotentiary or American envoy. Finally, I went to Atlanta, burst in on Dalton at his desk at the State Archives with an appeal: "Dalton, you must get me in touch with somebody who can brief me on European affairs!"

"Ah," he said, delighted again at a new challenge. "I know just the man."

Professor Swanson at Emory declared himself more than willing to help me on Dalton's recommendation. It was about that time that Dalton approached me for the first time about financial assistance for a project at the Archives. "We really need to preserve this material," he said, holding open a diary from another family. "It's very much like the documents you've found."

"There's nothing in the budget," I asked.

"Are you naïve," he said. "Of course not. The legislature has cut us again."

His putting me in touch with Professor Swanson cost me a thousand dollars, but it was worth every penny. My understanding of research tools improved a thousandfold over the next few months under the scholar's tutelage. I read all the usual histories in English and began to understand the larger picture.

In 1823 Central Europe had been pacified through the leadership of Prince Metternich. Liberals were put under pressure to shut up and leave, radicals were hunted, there was zero-tolerance for troublemakers. Metternich was determined to give the countries of the area some respite after the incessant wars of Napoleon.

Metternich's enemies were all those bright, educated democratic types of middle-class background who had hoped for a post-Napoleonic order with more open governments and better political access. As far as Randy observed in his diaries, the regular population of the country seemed pleased enough being left alone to mind their business and get back to the traditional normality of planting and harvesting.

Randy never gave any substantial clue in his diary entries that he understood or observed any of the struggles between the old aristocratic orders and the new middle-classes. He marveled at the busy productivity of the peasants and small farm holders whose daily labors he would often stop to watch, observing their methods of planting and harvesting.

"The European free-holder," he wrote, "is ever busy, never tiring." He might have said, of course, that any person working on his own land and for his own profit is more productive than slaves who have nothing to gain from their labor. He didn't, of course. Connecting the two remained yet outside his scope.

It was on a stormy Sunday afternoon that Jim came. The thunder and lightening were making me begin to think about leaving the attic when I heard the car drive into the front yard. He came up on the porch. I watched him from the window and was about to call down to him when he began to hammer on the front door, "Open up, Folly. I know you're there!"

"Jim," I called, "I'm up here. Let me get down to open the door. Wait a minute."

When I opened the front door, he rushed into the foyer in a great huff, all wet and angry. "Why did you shut the gates and lock them? You're holed up here like a hermit!"

"Goodness, Jim, what's wrong? I locked up last night and haven't been down to unlock the gates. How did you get in?"

"I took the damn thing off its hinges, and now I'm soaked, for Christ's sake."

"You look fit to be tied. What's going on?"

"I could ask you the same question. I had some men pay me a visit today. Why didn't you tell me you're trying to sell the business?"

He was short of breath, he was so furious. "Jim, let's go get something to drink."

"I don't want anything to drink, damn it! Don't think you can diffuse the situation."

"No, I just thought—"

"Why haven't you told me?"

"Jim, I haven't been out actively trying to sell the business. But you know that there are people out there who're looking for something like we've got. They don't wait until you tell them you want to sell."

"Come on. He said he'd heard…"

"No, then he was blowing steam."

"You don't want to sell?"

"Is there anything in business you wouldn't sell at the right price, Jim?"

He started to speak and then caught himself. "What's the right price then?"

"I don't know. But if they're really interested, let's let them give us an offer."

"Us?"

"You own part of the business, too, don't you."

"You're damned right I do."

"What about something to drink?"

"Okay, if you insist."

He followed me back to the kitchen. It may have been the sound of running water as I filled the kettle. Jim relaxed again. When I'd filled the kettle, I took it to the stove, turned on the eye and set it down. Then I turned slowly around and looked steadily at him.

He was watching me. His eyes were still inhabited by suspicion and anger. He had gained weight, but it added solidity to his person. He no longer looked too young for responsibility. It was deceiving, I thought. He was more foolishly involved with Laura than ever – something I couldn't imagine his doing earlier. Still, I had it from many sources..

"Why do you hole up in this…place," he asked truculently.

"I'm not holed up. I don't know what you mean by that. I'm out every day of the week doing my share in the business. But I'm working on something here I really enjoy."

"Yeah, that Lawson family crap."

The kettle began to whistle. I took out two cups, found the teabags and dropped one in each cup. "You want honey?"

"Yeah, sure. Or sugar."

"Okay. I administered the doses of honey and then poured the hot water into the cups. "Jim, this isn't like us. You've never made a scene with me before."

"It made me mad," he said, his voice less certain and more placating.

"It's not like us. What's wrong. Has Laura had anything to do with this?"

"Laura," he said. "What would Laura have to do with this?"

"Just wondering. We've always trusted each other before, haven't we? I've certainly trusted you."

"Fol, we're grown now. We're not kids, anymore. The world is real. It's not pretend."

"I can't argue with that," I said quietly. I took his cup, squeezed the water out of his tea bag and handed the cup to him. He took it. I tossed the used tea bag into the trash. Then I did the same for my own cup, then raised it to my lips and sipped. The liquid was still too hot to drink. A heavy roll of thunder rattled the kitchen windows. We both started, then looked at each other. He smiled first.

"Okay, sport. You're right. We can't help it if somebody wants to buy into a good thing."

"Yes," I said. "Just because somebody's interested doesn't mean we have to sell, either. Let's toast the future." I held my cup up.

"To the future," he said, saluting me with his cup.

In that year there were two hundred blacks in state legislatures across the U. S. There were sixteen in Congress, one in the U. S. Senate. During the previous decade blacks had become mayors of Cleveland, Los Angeles, Gary, Newark, and many smaller places. In very little time there would be black mayors in Birmingham, Atlanta, and New Orleans. There were more than six hundred blacks sitting on city councils, more than a thousand active as judges, aldermen, marshals, and school board members. And Jim would become another in a long line of white governors of the Empire State of the South.

I wanted to tell him that he was betraying all of his who had helped him by playing with Laura. Georgia voters wouldn't take kindly to an adulterous governor. That's what I thought. I was a little naïve.

~

"Karlsruhe, July 15th, 1823. Clarissa is extremely unhappy with staying here now that her mother lies ill in Charleston. Her restlessness is affecting the entire household. I believe much of her dissatisfaction lies in the letters her brother writes. Even the children are now distraught. Cassius pitched something of a tantrum this morning when I refused to wear the tie and shirt he had laid out for me. Everybody is on edge."

Randy was worried about the servants he had brought along and worried about his man Cassius the most. He had caught the valet "talking to one of Count Dohnhafen's maids in the back yard. After I ran her off, Cassius sulked for two days. I overheard him yesterday telling Miriam that they were actually free here in this country and could leave any time they pleased. There would be nothing I could do about it."

A Charleston gentleman had alarmed Randy only two months after their arrival in the autumn of 1821 by telling how he had lost two of his best house servants while sojourning at an Austrian spa. Randy reported in his diary that "a handsome woman and a fine young male house servant simply walked away and refused to return. The whole village protected them when Sam went out to drag them back. He found himself facing some fifty able-bodied and angry peasants and had to withdraw."

After that report Randy determined "to keep both Miriam's and Cassius's status secret." The question was, would they keep their status secret? Most worrisome was the fact that Miriam had become more fluent in French and German than anybody else in the household, including Randy. He wrote that she "must know that she can go free any time she pleases. Cassius is worth less than half of what Miriam is..." Randy broke off his thought, skipped two lines and resumed: "What the child is worth cannot be phrased in material terms! As soon as they tell the German or French servants that they are slaves, they will discover in no uncertain terms that slavery is against the law here. After that, one cannot tell what consequences will follow. I must be on my guard."

Again and again Randy laments that "it was a bad mistake to bring my two best house servants along. Especially now that I find Miriam speaks much better French and German than any of us. Clarissa – who seems unable to learn either language – depends on her in the most imprudent manner. She takes Miriam along with her when she mixes in Society. It is extremely awkward, but there is nothing I can do about it. Clarissa would insist, as she always does, on whatever she most desires. To oppose her is to trigger her terrible scenes. Since she could hardly expect Society to accept Miriam if it knew her true status, my wife has introduced her as a relative of the family. When I first heard this, I protested – but to no avail."

"Do you realize," I told Dalton at my next visit to the State Archives, "That Randy has allowed his wife to take Miriam with her into Society and to introduce her as a distant cousin?"

Dalton lifted his left eyebrow. He loved to affect such gestures. Then he smiled his 'I told you so' smile with curled lip: "This is, my dear, a new kind of history you've got. You're sitting on a gold mine. You could first publish the facts." He held up his hands and framed the book he was imagining, "First a sort of factual treatment of this thing developing. Later a kind of historical romance. It should make you rich and famous." Then he dropped his hands, "I forgot, you're already rich."

"But not famous," I said.

"No, but you really should start trying to write this up. I'm sure we can get it published. An article first in the historical journal."

"Dalton, I never went to college. I know nothing at all about proper style."

"I'll edit it. We can share credit. I can always use that. It's good for my reputation."

"Once I finish," I said, "perhaps we'll do it together. If I do it at all, you'll be co-author, then."

"Thank you," he said simply. Then he rocked back in his chair on the back two legs, "What you've discovered really is worth a dissertation. A person could make an academic career on it. Or at least begin one. I wouldn't mind spending the last decade or so of my career as a professor."

"Aren't you exaggerating? Can this material really be that important," I asked in disbelief.

"You just don't know. You're so innocent, my dear. So shrewd in business, so unknowing in scholarship."

Of course, I had no interest in publishing Miriam's story. It was all I could do to find the time I needed to continue reading. What I did is simply continue to decipher the diaries. Randy's problems with his wife, Clarissa, got worse that summer. On August 10th he wrote: "There is nothing for it. Clarissa must be sent back to Charleston. Worry and homesickness has made her ill. Her mother's illness is getting progressively worse. Stuart hints that she will not survive. Naturally, Clarissa has been keeping to her room since the last letter. She seems to be weakening. If I don't let her return, she may very well become truly ill or too weak actually to make the journey!"

Randy began to make arrangements for his family's return. Five days later they all set out on a Rhine steamer with the servants in tow. "The children are jubilant to be returning home. I think it a pity to curtail their European education so abruptly, for young Randy is doing very well, especially in German. His French seems rather sufficient, as well, and he is quite fluent in the local dialect. I was hoping to make a diplomat of him. John Adams did that for his son. Nothing does more to broaden the mind than an extended European sojourn," Randy wrote.

He dispatched Cassius with the family on a packet to London. "It is better to have him safely back in South Carolina than to keep him here and, perhaps, lose him altogether," Randy confided to his diary. "He is a good young man and will take care of the family on the journey."

Then he returned south again alone to Karlsruhe.

The first few pages after the departure of Randy's family for England, I wasn't sure where Miriam was. Had she gone with the family? Had she remained in Karlsruhe? And then, after visiting the cathedral at Cologne and other sights along the Rhine, Randy writes on returning to his rented mansion, "I found her at home, waiting. It was an enormous relief for me to find her presiding over the household. Her authority lies in her serene command of affairs, her fluency in both languages that any of the servants here in town use, and her presence. The combination of her beauty and her comportment are overwhelmingly genteel and lady-like. She seems more a great lady than all those born to it!"

He had won her at cards when she was seven or eight, sixteen years earlier, by his own account, and now Miriam had to be around twenty-one. Randy was forty-two. They were in the house together with, as far as I could tell, one or two other servants. If

Nigel Steeples had brought her back from Jamaica because of her great beauty (and she was seven or eight at the time), what must she have been at twenty-one?

If only I could have found a portrait of Miriam in 1823. That might explain the impression she was making upon all and sundry that was unsettling to Randy. I thought about her clothes. Being a man, Randy said very little about clothes. He recorded the cost of the material or the tailoring, but not often. These must not have generally figured as large expenses for him. There had been no mention at all of the clothing Miriam wore. Still, I guessed that Clarissa wouldn't have taken her along into society as a relative without having her decently clothed. It was safe to assume that Miriam was not shabbily dressed.

On September 2nd Randy received a letter he recorded almost verbatim. It was sent from London by Clarissa in which she related how "Cassius abandoned us. He simply left without my knowing it, vanished from the hotel on our first night here. We should have gone straight to the boat, but the captain advised us to take quarters in town for the week until he had the boat loaded. I think he had planned it all along, and I doubt that he had an accomplice. He has now disappeared into this great city of London. Pray take care that Miriam doesn't escape in the same fashion. Watch her closely, Randolph."

Such advice from the wife proved ironic indeed. In the meantime, Randolph did try to follow his wife's instructions. There were entries that spoke of his coming back during the day to check on her. Finally, however, he gave it up. "It is midnight. I simply don't have the time and energy to invest in watching Miriam. I will simply have to trust her. If she leaves, then she must leave. There is far too much to do at court. My consular duties are becoming more demanding, as well, especially in Munich."

Again, Randy confides to his diary that, "I believe I can trust Miriam. She is the warmest, kindest person in many respects, without being familiar. She is extremely competent. I also believe she is writing something. I think it might be a novel or a history. I find her often in the study, and there are many sheets of paper stacked up. This is good because it preoccupies her and may keep her mind off mischief."

Just how was this all possible? I needed to know more about society at these small southern German courts. The professor at Emory was not a specialist in that particular area. Dalton didn't know anybody since his specialty was the Southern United States. He promised, however, to contact somebody at the University in Athens but then phoned me one day and told me that he had found somebody else at Vanderbilt University in Nashville.

Though I didn't look forward to the drive to Nashville, I preferred it to flying.

2

I found Professor Josefewicz's office at the back of one of the older buildings on the Vanderbilt campus. Parking had been next to impossible, but I had finally just squeezed in between a truck and a tree and thought to hell with it. I only regretted that I was driving Judge Lawson's old Buick, which had been parked in the stables when I bought the house. If I got a ticket, I'd just pay, and that's all there was to it.

I had a xeroxed map of the campus Dalton had sent me, but I still had to ask twice before I found the place. The old quad of the school was lined with buildings that seemed a mixture of Gothic and other styles. The whole effect was one of beauty. If I had expected the professor to be housed in a splendor the buildings promised, I was disappointed. I found him in cramped office space. My impression was of stacks of papers and books literally filling the room, everything in a general chaos.

"You must be Mrs. Steeples," he said in what I took to be a German accent.

"Yes, sir."

"Let's step outside. I'm afraid there's no room in my office." He brushed at the wisp of white hair standing up from his skull. His eyes twinkled. What we did is go out and walk around the quad, he with his hands clasped in European fashion behind his back, I concentrating on explaining to him just why I needed to know more about the habits of the people who gathered at the smaller German courts.

"This Randolph Lawson," he said. "He was actually accredited at these courts."

"Yes," I said.

He rubbed his chin and stopped near a monument. I looked around and saw that we were standing very near the library building. There was a museum just up the walkway I had spotted as we passed. Then I saw Walt.

Walt was sort of loitering on the library steps, pretending to read something he held up fairly high. He then turned his back to us. My mind wavered. I began to doubt that I had actually seen him. It was absurd to think that he had followed me to Nashville. Still, I was disconcerted enough to say to the Professor, "Excuse me, Professor. Can we now go somewhere more private."

Professor Josefewicz's grandfatherly squint showed he knew something had happened in that previous moment. "You are tired of our strolling," He asked.

"I.—I can't think right walking around like this. I," I made a stab at smiling, hoping I would make myself sound natural, "I need to sit. Coffee would be good. Can I buy you a cup of coffee?"

"Ach," he said, "Kaffee" – he pronounced it like 'café,' "yes, of course. We can go to the faculty club. That should be comfortable and private enough at this time of the morning."

I looked back once and Walt was gone. I later decided I must have imagined it was him. The Professor was, at any rate, very helpful, so that my long journey to Nashville was not a waste of time. After listening to my description of what I knew of Randolph's circumstances, and with only his regular interruptions of, "extraordinary, extraordinary," he settled down in the heavily upholstered chair in the faculty lounge and gave me his opinion: "Remember, this is merely an unconsidered view. The American envoy had settled in to quarters in Karlsruhe. The Grand Duke was preoccupied at the time with an opposition parliament. He had permitted the establishment of a parliamentary government in 1818 and had sponsored the writing of a very liberal constitution. These particular South German courts were all rather liberal. He found that he was not prepared, however, to deal with a real parliamentary opposition. I would appreciate your excerpting any political passages Mr. Lawson wrote in his journals and sending them to me."

"I haven't really found too many," I told him.

"They may yet come. Surely he must have—"

"I have thought that he might have been afraid to commit diplomatic business to writing."

Professor Josefewicz thought about that. "A very shrewd man indeed. Few were that cautious in those days. Be that as it may," he went on, "this liaison with the young mulatto slave, as remarkable as it may seem to us, was not completely unheard of among Society. The noble classes were very tolerant of mistresses, you must understand. You say she had been presented as a distant kinswoman of the family by Lawson's spouse?"

"His wife," I said.

"Yes. Then it would not have appeared far-fetched to the nobleman gathered at court that a romance develop once the wife was – how does one say it? – out of the picture. I take it she was light skinned enough to be viewed as white?"

"Yes, I believe so. She had very light eyes. Like mine," I said. Then I felt my forehead burning. Had I exposed my own racial ambiguity to this benevolent old scholar? And if I had, what did it matter?

He looked at me a moment very shrewdly, but then he looked away. "Romantic liaisons were tolerated in such society."

Professor Josefewicz told me much about the politics of the time. He would not hazard a guess as to the character of Randy's mission in Southern Germany. He shook his head in the end, "We must see if he writes something about his mission. I will check this out with a few colleagues. I was unaware that there was any American mission to these courts at that time. The problem is, we need to talk to somebody conversant both with American and European diplomatic affairs at the time. I do find it odd that he chose to settle in Karlsruhe when he was dispatched to all three courts."

When I left Professor Josefewicz, it was past noon. I was hungry. On the walk to his office, I had passed what I thought must be a cafeteria. When I reached it, the kitchen odors were too much for me. I started in and then stopped. Walt stood up. As I turned to get away, I knew he was following me. I hurried out of the building, almost running.

"Folly!"

I began to run. It was ridiculous. I couldn't think. People stopped and looked as Walt came up behind me. He grabbed at my arm. I pulled away. "Please wait," he cried.

"Leave me alone!"

He grabbed at me again. I just managed to dodge, and he ran into a parked car and grunted. Behind me I was dimly aware of a vehicle stopping. A university policeman appeared. "Is there something wrong, m'aam," a uniformed policeman called to me.

"Yes, officer. This man is bothering me," I panted, hardly able to find the breath to speak.

Walt looked betrayed. "Officer, I know this woman. I know her."

The policeman looked at me. "Of course I know him, officer. That's why I *do not* want him bothering me!"

"You heard her, sir. Can I help you to your automobile, m'aam?"

"Yes, please," I said.

Walt was standing there between two parked cars like a statue. "Folly, you...How can you? I just wanted to talk to you. I followed you all the way from Atlanta!"

I let the policeman hustle me into his car, and he drove me to my car. At first I'd forgotten entirely where I'd parked, but we found it. He made a remark, meant to be humorous, about my illegal parking; then he stayed until I cranked up and drove off. At the first intersection I looked both ways, still so agitated I could hardly think. I expected to have Walt run up and try to open my door. But he didn't appear.

Back at Lawson Hall late that night, I climbed into the attic, switched on the desk lamp and took up where I'd left off. After my talk with Professor Josefewicz, I thought I understood a little better the kind of world Randy and Miriam inhabited. On October 30th, after attending a large diplomatic function with Miriam along, Randy sat down (as he wrote) "late at night" in an attempt to put his "thoughts together." He was beginning to feel "rather confused." In the next few paragraphs, Randy laid out his unfolding heart:

"This evening Lord Robert congratulated me on my good taste. He mistook my lack of understanding for discretion, clapped me on the knee, and said he understood. With that he looked significantly at Miriam, who was carrying on a conversation in French with Lady Harriet. It was only then that I understood what he meant. I suppose I must have colored because he laughed. The truth is, Society here obviously assumes that Miriam is my mistress! Lord Robert was congratulating me on my success! I discovered in that moment how intensely I dislike the fellow, fop that he is!

"When I completely understood what had transpired, I felt acutely embarrassed. I gathered my wits, however, and considered that such immoral behavior among this leisured class of aristocrat is not only accepted but approved. They have little else to do but gamble and pursue little affairs of the heart, as they call it, scheming their little rendezvous in secret corners of the park, whilst they actually expect Society to understand. It is a curious collusion in which secrecy is not really secret but an odd matter of public interest, its being secret making it more delectable. If they have made an especially admirable conquest, they want it to be known, though it should not be blatantly done.

"Now that I am here in the privacy of my study with Miriam safely in her chambers, I become fully aware of the significance of my discovery. My discovery! How naïve and provincial I seem to myself! That I had not fully comprehended what Society assumed as a matter of course. My wife and family have gone, and I am left here with a creature so beautiful, so accomplished, so exotic in figure and person, that all of Society is utterly taken by her. It defies imagination! How can I have been so blind?

"If they knew how innocent our relationship truly is, they would be honestly shocked. Innocence and moral behavior is something most of them view as ludicrous! The worst of this lot are the high nobles who daily exhibit their contempt for the sort of moderate life we in America cultivate and admire. They gamble immoderately, and their libertine mode of sporting with whores is despicable.

"There are, of course, those who seek to live as I have, men of business and affairs who come largely from the middle classes, men who were not simply born to high position and wealth. Be that as it may, the quality and tenor of our relations in Society are still determined by the great, independent lords who represent most of the governments here.

"I am so ashamed of my blindness, not necessarily to the perception Society has had of us, but of the genuine uniqueness of this person in my charge whom I have – I admit it to my shame – regarded in my callousness as my property and little more. Slavery had dulled my senses and hardened my heart. I fear what I must declare before God, for I have spent my life in the thrall of an accursed institution, I the master in appearance only but in reality made less than a man of genuine heart because of what I have done."

Late October it had been. I began to read the following entries that led into December, checking every letter, every word, putting the sentences together, trying to find some evidence, even between the lines, of what was going on between the two of them.

Randy was silent. He wrote about the weather. He wrote down his accounts scrupulously. He dealt with the issue of the other servants. He considered every matter but the one that mattered to me.

"Why doesn't he pack up and go home," Dalton jeered.

"He's working on some government business. I'm really beginning to think it's a secret mission. He rode to Stuttgart over the weekend. He is in conference."

"Doesn't he say what it's all about?"

"Too secret to put down in his diaries. That's what I'm guessing," I admitted.

"Not a word about her?"

"Not a word."

Dalton scratched his thick mop of graying hair and adjusted his wire glasses. I had noticed over the many months that we had worked together how he emitted a certain stale-sweet odor. It wasn't exactly old perspiration or ordinary body odor. It didn't exactly stink and was somehow oddly pleasant. I remember coming very close to asking him what it was that day.

The truth was, I felt so ecstatic about the way things were going in 1823 between Randy and Miriam, I could have burst out in song (and did on the drive home from Atlanta that day). Not only had I become very fond of Randy, I suppose I loved Miriam. They were more real to me than either Dalton or anybody else whom I was seeing on a daily basis.

The hard fact was that 1823 was far more interesting than my own life. There was no relationship that I had ever had that even came close to what Miriam was enjoying in Karlsruhe. She was conquering Society. Lords, counts, barons, and princes celebrated her at gatherings. They praised her fluent French. They marveled at her German.

Randy didn't like it very much, but when he failed to take her along, Society complained bitterly: "Countess Waldorf chided me today for not having Miriam along. All the usual affected phrases they use. I understood half of them. Lady Harriet came over and added her portion in English."

Randy had a German cook and two German boys on his staff. I kept a tally on a worksheet. He used one of the boys as a footman and errand boy. The other he was training to take Cassius's place as his personal valet.

In early December Randy announced to his diary that "Miriam can't be expected to do the housework. I have, therefore, hired two additional girls. Servants are ridiculously cheap here and in ample supply. I have heard, though I have had insufficient time to see for myself, that the populace is suffering near starvation at present and thus are extremely happy to have any situation in which they have regular meals. If we had the same conditions, there would be no need for slavery. I doubt very much, on the other hand, that these German peasants could work in the Georgia heat. When the temperature exceeds eighty degrees Fahrenheit, as it did last week once, our cook refused to do her work over the oven. Several people fainted on the streets in town. A man was said actually to have fallen out of his window with a head stroke. And that is eighty degrees, mind you!"

Randy toyed for awhile with the idea of hiring a trained butler to coordinate the household. His frugality won out, and he decided it was better to muddle through as they were. "German males of the lower classes," he noted, "become easily overbearing once they are given a little authority. They become martinets, I should say. The last thing I'd like to see is a butler infringing upon Miriam's prerogatives. Perhaps we will wait until a good Italian candidate comes along to fill the position."

Miriam's prerogatives, I wondered. What "prerogatives?" Miriam now had prerogatives? She can't do housework? Here was a man whose entire fortune had until now (and still did) depend upon holding some two hundred odd human beings as chattel slaves, yet, he finds that a young woman he won as a child at cards like people play today for chips or dollars possessed prerogatives?

December and Christmas presented Randy with his first really big dilemma concerning Miriam's status. An invitation to pass Christmas at the palais of Lord Carlton in Stuttgart, at the court of the Kings of Wurttemberg, led him to debate in an entry of December 6th with himself in his strong, legible handwriting:

"Lord Carlton, the English minister-in-residence in Stuttgart, has asked me to pass Christmas week with a company in his palais. He also asks me to bring my young 'cousin,' by which he means Miriam. Thus has her renown spread to other courts!"

The options were clear to him: "Must I take her? Must I leave her here? If I leave her here, it is not outside the realm of possibility that she will use the opportunity to seek her freedom. If I take her along, how will I be presented, how will we be understood. Surely Lord Robert has spread the news. He is quite a gossip, and he winks at me every chance he gets, giving Miriam that awful leer. The man is an impossible boor!"

Randy had been born in the previous century in August of 1781, the day being uncertain. By December 1823 he was, therefore, forty-two years of age. The portrait in the foyer of Lawson Hall had been painted in 1822, during the second year of their European sojourn. They had been spending June in Baden-Baden when a "highly recommended student of Mr. Tischbein, the painter of the fine portrait of Goethe in the Compagna," had agreed to do the work. Randy had been a virile specimen, as that male member puffing up his pant's leg showed. He was a man in his best years, successful, accustomed to command. Surely his dominant position translated into sexual vigor.

They departed for Stuttgart and Lord Carlton's palais on December 20th. Randy had decided to take Miriam along. There were no further remarks or speculation. The entry of December 23rd made plain enough what happened:

"Stuttgart, Palais Carlton. It is Miriam's first visit in another house. Lord Carlton's palais is, of course, much more elegant than our own modest house. There is a great company gathered here in town, at court and much festivity planned. She is enjoying it all exceedingly."

On the next day Randy recognizes as Miriam mixes in Society that "she is not dressed entirely suitable to the figure she cuts. She is not quite, as the Germans say, *standesgemaess*."

I looked up the word in Judge Lawson's German-English dictionary and read, "in accordance with one's rank." So that in Stuttgart Randy Lawson decided to dress Miriam "in accordance with [her] rank." How odd since her rank was slave. That was, at least, her rank in South Carolina or Georgia to which she was likely to return once the European sojourn was over.

In an attempt to hide this inadequacy from Lord Carlton, Randy sends about town, until he locates a tailor's "establishment" willing to do a rush job on getting Miriam a couple of proper dresses. Early Christmas Day the dresses are delivered, Miriam models them for him and he writes that, "she cuts the most exquisite figure. It is a very odd thing about nature that endows the great often with the most commonplace face and figure while creating in a young servant girl a singular and splendid personage! It is God's irony, I suspect!"

Miriam was "all the rage..." during the Christmas celebrations. There was a Christmas play for the court and gifts distributed to all the diplomatic corps. It was also the first time a certain Prince Zukovsky appeared in Randy's narrative:

"The young Russian Prince Zukovsky was all too attentive to Miriam this afternoon at the gathering in the salon. Word is that he is very rich and very reckless! Russians have something of a reputation here for dueling, racing, and gambling. I have seen some of the races on which men bet exceedingly great sums of money. The horses are usually Arabian and worth a fortune. Lord Carlton keeps a stable of sixty such steeds."

The next day he "found Miriam in a tete a tete with Zukovsky in Carlton's grand salon. I thought she had gone down to go strolling with Lord Carlton's maiden aunt! Such duplicity does not bode well." But then he adds later that evening, "Miriam explained that Zukovsky importuned her with an insistent and impatient manner. He literally took her hand, steered her away from Lord Carlton's aunt, Miss Tithers-Wood, and led her into the grand salon and the alcove where I found them after being warned by Miss Tithers-Wood (a most decent woman)."

On December 27th Randy discussed the troublesome Russian with Lord Carlton: "It seems my host can do little against this mad Russian. He assaulted the palais this morning in search of Miriam. The butler and the footmen had instructions to keep him out, but he is untamed. At one point he pushed two footmen off the terrace and forced his way into the public area. Zukovsky is highly connected, and Lord Carlton would prefer not to be brought as host into confrontation with the villain. I suspect Society is enjoying the episode, too. There is nothing left for us to do but leave Stuttgart secretly tonight."

It was about midnight when I got this far with the diaries. A car came barreling up the drive and slammed on brakes in front of the Hall, scattering gravel that I could hear in the darkness as it clattered on the tin of a covered flower bed.

I went to the porthole window and looked out. There was enough moonlight to see a figure scrambling from a sedan. He wavered as he moved to the front steps. Halfway up he veered, swayed, caught himself on the banister. "He's drunk," I said aloud. "Whoever it is, he's drunk." I turned back to the lighted circle where I had been working. I owned several guns, but they were all downstairs. I believe I thought it was Jim. I couldn't think of anybody else it could be.

The stranger began to hammer with his fist on the front door as I hurried down the mobile stairs into the library. I went to the dummy bookshelf, unlatched the secret latch and swung it open. I kept a .38 revolver there in a sock. Peeling the sock off the chrome revolver, I pressed the release button and the cylinder fell out to the left. I took the little box of cartridges and loaded six. By this time the intruder was beating the door with the flat of his fist, the sound echoed through the hall. "Hello," he screamed. It was a man. "Open up! I know you're there!" It wasn't Jim.

I left the library, took a right down the little hallway, then a left until I came to the foyer. "Go away," I shouted against the thick wood of the door.

"I've got to see you," the intruder answered. "Open the door!"

"You're trespassing – and you're drunk!"

"I'm not very drunk."

"Walt," I said, recognizing the voice at last. "I do not want to see you ever again!"

"Yes, it's me, Folly. Please give me a chance. I can't live without you. Please tell me what I did wrong and forgive me."

"Go away. I have a pistol. It's loaded. You're trespassing."

"You needn't wait for him any longer, Fol. Jim Hall is getting married. He's getting married, Fol. You needn't wait for him any longer."

I was leaning against the door, holding the pistol up like swat team members do in true police documentaries when they're about to go into a place to get somebody. "Go away," I screamed.

"You haven't heard. I know you haven't heard. I came to tell you. The Lawson woman is divorcing her husband. She's marrying Jim Hall. Don't wait on him any longer, Folly. White people stick with their own. And I love you. I'm sorry for what I did that night. I promise. I'll always treat you with respect. Please. I misinteperted what you wanted. That's what I did, Folly. Misinterpreted. I thought—"

"Misinterpreted," I whispered. Aloud I cried, "I'm phoning the sheriff. You have about five minutes to leave before he gets here!" But I didn't move. A terrible wave of nausea rose up out of my belly and swept over me in waves. I kept standing, a little crouched, leaning against the door. There was silence. I could hear him breathing. Then he burst out:

"Folly, he's getting married. It's the honest-to-God truth, Fol. I heard it from several people. She's pregnant. The Lawson woman is married. Her husband found out. There was a big, awful scene. I have it from a good source. An awful scene. He flew down from somewhere. I think he's a diplomat in Southeast Asia. I think he flew all the way in from there. That's what they're saying. He will get a divorce, and she'll marry Jim Hall. We're trying to do damage control because we think he's our best hope for this election. I'm sorry we're stuck with him, but we are. You're partly to blame, too. And I supported him, too – because of you."

"Don't try to blame me for your mistakes, do you hear!" I heard myself screaming, "I – do – not – want – to – see – you – again – EVER! Not ever again, Walt! Not ever! Go away! Go away!"

"Please, Folly. Give me another chance. I can't do without you. I miss you so much. I don't know what to do. I thought you loved me. I mean," he began to sob, "I thought you wanted to. Honest to God. I thought you wanted to that night. It's no use waiting for him any longer. He wouldn't have you any way. He's a politician, Folly. Can't you see that? He wouldn't marry a colored woman. It'd spoil his chances."

I shuddered as I remembered the back seat in the field near Milledgeville. "I trusted you," I coughed hoarsely.

"I know," he was weeping, "I know. I blew it. I blew it. Oh, God, give me one more chance, Folly. I'll make it up to you. I'll be the gentlest man on earth. I promise."

I pushed myself away from the door, "I'm going to phone the sheriff now," I said wearily.

"What if I come in through the window? I've got to see you."

"I've got a gun. I'll use it," I said. I listened. He was thinking about it. He was trying to decide if I really would use the gun. He was breathing heavily. "I'm going now to call the sheriff. I mean it, Walt." I only hoped the alcohol hadn't clouded his judgment too much and that he wouldn't try to get through one of the windows. They were all the way down to the floor. I'd kept thinking about getting good latches for them, but then I'd think again that it'd be useless anyway. An intruder could just kick through the panes. I'd have to do something about them. I made a mental note. I'd have to get them secure.

I waited another moment or two. He was still thinking. He was still weighing the evidence. The phone was on the wall just around the first turn of the hall made on its way to the library wing. "Folly," he wailed at last, "please! Don't kill me like this. Please! You're killing me."

"You'll get over it," I said, "everybody always does."

I got to the phone, took the receiver off the hook, dialed. The motor of the car started. I could hear the gears grinding; then the vehicle moved off down the drive. I hung up. I tried to remember if I had forgotten to lock the gate earlier. I thought I had done it. I would have to check in the morning. In the meantime, I'd sleep with the revolver until I could get the windows latched and secure.

3

Thank God even Jim's wedding seemed parenthetical to Miriam's story. It was a small, virtually secret wedding. I wasn't invited, of course. The Atlanta papers colluded with Walt's Civil Rights organization to hush up the scandal. It was just as Walt had said. Jim was the only candidate they had. The other candidate was a restaurant owner who purchased a weekly column in the newspapers and fulminated about the sanctity of segregation and the natural inferiority of the Negro. He had used a baseball bat to defend his restaurant when several young men had tried to integrate it, and now he passed out autographed baseball bats to tourists from little towns all over the South who came to pay homage to him.

I was still convinced that Jim was squandering his political capital unnecessarily with the Laura Lawson business. It would cost him, I thought. He was throwing away bundles of good will. Since politics wasn't my area, I didn't know how or where the payback would come. My experience of human nature and business told me, though, that it would come. Around some unexpected bend the collector would be waiting to call in the debt. Jim would pay. Maybe believing that made me feel better about Jim's marriage.

In the meantime, things looked good for him. The Atlanta establishment knew that, in order to continue rapid economic growth in the state, the old image of Georgia as a racist backwater had to be discarded. And they wanted to do it NOW. The political will was present. The network was in place. The civil rights establishment had every reason to go along, too.

One morning I opened the Sunday "Living" feature of the *Constitution* and found a full color human-interest feature on Jim. In the center spread photo he was shown kicking clods in the furrows of his father's fields. He was wearing blue jeans. Henry Hall's ramshackled, unpainted clapboard home place stood in the background. Jim was presented as a farm boy who had made good, a son of Georgia who had a heart for helping the state get on its feet.

The feature was a masterful example of political propaganda. It showed just how effectively journalists can promote a candidate they like no matter what kind of scandals there were lurking in the background. I laughed as I read the article. Jim was the bright hope for the future, the Vietnam veteran-hero, high school football star, homespun philosopher and farmer's son.

The writer touched every base. Jim was shown attending the little Baptist church near The Ridge and the Hall farm. Only I knew that he hadn't been to church since he got back from Vietnam. Finally, on the second page he was portrayed standing in front of Mr. Amos Hendricks' store. It was another very savvy photograph. The message was simple: If he had become affluent and powerful, the backdrop of his success was still a down-home storefront in a little, country town.

That center spread profile was only the first of a barrage that appeared over the next two months leading up to the election of 1974. While the media blitz continued, Jim barnstormed the state. He was shown in hundreds of photos in dozens of Georgia newspapers shaking hands with farmers like his father, kissing babies, and generally cutting the right sort of figure.

Jim developed rapidly into a remarkably adept and wily subject for radio interviews. Radio journalists loved him as much as did newspaper journalists. He could be counted on to give them what they wanted and needed. He was a quick study.

With the entire Civil Rights and business establishment of the state behind him, there was nothing Jim needed of me. I sold the business in October, shortly before he was elected. The settlement was complex, but the total came to more than three million dollars. Jim chose to keep his interest, but the new owners did finally buy him out with an offer he couldn't refuse (Jim had played them along, behaving like the dearest thing to him in the world was his ownership in Hendricks and Steeples).

Miriam's story wasn't the only thing that kept me busy after that. Bill Hawson put together some excellent net lease deals in the Atlanta area. I was heavily into Atlanta real estate during Jim's first gubernatorial year. In 1976 I purchased my first high-rise on Peachtree. It had an old penthouse apartment on the fourteenth story with a fabulous terrace overlooking Ansley Park.

The apartment encompassed about two thousand square feet of living space that nobody had used in ten years or more. It was like breaking into an Egyptian tomb with accumulated dust, dirt and cobwebs. There was even a special elevator connecting it with the lobby below that had been nailed shut but proved still to work. It didn't even need fixing and could still groan and rumble it's way up and down the shaft after the cage was closed.

I decided to make the apartment my own, but I didn't want to rush it. It would be a project to keep me busy after I finished working out Miriam's story. Walt didn't show back up in those months. Occasionally the telephone at Lawson Hall would ring, usually late in the evening, and when I picked it up there'd be nothing but somebody breathing. Then they'd click off. Once I said, "Walt, is that you?" The person hung up.

Laura had a child born in August, 1975. The Atlanta papers made the most of little Timmy. Having a kid growing up in the governor's mansion was worth good political coin. Laura's connections actually helped Jim, too. I had been wrong about it costing him, but I didn't mind. I realized that I wanted the best for Jim, no matter what.

By late 1976, I was convinced that I had misjudged the whole affair. Marrying Laura had been another of Jim's shrewd moves, perhaps his shrewdest. The marriage allied him with the Georgia plutocracy on a level that would have been closed to him had he simply remained the self-made, modestly affluent son of a redneck farmer.

There were occasionally rumors that the Boston family of Laura's former husband still fumed over the divorce. There were said to be a couple of unhinged, dissolute types in the family, very much like the Kennedys. One of them had sworn publicly that he'd kill Jim sometimes. It didn't sound like a thing a proper Bostonian would be saying, so I didn't take it seriously. They didn't have an Irish name, anyway, so I figured the Celtic wild card wasn't present in the genes (unless they had intermarried earlier).

Whatever the realities of Jim's relations might have been, they were hidden from me. In fact, it looked like the history of our friendship was pretty much a matter of history. Jim went into History and left our history behind.

I was relieved to find that I wasn't bitter. I hadn't heard much from Jim during the first two years of his administration. Everything I knew, I found out through the newspapers or Bill Hawson or just simply from the odd gossipy tidbit that came my way.

Being abandoned to History I found had its advantages. It gave me a freedom to go back to 1823-24 where Randy had been unable to escape Prince Zukovsky. He followed them to Karlsruhe after they left in the deep of night from Stuttgart to escape him. Their respite was only very brief before he showed up again:

"Zukovsky has shown up now here in Karlsruhe. I have talked to the Prime Minister about this nuisance, but he told me candidly that they left these matters to the gentlemen themselves. It is, in other words, up to me to settle the business once and for all. They are afraid of political or personal embarrassment, and Society judges a man by how well he handles such matters discreetly."

During the next few weeks, Randy put up barricades to keep Zukovsky at bay. The doors were locked, the servants given instructions not to let anybody in unless they were clearly identified and had nothing to do with the Russian. "I am virtually a prisoner in my own house," Randy complained. "When I leave, I must steal out a side door."

It was in late January when the dreaded moment arrived: "I was out riding today, trying to take the air and exercise my fine Arabian. We managed well in spite of the snow. The Arabian is more sure-footed than many of the breed. Zukovsky's approach was muffled by the snow, so it was a surprise to me when he came up behind me at a canter.

"He overtook me and, as we rode side by side, he began in French to insist that I open my doors to him. He professed to love my 'cousin.' My French is very awkward, especially when I am angry, but I think I made it clear to him that his interest in my 'cousin' was not welcome and could not be entertained under any circumstance.

"The man turned a bright violet that fairly alarmed me, to say the least. He began to rage against Englishmen in his fluent French. My rejection of his petition, he said, was an insult to his entire race, so far as I could decipher his language, his Czar, and the whole Russian people. Did I think I was better than he, a genuine prince of the realm, etc. etc.

"I did my best to remain calm. Our horses sensed our dispute and became nervous and difficult to handle. That, added to the general suspense of the situation, hardly helped. My very calm outraged him. He began again to accuse 'Englishmen' (I believe in his mind I am English) of having no real blood or feeling. At first I did not catch his meaning, but, as he continued in his excessive manner, I gathered that he meant that we are cold-blooded. At that point, he reached across, leaning deeply in his saddle, and slapped my cheek. It would be an understatement to say that I was astonished and then hard put to fight a rising tide of anger at such treatment.

"He shouted, asking me if it were not clear to me what he had done. I suppose I looked uncertain or puzzled, because he leaned over to slap me again. At this point, without thinking further about the matter, I grabbed him by his coat collars, heaved him from his mount, and tossed him on the ground. I took the reigns of his horse, drew up and turned back to see how he sat.

"Zukovsky was producing a pistol from his rather ample manteau, and I had to dismount quickly to disarm him. I reached him just as he was preparing to discharge the weapon. I kicked it out of his hand, hurried to pick it up myself and flung it as far as I could into the wood.

"Zukovsky was on his knees and flourished a dagger. Where he had it concealed I do not know, but he was well bundled against the January temperatures. He got to his feet, and we struggled. The man was not as strong as I might have thought, and I was able to wrench the dagger from his hand and throw it after the pistol. He set upon me with his fists, but I easily pushed him back. He was surprisingly inept at fisticuffs. I laid him out with a thrust to the belly and a left hook neatly placed under the jaw.

"While he was stretched out, I decided to search his horse for any other weapons. When I found none, and having secured the reigns to a bush, I turned back to see what condition he was in. He was sitting up, rubbing his belly and checking his jaw. I judged him to be about a hundred and sixty pounds and perhaps five foot ten, which is to say three inches shorter than I.

"I knew that by reputation he was a good shot, a fine fencer, and one of the best seats in Europe in a good race. For all that he would hardly have lasted long with his temper in Georgia or South Carolina. He was physically not strong enough. It was then that I realized how much these European aristocrats depend on being given quarter in any disagreement by their inferiors. Not many could stand against a good match on equal terms, and they could hardly expect it from an American.

"When he got to his feet, he was highly agitated and said that he had honorable intentions and I had no cause to be the obstacle to a match. I have obviously damaged his sense of honor. At first, I replied in anger that I didn't fancy being murdered, that it didn't seem honorable drawing a pistol on an unarmed man, etc.

"I controlled myself and then tried to appeal to this high sense of honor he claimed by pointing out that we were American commoners and obviously could not take any suit from a prince seriously, as we were not of his rank. This line of reasoning seemed to have some effect on the man, and we parted on tentatively amiable – no, less overtly hostile terms. I thought it possibly less likely that he would try to kill me again."

Later Randy wrote that, "Lord Robert came today to tell me the tale Zukovsky is spreading among Society. He claims that I am madly jealous and anxious to keep my relative to myself to use and exploit. I figure as the villain in his story, a selfishly lustful old man. This was a hard blow for me after yesterday's tossle with the man. I told Lord Robert that I felt I am the injured party, and now this Russian adds lies and insults to his importunities! Some honor these blue bloods exercise! Slander and outright murder are hardly beneath them.

"Lord Robert concluded his little presentation by telling me that he believes Society has taken the Prince's part, which doesn't surprise me. The very notion of America threatens Society here and arouses negative emotions among its members. They view us as brash, corrupt and – worst of all – democratic. When they exhaust themselves complaining about our vulgarity, they find new fuel in their hate for the institution of slavery (a hypocrisy if I have heard correctly about the state of their peasants in Austrian lands and Russia is true, though it doesn't appear so bad in these parts)."

Lord Robert suggested that Randy's only real option was to throw himself on the mercy of the Duke and ask for protection. At first Randy refused to consider the option, though later he decided to relent:

"For all his condescension, Lord Robert does view me kindly, I think, as a sort of colonial cousin. He had told me before how many younger sons he has known who set off to the colonies to seek their fortune. He said in leaving, 'It is a perfectly honorable course of action to appeal to the Duke, my dear fellow. You are here in service to your country, are you not, and it is, therefore, your duty to do what you can to stay at your post. The Duke's officers understand this. They also know that, since you are accredited here, it is incumbent upon them to offer you His Grace's protection from any in a private character who would intrude upon your peace of mind and safety. Zukovsky's behavior is not merely an insult to you personally, but to your government.'"

In an entry four days later, Randy wrote: "I waited two days, sent my petition to the Prime Minister, was told by a baron sent to me that the Duke couldn't see me. On Lord Robert's advice, I petitioned again, insisting upon my rights as the accredited envoy of a sovereign state, explicitly stating that I sought His Grace's protection against a foreign prince not present on his territory in any official capacity. That seemed to do it. It struck the right chord, though I had to overcome my pride to accomplish it."

The appointment with the Grand Duke of Baden followed at the end of the week. Randy was duly granted protection. He notes, however, more than once over the next weeks that Zukovsky was being sighted in the vicinity. At home the whole business with the Russian led to a face off between Miriam and Randy:

"Do I not treat you with respect, I asked her. To which she sat for a long time without answering. Neither did she seem particularly agitated. I can only say that her comportment is marked by a calm and self-possession most men would envy. However you treat me, she said finally, I am your slave. When we return home to Georgia, I can be bought and sold as property with no regard for my own desires and feelings. However well you treat me here, sir, as you must see yourself, it is hardly the same as when a Russian gentleman who appreciates and values my company and does not own my body seeks me out for conversation.

"I was much affected by what she said, but I asked her if she thought this mad Russian truly sought her for her company alone. 'I understand the implication of your question,' she replied, 'and I have considered it myself. It is clear to me that, in commerce with men, there remains the constant potential that their physical appetites might be aroused by some thoughtless gesture, some careless word. A woman must be on her guard against these things, of course. But I ask you, sir, what could the Prince do to me that might not happen to me a thousand times whenever I return to the United States? And be done with less consideration and thoughtfulness, indeed committed with violence upon my person? What is my status in your eyes and the eyes of your compatriots? Am I a human being with inherent dignity and legal rights? No! I am not even a person.' I asked her if I had ever given any indication that I regarded her as chattel property. To which she replied once again that the point that mattered was her legal status and her status in my household. Again I protested by way of asking her if she had not been treated well.

"'You, sir, have treated me well, and I understand that you rescued me as a child from lustful exploitation. But who is to say that you will live as long as I do, or that some unexpected misfortune might one day force you to sell me? My well-being hangs upon the thread of your continued good health, fortune, and happy mood. Can that provide me any assurance or security? I think not. As a slave and bondswoman I have nothing to complain about,' she continued, 'as a human being I have every cause to find my present circumstances unsatisfactory.'

"All of this was a reply to which I had and could have no comment. In order not to continue the interview, I found it necessary simply to stand up and leave the room. My position is, as I clearly recognize, untenable. I must speak to her as soon as I have given myself time to think about the implications. Clearly she cannot continue to be subjected to this torment that she is a slave. I feel indicted and perceive that it has been the accident of my birth that has placed me in a position to engage in the traffic of human souls in order to assure my own social and financial ascendancy. It is a horrible truth I must face. What I can do about it is yet to be resolved."

Three days passed before Randy risked speaking to Miriam again. He told her that he intended to free her, and that she would be legally free to go and do whatever she pleased. She asked if he would put his offer into writing and make it legal. He agreed. At the same time, Randy was in a difficult position. If he employed a German attorney, he confided to his diary, it would become public that he had been holding slaves illegally. He finally agreed to write up a document of manumission and stamp it with the consular seal of the United States. He would also issue her a passport to wherever she pleased to go.

"May I depart from you here in Europe, she asked me. I told her that she could, but I was hopeful that she would remain for awhile as my companion. At that point, she appeared agreeable. She then began to lay out her plans to me in the most trusting manner. She is writing a book in German about America and has tentatively found a publisher in Mr. Cotta of Tubingen and Stuttgart. She asked if I would support her in her work. She has some hope of earning a living by writing.

"Once I agreed to support her in her enterprise, it was not long before Mr. Cotta sent an agent to pay us a visit. He was himself one of Mr. Cotta's writers, a man of modest appearance and bearing the name of Huber. His mother, it seems, had served as editor of one of Mr. Cotta's primary journals for many years. Cotta published her novel just two years ago, and Mr. Huber led Miriam to expect good royalties from her work. By his report Cotta is a generous publisher and not niggardly in payment to his successful writers. He quoted a figure that would surely enable Miriam to live a year in Europe on her own, if worse comes to worse and she leaves me. At the same time, I found it opportune to insist that he pay Miriam a certain amount on delivery of her manuscript. He argued with me but finally agreed to do just that."

Randy delivered the documents of her manumission shortly thereafter and was rewarded by a kiss. "She kissed me. It was quite spontaneous. She is also nearly finished with her manuscript. I have not read it, as I have been too busy. I don't believe, at the same time, that she has offered me an opportunity. I do know that it is something of a memoir of her life."

The manuscript was delivered to Mr. Huber who took it to Stuttgart in June of 1824. Dalton and I found that five printings appeared between 1825 and 1830 under the authorship of Miriam Steeples and with the title *Denkwuerdigkeiten einer Sklavin in Amerika*. There had also been a French translation published in Paris in 1829. We were unable to find an English language edition. I ordered the book through interlibrary loan and soon had it to hand. It was printed in fraktur, the old German font. As I began to read, I was amazed.

Just as the German title indicates, Miriam had written an autobiography of her life as a slave. The first line was memorable enough to translate into English: "I do not recall much of my life in Jamaica except that I was taken from my family at an early age by a very pale man who smelt of drink. I remember nothing of the journey over the sea northward to Charleston but that he kept me in his cabin on board and would come each evening to fondle me. I both feared and hated him without comprehending the situation."

After finishing the book with, as he puts it, "the constant assistance of a dictionary," Randy committed his outrage to his next diary entries: "She has laid her soul bare in this book! Every line was almost too painful to read. There have been moments when I would have thrown the book against the wall, but I persisted. If it becomes known in Charleston, I will be ruined. Yet, is she not entitled to this? Somehow it is an effort of truth and justice. My own ruin is nothing when compared to the indignities and intrusions upon her person that she has endured in her short life. Much of it happened unbeknownst to me, but it was under my protection! Nigel Steeples was a drunken brute. His acts are too heinous to contemplate. I did not guess at the time how he had already exerted his perverted lusts upon the body of an innocent child. Had I known, I would have steered clear of him. In which case I would not have known about the child and thus would not have rescued her from his abusive habits. What else he did before dying of drink is awful to contemplate, and I trust he inhabits one of the inner circles of hell."

My own German was still quite good enough for me to read Miriam's memoir. If I kept a dictionary at hand, I used it rarely. She wrote clearly, simply and well. Her story was am emotional expose of life within the slave system of Georgia. She described the whole spectrum of an emotionally laden experience of dehumanization. Had the book been written in English and published in America, I thought it must have brought the system down decades earlier than it did. There was no way any but the hardest hearts could have read her book without being profoundly moved.

And, yet, Miriam's work was not an unrelieved account of the horrors of slave life. She told how she had been rescued from her first master (she changed and fictionalized the names of all involved) and treated almost like a member of the family by her new masters. She attributed her good fortune to her appearance, which, as she describes herself, was virtually that of a white woman. Indeed, she recorded dim memories of her father in Jamaica who, she thought, had been an English overseer.

The book was a short one, numbering one hundred and thirty eight pages. It brought Miriam's story up to the date on which the family was to take passage to Germany. Randy noted that, "she plans to continue a second volume of her experience and observations while here in Germany. She has said she does not plan an English edition in order to save me from embarrassment. I assured her that caution was not necessary. She is perfectly free to do whatever is best for her career."

And then at midnight Randy records the first move to intimacy: "We met on the stairs. Somehow I took her in my arms. It happened so naturally, the sweetest, gentlest thing in the world." Soon after Randy complained about the summer heat and recorded his resolve to go to cooler altitudes in Switzerland. "We will also find a place to be alone together," he added.

In July, 1825 he and Miriam traveled via Zurich and Bern to Interlaken. The mountain country gave them the respite they wanted both from the heat and from curious eyes. Randy rented quarters in a large farmer's house in the Lauterbrunn Valley surrounded by the connected peaks of the Jungfrau, Eiger, Monk, and Schilthorn.

They had travelled, as Randy put it, "incognito." Professor Josefewicz told me that simply meant they were traveling as man and wife under an assumed name. "What about their passport," I asked. "Couldn't people just ask to see their passport?"

"This is before the days of a passport," he explained. "And don't forget that Mr. Lawson was a consul. He could set out his own passports, a paper for each border crossing."

XXII

"I hear through the grapevine that you're doing pretty well in real estate," Jim said. We were sitting on my terrace on the fourteenth floor of my building. I had been pacing, looking out over Ansley Park. Then I sat down across the table from him. He had his long legs propped up on my wrought iron table and was leaning back in the chair, still slender, still graceful without meaning to be. "You certainly have picked yourself a choice spot here," he mused, grinning the old, satisfied grin. Jim was obviously as pleased with my success as if he were personally responsible. "Who'd have believed that you and I would come so far!"

"Least of all me," I said. "It's all been sheer luck. That's the only explanation."

"The good Lord," Jim said. "He did it for us. I knew it even when we were little."

"Knew what," I said with that smile people get when they are saying: get real! How can you be so absurd?

"That the Lord had this plan for us both."

Again, I tossed my head with that 'aw, man' kind of thing. "You're too much," I said.

"No. You know that song, 'he walks with me and he talks with me'?"

"'And he says that I am his own,'" I crooned.
"And the joy I felt as he tarried there was like nothing I'll ever own..."
"I don't think that's right."
"Well, it's something like that. Anyway, I knew. It was like he spoke to me. Many times."
"Told you you were something special, didn't he?"
"That there was a special mission for me."
"And this was it? Being governor and so forth?"
"Well, part of it."
The thing is, I didn't doubt that Jim was convinced that his was a special destiny. That's the way he had always acted. "Part of it?"
"There's something else yet. I haven't been able to see that clearly. At first I thought it was Timmy. And Timmy is part of it."
"Do you still have that feeling of closeness? That he's walking and talking with you?"
"Not lately. But it'll come back. I've just been so busy."
"Wow."
"Don't you?"
"I guess I never did. Some are chosen. Others aren't."
"Yes," Jim said, sitting up, leaning over the table earnestly, "But look at everything he's done for you."
"The good Lord?"
"Yeah."
"This is all luck and—and partly good advice."
"Then why can't other people do it?"
"Some do. And a lot more than I've managed to accumulate."
Jim fell back loosely in his chair, "So that's it for you. Blind luck." He shook his head and grinned. "You're always going to be the tough little waif, aren't you, Fol. Tough it out. Life's a bitch, but I'm gonna make it through."

"What choice do I have," I asked rhetorically. Then we both looked at each other and laughed.

"You're a case. You really are. You're a sight, sport. The Lord makes a lot more sense to me. You can't feel any joy just toughing it out. It's not the way it's meant to be."

"Yeah yeah," I said.

"Haven't you just rejoiced in some of all of this you've been able to do? Just felt great. You know. Felt blessed?"

"Blessed." I felt my brow crumple into a frown. I'd never thought of it that way. "I guess I sound pretty ungracious, don't I?"

"First of all, you were born gorgeous. You're still gorgeous. But you hide your beauty under a barrel, as the scripture goes. It's like you don't want anybody to know. You're trying to keep your whole life a secret, baby, but who're you keeping the secret from? Do you think God doesn't know? Do you think I don't?"

"I hadn't thought about it until now," I said, "but I guess I've always been waiting for something really bad to happen. Like Laura tripping me, or Miss Ellen dying, or my mother going off up north. Or Judge Lawson dying right there in front of—me. It seems like with everything that seems like a might be good, there is something really bad, you know. I've just tried to brace myself."

"That stoic business is a sad way to get through life, hon. Loosen up! Have a little fun."

I looked at Jim more candidly than I had intended (because I saw him shift ever so slightly) and asked, "How?"

"Geez, sport. Take a trip. Go to Europe."

"Alone?"

"Well..." He seemed to be actually considering something, "Maybe not alone."

"No, that's what I mean," I said, throwing up my hands.

"Laura's leaving me, Fol. She'd have already gone, but I talked her into at least pretending to stay until I finished this term."

I couldn't pretend any sympathy. I stopped myself from blurting out something really stupid like "wonderful" or maybe "great" or even "good riddance." So I finally didn't say anything, which was best.

We both sat there looking down at the table awhile. I was thinking about Laura Lawson going. She would leave him Timmy, their child, whom I only knew from photos in the newspaper and maybe a brief short a couple of times on some news program. The People of Georgia has apparently liked a child being in the governor's mansion. That is, if you can believe the happy features the columnists wrote, though I never did know how a few reporters could really know what the People of Georgia felt about any issue.

"Folly, I'm not sorry. I'm not sorry she's going. She's a cold-hearted, scheming woman, just like you said. She's involved with Baker Gooding."

"Baker Gooding?" I started to say, but he's married, and then I remembered that wouldn't make any difference to Laura.

"Yeah, he's got the money she needs. She says I'll soon be a has-been when this term is over. She has to move on."

"And Timmy?"

"Timmy's no problem. He stays with me. She doesn't," real bitterness stole into Jim's voice. It was an unaccustomed sound, "she doesn't give a – doesn't care about children. She says she thought she was barren. Didn't want to have any, in the first place."

"Ugh," was all I could manage.

He had phoned that afternoon out of the blue. He hadn't even said, "Hello, this is Jim," like you'd expect. He simply said, "Can I come by to see you – about four or so?"

"Jim?"

"Sure. It's me, Fol. I need to talk. Are you free?"

"When? Today at four? Tomorrow?"

"Today. About four. I'll need to get in soon enough to beat the afternoon traffic."

I had hesitated a moment, trying to think. Should I do this? I hadn't seen him in three years. Three years! And he suddenly phones and wants to come by. Then I heard myself saying; "Yes. Come on. I'll be here."

While I waited I thought about the time that had passed since his marriage. He had been a lot in the news, more than most governors before him. He had been the darling of the media. Now he had about nine months to go in his four-year term. I wondered what had happened that he'd just suddenly want to see me. My intuition had been that it had to do with Laura Lawson, and I had been right.

They'd be splitting up, I thought. Something like that; yet, even as the thought occurred, I rejected it, though something still caught in my throat. It's true when they say that something 'leaps' in your chest, like your heart shifting into overdrive when you break through that fourth mile.

When Jim arrived, it was as if we'd just seen each other the day before, as far as he was concerned. He gave no explanations but just pecked me familiarly on the forehead, bending forward, his lips doing nothing more than brushing my skin. Then he breezed in.

He wanted to see the apartment, and then it was he who saw the terrace through the windows of the French doors and said (like we were still partners and he co-owned the place with me), "Let's sit out there awhile. I could use some of that sunshine."

"It'll be a little chilly," I said, but I opened the door and we walked out onto the red tiles. "So what did you find out about your family and the Lawsons," he asked suddenly.

"Oh? You mean—"

"Yeah, all that work you were doing on the journals you found."

"It's a long story."

"Everything's a long story, Fol. Everything. Tell me."

I had given him a summary of what I knew about Randy and Miriam, at least up to the time they were in Switzerland together alone. He had sat listening like he enjoyed it, so I was encouraged to go on more than I ordinarily would have done. And then he had talked about God and so forth, then gotten to Laura leaving him. And so we were both sitting there. I didn't know what he was doing, but I was trying to sort out my feelings – and the whir in my mind told me that wasn't going to be easy.

"Timmy looks like a cute kid," I said. "In the photos."

"You don't know him, do you?"

"How could I, Jim? This is the first time I've seen you in three years."

"Three years," he said, as if the number surprised him.

"Yes."

"You're sure?"

"Yes, I'm sure. I haven't ever met your child."

"I thought about calling you often enough, Fol. But it never seemed like the right time. There was a time I was seriously thinking about asking you to come on board and be my advisor or aide-de-camp."

"I couldn't have done it. I've been far too busy with my own business, Jim."

"I figured as much. It wasn't realistic. But you were always kind of there in my thoughts. Believe it or not."

I didn't tell him that I'd decided I had become the part of his history that was frozen and past. "I guess I believe it. I don't seem to have any trouble believing it," I laughed. I didn't know why I thought that was funny. Jim was sort of chuckling, too.

"I'm gonna have a few months, Fol. When this term is over."

"Just a few months?"

"Well, I've got it from good sources that Gil Daily may not be running again."

"Senator Daily?"

"Yeah. He's got some kind of disease. I'm not sure what it is. They're keeping a tight lid on it. He'll be coming up for reelection in two years."

"So you'll have a few months in between," I said.

"Yeah. Who knows? It may not be right. About Gil's disease. You know how rumors are."

"Sure. Sure, I know how rumors fly."

"I don't feel washed up, Fol."

"Of course not. You're in the prime of life, Jim."

"That's the way I feel. I feel like there's something else waiting."

"You know there is," I urged, not knowing really what I meant.

"Course, Laura may try to mess things up. She's good at that. Has a real nasty streak. I don't know what she'll do. Hey, does she know about all this – about you and the Lawsons?"

"I don't think so. She might sort of guess at it, but I don't think she really knows."

Jim grinned, "That's kind of funny, isn't it. You being more a Lawson than she is. And now you own the old mansion. That's pretty funny, when you think about it."

"I guess it is," I agreed.

"I never heard Laura say a word about it, though. I mean, you owning the Hall. Never heard her say a word."

"She's probably blocked it out of her mind," I said.

"Maybe it's one of those things that are beneath her noticing," Jim actually laughed at that.

"I'm sure it is."

"Are you…are you going with anybody or anything like that, Fol?"

"Not right now," I said.

"Do they still call it dating at our age?"

"Who knows what they call it. God, Jim, I'm thirty-six. Men like nubile girls. No wrinkles."

He looked across the table at me, "You're still really beautiful, Fol. Honest to God, I can't understand how you're still single."

"Beats me."

"Probably because you're so smart. You're too smart for most men. Sometimes even I wonder about it, Fol. It must be awfully lonely being so smart."

I felt puzzled, "What do you mean, Jim?"

"There's a busy life going on in that lovely skull that you can't share with many people."

"There's not much going on in there, Jim. Not of any particular interest to anybody other than myself."

He began to gather himself, pushing the chair back, "Well, it's been every bit as good as I thought it would seeing you again, sport. So much like old times. Hey, I gotta get going. Timmy'll be waiting. It's getting late."

We both got up. He put his arm around my waist and pulled me against him as we walked back into the apartment, but loosely, casually, as if it didn't really matter and he wasn't actually thinking about what he was doing. We got to the lobby that way and were standing in front of the elevator. He had punched the button, and we heard the whir of the cables, when he said, "By the way, what did Randolph Lawson do about his slaves when he got back from Europe? Did he free them?"

"He died suddenly on a trip north to visit his friend, Albert Brisbane, in New York. I guess he didn't have time to do anything—if he intended to."

"Who the hell is Albert Brisbane?"

"He was a social utopian," I began. "A Fourierist Randy met in Europe." The elevator arrived with a bump and grind. The doors glided open.

"What is that?"

"Sort of socialist," I said.

"So he went up to see this guy and got sick?"

"A fever. I haven't been able to find out anything else." I reached into the cabin of the elevator and pressed down the 'hold' button.

"And Miriam? What happened to her when he left?"

"She did all right with her writing. She gave lectures. Her books went through multiple editions."

Jim stepped into the elevator. "Tell me this, Fol. If you are descended from Miriam – I mean, how did that happen if she stayed in Europe?"

"Her son came over as a missionary after the Civil War. He started a school for freedmen there in Lawson County. He was lynched by the KKK, but his two children survived. Randolph the Third took them in, I think. I'm still working on that." I released the button and backed away.

"Lynched," Jim said. He looked genuinely shocked. As if I had told him something terrible that happened to somebody he actually knew.

"Goodbye, Jim," I said releasing the hold button. The doors began to slide shut. I had one last frame of Jim standing there in the white light of the elevator, his handsome features distorted, his eyes covered by a glaze of internalized concern

~

Randy had bought a cottage near Stuttgart for Miriam. He had, as he put it, "settled the largest sum I could afford upon her," and then returned to Charleston where he had more than enough to do rescuing his fortune from the mismanagement if not outright thievery of his brother-in-law.

The work of getting his business back on solid footing took the rest of the decade. In 1837 Albert Brisbane wrote him an urgent letter I found pressed between the pages of the diaries. It was characteristic of the eccentric polyglot to write the letter in German: "Lieber Herr Lawson, Sie interessieren sich fuer meine Projekte hier in New York, und ich kann Ihnen versichern, dass freiwillige Arbeit die Antwort zu den Problemen der Welt ist. Kommen Sie und beobachten Sie! Wir machen grosse Fortschritte hier in unserer Gemeinschaft. Jeder tut das, wofuer er Neigung und Begabung besitzt..." He went on to assure Randy that he would discover how he could transform the system of slave labor into a cooperative community.

In his last entry Randy set out his moral dilemma, "I have continued to delay the step I must take because, without finding some alternative to simple manumission, it will simply set my Negroes at the mercy of a hostile world without arming them to make their way. Brisbane may have come upon just the right formula in his Fourierism for establishing a community in which they may be both free and secure. I can then return in peace to Europe to find my heart!"

There follows an empty page, a sort of piety, and the narrative is taken up again in the strong, unwavering hand of Randolph II: "We received word today that our dear, honored father succumbed to the fever in Batavia, New York almost a fortnight ago. The responsibilities of the family now fall upon my shoulders. We are all disconsolate."

The only hope the slaves might have had was gone, and the Lawson plantations continued to be operated as before. Like his father before him, Randolph II brought only momentary respite to the plantations he visited. His presence was intended to moderate the cruelty of the overseers without in any way modifying or abolishing the system that made their tyranny possible.

9 780595 190706